# KNOCK 'EM DEAD

## A CAPTAIN DARAC MYSTERY
### #4

## PETER MORFOOT

Galileo Publishers, Cambridge

Galileo Publishers
16 Woodlands Road
Great Shelford Cambridge
CB22 5LW UK

www.galileopublishing.co.uk

Distributed in the USA by:
SCB Distributors
15608 S. New Century Drive
Gardena, CA 90248-2129

ISBN 978-1-912916-18-4
First published in the UK 2020
© 2020 Peter Morfoot

Printed in the EU

**PRAISE FOR TH**

**IMPURE BLOOD:**

*"Engrossing... An auspicio*

*"Great plot, appealing her*
*winner"* – Martin Walker,                              ~~Bruno Courreges~~
novels

*"Impressive... will delight fans of international crime"* – Booklist

*"A vibrant, satisfying read"* – The Crime Review

**FATAL MUSIC:** One of *Strand Magazine's* Top 25 Books of 2017

*"A thoroughly satisfying novel... Morfoot brilliantly captures the sights, smells and attitudes of southern France as well as giving us an engaging hero"*– Mike Ripley, Shots eZine 5 Picks of 2017

*"In Morfoot's intriguing second whodunit featuring French police captain Paul Darac (after 2016's Impure Blood)... The road to the logical solution is full of surprises"* – Publishers Weekly

*"Pulls you along like an iron bar to a magnet. Crime and mystery readers will consume every last morsel of this book."* – David Cranmer, Criminal Element Magazine

*"Deftly interwoven plot lines... vividly captured Riviera setting... This strikingly well-written crime novel should appeal strongly to many."* – Bruce Crowther, Jazz Journal

**BOX OF BONES:**

*"An accomplished piece of crime fiction. Captain Paul Darac... has become, without doubt, my favourite foreign detective created by a Brit since the late Michael Dibdin gave us Aurelio Zen."* – Mike Ripley – Shots eZine, 5 Picks of 2018

*"The plot, filled with enough twists and turns for a corkscrew, is intriguing while never losing touch with either reality or humanity."* – Crime Review

*"Darac leads an engaging and distinctive team of officers, all of whom grow as the reader learns more about them. Not only are the good guys well drawn, but so too are the bad guys and the plot is intriguing and filled with many twists and turns."* – Bruce Crowther, Jazz Journal

Captain Darac Mysteries

Impure Blood
Fatal Music
Box of Bones

For Katherine

# PROLOGUE

The man was no longer watching the trains go by. He had seen quite enough of the *Régionales* clattering off towards Nice or Cannes. Even the Vintimille-bound TGV, pushing a pressure wave that thumped the windowpane next to his ear, had failed to claim his attention.

Two empty bottles of La Poche's house red sat on the table in front of him. For a moment, he considered ordering a third but decided against it. Time to call it a night. Casting no more than a glance across at the station, he got to his feet and made for the bar where a boy wearing a rapper T-shirt and earphones was swilling out glasses and muttering something rhythmically to himself.

'I may as well go up,' he said to the boy's back.

No response. The man shrugged and, slapping a beaded curtain aside, began picking his way through a dank-smelling storage area towards a windowless stairwell, its entrance flanked ceremonially by a pair of defunct fridges. He heard a click and the overhead light went off. Timed out? He could hardly have covered the ground any faster if he'd sprinted.

'Hey!'

He waited for his eyes to adjust to the darkness. They didn't. He called out again, louder this time. The only response was a sound of scuttling somewhere away to his left. Hoping to trigger further meted-out illumination, he took a couple of faltering steps but succeeded only in bumping his knee against something hard. He explored it. Cast iron, louvres, some sort of rack on top – an old radiator. He stepped back and, feeling blindly for further obstacles, edged forward on a different line. After a moment, a strip light flickered into life on the landing above. He hurried to the stairs, taking them two at a time until a maddening realisation stopped him. He'd left his shoulder bag in the bar. The bag containing all his notes and photos. And he a pro, too. Now he would have to run the gauntlet of the lighting all over again.

'Monsieur Férion?'

Salvation.

The voice was coming from the storage area. It had to be the boy from the bar: they were the only two left in the place.

'Here.'

'Where are you going, Monsieur Férion?'

He gave a dry laugh. 'Where indeed?'

One earphone dangling free, the boy appeared below. 'You left this.' He tossed the bag on to the bottom step and, plugging himself back in, was gone as quickly as he had come.

'Too kind.'

Férion was half-way down the stairs when he heard a click and the lights went out once more.

# 1

The voice in Mayor Hervé Montand's ear was loud, angry and in a hurry.

'Yes, I was just about to call you, Monsieur...' Clamping the phone under his chin, Montand fished the letter from the pile on his desk and rolled his eyes. '... *Lhatib.*'

As he waited for the noise to cease, Montand swivelled in his chair and gazed out over the Var river basin below. Laid out on an east-facing shelf on the ground rising behind the coastal resort of Saint-Laurent, the village of La Crague overlooked an uninspiring stretch of the waterway. Ten or so kilometres from its egress into the glittering Baie des Anges, the Var was no gorge-quickened torrent; it was little more than a network of parched, gravelly shallows flanked by the sprawl of a *zone industrielle*. Yet it was one of Montand's two favourite views in the world. The other was the reverse angle, the massif of La Crague viewed from the *zone*.

His eye settled on the bottle-shaped chimneys of a white-walled factory unit. From the mayoral chamber, a visitor would have needed binoculars to have made out the name emblazoned on the flag flying over the site. On this still July morning, it was hanging limply against its pole, anyway. But it was Montand's flag, Montand's factory, and above it, La Crague was Montand's commune and always had been.

'I can assure you that the account will be paid in full, Monsieur Lhatib, but we need a little breathing space. A little more time. A deferral, in fact.'

Lhatib responded with a stream of abuse.

'I understand your anxiety but as our long-term position has *never* been so assured, I am willing here and now to offer you a generous one-off payment to be made at the conclusion of our—'

Lhatib's stream turned into a flood. Surely, Montand thought, the man understood the principle of the inducement? The others all had. He decided to spell it out. 'Monsieur, you have my word as mayor of the ancient commune of La Crague-du-Var, that—'

Abuse gave way to laughter. When Lhatib spoke again, it was to state his conviction that in no other country would La Crague, among the smaller of the 36,000-plus communes in France, merit a parish councillor, let alone a so-called mayor; one, moreover, who couldn't pay his bills on time and had to resort to offering his creditors bribes.

Montand's bald head flushed red as a cock's comb and it was all he could do not to tell the nonentity to piss off back to whichever cesspit in the sand he'd crawled out of. But Montand kept quiet long enough to hear that if his outstanding account were not settled by the end of business today, he would soon be explaining himself to the regional prefect. He and his office would be exposed, shamed and sued. Criminal charges were likely.

As if summoned, his gaze rose to the portraits hanging on the wall opposite him, each a Montand wearing the sash of mayor. His head dropped. 'Monsieur,' he began again, but Lhatib had hung up. Montand looked at the bottom line on the account. Could he cover it personally, right away? Probably, but not without attracting some awkward questions from his wife, Mathilde, in whose name his business was registered.

He was still considering the matter when the phone rang again. A different voice and a different threat, this one promising a more straightforwardly painful outcome if payment were not made forthwith. And when, only minutes later, Montand took a third call, he was forced to acknowledge that a new picture was emerging. From all sides the ante was being upped and he couldn't allow it to rise any higher.

His eyes bored into the piles of bills sitting in mute accusation in front of him. Something snapped in his head and with a series of thrashing swipes, he cast them wildly to the floor. The effort shot a searing pain up his back and he yelped. Now, on top of everything else, he would have to squeeze in a visit to the surgery but at least his painful little fit had cleared his head. As his forebears looked down on him, Montand reached for the mayoral phone and tapped in a number. After several unanswered rings, he heard three sounds in succession: a soaring and swooping Swanee whistle; a crash of breaking glass; and finally, the forlorn fart of a deflating whoopee cushion. That it ended in a triumphant upward flourish offered scant solace as he began leaving his message.

# 2

A slender shadow fell across the bar.

'Perrier.'

The boy's fingers stopped dabbing at his iPad. Pulling out one of his earphones released a tinny barrage of voices into the air. 'Huh?'

The woman had the case-hardened look of someone who wasn't used to asking twice. 'Perrier,' she said, mooring her shades in the artful casualness of her brushed-over bob. 'A cold one.'

Caroline Rosay dropped her car keys into her black leather daysack and glanced around. There was no sign of the client she was meeting, nor of anyone else. Approaching lunchtime and the place was deserted? La Poche was evidently not Saint-Laurent-du-Var's answer to Les Deux Magots. As a train pulled into the station across the street, Caroline heard the chiller cabinet door close stickily behind her.

'Make sure it's in-date.'

'Huh?'

She checked the label herself. 'Forget it.' She considered returning to her car – she had a couple of litres of the stuff in her cool box – but decided to stay put. 'Alright if I sit in the shade? Of course it is.'

The boy's eyes followed Caroline as she walked through a swirl of sunlit dust motes into the seating area. Hoping her Dior silk would survive the examination of the folding aluminium chairs, she found a clean one and set it down at a table next to the window. It was open almost to the floor, a boon on a hot July day. She found the view itself uninspiring. Masked intermittently by trees, the platforms of Saint-Laurent station were bounded by a chain-link fence. Standing in sharp silhouette against the mesh, passengers lined up on the Nice-bound side looked to Caroline like prison camp inmates waiting for news from outside.

She understood now why her client had chosen to meet here rather than the station's other café, a popular alfresco spot outside the booking hall. "I have a train to catch," he'd said. "But I'd like a few quiet words with you first." If by "quiet" he had meant "unlikely to be overheard", Monsieur Ambroise Paillaud could hardly have chosen a better place.

'The bitch ain't straight!' declared the boy at the bar, loudly and out of tune.

Caroline glanced at her Piaget. Paillaud had better be on time. It was less than three-quarters of an hour to her tennis lesson and the meter would start running whether she was there or not.

With the window wide open, Caroline could hear the station PA as clearly as if she had joined the inmates on the platform. Heralding a spoken announcement, a four-chime refrain sounded, the first three notes rising strongly and evenly, the fourth, a faint, falling echo cut short. She had never noticed before how much drama those four little notes conveyed. How much anxiety.

Voices in the doorway made her turn. One belonged to Paillaud.

'I know you!' the other man said, grasping Paillaud's elbow from behind. 'You're the old film star. The comedian. "Monsieur La Chute", they called you. "Monsieur La Chute, the Prince of the Pratfall!" You're brilliant! What *is* your real name? Uh... Tati! That's it. Jacques Tati. You are him, aren't you?'

'Yes I am,' Paillaud said. 'Now piss off and leave me alone.'

The PA announcement kicked in. News of a delay.

'Was that the Marseille train?' the man said, undeterred. Paillaud continued into the café, ignoring the question. 'Well, I'd better go. Wonderful meeting you, monsieur!'

As the boy at the bar was still lost in the unsociable world of his social media, Paillaud entered without acknowledgement and went to join Caroline. Slipping his shades into the breast pocket of his white cotton jacket, he kissed her hand and sat down.

'Forgive me, Jacques,' he said, casting a heaven-ward glance.

'Monsieur Tati might forgive you, monsieur, but what about your fan?'

'Fan?' Contrition gave way to disdain. 'Didn't even know who I was. Screw him. Screw the lot of them.'

Had his career taken a different turn, Caroline reflected, Paillaud would have aced *The Misanthrope*. 'So – what is so urgent that we needed to meet here and now, monsieur?'

He handed her an envelope. '*Ambroise*, please.'

'I hope this isn't...' She took out a hand-written sheet of A4. 'Oh, Lord. You should have come to my office.'

He shrugged. 'You can register it when you get back. I trust you.'

If the remark were intended as a compliment, it missed its mark. 'Monsieur—'

'I didn't know whether to initial and number the page as there's only one. I did, as you see. Is it alright? Technically?'

'I'm sure it's all fine.' He had had plenty of practice, after all. 'But that's not the point.'

'Read it, then.'

Her brow furrowing, Caroline read the opening few lines, then, lowering the document, took a quick glance over her shoulder.

'Deaf lugs can't see us,' Paillaud said. 'Pillar in the way.' He smiled. 'Like a side aisle seat in the old Théâtre Souris.'

Her steel-grey eyes met his. 'You're not serious about this? It's a joke, surely.'

'Caroline, *this*...' Maintaining a straight face, he turned his toupée sideways. '... is a joke. Read on.'

14

Betraying not a flicker of amusement, she returned to the document. The handwriting was small, the pen strokes incised deeply into the paper. 'You've dated it today, I notice.'

'I wrote it just before I came out.'

'In haste. A tearing hurry, even. Monsieur, I strongly suggest—'

She went to give it back to him but he threw up a hand. 'I've been thinking about this for years.' He repositioned the toupée. 'I mean every word of it.'

Caroline ran her tongue over her lips. Perhaps it had been a mistake to have rejected the Perrier. 'Monsieur...' She marked the correction with a cool, professional smile, '*Ambroise*, does anyone else know about this?'

'I've never discussed it with anyone until this moment.'

She believed him. Paillaud, a virtual recluse, was the most secretive person she had come across in her ten years as a notary public. 'And this is the only copy?'

It was Paillaud's turn to look surprised. 'It's a handwritten document, as you see.'

'You could have had it photocopied.'

'Why would I do that? No, no. Read on, mademoiselle.'

'Caroline,' she said absently.

'Read on, *Caroline*.' Inclining his head extravagantly, he made a sad clown face. 'Do it for Monsieur La Chute.'

From nowhere, a figure materialised at the open window. A blur of heaving breath and sweat. Instinctively, Caroline's hand went to her daysack but the man, a jogger wearing a grey hoodie, ran safely past. She continued without missing a beat. 'You are certain you want to go ahead? You've changed your mind so often.'

'No, I haven't.' Paillaud discarded the clown face. 'Ever.'

Another tense little four-note clarion drifted across from the station.

'Is that your train?'

'Not quite yet.'

'Alright.' She glanced at her watch. 'Would you excuse me for a moment?' She extracted her mobile from her daysack and stood. 'I need to make a quick call.'

Paillaud lowered his black-dyed eyebrows in a look of such coy suspicion, it would have played to the cheap seats in any theatre. 'To whom?'

Caroline pursed her lips. In any circumstances, it was an impudent question and she would have allotted more time for their meeting if she'd known its true purpose. 'I won't be a moment.' She stepped over the window's low sill and headed a little way down the street.

Paillaud's face was suddenly damp with sweat. 'Don't be too long,' he called out.

'Got no axe to grind!' the boy announced. 'No backs to mind!'

Paillaud dabbed his face with a handkerchief as he watched Caroline walk back and forth, her mobile against her ear. Unable to pick up what she was saying, his thoughts turned to his plans for the day. A disquieting thought struck him. The network of lines bit more deeply into his face as he thrust a hand into one inside pocket and then the other. He blew out his cheeks. Yes, of course he still had his wallet. He opened it. And yes, of course he still had the tickets for the train and for the exhibition. It couldn't have been otherwise. He'd checked twice already since leaving home.

'Done.'

Startled, Paillaud dropped the wallet. Trying to catch it, he succeeded only in knocking it under the table where it landed in a miniature explosion of dust, the tickets parachuting down after it. 'You know, I did a *comedy* conjuring act at one time.' He let a raised eyebrow make his point for him as he pushed back his chair.

'Allow me.' Caroline picked them up. 'Ah, you're going to the Brassaï show.' She slipped the tickets back into the wallet and handed it over. 'I'm going myself in a couple of weeks.'

'Yes? I've always loved his photos. So sure-eyed.' He planted the wallet firmly back in his pocket. 'As I used to be sure-eyed, sure-handed, sure-footed... Now I'm not sure of anything much.'

She indicated his document. 'Except this.'

'Except that.'

She read it, eyes wide, until the final line.

'Well?'

'You realise what this will do to your standing in the community, monsieur?'

The idea amused him. 'The oh-so-mighty community of La Crague-du-Var? So what?'

'With respect, no one asked you to move back to the area.'

'I was going to live out my days in Paris? You know what the winters there are like?'

'Winters are milder still down here in Saint-Laurent.'

'But this isn't home, is it?'

'I guess not.' Caroline had just one question left. 'Why now?'

Paillaud looked towards the station. 'People say "I've got cancer," don't they? "I've got a bad heart." Got this. Got that. I don't. I say they've got me. But what they don't know is *I* am going to have the last laugh.' He turned to face her. 'Not when it suits *them* but when it suits *me*.'

'I see.' Form dictated an expression of sympathy and Caroline thought about putting her hand on his. But she couldn't, somehow. 'Your life is your own, monsieur.' At length, she picked up the document. 'So this is what, really? Your way of..?' She searched for an appropriate term.

'It doesn't matter what it is. Sign it.' He looked deeply into her eyes and gave her a smile that would have broken the hearts of film-goers anywhere. 'Please.'

'If I don't, you'll find another notary, anyway.' She signed and dated the document, and then slipped it into a zipped pocket in her daysack. 'I'll register it later today.'

'I thank you from the bottom of my heart.' He patted his

pockets and fished out a cheque book. 'I almost forgot.'

'No, no. Please put that away. So when is your train?'

'A few minutes.' He indicated the cheque book. 'Are you sure about your fee?'

'Quite sure.' She stood and, producing a more natural smile than before, offered her hand. 'Enjoy the show, Ambroise.'

Looking into her eyes, he took her hand and kissed it. 'I will,' he said.

# 3

Directives from Divisional Command rarely brought good news. The one sitting on Captain Paul Darac's desk bore the heading: "Re: Lieutenant Roland B. Granot."

'We have not taken this decision lightly, Captain.'

Darac glared at the handset, took a deep breath and let it out slowly. 'With respect, Commandant, you are not listening to what I'm saying. Granot's worth as an officer is inestimable. His value to the Brigade Criminelle, to Commissaire Agnès Dantier, to me and to the other members of our team—'

'You have your instructions.'

The line went dead. Darac slammed the handset into the cradle. Granot was due in five minutes. Five miserly minutes to conjure something positive. A plan was needed. Darac picked up the internal phone and called Vice Squad Captain Frankie Lejeune.

'You *are* acting commissaire,' Granot said, his moustachioed chops flushing a livid, lobster red. 'Act like it!'

Darac absently ran a hand into his black wavy hair and kept it there as he slid the letter across the desk to Frankie. He tried to catch her eye but she seemed tuned to a different channel today.

'Perhaps there's a way around it,' she said, the dark contralto register of her voice somehow giving credence to the idea.

'And Agnès half-way to New Zealand! If *she* was here,

there'd be a way.' Granot sat back in his chair, folding his arms over the flabby bulwark of his belly. '*She* knows how to handle these arseholes.' And then he spotted the tell-tale yellow paperclip fastening the note to the letter. His shaggy brows lowered. 'Let me see that... "Paul," ' he read aloud, ' "It seems Divisional have finally rumbled my stalling tactics. I've been over it with the union, by the way. There's nothing they can do." ' Granot looked up. 'Thanks a bunch, comrades!' He returned to the note. ' "Sorry, but you'll just have to convince the big man to comply. *Courage*, Agnès." ' Granot crushed the note into a pellet and flicking it away, landed it flush in Darac's empty espresso cup. 'He shoots, he...' Granot slumped back in his chair. 'Who cares anymore?'

Frankie scanned the letter itself. 'Theses targets are not unachievable, you know.'

'What – lose twenty kilos? Get my blood pressure down "significantly"? Ditto blood sugar. Ditto cholesterol or else it's "Thanks for everything, now bugger off." All in six months?'

Darac's hand was still in his hair. '*Three* months.'

'*Three*? Impossible!'

Frankie shook her head. 'If you make a concerted effort, you can do it. And think of the long-term benefits to your health. You could be in serious trouble one day if you don't do something about it.'

'You don't want a stroke, do you?' Darac said.

'Thanks, maybe later.' Granot shook his head. 'Twenty-eight years a *flic*! Twenty-five of them in the Brigade Criminelle!' He looked earnestly from one to the other. 'I don't want to be redeployed. I want to be out there on the street. With you and Bonbon, like always.'

'Of course,' Darac said.

'Just wait and see what *he* says about this when he gets back from leave. He'll be devastated!'

Bonbon would be contemptuous of the directive, Darac knew. But it wasn't the way to go. He was all positive body language, suddenly. 'Look, let's hope you do beat this thing but just suppose for a moment you don't and they wind up parking you behind a desk. It's not so awful. Let's face it, you're not exactly the action hero type, anyway, are you?'

'Whose side are you on?'

'All I'm saying is that your forte is, and always has been, more cerebral than physical. When it comes to chasing paper, following money, finding the one figure or timing or... *anything* in a report that doesn't add up, there's no one to touch you. And you do all those things sitting at a desk. Usually. This could be more of an opportunity than a disaster.'

Granot examined his lovely new opportunity with all the wariness of a toddler presented with an unfamiliar plate of food. 'Twenty kilos to lose!' he said, shoving it firmly away. 'Twenty! I'll never do it.'

Darac leaned in to Frankie. 'Listen, have you got any diet books or exercise DVDs you can...?' Her soft green eyes hardened to jade, a look he had seen many times before but never directed at him.

'You're confident I do, it seems.'

Grasping his T-shirt, Darac felt the need to waft a little air around his torso. 'And I know *you* know...' he lowered his voice still further. '... what I think about that, too.' He gave her a look. 'Are you alright, Frankie?'

She shrugged. 'Perfectly.'

Darac's desk phone rang and he took the call. 'Monsieur Frènes,' he said, unable to mask the contempt he felt for the public prosecutor. 'And what can we do for you?'

Frankie turned to Granot. 'Look, there's no alternative, is there? If you want things to go on as they are, you *have* to shape up and fast.'

'So *do* you have any diet books and things?' The words stuck in his craw but he got them out. 'I need all the help I can get.'

'That's better. I may still have a couple somewhere. I'll bring them in.'

Darac ended the call. 'One for us Granot, by the sound of it.'

'I can come along, can I? Not scared the car might tip over or anything?'

'We'll just have to risk it.'

'Three months...Three!'

As they filed into the corridor, Darac moved in next to Frankie and put his arm around her shoulder. 'Sure everything's fine?'

'Yes?' she said, as if mystified by the question.

'This isn't like you.'

'What isn't?'

'So where are we going?' Granot said, lost in his own problems.

Darac withdrew his arm. 'Saint-Laurent-du-Var station. Problem with a passenger on the 11.50 TGV.'

'What sort of problem?'

'The trying-to-get-on-it-while-it's-going-flat-out sort of problem.'

'Ah. The victim was pushed, obviously.'

'According to the train driver, poor sod. There's no sign of the perp.'

'Witnesses? See – I may be on my way to the knacker's yard but I still know the ropes.'

Hoping that Granot's affection for self-pity might cool at some point over the next three months, Darac pressed on. 'As yet, the driver is all we have. The Transport Police are talking to him at Gare Thiers. We'll look in on him and then go off to Saint-Laurent. Pathology's already there.'

'Deanna?'

Darac shook his head. 'She's not back until Monday.'

'Not Barrau?'

'Off sick, thank God. It'll be Map.'

'So we've got no Agnès, Deanna, Bonbon or Barrau? There's no bugger on, hardly.'

'We are a bit – Darac was about to say "thin" but he stopped himself in time. ' – light.' *Brilliant.* 'At the moment.'

22

The elephant well and truly back in his room, Granot missed the *faux pas*. 'Twenty kilos... *And* I only got Mark Cavendish in the Tour draw.'

'I thought he was supposed to be good.'

'As a sprinter, yes. Superb. But he's not going to win the Tour overall, is he?' Another shake of the head. 'Twenty kilos and Cavendish. Who'd you draw, Frankie?'

'What? Oh, can't remember. Bonbon had never heard of him so...' She shrugged, a characteristic gesture to which she added a curiously ambiguous smile. 'No great loss, eh?'

'Unlucky.' He gave Darac a look. Clueless when it came to sport, his boss had previous when it came to drawing the favourite. 'Chief? And don't say Cadel Evans.'

'I was going to say *Bill* Evans but that's jazz talking.'

Once more, life had dealt Granot a bad hand. 'You *did* draw Cadel Evans?'

'Now that you mention it, yes. Funny name. You'd think I'd remember it.'

'This is a black day for justice!' They had reached Granot's office. 'I'll just pick up a couple of pizzas and my walking frame and I'll be right with you.'

Darac was too concerned with Frankie for a comeback. 'No hurry.' He turned to her. 'Got a second?'

'You could have told the man you'd miss him if he did have to go.'

'*Miss* him? It would be little short of a disaster for us.'

'Personally, I mean.'

'I did, more or less. He knows that anyway.'

'Really?'

He kept his eyes on Frankie as he called through the doorway. 'Granot?'

'What?'

'I'd miss you if you had to go.'

'I know you would, you arsehole.'

Darac blew out his cheeks. 'It was tough going but I think

that finally cleared the air.'

The routine seemed to do nothing for Frankie's mood. 'You wanted a word?'

'Ye-es...You know the Quintet have got the Jazz Festival gig coming up in a couple of days? It's a much bigger and better event this year. No more Cimiez. We're in Jardin Albert now.'

'Paul, you are literally wearing the T-shirt. And you've talked of little else for the past two months.'

Was *that* what this was about? Surely not. 'We're playing the Théâtre de Verdure stage. Anyway, I was wondering, just this once, if you'd like to come. As my guest, of course.'

'Alright.'

'And after our set, there's this fabulous trio out of London and then finally... What? You don't want the usual week to think about it and then say "Sorry, can't"?'

'No, I was thinking I should go along this time.'

'That's wonderful.' He smiled but it faded almost immediately 'And Christophe, too if he can.' *Say he's out of town.* 'Or is he..?'

'No, he's around at the moment. I'll ask him.'

'OK.' Darac smiled and, pursing his lips, gave an enigmatic nod. 'Right.' He nodded again, part of a dumb show intended to convey that he recognised something was amiss between them; that it needed putting right; and that he hoped they might start right away.

'Back to Sepia Joe,' she said, taking her leave.

'The retro pornographer?'

'The same.'

'Lovely,' he said to her retreating back. 'See you later.'

Without turning, she gave a little wave and walked away down the corridor.

Granot was struggling into a fresh shirt as Darac stepped into his office. 'Something's on Frankie's mind. She's not herself.'

Granot checked his desktop screen and logged off. 'It's not surprising, is it?'

'It's not?'

'She's worried about me, obviously.'

'That's... probably it.'

'And I tell you what, the news will kill Flak. She really looks up to me, that girl.'

At the desk, Duty Officer Charvet had a word for Granot as they signed out of the building.

'Blueberries. That's what you want. They're a superfood.'

'That and steak frites,' Granot said, slipping on his shades. 'Especially if you throw in a few Chimay Blue Tops. Or Duvel Tripels.'

Charvet turned to Darac. 'It may be hopeless,' he said.

# 4

Mayor Hervé Montand was lying face-down on the table, his head half-submerged in a horse collar-shaped cut-out. Attending him was a bright-eyed, slightly built woman of about 30, wearing navy blue trousers and a crisp white tunic. Her ID badge read: JODIE FOUCAULT, MASSEUSE. Montand was her eighth patient of the morning.

'Here's the tight one,' she said. 'This may hurt a little.'

Jodie may have looked ill-equipped for such physically demanding work but her short, lean frame was deceptive, the legacy of a youth spent in top-level gymnastics. The crescent-shaped scar on her cheek was not the only souvenir of the years she'd spent defying gravity in ever more impossible ways – there was steel in Jodie's sinews still. Her oil-filmed hands began to work and then relax the muscle, rolling it out into the surrounding tissue. 'Knead... Relax... And roll...' Her tone was as soothing as if she were lulling a child to sleep. 'There, how does that feel?'

Montand replied in a series of breathless blurts. 'If I were a betting man... I'd hazard a good few euros... that you bake the finest baguettes...' He flinched '... in all of La Crague.'

'*All* of La Crague?' Jodie grinned, unable to keep the amusement out of her voice. 'Fame at last.'

'A little more respect... If you *don't* mind!'

Jodie squeezed harder.

'*Argh!*'

'Easing down now... Anyway, I'm not even the best baker in

this surgery. Or at Centre Sicotte, come to that. Oh, and if you take a nice deep breath before you speak, you'll find it more comfortable.'

He made a perfunctory croaking sound in his throat. Jodie felt the soft pink flesh of his back rising as he filled his lungs.

'How many sessions might I need?'

'Let's assess things again after three. But what would help you in the long run is to build up the muscles around the strained ones.'

Another breath. 'It's not easy to find the time. With all my mayoral duties.'

'And what has the mayor been up to this morning? To do this to himself?'

'Nothing,' he said quickly. 'That I recall.'

'You don't know how you did it?'

'Mademoiselle Foucault... I am not in the habit of telling falsehoods.'

Ten years old again, Jodie stuck out her tongue. The back of the mayor's head, as bald and round as a toilet bowl, seemed to take no offence. 'I can tell you how you did it.' She felt his muscles tense all the more. 'Easing down once again... if you're interested?'

'Yes, of course I'm interested.'

'Injuries to the latissimus dorsi typically occur as a result of pulling, dragging or shoving a weight. Injury is especially likely if the patient is off-balance or twisting at the time.'

More tension still. Jodie took her kneading up a notch.

'Now I think about it, I did... move some documents around... in the council chamber.'

'They must have been heavy old documents.'

'You recommend building up the muscles?' Montand said, moving on.

'Definitely. You're what – sixty now? Pilates works well. Also, yoga. And weight training, properly supervised.'

'All available at Centre Sicotte, no doubt. And at great expense.'

'Applying a *little* more pressure now... Monsieur, I work here

27

at the surgery part-time and I work at the Centre part-time. I have nothing whatever to do with the running of either establishment.'

'*Argh!*... I wasn't suggesting you did. I need to go there on another matter later so I'll make enquiries then.'

'I'd start with Pilates.'

The session kneaded, relaxed and rolled on for another five minutes.

'Now the easy part,' she said, covering his torso with a towel. 'Just relax for a few moments.'

After washing her hands, she grazed a side table stacked with printouts, selected one and took out a pen. Hoping he would fall asleep, as patients often did during these *après* moments, Jodie said nothing further until she had finished annotating the sheet.

'Still awake?'

'Of course.'

She helped Montand to his feet. Lying prone for half-an-hour had distended the fleshy masses of his face and Jodie waited until blood had drained from the loose pouches of his cheeks before leading him through a few rudimentary stretches.

'How does that feel now?' she said, looping a hair band into a figure of eight around her stubby ponytail.

'Better.'

'Good. Need any assistance getting dressed?'

'I can manage.'

'Here's an instruction sheet. Please pay particular attention to my notes. Now if you'll excuse me? I'm due elsewhere.'

Jodie left him to it. Crossing the waiting area, she kept her eyes open for any familiar faces but saw none. It was a typical cast of characters: cheerful middle-aged man explaining how he'd broken his ankle; young mother texting while baby cries for attention; elderly man staring at floor, sighing and saying "oh dear" intermittently; stone-faced elderly couple, seasoned trappists, trainee corpses; finally, beset father trying to read *Le Petit Prince* to twin bespectacled six year-olds with ADHD.

Managing the traffic was a heavily made-up receptionist

wearing a T-shirt shouting up the forthcoming La Crague Iron Man event. She glanced up from her property magazine as Jodie joined her behind the counter.

'Hi Jodie,' she trilled. 'Finished for the day?'

'Yeah, I thought I'd sail my luxury yacht over to Monaco for the afternoon.' She picked up a board with various forms clipped to it. 'Want to come?'

'Oh, why not?' Her computer produced a muffled gong-like sound. 'Wouldn't it be marvellous?' She checked the patient list on the screen. 'Monsieur Floine?'

The sighing man stood as "Delete Monsieur Floine?" came up on her display. 'Room Two, monsieur.'

He nodded and trudged away, deleted.

The receptionist lazily turned the page of her magazine. 'Goodness – look at *this* place... So what are you up to really – home calls?'

'Not until this evening.'

The woman turned to Jodie, her bland expression taking on the hauteur of an old-fashioned schoolmarm. 'You are a little miracle, the way you fly around.'

Pausing in mid pen-stroke, Jodie glanced at the woman's T-shirt. 'Save it. Arnaud's already stung me for ten euros.'

'I'm serious. And I'm not just talking about how hard you work, I'm talking about how well you manage your condition.'

'Oh, that,' Jodie said, still refusing the tyranny of the woman's favour. 'Nothing to it.'

'Nothing? All those needles?' The receptionist shuddered at the thought and returned to her magazine. 'So where *are* you tearing off to next?'

'Centre Sicotte. I'm there until 4.30 today.'

'Rubbing down a lot of muscular young men all afternoon? Why not!'

Jodie smiled, tilting the crescent moon-shaped scar on her cheek into a different phase. 'They're not all sports injuries. I've got yoga ladies. All sorts, really.'

'I fancy yoga. Or rather the instructor. What's he called, the delicious one?'

'Deepak. Deepak Abhamurthi.'

The receptionist seemed to go off the idea. 'He doesn't look like a... Deepak.'

Jodie's pen began to falter. She gave it a coaxing shake. 'He wasn't called that originally. It's a sort of stage name.'

'Ah. I might sign up, as I say. I think he could get me into some very interesting positions, young Monsieur Deepak.'

'You wouldn't be the first. Damn... ' With one entry still to make, Jodie's pen gave out. 'You haven't got..?'

'Of course.' The receptionist opened a drawer containing bundles of ballpoints in assorted colours. Each bore the legend: "*Centre Médical de La Crague-du-Var, Docteur Arnaud F. Zep, Médecin Géneraliste*" in gold, followed by an indecipherable splodge of figures. 'Good thing you know what the phone number is. Take your pick.'

Jodie chose a blue one and began scribbling incomplete circles on a piece of waste paper. 'I think this thing has dried... No, here we go. Sort of.'

The receptionist lowered her voice. 'Cheapo rubbish. You know how tight our good doctor is.'

'He's generous with his time. And with his charities.'

'A little charity closer to home wouldn't go amiss.'

A heavy knock on the counter.

'Monsieur Montand,' the receptionist said, closing her magazine. 'I am *so* sorry. I didn't see you.' She took his appointment card. 'Same time next week for you?'

'I suppose so. Would Doctor Zep be available? Just for a word, not a consultation.'

'He's not back from his run yet, I'm afraid. Or his swim or bike ride. He's in training.' A look of deep concern. 'Have you sponsored him yet, by the way? It's for a school in Angola, this time.'

Montand appeared unmoved. 'Yes, I know.'

'Right, my darling, I'm away,' Jodie said, her bold bud of a face breaking into a smile. 'Thanks for the pen. I may start recommending them to my wrist patients. Good exercise — having to go over everything twice.'

'And then he has the rest of the day off,' the receptionist continued, ignoring Jodie. 'Apart from home visits, emergencies and so on. So if you could wait? He's due any minute.'

'Just for a minute, then, alright.'

The receptionist heard the door close behind her. 'Oh, you've gone.'


Jodie ran into Dr Zep in the car park; or rather, he ran into her. A short, stocky individual in his early forties, Zep's bristling red hair and whorled, pock-marked skin gave him an overwrought, eaten-up look even at rest.

'Sorry,' he gasped, his chest heaving as he bent forward, hands on knees.

'No harm done.' As long as she had known him, Zep had made the average fitness fanatic look like a couch potato. But today, his grey hoodie almost black with sweat, his ruddy complexion pale as paper, he'd obviously pushed things too far.

'Are you OK, Arnaud?'

He spat out a string of gobbets between his feet. 'P.B.'

'Congratulations.' Thinking that posting a personal best wasn't worth killing yourself for, Jodie's eyes narrowed as she glanced at the stopwatch on his wrist. 'Which route? Not Saint-Laurent and back?'

He nodded.

'That's absurdly fast.'

'Thanks.'

'In a bad way, I mean.'

Zep straightened as a voice hailed him. 'What's Montand doing here?'

'Ricked his back. I was a bit rude to him on the table. Probably wants to complain about me.'

'That's it, Foucault – you're fired.' Zep took a couple of deep breaths. 'Until tomorrow. Here goes.'

'Don't run!' she said, getting into her car.

Jodie kept her eye on the two men as they came together. She could neither hear what they were saying nor read their lips but it was clear that Zep wasn't buying the mayoral argument. Increasingly frustrated, Montand jabbed an index finger in the direction of Saint-Laurent. *Or is it at me?* Jodie wondered. Montand repeated the gesture, pointing right at her, this time. Although she had been half joking, perhaps he *was* bitching about her. For a little routine ragging of La Crague? She felt her muscles tense as a more troubling explanation occurred to her. But how could Montand have found *that* out? Whatever it was, Dr Zep had clearly heard enough. Shaking his head, he strode off towards the surgery but then, coming to a halt with a click of his fingers, he turned to make a point of his own. *You tell him, Arnaud.* An afterthought it may have been but for some moments, Montand stood as motionless as the statue of his great-grandfather, the centrepiece of the village's Place Charles Montand.

By the time Jodie pulled away from her space, Montand was approaching his own car. She slowed and rolled her window. 'Are you alright, monsieur?'

He said nothing as he continued on his way.

# 5

'Impressive, the way the TGV driver's holding up,' Darac said, nosing his Peugeot on to the apron of Saint-Laurent-du-Var station. 'Considering.'

Granot shook his jowly chops. 'It's all bluff.'

'Denial? Perhaps. I wouldn't blame him.'

'Call it what you like, he'll be crying into his cognac later.'

They got out, collected a laptop from the boot, slipped on their police armbands and began picking their way through the crowd.

With no trains running in either direction, SNCF had laid on a shuttle service of replacement buses. Officials were advising those not waiting for one to vacate the area, an instruction aimed principally at rubberneckers.

'Look at all these raised hands,' Granot said. 'Like someone's called for a straw poll.'

Darac nodded. 'Not content just to gawp now, are they? People have got to take photos as well. There's nothing to take from back here, anyway.'

'And where do the snappers go in between times? They're never around when they might be of some use, are they?'

'Gangway! This is something you won't miss if they bump you sideways,' Darac said, still trying to sell the idea. And then he played the killer card. 'And you certainly won't miss the new protocols from Luxembourg.'

'The European Court of Justice.' Granot muttered the words in a snarl. 'European Court of Meddling Shitheads, more like.'

'Not entirely fair.'

'What's fair about making our lives more difficult?'

Darac the maverick was averse to hierarchies, directives and red tape of all kinds. Nevertheless, he supported Luxembourg's reforms in the main, including its most controversial: the removal of some of the restrictions governing a suspect's access to legal representation. Yes, amoral, smart-mouthed lawyers could soon be present during the questioning of all suspects in custody, not just those in cases initiated by the examining magistrate, and that was an unappealing prospect even to the most upright officer. But there was a saving grace. The lawyer in question would not be permitted to intervene, merely ask questions at the end of the interview. For Darac, this represented a fair balance; it granted the accused a new level of protection but shouldn't interfere with interrogations in any serious way.

The change would represent a bridge too far, he believed, for only two types of officer: those who relied on beating confessions out of suspects, guilty or not; and those, like Granot, who were set in their ways and were irritated at having to do things differently. Both camps had already seen a rise in resignations and early retirements. For the time being, Darac was content to see how things worked out in practice. But if ever a murderer, rapist or kidnapper walked free on his watch because of the change, *that* day, Darac knew, might prove his last on the job, too.

'So there you have it, Granot,' he said. 'Perhaps you'd be better off out of our brave new world of policing.'

'No I wouldn't. I like moaning. Being hacked off is my natural state.'

Darac couldn't argue with that one as they passed with some relief into the safe haven of the cordoned-off area.

'Where's Patricia?' Granot said to a young technician signing officers in and out of the red zone. A box of overalls sat open on a cart next to him.

'On leave, Lieutenant.'

'Ah.' A moue of disappointment. 'Right.'

First, Bonbon on leave and now Patricia? Darac knew exactly what Granot was thinking. Where was the fun in facing a hellish challenge if you couldn't share the pain with your mates?

They suited up, never a welcome prospect for Granot in hot weather, and the pair walked through the booking hall out on to the Nice-bound platform. Standing in the shade was a young black woman wearing the uniform of a captain in the SNPF, the National Rail Police Service. 'Captain. Lieutenant.' She smiled and extended a hand. 'Been expecting you. Florence Feilleu.'

The introductions made, Darac got straight to the point. 'Your role here?'

'To tread on your toes, naturally.'

Cute, Darac thought. 'Seriously.'

'I'm the rail incident officer. I've already informed your forensic and pathology people that the fatality appears to be a clear case of murder and that we are here chiefly to manage the railway context of the investigation. To clear up and to assist you and your teams, basically.'

'For our safety and so on,' Granot said.

'Yes.' She gave Darac a look and held it. 'And to ensure there is no repeat of the sort of unauthorised shenanigans that took place at Nice's Gare Thiers, recently.'

'Ah, yes,' Darac said, feigning innocence. 'Real mischief-makers, some of my colleagues.'

Florence was still holding the look. 'So I've heard.'

'Got any big fast locos handy, by the way? Love to take one for a spin.'

'Get an X-Box.'

He grinned. 'But back to business...' He went no further as a message crackled in on her lapel radio.

'Copy that. Over. You'll have to excuse me just for a moment, gentlemen.' She raised a hand. '*Don't* go anywhere.'

' "Gentlemen," ' Granot mouthed, as she took her leave. 'Not used to such courtesies.'

They looked around them. Open to the elements, the

station had a layout as basic as a child's train set. Running east-west, two sparsely furnished platforms were connected by a footbridge at the western end, where they were standing, and by an underpass at the eastern end. The booking hall and a few ancillary structures were grouped next to the footbridge on the northern, Nice-bound side of the station. Soft-leaved shrubs and the razor-edged tentacles of aloes relieved the stark symmetry of the chain-link fence that bounded the length of the platform. Beyond, blocks of flats, classier apartments and business premises layered back into the town at a variety of angles.

Route Nationale 7 ran immediately behind the Marseille-bound platform, opposite. On the far side of the road, a parade of apartment-topped shops looked as if it had seen better days.

'Talk about the other side of the tracks,' Granot said, wiping his forehead. 'Can't be easy running a business when the places either side are boarded-up and splattered in graffiti, can it?'

At that moment, young Officer Max Perand loped lazily out of one of the shop doorways. Catching their eye, he gave a shake of the head and a thumbs-down. No eyewitness as yet.

Florence Feilleu had finished her call. 'That was Eric, your safety liaison officer. All train services and movements are suspended in both directions through this sector—'

Granot harrumphed. 'No change there. They're on strike more than they actually work, these people.'

'Be that as it may, there are still dangers out there on the tracks so take your cue from Eric before venturing away from any of the public areas of the station.'

Darac nodded. 'Are the overhead wires live?'

'Power was turned off but it's back on now. We had to check for damage from flying... let's just call it debris.'

Darac winced. If, as he suspected, Florence was playing the "I've seen it all" game, she was winning it.

'Obviously,' she went on, 'the network's priority is to reinstate services through the station as soon as possible so I'd appreciate it if you'd let me know the moment you deem that feasible.'

'Sure. Anything from CCTV yet?' It was worth a try. 'Anything conclusive, I mean.'

'Your crime scene coordinator... Lartou, you call him?' Darac nodded. 'He's going over the footage now. There should be something – there are cameras all over the station. In terms of eyewitnesses, we had a team here very soon after the incident and they spoke to every potential witness. No one saw anything.'

'Naturally.'

Across the road, Perand emerged from another shop door. Catching Granot's eye, he pointed to the floors above and disappeared around the side of the building. Reflecting that he himself would have started his questioning on the uppermost storey, where the view of the station was more comprehensive, Granot gave him a slightly tired nod in acknowledgment.

'Florence, do you think we might get any more from the driver?' Darac said. 'Counter-intuitively, eyewitness statements typically become more detailed over time. For the first few months, anyway.'

The question seemed to raise her hackles. 'First and foremost, I'm a police officer, Captain, not a rail worker. I know all about the Witness Detail/Time graph. And the reward system that typically shapes it.'

Granot produced another harrumph.

'Forgive me,' Darac said. 'I was thinking more about the shock aspect. The driver is dealing with it remarkably well—'

'For the time being,' Granot interjected. The last word on the subject.

Darac continued without missing a beat. '—but *might* he remember more, say, tomorrow?'

'You'll be the first to know if he does but, having spoken to him myself, I think it unlikely. In fact, he did well to see the individual being pushed at all. With their eyes on the track and travelling at high speed, most TGV drivers report only hearing the thump and seeing the splatter.'

*Seen it all and pretends she doesn't care.* 'Actually, he neither saw the push, nor the pusher, did he?'

Hackles higher still. 'He saw the victim careering off the platform edge in front of him.'

'That's the outcome of a potential push, isn't it?' Darac said.

Her radio crackled into life once more. 'A moment,' she said, stony-faced.

Granot turned to Darac as Florence gave herself space. ' "Gentlemen" didn't last long,' he said, ventriloquially. 'Chip on her shoulder, hasn't she? I'll bet she failed her P.N. entrance.'

Darac gave him a look as he took out his mobile and hit one of the hot keys.

'What?' the big man said. 'No chip on *my* shoulder. My pain is justified.'

'Of course... Flak?' Darac scanned the blocks of flats behind them. 'How far have you got?' He listened. 'Anything?' He gave Granot a little shake of the head. 'We're down in the station now. Check in later.'

'She's working the floors top to bottom?' Granot said.

'She is.'

'Perand's doing it the other way round. Idiot.'

'*Skinny* idiot, you mean,' Darac said, reading between the lines. 'Skinny, never-to-be-given-an-ultimatum-about-his-weight idiot.'

'Rubbish.'

Florence finished her call. 'Here's Eric now,' she said, looking past them. 'And he's got your radios. Good.'

A short and shaggy individual wearing a grubby high-vis gilet, Eric resembled an old tennis ball.

'Before you move off, he's going to brief you on safety. Please listen carefully.'

Eric dispensed the radios as Florence took her leave. 'So gents, the prime thing to remember when you're down on the tracks is: don't fall over. You could sprain your ankle on the rails – done it myself – or sustain a nasty graze from the chippings.

Done that as well.'

'It must have been horrible for you,' Granot deadpanned. 'Is that it?'

'Yes, that's your briefing. I'm off for a coffee. Want me to bring you a couple?'

Their orders duly placed, Darac and Granot left the shade and stepped out into the full glare of the sun. Their first port of call was the hazy form of a tall, white-clad figure standing, head bowed, at the far end of the platform. Speaking into a voice recorder, pathologist Djibril Mpensa was concluding his initial report as they joined him.

Darac gave his shoulder a pat. 'What have we got, Map?'

'What we've got is body parts spread high and wide. At the speed the train was going, the victim's body exploded, effectively. The track crew have done a brilliant clearing-up job.'

Numbered card markers were scattered over the scene, each sitting on a mat of green disinfectant powder. In the roiling blur of the heat, the white-flecked patches of green put Darac in mind of a Monet. *The Water Lilies*, perhaps. Or maybe he too was in denial.

'Got a name?'

'Not as yet but I'm hopeful. Things like wallets and cards fare much better than their owners in this sort of incident. They get blown all over the place, though, so R.O. has a team combing a wide arc. As far as the pathology goes, the victim was male and elderly. That's about it at the moment. Obviously, I'll be waiving formal ID.' The young man opened his overalls down to his waist. '*So* hot today.'

'Is it ever?' Granot said, rearranging his own into a little off-the-shoulder number. 'That's... no better.'

'But you look stunning.' Darac turned, peering along the tracks at a shape emerging through the haze.

'Here comes R.O.,' Granot said, making out the brawny figure of chief forensic analyst Raul Ormans.

'Nothing wrong with your eyes.' Darac was still unable to

identify the apparition. 'That's one tick in the health column.'

Granot turned to Mpensa. 'I've got three months to lose twenty kilos and other things. Or it's...' He made a throat-cutting gesture. 'Got any advice?'

'You could try eating less and moving more. Preferably quickly.'

'Thank you.' He gave it the full Oliver Hardy moue. 'I never thought of that.'

The mood picked up considerably as Ormans joined them. 'Treasure trove,' he announced in his rich *basso profondo*. 'You'll never guess who these goodies belonged to?' He held up a poly bag. 'None other than Monsieur Ambroise Paillaud.'

Mpensa looked none the wiser.

Granot gasped, almost happily. 'Ambroise Paillaud?'

'Yes.'

'Monsieur La Chute?'

'Yes.'

'That's made my day.' A crow with powder-speckled feet hopped on to the track bed in front of him. 'In... a manner of speaking.'

'You've never heard of him, Map?' Darac said.

'Sorry.'

'Comic actor. A bit like Tati. Not so interesting, nor as big a star, but if you're in the mood for them, his films are hilarious.' Darac opened the laptop. 'I'll bring him up.'

Before he'd even entered the password, Ormans had launched into a definitive summary of the comedian's life and works. It had been, he held, a rags-to-riches story that had begun in nearby La Crague-du-Var and 'come into its full flowering' in the Paris of the early sixties. Paillaud's refusal to go with the times was generally thought responsible for the gradual decline in his celebrity, a state of affairs which appeared to have had no deleterious effect on his skilfully managed fortune. 'As you might imagine, the locals welcomed the wealthy star's return to La Crague a few years ago with open begging bowls.' He grinned. '*Arms*, I mean.'

One point stood out irresistibly to Darac. 'Paillaud's speciality was the pratfall, right?'

Ormans nodded. 'Hence the soubriquet. Ironic, considering.'

'That's one word for it.'

'What – you think he might have fallen voluntarily?' Ormans gave the line an actorish flourish. 'His last great performance?'

The half-smile that invariably played around Darac's lips widened. 'Well, it crossed my mind, yes.'

Ormans's gloved fingers delved among the credit cards and keys in his goody bag. 'In that case, you'd better take a look at these tickets.'

Map and Granot looked on as Darac examined them.

'Advance senior return to Nice, validated at 11:43 today.' He pursed his lips. 'Return, note. And... a timed entry ticket for the Brassaï photography show at MAMAC. For 3 o'clock this afternoon.'

'If the great man jumped, it must have been on a pretty sudden impulse,' Granot said. 'Doctor?'

'It happens. Remember that teacher we attended, Darac? Frémet? No, Frémarde. The man spent all day booking a couple of holiday flights and then hanged himself.'

'These no-frills airline sites can do that to you. You've got house keys, credit cards and so on, R.O. Any sign of a mobile?'

Ormans shook his head. 'No mobile in bits or otherwise as far as we can see. He may not have had one, an old-school type like him.'

'So that's the search completed?'

'As far as the station approaches are concerned. We can check the flanks, adjoining streets and so on later.'

'I'd better just take a look,' Darac said, gazing along the tracks. He handed the laptop to Granot. 'Send Lartou the most recent shot of Paillaud you can find. It'll help ID him on the CCTV footage. Assuming the victim and the effects actually match up.'

'Perhaps *that's* Paillaud's last great performance.' Granot looked half-intrigued, half-appalled at the complications it would involve. 'A disappearing act.'

'We won't go *there* unless we have to.'

'On that less than happy thought,' Ormans said, ' I'll be at my van, logging these in.'

'Thanks, R.O.' Darac turned back to Granot. 'Get hold of crowd control, will you? Needs beefing up. Should a blood-stained bit of paper with Paillaud's name on it have fluttered in through somebody's window and they contact the media – need I say more?'

As if seeking the sympathy of an invisible companion, Granot shared a look with thin air before replying. 'Anything else, master?'

'You love all this, remember?'

Leaving Granot to simmer, Darac redundantly looked both ways and stepped on to the track bed. With the tang of hot metal in his nostrils, he had taken no more than a couple of paces when his thoughts turned to Frankie and an altogether sweeter scent suggested itself to him; her signature *Marucca* perfume. Frankie... Had she ever exhibited even a hint of coolness toward him before? He couldn't think of a single occasion. As if it were a case, he began searching for a motive. Whatever it was, Frankie hadn't wanted to share it with him. Indeed, she hadn't acknowledged that anything was troubling her. Yes, it had been tactless of him to refer to the use Granot might have been able to make of her old diet books but she would normally have made a joke about it, produced a crushing put-down and come out of the exchange on top. Nothing was off-limits usually.

It had been in the one-on-one confessional atmosphere of an all-night stake-out that Frankie had first revealed her misgivings about her figure. She would have given anything, she'd said, to have been "blessed" with the elfin frame of Darac's then lover, Angeline, and not "saddled" with the hour-glass curves she had. At the time, Darac had felt that Frankie's figure was something he couldn't really comment upon and had gone no further than bland reassurances. Lately, he had had no such qualms.

His radio crackled into life. 'Found something?' Mpensa's voice. 'Over.'

'What, Map?' Darac hadn't realised he was staring at one of Monet's water lilies. Up close, it looked less cheerful. 'No, no. Just... thinking. Over' He felt a degree of guilt about it but the tracks had been searched thoroughly, hadn't they? A couple of minutes lost wouldn't harm the investigation. And what was more important, anyway? Deciding he could keep his eyes open *and* think, he set off again.

*Start at the beginning.* For three years, he and Frankie had worked on virtually every case in tandem. Murders. Rapes. Kidnappings. Armed robberies. Thousands of hours side by side. "Spending low quality time together" was how they characterised their relationship, a joke but also a way, he now suspected, of playing down its significance for the benefit of Frankie's husband Christophe, and Darac's lover, Angeline. That was fair enough. They were no more than friends, after all.

Then one day, out of a clear blue sky, Frankie told Darac she needed "a new challenge" and was leaving his team to head up the vice squad. Some time later, Angeline told him she was leaving him, also – to head up a whole new life. It had taken him months to get over losing her but it wasn't until the following year that his submerged feelings for Frankie had finally come to the surface, and in expressing them, he discovered she had felt the same all along. Ever since, the two of them had been in a *shall we*? *shan't we*? situation that would have been easy to resolve but for one thing. Angeline may have flown the coop; Christophe had not.

But what was happening now?

When he returned to the platform, Rail Liaison Officer Eric had arrived with the promised double espressos, and a surly-looking kid wearing a rapper T-shirt. Before they went any further, Granot relayed the info that the assumed victim had had neither driving licence, mobile phone, nor next of kin.

'And this young man, chief,' he said, as if announcing something remarkable. 'Is one Rafal Maso. He runs La Poche over the way, there.'

'Runs? Good for you.'

Rafal shrugged. It was nothing.

'His mother owns it,' Eric said, brightly, as if enjoying denting the boy's cred. 'Owns a few places locally. Lives upstairs. Him, I mean, not the mother.'

'Alright son,' Granot said, as Darac peeled back his overalls down to the waist. 'Tell the Captain here what you just told me,'

Rap fan Rafal ran an eye over Darac's Nice Jazz Festival T-shirt. If he felt any affiliation with him over it, he kept it to himself. 'I've got to get back to my bar.'

'That wasn't it,' Granot said.

Rafal sighed and began retelling the story of the meeting between a "stuck-up, hot-looking " woman and a "funky" old man. He had been too busy to hear what they discussed, the boy said, but he'd seen things, including the later moment when the train and the old man met head-on.

'We're standing more or less where it happened and your place is at ground level, right?' Darac scanned the greenery behind the platform. 'So how did you see it?'

'Uh... through a gap?' Rafal said, with practised condescension.

Darac downed his espresso. 'Which gap?'

The boy extended an arm. 'That brown patch in the shadowy bit? That's the café awning.'

'Thank you. You say the angle cut off the part of the platform where the victim was standing?'

'I saw the train hit the guy. Awesome! But that's all I saw.'

'Anyone else in the place see the incident?'

'I was the only one in there.'

'It's usually empty,' Eric volunteered. 'That's why I go.' He turned to Rafal. 'Nobody in the B&B bit upstairs, then?'

Some officers might have reminded Eric that it was the

police's job to ask questions but it was a valid one and Darac let it stand.

'I did have a booking last night,' Rafal said. 'But he left after breakfast.'

'OK.' Darac wiped a bead of sweat from his forehead. 'The call the woman went outside to make, did she get through?'

'She was talking into it and listening, so what do you think?'

'After she returned, she and the old man carried on for fifteen minutes or so, you said?' Rafal shrugged assent. 'How long did the old man stay on?'

'After maybe... five minutes, he got up, went to the bog and left.'

Keeping Paillaud's celebrity a secret, Granot closed the image page on the laptop and brought up a passport photo. Scrolling the holder's name off the screen, he turned it to Rafal. 'This him?'

'Looks like him.'

'You gave a pretty full description of the woman to Lieutenant Granot,' Darac said. 'Anything else you can tell us about her? How did she arrive at the café?'

'She had car keys.'

'Where did she park?'

'On a road, somewhere?'

Darac's sarcasm threshold had been crossed twice already. 'Answer the question, kid.'

'There's a couple of spots you can park down the street.'

'You didn't see the car?'

'No. Look, can I go? I had to close up to come over here. I'm losing money.'

Darac concluded the interview with the usual caution that further questioning may be necessary. As Granot circulated the woman's description, Darac took a call from crime scene coordinator, Jean-Jacques Lartigue.

'I'm putting you on speaker, Lartou... So how's the CC looking?'

45

'I've got Paillaud arriving at the station. I've got him validating his ticket. I've got him walking to the end of the platform.'

'And the "but" this time is?'

'You'll see if you look behind you, chief.'

He and Granot turned. Mounted on a pole were two cameras pointing in opposite directions.

'Paillaud positioned himself directly under that pole. If he'd stood anywhere near the platform edge, he would've been in shot. The base of the pole is the one place you can't be seen on camera. Same applies on the Marseille-bound platform.'

A deliberate choice or just chance? Darac didn't believe in coincidences, usually. 'That could be significant in itself, Lartou.'

'I tell you what I've also got, chief. I've got a couple of individuals approaching him. Separate incidents, one directly after the other. Click play on the first of the files I've just sent you. It's footage from the forward-facing camera. Not good quality, I'm afraid.'

They watched as a fleshy, bare-headed man emerged at the top of the underpass steps and walked with a sort of excited surprise towards the camera.

'He's hailing Paillaud, look,' Granot said. 'An old friend, by the look of it. He's certainly excited to see him.'

Darac gave a little shake of the head. 'Too excited, I think. He's approaching Paillaud more or less as I approached Sonny Rollins, the one time I met him.'

'You think he's a fan?'

'He's waiting on the opposite platform when he looks across and sees his hero. Decides to come over and pay his respects. That plays, doesn't it?'

As the man approached the foot of the CCTV pole, he disappeared out of the bottom of the frame.

'Keep watching, chief,' Lartou said. 'What happens next is interesting.'

With their backs to the body of the station, Paillaud and the man crabbed arm-in-arm into the CC shot. Paillaud looked behind him a couple of times, took a half-pace to the side, and then, wreathed in smiles suddenly, embraced his new friend around the shoulder. The man held out a camera at arm's length.

'Taking a selfie,' Granot said. 'He's a fan, alright.'

The shot taken, Paillaud dismissed the man, ignoring his entreaty for a parting handshake. His adoration seemingly undimmed, the fan bounced away toward the underpass steps as a train pulled into the Marseille-bound platform opposite. Paillaud, meanwhile, had slipped back into his pocket of invisibility.

'Good old Monsieur La Chute was a bit of an arsehole by the look of it,' Darac said.

Granot selected "You Haven't Thought This Through" from his repertoire of looks. 'Imagine being the centre of attraction all the time, though. I'd be just the same.'

'He seemed very particular about where to stand to have the shot taken, didn't he?'

'That's the old pro in him. Perfectionist.'

Darac wasn't convinced. 'Maybe. Lartou, what next?'

'A couple of minutes later, it gets more interesting, still. As the Marseille train is on the point of leaving, I've got a well-built male, aged anywhere between 30 to 50, walking purposefully down the Nice-bound platform in Paillaud's direction. This one is no fan. By his body language, he looks as if he wants to give Paillaud a pasting. I've split-screened the footage from both cameras.'

The man was wearing light-coloured knee-length shorts, sandals, and a blue-ish short-sleeved shirt, the summer uniform of half the men in France. His face was a pixilated mush under the peak of his dark *casquette*.

'That's what you call making a bee-line for someone,' Granot said.

'He certainly seems to be on a mission. No looking around; angry set to the shoulders.'

'He *could* be about to pick a fight.'

47

In the frame, the peak of the man's *casquette* acted like a falling curtain over his face as he advanced toward the foot of the camera pole.

'And so... he disappears.' The pair kept watching. 'And doesn't reappear the other side. So he's joined Paillaud under the camera.'

'How long before the train hits?'

'Another fourteen seconds,' Lartou said. 'The forward-facing camera catches it. Brace yourselves.'

Suddenly, there was Paillaud, his life held in suspended animation over the rails, his body strangely graceful even as it was offered up to instant, unstoppable, annihilation. And then the TGV whooshed through the frame and bloody fragments misted the air. As Darac and Granot revisited language expressing the relationship between sex, defecation and hell, the rear-facing camera had a story of its own to tell. No flying debris here; the momentum of the train shot everything out in front. But it did show the angry man retreating in some haste.

'Let's get this timing sorted out,' Darac said. 'Could Casquette have pushed Paillaud?'

They played the twin sequences twice more. 'What's your take on it, Lartou?'

'Inconclusive. Just before the impact, Casquette is not in the frame so yes, he could've pushed Paillaud. But he may've already been leaving the scene before that.'

Running the sequence again, Granot put in his own two cents-worth. 'When he appears back in the frame, he takes a pace or two and *then* turns. And he throws up his hands. We can't see his face but it's a shocked reaction, isn't it? It was news to him, what happened.'

'Nevertheless, he still may have pushed the old man. We don't know how far he may have staggered before he went over the platform edge.'

Granot nodded. 'If it took a second or two, Casquette might well have reached the point we see in the frame. If he had pushed him, it may not have been deliberate, though. He goes over to Paillaud to have it out with him over something. They scuffle. Shoving match. He's a much younger man so Paillaud inevitably winds up flying off.'

'It could have been that way. Casquette doesn't hang around, notice. Makes him look guilty of *something*.' Another thought struck Darac. 'Not many people around, Lartou?'

'A train hadn't long gone, clearing the platform.'

'Ah.'

'If you run that footage on, chief, you'll see Casquette disappearing back down the platform towards the booking hall. He doesn't look around again and the few passengers who are there don't look at him. Their eyes are on the tracks.'

'We need to find Casquette, obviously.'

'There's not much point flying a still from these images, chief.'

'Not yet, anyway. What about the departing Marseille train, the one Selfie Man got on? Could anyone on board that have seen what happened?'

'Someone in the rear part of the very last carriage *might* have, I suppose. But I think even they would have lost the sightline by then.'

'We need to follow that up and talk to Selfie Man. For one thing, someone may have been standing in the blind spot with Paillaud when he went over to him.'

'Before Casquette got there, you mean?'

'Indeed. And it may be *that* person who shoved Paillaud. Have you had time to check whether everyone who was in the frame earlier is accounted for?'

'No one goes missing as far as I can tell.'

'That's something.' Darac glanced at his watch. 'If Selfie got off at Antibes or Cannes, he'll be well away and we'll have to do the usual things to find him. But if he was travelling some distance, he might still be on the train.' He gave Granot a look, all that it took to kick-start the operation – radioing Florence Feilleu. 'Anything else, Lartou?'

'No, except to say that our best hopes for an eyewitness have got to be Flak and Perand. Quite a few windows overlook the station.'

'Indeed.' Nothing was said for a moment. 'Run the collision sequence again, Granot.'

They watched it three further times.

Granot knew the look. 'Something bothering you?'

'Just once more,' Darac said.

\*    \*    \*

Over in the flats, an elderly, rotund woman with thinning hair opened her door to Max Perand. In the room behind her, a male clone lay stretched out on a day bed moored by an open window. Perand could feel it in his young bones. An elderly brother and sister with nothing to do all day but watch the world go by? He was sure that this would be the breakthrough moment.

'We didn't see anything,' the woman said. 'Did we, Jacques?' Before Jacques had the opportunity to reply, she was already closing the door in Perand's face.

'Just a moment, please, Madame and Monsieur..?'

'Recolte.'

'Thank you.' He showed his ID. 'May I come in?'

The woman shrugged. 'Do I have any choice?'

'No,' Perand lied, thinking it unlikely that the Recoltes would be au fait with judicial developments in Luxembourg.

She shrugged once more and waddled aside. The room smelled of cat food and cigarettes.

'Do you look out much?' Perand said, joining Jacques at his window. Three floors below, the entire length of the station lay stretched out in plain view.

Jacques took a breath in.

'No, he doesn't,' Madame Recolte said.

'Please allow your brother to answer for himself.'

Madame Recolte stiffened. 'Jacques is not my brother!' She held up a work-worn hand, her ring finger garrotted by a gold wedding band. 'Yes?'

Perand shrugged. 'Alright, please allow your *husband* to answer for himself.'

'Pah!'

In the bed, Jacques looked torn between condemnation and admiration for the visitor. Madame was evidently unused to being gainsaid in her own apartment.

'We didn't see anything,' he said, tipping Perand a wink. Or was it a nervous tic? 'I was engaged in other matters if you follow me when it happened. Didn't see nothing.'

The wink once more. Did it mean something? Perand turned to Madame. 'Would you make us some coffee?'

'No.'

'Or just bring a glass of water? It's very warm today.'

Folding her arms, she made a show of standing her ground. 'I'm not moving from this spot.'

'We didn't see nothing,' Jacques said, winking repeatedly.

Standing with her back to the kitchen, Madame couldn't see the fat ginger ball of fluff that was setting course steadily toward her. 'So if that's all?' she said.

Like an overloaded ship attempting to pass under the Colossus of Rhodes, the cat butted between Madame's feet suddenly, making her start and kick out. Brained by its own mistress, the animal became a hissing bladder of fury.

'My baby, I didn't see you!'

In the avalanche of self-recrimination and promises that followed, Jacques drew Perand toward him. 'Come back about 4.30.' he whispered. 'The bitch is going out. Bring a bottle.'

'What of?'

'Anything.'

# 6

Hot at either end, an inferno in the centre, the firing tunnel was a hundred metres of graduated heat control. This morning, it had been a hundred metres of trouble.

'How many cart loads?' Hervé Montand shouted over the rumble of a lorry heading for the slip tanks.

'It was...' The foreman consulted his clipboard. 'Eight.' He made an effort to brighten. 'But it's all fixed now, monsieur.'

'How many pieces were lost?'

The man braced himself. 'Forty-four urinals, thirty shower trays, sixteen bidets.'

'All *after* firing?'

'After, yes.'

'Unusable, therefore.' Montand's eyebrows rose, crazing his forehead. 'Waste.'

'I'm afraid so.'

'Oh, don't be *afraid,* Bernis. Be *sacked*!' He turned on his heel. 'Go and see Zoë. Now!'

Montand's next stop was the moulding shed. No issues there, he moved on to the glazing bays. It was a further twenty minutes before he got back to his desk and checked his landline phone. There were no messages which, under the circumstances, was a mixed blessing. He swivelled in his chair and gazed at the ground rising above the far bank. Wedged beneath its scrub-covered crest, La Crague was sunk in shadow, a closed eye in the face of the massif. Montand closed his eyes, too.

The office door slammed.

'Napping, Hervé?'

Radiating a potent combination of brutality and sensuality, the unannounced visitor could have been anything from a slaughter-man to a gigolo. His cocksure expression said that killing floor or bedroom, it was all the same to him. If it had legs, it was going down.

'What do you want, Guy?'

Guy Vaselle drew up a chair and sat down, knees wide apart. 'You don't look pleased to see me.'

'If you were not my brother-in-law, I wouldn't be seeing you at all.'

Vaselle looked affronted. 'That's no way to talk to your head of quality control. Even on his day off.'

'What do you want, Guy? And remove that bloody hat!'

'Sure.' He tossed his blue *casquette* on to the desk, skittling a photo. 'Don't worry about Mathilde. She's used to falling over, these days. Funny – hardly ever did it when we were kids.'

Montand let the remark, and the photo, lie. '*What* do you—'

'I tell you one thing I want,' Vaselle said, getting to his feet. A drinks cabinet stood behind Montand's desk. 'So what's eating you today?' He downed a whisky, and poured another before going back to his seat. 'Same as yesterday and the day before that?'

Montand let out a long, slow breath. 'It's worse,' he said, with the air of a suspect finally coming clean to his interrogator. 'Far worse.'

'I've told you where you're going wrong. There are too many people working here. People who screw up, join unions, take breaks, get sick.'

Montand gave him a look. '*And* have days off.'

Vaselle leaned forward. 'I'm not people. I'm management.'

'And you should be grateful you bloody well are.'

Humiliation vying with bitterness, Vaselle sat back. 'We need robots. Every other company in the area uses them extensively.'

Montand shook his head. 'There may be some production advantages in automated technology but we have wider responsibilities here, do we not? What about the damage unemployment does, both to the individuals concerned and to the community?'

'What about it?'

'Almost everybody who works here lives up in La Crague. There are communes far nearer the factory but just in case you don't know, it's company policy to favour our own. If I laid off half my staff and replaced them with machines, what kind of place would La Crague become? I'll tell you. A rural *banlieue*. A second L'Ariane. A place full of layabouts with nothing to do but get drunk, take drugs and worse.'

Vaselle grinned and shook his head. 'You don't give a shit about the *individuals* who work here. I've just seen Bernis coming out of Zoë's office. In tears, the idiot. It's money. Or the lack of it. You'd invest in robots tomorrow if you could.'

'I... had to get rid of Bernis. I've told him before about the—' He batted the point away, tweaking his back. 'I don't have to justify my actions.' He stood and, resting his hands palms down on the desk, leaned forward. 'My record shows I care just as deeply about La Crague and its people as my ancestors before me.'

'You're wincing, Hervé. Stand up too quickly? Sit down and I'll tell you what I really wanted to see you about.'

'I'll remain standing.'

'Then you can get me another drink.'

Montand thought about it, but muttering 'Like brother, like sister,' he did as he was told. Avoiding Vaselle's outstretched hand, he rapped the glass down on the desk.

'Cheers.' Vaselle downed it in one, finishing in a teeth-bared snarl. 'Hervé, my friend, I've been stringing you along. I've got good news. I was down in Saint-Laurent earlier. The station. Saw someone we both know. Someone who's quite important to us.'

Montand sank slowly on to his seat.

'Thanks to my... *involvement*, let's call it, I can report that all your troubles as the owner of this company *and* as mayor of good old La Crap-du-Var are at an end.' He shrugged. 'Once I've got over a little local difficulty, that is. But I'm working on that.'

Feeling the weight of his forebears on his shoulders, Montand sat forward.

'What are you saying?'

'What am I saying?' Through the window, Vaselle watched the firing tunnel's rejects being tipped into a skip with a great shuttering crash. 'I'm saying that Paillaud is dead. Hit by a train.'

Montand let his head fall back. 'Oh, my God.'

'Say goodbye to debt, Hervé. Say goodbye to inefficient working practices. In short, say goodbye to the past.'

Montand didn't reply immediately but when he did, his eyes appeared to be in danger of popping out of his head. 'So Paillaud is dead?'

'As dead as dead can be.'

'And *that, Guy,* is your good news?'

Suddenly, the cock seemed not quite so sure. 'But I thought—'

'No you didn't.' Montand's high-domed forehead was as red as a final reminder.

'You're not capable of thought.'

'Watch yourself or I'll kick you through that fucking window. What *is* this?'

'Did you kill Paillaud?'

'No.'

Montand stared at Vaselle's large, wide-set eyes, his square jaw, his muscular torso. But he couldn't see behind them and never had been able to. He really didn't know whether the man was telling the truth or not. 'Are you aware who Paillaud had another little tête-à-tête with this morning, Guy?'

'Spit it out.'

'It was Caroline Rosay.'

Vaselle reacted as if he'd been slapped. 'What? How do you

know that?'

'Zep saw them together while he was out training. You think our troubles are over, Guy? They're only just beginning.'

# 7

His arms tore into the water as if it had personally offended him.

'Go hard now!' the coach in Dr Arnaud Zep's head shouted. 'Come on!'

His tumble turn had all the grace of a threshing machine but it got the job done: thirty-six laps swum, fourteen to go. Fifty laps in Centre Sicotte's pool, a thirty-metre affair, added up to just fifteen hundred metres. But at the pace Zep was maintaining, it made for a suitably punishing swim, the first of three in this session. In between them, the weight room beckoned and it was a call he usually answered. And at 10 o'clock in the evening, when everyone else was obliged to leave, he would return and have the pool all to himself; a perk for the local doctor from the Centre's founder and owner, Martina Sicotte herself. He could swim all night if he wanted to. And on a couple of occasions, he had.

Over in the Centre's main building, the Roland Garros Suite, masseuse Jodie Foucault was scrolling down her client list for the afternoon. 'OK, what have we got?'

Sitting cross-legged on the floor behind her, a shiny, loose-limbed man wearing shiny, loose-fitting pyjamas was reciting a short prayer to an empty saucer.

'Newsflash,' Jodie said. 'I'm not fully booked.' She closed the file and brought up a page headed "Abha Yoga." 'You've got some gaps, yourself.' She looked down at the cross-legged man. 'And I'm not talking just about those pants.'

'The wheel will turn.'

' "*The wheel...*" Park the patter, Deep. There's no-one here but us.'

'I know not what you mean.'

Deepak Abhamurthi could do spiritual strength. He could do erotic promise. Innocence was out of his range.

'Save it for the customers. What there are of them.' Jodie picked up her bag and headed for the door. 'I'm off to my one-thirty. And remember what Tina said. No wandering off until Sonia gets back from her lunch.'

In one liquid action, Deepak stood and, letting out a long burp, leaned forward to check out the screen. But living ever in the moment, his attention was drawn immediately elsewhere. Two girls wearing skimpy tops and skimpier denim cut-offs were crossing the foyer. One of them glanced his way. Deepak's long-lashed eyes glinted with wonder; the look of a fawn who had just discovered there was more to life than grass. The girl whispered something to her friend, drawing her glance, too. He smiled. The girls giggled, linked arms and went on their way.

He finally took in the page on Sonia's screen. 'Shite,' he said.

The door opened behind him and a woman in her late forties walked in. 'Hi Sexy,' she said, giving Deepak's backside a slap.

'I'm not fond of that pet name,' he said, hurriedly exiting the screen. 'For me, sex is sacred.'

Martina Sicotte threw back her head and laughed. 'For me too. I call out His name every time I screw.' Her grin faded but the upbeat vibe persisted. 'I have just heard something on *Télé Sud*. And it could be the best news ever.'

'News?'

The desk phone rang.

'Where's Sonia got to, for Christ's sake?'

'Still on her lunch break. News?'

'Wait a second.' Her gold necklace swung away from her chest as she picked up. 'Centre Sicotte, Tina speaking... Caroline!' She made a moue. 'I'll be on court in two minutes... No, the meter is *not* running. Two minutes. Three max.'

The door opened and through it floated a little slip of a woman wearing a white blouse and a serene smile. Settling at her desk like a slowly falling mist, she reached quietly for the mouse.

Her call over, Martina hung up. 'Nice lunch break and fifteen minutes, Sonia?'

'Oh yes, quite nice, thank you.' Sonia smiled, a feather evading the forehand smash of Tina's censure. 'Quite nice, indeed.'

'It throws everything out if you're not back in time. Don't do it again.'

'Yes, thank you.' The greater the displacement of air, the surer Sonia's protection from the blow. 'I'm leaving at 3.30 today, so...' Her carolling tone conveyed that if her boss didn't mind, she had work to do. 'I must get on.'

Martina led Deepak out into reception. 'I'm telling you, Madame Sonia Bera will have to go.'

'Everything must pass. The news?'

Tina waited as a couple bound for the fitness room were safely out of earshot. She looked into Deepak's eyes, their centres dark and silky as chocolate ganache. 'Ambroise Paillaud,' she said. '*He's* passed, alright. Passed big time.'

# 8

Crowd control was living up to its billing as Darac and Granot crossed the station apron.

'Let's get out of here before *Télé Sud* arrives.' Darac put the Peugeot in gear. 'It's only a matter of time.'

'An "anonymous tip-off." Pah! That Annie Provin woman will run *any* story. And of course, the caller used a public pay-phone, she says. And of course, he didn't see the incident itself, just recognised Paillaud beforehand.' Granot let out a belch. 'Stop at Le Panier on De Gaulle. I'm in need of croissants after all this.'

'This is where it begins Granot, alright? We'll stop at Rosenblum's. I'll treat you to a box of matzos.'

'*Treat?*' Granot shook his jowls. 'May as well chew the box. Or air.'

Darac's mobile rang in the dock. The number belonged to Public Prosecutor Jules Frènes. 'That didn't take long... Yes, monsieur?'

'Is there any truth in the rumour?'

'If they're saying you've lost your reason,' Granot said. 'Tell him it's true.'

Darac pressed on. 'The rumour that the deceased is none other than Ambroise Paillaud? It looks as if it is, yes.'

'You realise what this means?'

'That they're likely to re-run a few of his old movies on TV? I love the one in which he falls off the Arc de Triomphe on to a passing whoopee cushion.'

'Stop that! Stop it now! The possible murder of one of France's most beloved sons is a tragedy of national, indeed, international import. In the regrettable absence of Commissaire Agnès Dantier, you are leading the investigation on the ground. You are to remember at all times that you are acting under *my* orders and that you will carry out those orders to the letter. You will not deviate. You will act with decorum. If you do not, your previous record of, well, yes... *success*...'

'That must have hurt him,' Granot said.

Frènes continued: 'That record, Darac, will count for nothing and I will strive with all the means at my disposal to make your life as a senior police officer untenable.'

'That sounds almost like a threat, Monsieur Frènes.'

'I haven't finished. You and I are to be the public faces of this investigation. We will be under scrutiny both here and abroad. I shall be giving a press conference later which will be beamed around the world. You shall be at my side.' He gave the details. 'And you shall behave yourself.'

'My availability later depends entirely on where we get to. Now I have a crucial task to perform.' He pulled up outside Rosenblums. 'I'll be in touch.'

'If that arsehole has anything to do with it,' Granot said. 'I may not be the only one clearing out my desk.'

'I can play the notes as written.' Whether Darac would feel like doing so was another matter. 'If I have to.'

Had Granot's grizzled old chops sprouted tusks at that moment, his impression of an astonished walrus could not have been more complete. 'Captain Servile? Don't be ridiculous.'

'*Acting Commissaire* Servile if you don't mind. Let's go buy some air.'

As Darac grabbed his mobile, it rang again.

'Florence Feilleu, Captain. I have an update. Following Lieutenant Granot's call, I instructed a team to board the westbound train from Saint-Laurent. They did so at Le Muy.' She gave it a beat. 'You were supposed to say "But Le Muy doesn't have a station anymore" so I could impress you with the fact that we can board and deboard wherever we like.'

Darac grinned. Florence appeared to have regained her sense of humour but she was making a point, too. 'Actually, I didn't know Le Muy ever had a station. How did it go?'

'From our interviews, it's clear that no one on board could have seen the incident at Saint-Laurent.'

Darac shrugged. 'It was a long shot.'

'However, we were able to apprehend one Claude Grange, the passenger you dubbed Selfie Man. He'll be only too happy to talk to you, he says. He was travelling to Les Arcs and that's where we're holding him. I can patch you through if you're ready.'

'Great work, Florence. Compliment your team, too.'

'You see, we do have our uses.'

"Happy to talk" proved to be something of an understatement.

'I'd seen Monsieur Paillaud on my way *in* to the station to begin with. Outside a café. But stupid idiot that I am, I called him Jacques Tati. Can you believe it?'

Granot and Darac shared a look. Grange was two witnesses in one? Unheard-of riches.

'And me, his biggest fan, Captain. And look what happened in the end. They've just told me. Unbelievable!'

'We'll get to that. When did you encounter Monsieur Paillaud at the café?'

'Be about 11.15.'

Granot made the note, adding that it corroborated young Rafal Maso's account.

'He was meeting a woman.'

'Did you see her, Monsieur Grange?'

'Before he turned up, yeah. Well dressed, good looking. *Very* smart woman.'

'We'd like to talk to her. Can you tell us anything that might help us find her?'

'See where this gets you. I'd gone over to Saint-Laurent to see a man about a car. It's a long way, especially with mine in the garage, but you don't come across all that many—'

'Monsieur. Keep it relevant, please?'

'Sorry, yeah. In the end I didn't go for it but me and the guy got talking. And then she drives up and parks right next to us. Boxster convertible, glacier white, red leather upholstery. Beautiful car. Didn't get the registration before you ask. Why would I? But I can tell you one thing – she was off to play tennis after the meeting she'd come in for. Not that I knew who it was with then. The meeting, I mean.'

Darac shared another look with Granot. 'Do you know how soon after the meeting the woman was intending to play?'

'Dunno.'

'How do you know any of this?'

'Once she'd parked, she got on her mobile as she went round to the boot to get something out. People don't realise how loud they're talking, do they? Even so, I didn't catch it all. Just bits.'

'She didn't open with, "Hello, it's Alicia," or anything? Think.'

'Uh... No. She said, "Hi, it's me." '

'So she was calling someone she knew well.'

'And that came across in how she was talking. Warm. Casual.'

Darac glanced at his watch. If the woman had gone to the court immediately after the meeting with Paillaud, was it possible she was still playing? Even if she were, there were an awful lot of tennis courts in the area. 'She didn't mention the venue, did she?'

'No, but I know *who* she was playing, if that's any use.'

'I'd swap this guy for Perand any day,' Granot whispered, pen still at the ready.

Darac grinned. 'Excellent, Monsieur Grange. Tell us.'

'It was somebody called Tina.'

'Tina..?'

'No surname. Sorry.'

Darac's face fell. 'Ah.'

'Good player, this Tina, apparently. The woman joked she'd never scored a single point against her.'

Granot wrote "Tina = Martina Sicotte???" in his notebook and underlined it.

'Anything else you can tell us before we move on to what happened later?'

'Just a minute – the officer's saying something to me... Right. He says he's sending the selfie I took to your lieutenant right now. Don't get your hopes up – it's terrible.'

'Don't worry about that. Anything else on the woman in the Porsche?'

'Not that I can think of.'

'Did you hear the end of the call or had she gone to the café by then?'

'She was just going but I heard it.'

'How did she sign off?'

' "See you tonight," it sounded like.'

'I see. So back to Ambroise Paillaud.'

'Monsieur La Chute, himself. Of all the people to run into! I'm still in shock. I nipped over to the other platform to apologise to him to begin with. For calling him Tati. I knew it wasn't him. I don't know why I said it.'

'He was standing under the CCTV pole, wasn't he?'

'Was he? I didn't notice.'

'Was he with anyone?'

'No, he was by himself. That's the way he liked it, they say.'

As Grange recounted the way Paillaud's initial coldness had turned to enthusiasm at the request for a selfie, a copy of the photo itself pinged in on Granot's laptop. He and Darac smiled. The camera's zoom and autofocus settings had combined to bisect its twin subjects, picking up instead an angry-looking individual getting out of a car in the street behind them. Wearing shorts and a blue shirt, he was raising a blue *casquette* to his head.

'Full face, look,' Darac said, under his breath. 'What a break.'

Granot was already routing the shot to the forensic lab at

their home station, the Caserne Auvare. From there, images would be emailed to all concerned officers, TV and print media. 'I'll ask Lartou to get stills flown all around the neighbourhood, as well,' he said.

'Good.' Darac continued to Grange. 'The guy your camera focused on by accident, monsieur – did you notice him at the time?'

'No. Sorry.'

Grange's part in the call ended with his assurance that he'd seen nothing of the "accident" itself. And that he would thank God for the rest of his life that he hadn't.

After signing off with Les Arcs, Darac made another call. 'Flak? Any second now, a really nice shot of Casquette is going to buzz into your inbox. Ditto Perand's. You know what to do.'

'Right, Captain.'

He shared what he'd just learned with her. 'Anything resembling a lead so far?'

'Nothing. A lot of people were out, though. I've put cards through.'

'One of them might get back to you with something. It has happened, they tell me.'

'Could you just pass on a message to Lieutenant Granot?'

'Pass it yourself. I'll put him on.'

Giving Granot a second mobile to deal with occasioned a display of such cack-handed confusion, a set of juggling clubs would scarcely have created more difficulty.

'Rahsaan Roland Kirk used to play three saxes at once,' Darac said, helpfully.

'I'm a detective, not an octopus...Yes, Flak?'

'If there's any help I can give you with this Divisional Command directive, just ask.'

'That's kind. Won't forget it, Flak. Signing off, now.' He elbowed Darac in the ribs. 'Told you. Worships me.'

'She can't be right about everything.'

In his juggling act, Granot had dropped his notebook and it

had somehow found its way under the clutch pedal. Darac had to get out of the car to retrieve it and as he handed it over, three underlined question marks caught his eye.

'Who's Martina Sicotte?' he said.

# 9

'Thanks for responding to the card I left, mademoiselle,' Flaco flashed her ID. 'You saw the whole thing, you say?'

'It was disgusting.' She forced a smile. 'Please, come in.'

Wearing stone-coloured shorts and a strappy top, the woman was in her early thirties, tall, slender and with shoulder-length, dyed-blonde hair. She owed her full, high-set breasts to implants, Flaco guessed; and her small, even teeth had been veneered so blindingly white, they had the unnatural look of old-fashioned dentures.

With the sun streaming in, the living room was a brightly cheerful if, by Flaco's own standards, untidy space. Among the painted lightweight furniture, an old-fashioned mahogany side-board caught her eye. On its cluttered top, the footprint of some-thing recently removed was the only part of it not overlaid by a film of dust.

'You were out on your balcony when it happened?'

'Yes. Go through.'

Flaco went to the rail and checked out her twentieth different view of the station that afternoon. Not one of the more compre-hensive views, in truth.

'Great cornrows you have,' the woman said, joining her. Standing next to one another, the pair looked about as different as it was possible for two women to look. 'I had it done once but it looked stupid.' She smiled, artlessly. 'You've got to be black, I suppose.'

Now wasn't the time. 'So exactly what did you see?'

Somewhere behind them, a kettle came to the boil and clicked off.

'I saw this well-built guy run, well not run, walk – walk quickly up to the old man standing at the end of the platform.'

'How come you noticed? Everyone else I've spoken to has said, "you don't expect me to stand looking out of the window all day, do you?" '

The woman indicated her sun lounger. Under it was a low, flat object covered by a plastic sheet. 'My treadmill. I have to watch my...' She hesitated, giving her short, strapping visitor a half-sympathetic, half-patronising look. 'I'm a workout junkie.'

'Me too. Kick-boxing is my thing. Is that where it lives, the treadmill?'

The question seemed to wrong-foot the woman. 'Yes... I just pull the lounger to one side and it's good to go where it is.'

'Would you show me? I'm thinking of getting one.'

The request further unsettled her. 'Alright. It's not powered or anything. Just a roller.'

'That would suit me. Useless with technology.'

The demo took up no more than a minute. At the end of it, the woman's breathing had increased but her anxiety level appeared to have diminished.

'Thanks for that.' For the first time, Flaco thought she could detect alcohol on the woman's breath. 'Alright to continue out here?'

'Sure.'

'This well-built guy – have you ever seen him before?'

'No. Never.'

'Uh-huh.' She showed her Grange's accidental close-up of the man on her mobile. 'This him?'

'I think so... Yes. It is. Definitely.'

The reward smile not coming easily to Flaco, she gave a brisk nod. 'What happened when the two of them came together – the guy and the old man?'

The woman began twisting a strand of hair around her finger.

'They went off on one.'

'They fought physically?'

'No, no. They just had words. Only lasted a few seconds.'

'Right.' Flaco moved in closer. Yes, the woman had been drinking alright. A spirit of some kind. Unsurprising, perhaps, under the circumstances. 'And then what happened? Take your time.'

The woman put her hand to her forehead. 'The guy had got off his chest what he'd wanted to, I guess, because he turned and left. And then...' She reached for the handrail in front of her. 'The old man took a running jump... straight in front of the TGV.'

'He jumped? Completely of his own volition?'

The woman straightened. 'Yes. There was no push. Nothing. He ran and jumped.'

'You'd be prepared to say that at an inquest?'

'Yes.' She reached for Flaco's forearm. 'Could we go back in? I'm sick of this view today.'

After what she'd just seen and heard, Flaco's thoughts were already returning to the sideboard. 'Of course.'

Repairing to a sofa occupied by a menagerie of soft toys, the woman made a space for herself and gestured Flaco into the armchair opposite.

'This is cheeky but I missed my coffee break earlier.' Now was the moment for a smile. 'I heard the kettle. If you were about to have one, I'd join you.'

'I was going to have an Earl Grey tea. Would that be alright?'

She had never tried it. 'My favourite, thank you.'

As the woman padded into her kitchen, Flaco moved quickly to the sideboard and slid open a drawer. And then another. Nothing. Perhaps she had jumped to the wrong... The third drawer came up trumps and she offered the object to the dust-lined footprint. It fitted exactly.

'A slice of lemon?' the woman called out.

'Perfect,' Flaco said, slipping her phone out of her pocket. She took a shot of the object and put it back in the drawer. When her hostess returned, Flaco was playing innocently with her mobile. 'Sending a quick email,' she said. 'Just routine.'

'Right.'

The station PA's four-note clarion drifted in from the balcony. A lengthy live announcement followed, every so often eliciting a groan from the waiting crowd.

Flaco took her tea. 'Sounds as if people aren't getting what they want.'

'Well,' the woman said, a harder edge in her voice. 'Isn't that so often the way?'

# 10

Darac pulled up at temporary lights, the second stop for road works he had had to make since passing the sign to La Crague. 'So tell me about this Martina Sicotte.'

'She'll be in her mid-forties now, I should think,' Granot said. Vehicles dribbling through on the open carriageway began to dry up. 'Twenty-year pro on the tennis circuit. She could well be the Tina our mystery woman is or was playing.'

'Hot, then?'

'I certainly am.'

'You do have a certain boil-in-the-bag look.' The light went to green. 'But I meant Martina.'

'Martina hot? She was not. Luke-warm at best.'

'Did I miss something? I thought you said she was a long-term pro?'

'She was and I'm sure she hammers the locals. Including the men. But her mother, Yolande – now she *was* a tennis player. A true champion. Hard as nails.'

'So it's her centre, Yolande?'

'No, she kept her maiden name, Yolande Bertrand.' Granot gave Darac a look. 'Don't tell me you've never heard of *her*.'

'You know me and sport.'

'Wait a minute.' Granot laid a hand on Darac's forearm. 'I've just told you Yolande was a top-ranked tennis player, right?'

'What's with the death grip?'

'She marries a Monsieur Sicotte and in time, gives birth to a girl. She calls her Martina.' His shaggy eyebrows rose, creasing his forehead like an old dog blanket. '*Martina*. OK? Now why might she have chosen *that* name?'

Darac shrugged. 'After her own mother? How should I know?' He saw it. 'Ah.'

Granot brightened, a teacher encouraging a slow pupil. 'Yes?'

The lights turned green. 'She named her after Tina Brooks.'

'Who the hell is Tina Brooks?'

'Hard bop sax player. Great improviser. A man, oddly enough.'

'It was after Martina Navratilova, you imbecile. Best woman player of all time.'

'Navrati... Oh yes. Rings a bell now.'

At a sign, Darac turned towards an uninspiring ensemble of buildings dotted around a small, unimaginatively landscaped green space. 'Here we are, the Sicotte Centre for Mind, Body and Spirit.' He ran an eye over the glass and concrete. 'Eighties Mediocre – a style that never dates. It's always crap.'

Granot's eyebrows rose. 'I tell you what isn't.' He pointed at the one shade tree in the lot. Parked underneath was a smart white convertible. 'Voilà.'

Darac headed for it and drew up alongside. The car was a white Porsche Boxster with red leather seats. 'Got her.' Darac gave Granot's knee a slap. 'Good shout, man.'

'All part of the service.'

Darac retrieved the laptop and fed in the registration. A couple of quick searches provided the basics. 'One Caroline Rosay is the owner, a notary public residing in La Crague. Single. Clean record.' He angled the screen. 'This is her. What do you think?'

Granot flipped open his notebook. 'Considering Rafal Maso was plugged in to his own little world at La Poche, he did give a pretty detailed description.' He read it out and peered at the screen. 'It's her, alright.'

'Agreed.'

They set off on a path signed, presumably without irony, to "The Complex". 'She's a notary, Granot. A notary who has a

72

meeting with a man who only half an hour or so later winds up dead.'

'At college, that is what we would have termed "a significant connection". We don't know if she was *his* notary, of course.' Granot swiped his mobile. 'Easy enough to check, though. I'll get Charvet on it. He likes having something proper to do in between buzzing people in and out.'

Granot called the duty desk at the Caserne and asked Charvet to search the national registry of wills database, the FCDDV. 'Soonest, please.' He went to ring off but Charvet had more. Granot listened, nodding forbearingly. 'Blueberries, yes, I remember. Superfood... I'll get one... Several then, alright? Thanks.' He rang off and after a few paces returned to his theme of the moment. 'You know, one of these days, it might matter that you don't know a blind thing about sport, chief. Might affect a case, I mean.'

Darac adopted the look of a wild-eyed street boy. ' "Who's the world ping-pong champ, *flic*? Tell me or I'll blow your freakin' head off!" ' He dropped it. '*That's* going to happen.'

'Sport's a part of life. It's all around you. And what does Agnès say? "No knowledge is wasted." True?'

'True, but while I've got sports nuts like you and Bonbon around...' He went no further, running aground on the tide ebbing away in Granot's eyes. 'Listen, they haven't banished you yet. And they won't if you get your act together.'

' "They haven't *benched* you yet," works better. You'd know that if you knew anything about sport.'

Darac's mobile rang. 'It's Flak. I'll put her on speaker.'

Drawing into the shade of the main building, they paused to take the call. .

'One of my card people got back to me, Captain.'

'If you've got a flag on you, raise it.'

As Flaco gave the contact's name and address, Granot's eye was taken by a line of scantily-clad individuals filing giddily out of reception. Leading them was a glossy individual wearing the expression of someone who was used to being adored. As if a button had been pressed, Granot felt an urge to adore him with a sharp jab to the nose.

'We're the seekers of truth,' the line's tail-end Charlie volunteered, answering Granot's unasked question as he skipped by. 'Deepak's doing it outside, today.'

'*Is* he?' Granot said, his smile fading quicker than a sliced backhand.

'The woman has a treadmill set up on her balcony, Captain. She was working out on it when she saw the whole thing. Paillaud jumped all by himself.'

'Suicide? And she'd testify to that?'

'She would. There's only one problem. She's lying.'

'Hold it a second, Flak,' Darac said, as a couple of muscle-bound men in shorts tottered past them like a pair of giant babies. 'OK, go on.'

'She could have seen what she claimed only if she'd been standing on the extreme right-hand end of her balcony. The treadmill is set up on the opposite end, though, and she confirmed she didn't move it.'

As Granot listened, he watched the babies disappear into reception. A moment later, a woman in a white short-sleeved tunic appeared framed in the doorway. Following a brief exchange with someone at the desk, she began jogging briskly towards them. Her fair hair gathered into a stubby ponytail, there was more than a suggestion of a tomboy in the way she looked and moved.

'Left something in my car,' she said to Granot as she ran past, offloading the line like a rugby player's pass. 'So much for our memory course!'

Granot gave a fruity little chuckle. The staff in this place weren't all wankers, it seemed.

'So why did she lie?' Darac continued to Flaco.

'She's Casquette's girlfriend. There was a framed photo of the pair of them freshly secreted in a drawer – so I wouldn't make the connection, obviously. I found it when she left the room, briefly. I let her talk for a while before confronting her about it.'

'Excellent. Was he with her before the confrontation with Paillaud?'

'No, he rang her afterwards.'

' "Hi sweetie, would you do me a big favour?" '

'More or less exactly what he said.'

'How big a favour is it, do you think?'

'He swore to her that he hadn't done anything. He and Paillaud rowed. There was no pushing or shoving and then he left. The train hit when his back was turned. That's what he told her.'

'His name?'

'Vaselle, Guy Antoine.' She spelled the surname. 'Motoring offences only. You should be getting his photo from the Caserne any second now.'

'Tell us about him.'

'He's the quality control manager of Montand Sanitary Ware, a ceramic business in the *zone industrielle* just up the Var. He's the brother-in-law of its owner, a Monsieur Hervé Montand, who's also the mayor of... La Crague.' She spelled that, too. 'Wherever that is.'

'It's stuck half-way up a mountain on the other side of the river from the factory. Not far from Carros.'

'Really? Carros, I know. I've never heard of La Crague.'

'Odd little place. Got a sort of Land That Time Forgot feel. Where does Vaselle live?'

'In Cagnes.' Flaco gave his address, landline and mobile number. 'The mobile he gave to this particular girlfriend, at least. I rang it there and then. It's switched off. And there's no one at home. No one answering the phone or the door, anyway.'

'So the girlfriend doesn't know Vaselle's whereabouts?'

'She says not.'

Darac pulled at his T-shirt, fanning a little air around his chest. 'Do you believe her?'

'Yes I do. I told her to contact us if he rang again or showed up. I really scared her – I'm certain she will – but shall I take her in, anyway?'

'No – better to leave her in situ. In the meantime...' He glanced across at Granot but the big man, ahead of him on the play, was already calling Mobile Response. '...We'll get a couple of uniforms round to Vaselle's place and we'll post a plain-clothes where you are, just in case.'

'Understood.'

'Good work, Flak.'

He could picture the modest little smile the young woman from Guadeloupe was allowing herself.

'Oh, Perand rang me, Captain. He's got a call-back with a potential eyewitness, as well, a Monsieur Recolte who lives over the shops on the opposite side of the station.'

'Ah yes?' A maverick himself, Darac cared little for matters of form but free spiritedness in a junior officer was one thing; not respecting the team ethic, another. 'Perand hasn't shared this with us.'

'Probably because he suspects Monsieur Recolte is senile or lonely or both. Anyway, 4.30, he's seeing him.'

'Fair enough. That's it.'

Granot's call to Mobile Control over, he turned as Ponytail came jogging back from the car park. She was breathing as easily as if she were walking.

'Got it,' she smiled, brandishing what looked like a travel brochure.

The big man smiled back at her, an occurrence so rare, Darac almost dropped his mobile as they continued on their way.

'I don't think you're Roland Granot. You're an impostor from the Planet Charm.'

'What are you talking about?'

'You actually smiled. Warmly. At the jogger.'

'Bollocks.'

Order restored.

Reception was a thing of tongue-and-groove pine, leather-clad seating and chequered carpet tiles; a somewhat down-at-heel space presided over by a photo of a young tennis player receiving a small silver cup from a small silver-haired man.

'Martina?' Darac said.

Granot nodded. 'Just about the only tournament she ever won.'

At the desk, a smartly dressed little wraith of a woman aged, Darac guessed, in her mid-fifties, was already smiling before she looked up from her keyboard.

'Good afternoon,' he said, flashing his ID and checking hers, 'Sonia. Could you tell us if Madame Sicotte is still ..?' He searched for the term.

'On court?' Granot said.

'Yes, she is.' Sonia checked her screen. 'Court One.'

'And she'll be free when?'

'The lesson ends in... ten minutes.'

'Her opponent...'

'Pupil,' she said, the smile unchanged.

'Her *pupil* is one Caroline Rosay, yes?'

Sonia half-rose from the cover of the desk and scanned the area. The coast was clear. 'May I ask what this is about? We do have certain guidelines now to do with...' She lowered her voice. '... confidentiality.'

'What it's about, Sonia, is also...' Darac lowered his voice. '... confidential.'

'Of course. And personally, I do think it's all nonsense, this new thing.'

'We need to talk to her and briefly to Madame. Is there somewhere private we'll be able to conduct the interview?'

'Martina's office. Just back along the corridor, there.' Pursing her lips, Sonia gathered the loose papers in front of her and soundlessly squared them up. 'That is *very* private.'

Learning that once off court, Caroline would have to cross reception en route to the locker room, Darac and Granot withdrew to a row of chairs lining the side wall.

*Sans* travel brochure, Granot's jogger friend appeared at the desk and after a word with Sonia, walked across to greet them. 'You're waiting to talk to Martina and Caroline? They won't be long.'

'Thanks,' Darac said, wondering how she had acquired the unusual scar on her cheek.

Granot produced an avuncular grin. 'Glad of the sit-down, to tell you the truth, mademoiselle. And you are?'

She extended her hand. 'Jodie Foucault.'

*Foucault.* The name, courtesy of philosopher Michel, put Darac in another time and place. His former lover, Angeline, had written extensively on the man's theories and was wont to discuss them with Darac over a late-night glass or two. He could still articulate the arguments. Where he detected contradictions in Foucault's thinking, Angeline saw paradoxes. And wasn't it the paradoxes, she suggested, that pointed to the deeper truth at the heart of all modern French thinking? He could picture her now, sitting out on the roof terrace of his apartment, from time to time noting down a new idea, a discussion topic for some future class. Then they would sip more wine and listen to more music before wandering back into the apartment, and to bed.

This was the second time today, he realised, that he'd had thoughts of Angeline. It triggered another memory of the night Frankie had first shared her reservations about her figure; and how she envied, she had said, Angeline's slender, "wear anything" frame. Because it had seemed disloyal, Darac hadn't told Frankie that Angeline, despite everything she knew and lived by, had occasionally expressed a reciprocal envy for her.

Frankie... Darac needed to talk to her. He was rehearsing with the band at the Théâtre de Verdure later, the alfresco venue in Jardin Albert. Perhaps she would be free afterwards.

'Won't be long,' Granot said, rising.

'What?'

'Didn't you hear what we were saying?'

Darac looked past him at Jodie. 'Foucault – any relation to Michel?'

She gave him a quizzical smile. 'Michel? There's a great-grandfather, I think. But he's on my mother's side.'

Darac shook his head. 'Sorry. Irrelevant.' He turned to Granot. 'Where are you going?'

'To the workout room.'

'You are?' Granot was definitely an impostor. A poorly briefed one. 'Why?'

'Jodie's going to give me a quick tour. She's got a plan. Reckons she can get my weight down – the lot.' The rolling hills of his chins took on a lofty resolution. 'With her help, I think I can beat this thing.'

'Good. Excellent.'

'Follow me.' Jodie smiled, leading Granot away. 'Don't be put off by all the rowing machines and things. They can look a bit daunting...'

Grinning at the strangeness of it all, Darac glanced at his watch. There was still a good five minutes before the interview so he had time to call Frankie. He stepped through the front doors, and checking he had a sightline back into reception, took out his mobile. No answer. He left a message.



The two women wore white tennis dresses, expensive wristwatches and red shale-clouded shoes. And that was where any similarity in their appearance ended. As if she were carrying around her own personal fairground cut-out, Martina Sicotte had an oddly mismatched appearance. Her pinched, sun-scored face reminded Darac of photographs of dustbowl era sharecroppers in the U.S. but her muscular frame and legs were unmistakably those of a professional athlete. The mismatches didn't end there. Her right forearm was twice the circumference of her left. Darkly powerful, she looked as if she might have been sitting in an armchair for the past forty-five minutes.

One towel draped across her thighs, another around her neck, the lean and fair-haired Caroline Rosay was sweating profusely.

'You teach for half an hour and then conclude with a short game?' Darac said, hoping Granot was surviving his tour of the workout room; the big man still hadn't shown.

'Yes, I run through a core programme and then we play a set or for fifteen minutes whichever comes first.'

'Believe me, the set *always* comes first,' Caroline said, checking out Darac's T-shirt. 'Are you going to the jazz festival?'

'Yes. You a fan?'

'In a soft-core sort of way. I like Brazilian music. Astrud Gilberto – that kind of thing.'

'OK,' Martina said, rising. 'You two need to talk.' She picked up a pile of papers from her desk and strode to the door. 'Don't leave it too long before you hit the shower, Caroline. You can catch cold even in this heat.'

'That depends on the Captain, here.'

'I'll be as quick as I can.' He stood and extracted his notebook from his trouser pocket. 'I may need just a brief word with you, later, madame. That alright?'

'Sure.' Martina ran an eye over him. 'You play tennis? I'm offering six lessons for the price of five, today.'

'Sorry. Ball sports are not my thing.'

'Pity. Catch you later.'

'You are a wise man,' Caroline said, as Martina closed the door behind her. 'You are also puzzled about something.'

And you are a very observant woman, Darac thought to himself. 'It's her accent. I've got a pretty good ear but I can't place hers, at all.'

'That's because you're aiming at a moving target.' She took a long swig from a bottle promising "Pro Rehydration", then patted her forehead with the neck towel. 'Tina grew up on the tennis circuit. Americans, Russians, Australians – it's a polyglot world.'

'I see.' Finding an empty couple of pages, he turned to Caroline and smiled, a benign signal that they were moving into deeper waters. 'This is quite informal,' he said. 'Just a chat, in effect.'

As if finding some amusement in his assurance, she gave a

little involuntary laugh. 'Really?'

'Nevertheless, I do have some questions and I would be grateful if you would answer them.'

'I'm sure you would.'

'Earlier today you had a meeting with Monsieur Ambroise Paillaud?'

Beads of sweat already pocking her forehead, she put her towel to use once more. 'I did.'

'At La Poche, opposite the station in Saint-Laurent?'

'Indeed.'

'He was a client?'

'So it's true. He *is* dead.'

'Someone is and it seems certain that it's Monsieur Paillaud. He was a client?'

'He was.'

'Can you remember what he was wearing this morning?'

Caroline stared off for a moment and then gave a description so complete, it included Paillaud's toupée. Her list matched the findings at the scene.

'Thank you. Did you or Monsieur Paillaud set up the meeting?'

'The latter.'

'And to establish a time frame, when did you arrive at La Poche?'

'Around 11.15.'

Darac had a question he knew Caroline would realise strayed beyond the bounds of informality and from which other searching questions might flow. 'Would you mind telling me the purpose of your meeting?'

'Yes I would but since your next move could be to suggest we continue our "chat" all the way over at the Caserne Auvare, I really have little option, have I?'

'Mademoiselle—'

'Oh, don't worry – I would do the same in your position.'

'Thanks for understanding.'

'Actually, I didn't know what the purpose of the meeting was. He just said he wanted to see me.'

'Uh-huh. And just going back to the time frame for a moment, I understand you went outside briefly. When was that?'

'11.20 or so. To make a phone call.'

'And who might you have been calling?'

'*Might*? We've already established the ground rules, Captain – there's no need to pussyfoot around. After just a few minutes, it was clear to me that the meeting was going to take longer than envisaged, and I was concerned it would eat into my court time.' Another dab of the towel. 'So I called Tina to ask if she could squeeze me in later. These twice-weekly thrashings are expensive, and having already paid for the pain, I wanted my money's worth.'

Darac grinned. 'I suppose scoring points against a former pro can't be easy.'

Caroline took another long draft from her bottle. 'One doesn't score points in tennis, Captain. One wins them.'

'Ah, yes? And was it necessary?'

'Was what necessary?'

'Having the lesson put back until later.'

'Do you actually believe I've been running around the court all this time? In the middle of a scorching July day? I don't know whether to feel flattered or offended.'

Darac could see little point in bashing balls around in any sort of weather. 'It *was* put back, then.'

'By an hour, yes.'

'You left Monsieur Paillaud in the café at about?'

'11.35.'

This all tallied with Claude Grange's and Rafal Maso's accounts. 'And your lesson began an hour later than planned. How did you spend the interim?'

'I drove round to Cap 3000. Bought a new swimsuit at Cala. If you'd care to check, it's in my boot – the white Boxster. But I'm sure you already know that that's my car.'

Hot and sticky though she may have been, Caroline Rosay's cool self-assurance put Darac in mind of a young Lauren Bacall. Or rather, Bacall's early Film Noir persona. On a different day, he might have posed his next question à la Bogart but he continued as before. 'So, going back to the meeting itself. Why did Monsieur Paillaud want to see you?'

Caroline took another swig from her bottle and patted her forehead. 'Do *you* rate Astrud Gilberto, Captain?'

He rated Nara Leão higher; Elis Regina higher still. 'She has something, certainly. Especially when accompanied by Jobim.'

'I agree. *Why* did Monsieur Paillaud want to see me? To tell me he was ill. Terminally ill, in fact, and that he intended to take his own life.'

Darac's brows lowered. 'He told you he was going to kill himself?'

'Yes.'

'And knowing that, you went off to chase a ball around a tennis court?'

She made an exasperated sound in her throat. 'I obviously didn't expect him to do it there and then. He was going to the Brassaï show in Nice, for one thing. It's ticket-only and he had one. He also had a train ticket. A return, I think.'

'How do you know that?'

'He dropped his wallet. They fell out and I picked them up for him. Anyway, that's why he wanted to meet me at the station. And even if I had known his intentions, you have to remember that I act *for* my clients, Captain, not against them. I frequently advise but if someone is set on a particular course of action, it's not my role to try and prevent them. So long as there's no illegality involved.'

Darac pursed his lips. As dispassionately as she had made it, perhaps Caroline had a point. 'Can you recall his exact words?'

'Uh... "Cancer has got me but I'll go when *I* want to; not when *it* does." It was something like that.'

'Thank you. What was his motivation in telling you this?'

Slipping off her neck towel, she gave him a disappointed look. 'You're asking me to comment on another party's—'

'Alright, why do you *think* he told you? What could be gained by it?'

'Gained? Nothing except perhaps to share his situation with someone. He lived alone, had no family at all, and no friends. A recluse, really. And although I wouldn't exactly say I was his confidante, I believe he regarded me as someone he could at least trust.'

'His will is lodged with you, I take it?'

'It is.'

'Your office is where?'

'At home, La Crague. Avenue Montand.'

'I see. Did Monsieur Paillaud at any time in your meeting refer to the will?'

She gulped down more fluid from the bottle. 'No.'

'So he didn't want you to record a change, or anything?'

'How could he without referring to it?'

Feeling Caroline's mien turning a degree or two cooler, Darac decided to ease off a little. 'Quite – stupid question. Could you tell me when he made his will?'

'December last. Check on the national database if you like.' She got to her feet. 'And now, Captain, I really should head to the shower.' She swung her kit bag on to her shoulder. 'You don't want me to catch that cold, do you?'

As they made their way into the foyer, Granot appeared, finally returned from his guided visit to hell. But instead of the sweat-drenched wreck Darac was expecting, the man looked relaxed, even strangely, *uniquely*, serene. 'This is my colleague, Lieutenant Granot,' Darac said, making the introduction. 'At least, I think it is. Another question, mademoiselle, while we walk?' He scrolled screens on his mobile. 'Just a quick one.'

'Alright.'

'Would you look at this?' He handed it over. 'The fuzzy faces belong to—'

'Monsieur Paillaud and the almost fan I mentioned from the café,' she said, slowing. 'So he caught up with him again at the station?'

'He did but it's the man in the background I'm interested in. The one in focus. Do you know him?'

She gave a disdainful snort. 'Twice in one day. My, I am lucky. It's Guy Vaselle.' She handed back the phone. 'We passed each other in our cars. Slowly enough to exchange looks; *his* conveying that he was sure my seeing him would have made my day.'

'And it didn't?'

'Some may find Vaselle irresistible, Captain. I am happy to say, I am not one of them. The man is an arrogant, ignorant boor.'

'How do you know him?'

'He was a builder until a year or two ago. There was some work I needed doing and had a few local firms in to give estimates. Monsieur Vaselle made it crystal clear that if I opted for him, he would be happy to provide certain extra services. And, praise be, at no extra charge.'

'On behalf of my gender, I apologise.'

'No need, Captain, I assure you. Why are you interested in him?'

'Monsieur Paillaud was involved in an altercation immediately before the speeding train hit him.'

The news brought Caroline to a halt. 'And the altercation was with Vaselle?'

'It was and although Monsieur Paillaud disclosed his suicidal intentions to you, we are far from certain he ended up under the train of his own volition.'

'Pushed?' She pursed her lips, thinking about it. 'I suppose when you consider Monsieur Paillaud's exhibition ticket and so on, it makes more sense. But Vaselle? He has a filthy temper, I would imagine, but I can't quite picture...' She brightened, returning to her signature look. 'Still, I don't have to, do I?' She walked on. 'That's your job.'

'Mine, Lieutenant Granot here and several other officers.'

'Interesting question, isn't it?' she said. 'Does it count as murder if the victim intended to kill himself, anyway?'

It was Darac's turn to be knocked off his stride. 'Of course it does.'

'Morally, I mean.'

'That's a little more difficult.'

At the first hint of philosophical speculation, Granot had been known to emit heart-rending groans. Darac gave him a look. There was no grimace. No eye-rolling. Just that same look of almost post-coital reverie.

They had arrived at the women's locker room.

'This is where I live,' Caroline said. 'Don't hesitate to contact me if you require anything further, Captain.'

'Thank you.' They shook hands. 'Just one final question. It's something we can't check on the database but you *could* just tell us.'

'Try me.'

'Monsieur Paillaud's estate is a large one, I imagine?'

She pushed the door open, releasing sweet and sour scents into the air and a peal of girlish laughter. 'It could be.'

'To whom is it bequeathed, principally?'

She smiled. 'See you at the jazz festival, perhaps.'

And with that, Caroline Rosay disappeared into the fug of the locker room.

He turned to Granot. 'Impressive woman. I'm Paul Darac, by the way. And you are?'

'Mademoiselle Foucault gave me a massage. That's all I know.'

They headed back to the foyer.

'I thought she was supposed to be showing you the ropes?'

'She did, but first she ran a video of the things they do here. Up came this clip of her in action on this guy's shoulders. I mentioned how tight mine were and she gave me five glorious minutes. Strong hands, I tell you. A slip of a girl like that! And she didn't charge me.'

'This is how they get you. First five minutes free; next thing, you've signed up for a thousand euros-worth. Let's go.'

'No, no. She wouldn't do that. And you should see her on the cross trainer.'

'The what?'

'Cross trainer.'

'Unbe-cocking-lievable.'

'With her help, I'll hit all my goals – you'll see.'

'*Goals?*'

'Laugh. It's fine.' Granot composed himself into a roughly Granot-like form. 'So – Caroline's meeting with Paillaud?'

'She said he told her he was going to top himself. Terminal illness.'

Granot's aura darkened a shade. 'And then she just drove off?'

'She hadn't realised he meant right away, she said. But whatever the timing of this thing, we've got Guy Vaselle to think about, haven't we?'

'Coercing your girlfriend into lying for you doesn't look good. Where to next?'

'Paillaud's place. We might find something there. But first, I need a quick word.' Hearing a loud, strangely-accented voice, he turned. 'With *that* lady.'

As Martina Sicotte issued an instruction across the receptionist's desk, Granot studied her four-square frame. 'She's built like her mother. Pity she couldn't play like her.'

Before they reached the desk, she was joined by the short, shiny yoga teacher fresh from his stretch in the woods.

'The smarmy swami's back,' Granot said, all vestiges of serenity gone. 'Look at him.'

'This might only take a second. Light and casual, now.'

As they approached, the shiny one put his palms together in greeting.

'Deepak Abhamurthi,' Martina said, speaking for him as if it would have been sacrilegious not to have done so.

'How's it going, mate?' Darac said to him.

'He teaches Abha Yoga here,' Martina continued. 'His own system.'

'Good for him. If you'd like to leave us for the moment, monsieur? Earthly matters.'

Deepak bowed slightly and took his leave.

'Madame, in my chat with Mademoiselle Rosay, she mentioned she'd phoned you earlier. Just need to tick that box if we can.' He gave a nod in the general direction of Nice. 'For the suits, you know.'

'Don't talk to me about them! Yeah, she phoned. Twice, about an hour and a half apart. The first would have been at around...' She rolled her eyes. 'Idiot, I don't need to tell.' She grabbed a mobile from her bag. 'I can show.'

Another *raise the flag* moment – Darac had anticipated no more than a verbal confirmation. 'Excellent.'

'I can show the first one, anyway. The second was to the land-line in the office.' She performed a little girl's apology face. 'I was late on court.' She tapped away at the screen. 'There. Check for yourself.'

The Calls Received list showed an entry name-tagged for Caroline Rosay ringing at 11.17, more or less the time she had stated.

'This is really helpful.'

'You're welcome.' For a second time, Martina looked him up and down. 'What's your game, Captain?'

'Pardon?'

'You said you're not into ball sports but with that physique, you must play *something*. Judo? Wrestling? Water polo?'

As Granot's laughter turned into a coughing fit, Darac explained that as a non-swimmer, water polo was out of the question and the others were not his thing, either. Except when they were called for on the job. 'All I play is guitar, I'm afraid.'

'Listen, I'll give you six lessons for the price of *four*.'

'That's generous but there's really no point.'

'You should at least think about learning to swim. We run courses.'

'Some other time.' Darac shook her racquet-hardened hand. 'Thanks for your help.'

Granot had a parting shot to deliver; one, it seemed, he was confident Martina would be happy to receive. 'I saw your mother win at Roland Garros back in '77.'

'Uh-huh?' she said. And headed back to her office.


As Caroline Rosay showered away the sweat and shale dust, a figure strolled into the changing room, made a circuit of the benches and inserted a key into locker number 17. There were two bags inside: a white plastic holdall and a black leather daysack. Slipping an envelope into an inner compartment, the figure saw something unexpected. Something that demanded a second look.

# 11

'*Window number three.*'

Hervé Montand detested queuing but there was no alternative: the concept of entrusting the internet with any sort of financial transaction was anathema to him. And so, although it pained him to relinquish the reins of power even for a minute during working hours, he had set off for the Saint-Laurent branch of Société Pro-Corse in good time to meet the mid-afternoon cash transfer deadline. Messieurs Lhatib and the other members of the "do it today or else" crowd were going to be paid after all.

'*Window number one.*'

Montand had raised funds in the least damaging way he could: by having the company's line of credit extended and by drawing down an amount equivalent to his salary until Christmas. After the events of the morning, the threat of facing awkward questions from his wife Mathilde, the registered owner of Montand Sanitary Ware, had ceased to matter. And with any luck, he concluded, she might be too drunk to notice anyway.

'*Window number three.*'

His longer-term problems, he knew with certainty, would be far more difficult to overcome. Just how difficult, he wasn't sure. But he intended to find out. And he intended to act.

'*Window number two.*'

Montand strode confidently forward.

'Monsieur?'

'Effect these transfers, would you?' He passed them through.

'Everything is filled in.'

The teller glanced at the wall clock. 'You have missed the deadline for today.'

'What?'

'The deadline. You've missed it. By two minutes.'

Montand looked at his watch. Where had the time... 'Get me the manager.'

'Monsieur, that will not achieve—'

'Get me the fucking manager!' All eyes upon him, his own slid to his shoes. But he quickly recovered. 'Monsieur Roux is a personal friend.' One he had had no intention of confronting with the situation but again, needs must. 'Get him now.'

'Monsieur Roux has moved on. Our new manager is Monsieur Sidiqui.'

'*Sidi..*?' It took a moment to gather himself. 'Then... get *him*,' he said.

# 12

Carrying a laden laundry bag, Mademoiselle Daniela Wien-awska marched into La Poche as if she owned the place; but it was the diminutive figure of her mother, floating along behind like a tethered cloud, to whom it actually belonged. At the bar, Rafal Maso, for once without his headphones, was serving beers to a quartet of fat men wearing rugby shirts.

'Raf,' Daniela said, by way of greeting – half a name for half a brother. 'Stripped the bed?'

'It's in the basket.'

'Back in a minute. Make us a citron pressé, will you?'

'Don't forget the bog.' Rafal opened the till. 'Twelve euros eighty,' he said to one of the fat men.

Daniela pushed through the curtains and headed for the stairs.

'Is everything alright now, darling?' Sonia said, smiling serenely as she kissed her son lightly on both cheeks.

'Weird morning. Really weird. Busier than usual, too.'

'Why didn't you call me right away?'

'Didn't want to worry you.'

'You good boy.' Still smiling, Sonia ran an eye over the gathered faces. 'Wonderful for business, a death on the line.'

'They axed the trains. When they put them back on, these guys just stayed.' He poured a slug of slivovitz into a cup. 'Latte with it?'

'Lovely.'

Sonia went to sit at her usual table. From across the street, a four-note refrain heralded an announcement. The *Régionale* to

Grasse via Cannes was running eight minutes late. It proved an optimistic forecast. The service still hadn't arrived by the time Daniela returned from upstairs and sat down opposite Sonia.

'I finished the Cif. And we're nearly out at home.'

'Rafal?'

He joined them.

'When's your next booking for the room?'

'Not until the end of August.'

Sonia's cheek muscles took a well-earned rest. 'Nothing for six weeks? At this time of year?' The smile was already back. 'But you never know so let's re-stock anyway. There's a whole carton in the garage up at the Saint-Jeannet house, Dani.'

'Right.' Daniela grinned as she stirred her juice with her straw. 'So, Raf. You finally met Caroline.'

'Yeah, and I didn't even realise it was her.'

'Duh! And?'

'Talk about up herself but who cares?' He shook a loose fist. 'One cool lady.'

'*You* don't have to clean for her.'

'She's always nice to me at the Centre,' Sonia said. 'A little brisk, perhaps. But nice.'

'She can be really sweet, at times.' Daniela sucked up a mouthful. 'At others, she can be a real bitch.' She squeezed her mother's hand. 'Sorry, *maminka*.'

'Don't worry, darling.' Sonia's expression retained its habitual serenity. 'I've known a good many bitches in my time.'

'Does that include Tina?' Rafal said.

'Tina's more of a loser than a bitch. A loser, a whore and a skinflint.'

'Never mind about her – what about Monsieur Paillaud?' Daniela's straw made a loud draining sound as she sucked up the dregs of her juice. 'How long before all the fun begins?'

'Soon,' Sonia said. 'Very soon, I should think.'

# 13

The sign was hiding in a wall aglow with bougainvillea.

'Which way?'

Granot narrowed his eyes. 'Left.'

As Darac made the turn, his mobile rang and he glanced at the number. 'Go ahead, Map.'

'Darac, I tried to call a few minutes ago.'

'There are several dead spots on the La Crague road. Go ahead.'

'I know there wasn't much doubt but just confirming that the dead man was indeed Ambroise Paillaud. Blood from the scene matches samples taken by the Clinique Albert Magnesca in the city.'

'Right.' He thought back to his meeting with Caroline Rosay. 'So he did have cancer?'

'They treat other things there, too, but yes – he had a rare form of leukaemia. Terminal.'

'OK, Map. Thanks for that.'

Granot shook his head. 'I was half hoping it was someone else.'

'A strange thing, fandom, isn't it? Feeling drawn to people you don't personally know simply because they make you laugh. Or cry. Or groove.'

'The last one is particularly strange.'

He turned to Granot. 'What are you on tomorrow?'

'Micro-managing bastard. All the same, you acting commissaires.'

'It goes with the territory, sweetheart,' Bogart said, three conversations late.

'I'm due a half-day off. I'll be spending some of it with Jodie.

At Centre Sicotte, I mean.'

It was too good an opportunity to miss. '*Jodie*. And what will Madame Granot make of that?'

'My mother?' He indicated the road. 'Carry on to the end.'

'I was thinking of Odile.'

'Odile will be glad I'm finally doing something about my health.'

'With Jodie.'

'With the finalists of Miss World, if necessary.'

'Too good for you, that woman.'

'She would be the first to agree with you.'

'How many wives have you had, Granot?'

'Including my own?' He gave a weak smile. 'Three.' More peering. 'Is that Chemin des Mimosas? Yes, turn right. It's on its own, the villa, so we shouldn't have any... Uh-oh.'

Ahead, a posse of reporters and other hangers-on had gathered at the cordon tape.

'Hyenas,' Darac said. 'All they're missing is the carcass.'

As if he had a remote camera on Darac, Frènes rang at that moment.

'What was the last thing I said to you, Captain?'

'Was it how you'd kill for a ticket to the jazz festival?'

'It was to remind you to keep me constantly informed on your progress. I haven't heard anything from you since I rang earlier.'

Darac could feel his chest tightening. 'Listen, if we'd had anything...'

Granot held up a cautioning hand. 'Don't give him an excuse,' he whispered.

It was a timely reminder. The last thing Darac wanted was to be taken off what might prove to be one of Granot's last cases with the team. 'I was about to call, as a matter of fact. Just a moment ago, Djibril Mpensa confirmed that it *was* Ambroise Paillaud who was killed in the incident at Saint-Laurent-du-Var station.'

'That's *something*, at least.'

'Lieutenant Granot and I are making significant progress on

the question of whether Paillaud was pushed into the TGV's path by one Guy Vaselle deliberately, accidentally, or whether he took his own life.'

'And the others? Busquet? Flaco? Perand? What are *they* doing?'

Darac's patience wearing ever thinner, he gave it a good couple of beats before answering. 'Lieutenant Busquet is on leave. Due back tomorrow. Officer Flaco has already made a key breakthrough and is following a number of leads. Officer Perand will be interviewing a potentially crucial eyewitness later this afternoon.' Though it seemed unlikely from Flaco's earlier report that old Monsieur – Recolte was it? – would give Perand anything useful. 'When we have more, you will be the first to know, monsieur.'

'You're damn right I will be and you'll be quick about it. Instil that imperative in the others. We need the speediest possible outcome on this one. Do you understand? Speedy and secure. I want to make tonight's 9 o'clock news at the latest. Alright? In the meantime, ensure you are contactable at all times and should you encounter the media, remember whom you are representing.'

'Yes, yes.' More tightening in the chest. 'You're slowing us down, monsieur. Out.'

The press pressed forward. Ignoring all entreaties for a comment, the pair pressed back and with Granot's bulk to the fore, they gained the cordon tape and signed in with Patricia's temporary replacement.

'Keep the bastards well back,' Darac said. 'Shoot them if necessary.'

'He's joking,' Granot added, quickly. 'The house keys?'

They took them and headed for a wicket gate set into the tree-lined wall that screened the garden.

'No pool,' Granot said, as they walked through into the back yard. 'No alarm, either.'

'I'll check the recycling.'

The bins were empty.

The back door opened into a clean, routinely stocked kitchen. Darac opened the fridge. 'Plenty of in-date stuff in here.'

'That only *suggests* Paillaud may have intended to return.'

'True. By the same token, though, we'd better check the water and power.'

They proved to be still connected. In itself, it didn't mean much but it might have strengthened the suicide call had Paillaud turned them off before leaving for the station.

In view of the man's fame and the reputed size of his fortune, the rest of the villa was not what Darac and Granot would have expected. It was an attractive place and large, especially for just one person, but it was not lavishly appointed. There was no projection room to show the dozen or so full-length features and countless short films in which Paillaud had starred. There was no music or games room. No elaborate sound or vision system. And unless they were hidden, there was no computer or laptop.

'Not spending your money,' Granot said, as they headed back into the living room. 'That's one way of building up a fortune.'

A pulsing red LED drew Darac's eye towards a table set against the far wall. Sitting between a pair of clown figurines was Paillaud's landline phone. 'Someone's been in touch, by the look of it.'

'Let's hope it's Guy Vaselle.'

'What – "I'm going to kill you. Meet me at the station" ?'

'Wouldn't something like that be good? Just once in a career?'

'Let's see if we can get the thing to work, first. If it's password-protected, we'll have to take it back for Erica.'

Darac hit the play button.

'You have one new message,' the machine announced. 'Today, at 10.42 a.m.'

'Unlucky, caller,' Darac said. 'You only just missed him, probably.'

'Message number one,' the machine continued.

The voice that kicked in sounded thin and anxious.

'*Monsieur Paillaud? Ambroise, if I may. I hope I'm not disturbing you. This is Mayor Hervé Montand.*'

Darac and Granot shared a look.

'*Something has come up here at the Mairie. It's something rather pressing and I would very much appreciate a meeting to discuss it with you. Today, if possible. Your long-term commitment to the ancient commune of La Crague-du-Var of which you are, of course, its most celebrated son, is of inestimable comfort to us. However... Well, we can talk about that. You have my numbers for the Mairie, the factory, my home, and my mobile...'*

Granot looked for an address book as the message continued. There appeared to be none.

*'Would you be kind enough to call me back? I anticipate remaining at my desk here at the Mairie for a little while longer, and then, as usual, I shall head down to the factory for the remainder—'*

'End of message,' the machine announced.

Darac absently picked up one of the clown figurines. 'A crisis at the Mairie; heavy hints about Paillaud's generosity, but also his obligations, towards his native commune; the scarcely masked anxiety in the mayor's voice. What did R.O. say about begging bowls?'

'It did sound as if a request for a hand-out was coming. One Paillaud never got to hear.'

'And an hour or so after Montand leaves that message, his brother-in-law and employee, Guy Vaselle, meets Paillaud at the station.'

Granot nodded. 'He puts Montand's case. "We need some money, please." Paillaud replies "Bugger off" and the volatile Vaselle throws him under the train.'

'Perhaps.' Aware of its awfulness suddenly, Darac set down the clown ornament next to its partner. 'And don't forget Paillaud's meeting with Caroline Rosay, beforehand. I'm not sure I completely believe her account of it.'

'What's going on here, chief?'

Hands on hips, Darac stared at the floor; Granot stood twisting an end of his moustache.

'Any thoughts?' Granot said, at length.

'Plenty. Nothing cogent, though.' Darac looked up, catching a sight of the two of them in a full-length mirror. 'Except that we look like a pair of clowns, as well.'

'Speak for yourself.'

Darac scanned the room. 'So what sort of a man was Ambroise Paillaud?'

'Normally, I'd say the contents of a person's bureau tell us all we need to know but as this is Monsieur La Chute...' Granot turned to the room's two bookcases. 'Perhaps this might be as good a place to start as any.'

Darac's eye was taken by the wall space between the cases. He indicated a dust-hung rectangular shape a shade deeper than the surrounding pale yellow emulsion. 'Something has hung there, hasn't it? A painting, a poster or something. A large one.'

Granot was already checking out the books themselves. 'And?'

'Just wondering what had graced that space. It's significant what people put in pride of place on their walls. That football photo in your living room, for instance.'

'*That* is no ordinary football photo. It's the '98 World Cup-winning side which, FYI, just happened to be us. France, I mean. Signed by the whole team.'

'Does Odile approve?' As if drawn by a force beyond his control, Darac moved to an alcove crammed with vinyl LPs. 'It completely dominates the room.'

'Approve? It's Odile's photo. She doted on that team.' Encouraged by its title, Granot pulled an old clothbound volume off the shelf. 'Especially Monsieur Patrick Vieira for reasons best known to Odile's hormones.'

'So if you ever took the photo down, it would be significant, wouldn't it?'

'Yes. It would mean I'd had to sell it. Through being put out to grass. The bastards.'

*Hallelujah*, Darac thought: Granot the grump was well and truly back. 'They're not talking about giving you the heave-ho, just a sideways move.'

'*Sideways*,' Granot muttered. 'I don't like sideways. I'm a man not a crab.'

'It's not going to happen now, anyway, remember? Thanks to

your personal trainer.'

'Oh yes. I forgot for the moment.'

No sooner had Darac begun running an eye over Paillaud's record collection than he remembered Angeline's observation that in every situation, there were people who looked for points of engagement with others, people who looked for points of opposition, and finally, people who looked merely for points of information. "Which are you, Paul?" Darac had replied that when he was off-duty, especially when he was playing with the Quintet, he was the first; the rest of the time, the third. It hadn't occurred to him to challenge the categories with which Angeline had presented him, a response she invariably adopted. Another test flunked. It was the third time today, he reflected, that Angeline had popped into his head. The last time that had happened, he had run into her in person almost immediately.

'Anything?'

The record collection was heavy on shows, popular songs and light classical pieces.

'Update: Paillaud and I have nothing much in common musically.'

Granot's reply was submerged in a rumble of laughter. 'This is brilliant.' He checked the spine. '*A Pictorial History of French Comedy*. I'm on 1961. Come and look.'

Filling a whole page, the photo depicted a young Paillaud in one of his most popular guises: a willing but hapless waiter. The elements were familiar. The location: a café terrace in Paris. The task: responding to a diner's finger-clicking summons. The complication: Paillaud can see only at a right-angle to his direction of travel, his view ahead blocked by the two-metre high stack of trays he is carrying. The hazard: the Seine, flowing alongside the terrace a good four metres beneath the quayside and with no barrier intervening. Entitled *Coming, Monsieur!* the photo captured the moment Paillaud, oblivious of the watery consequences, took a full, extravagant stride off the quay. Facing the camera, his cheek pressed against the tower of trays, the young man's expression conveyed such whole-hearted effort and such innocent confidence that Darac didn't know whether to laugh or cry. He laughed.

'That face,' Granot said.

'I know. I've seen this movie countless times. Always gets me.'

'He looks indestructible.' Granot made a sad little plosive sound. 'Would you say I was a sentimental soul?'

It was as well Darac was still chuckling. 'Under the surface, perhaps. *Far* under. In fact, so far under—'

'Stop there.' He gazed at the photo. 'Well, this gets me a bit, let me tell you.'

Darac's grin faded as he checked the credit at the foot of the page. 'Curious. It's a Brassaï, this photo.'

'So it is.' Granot's shaggy eyebrows rose. 'He was there at the beginning of Paillaud's career; and he was there at the end, in a way – the exhibition he never got to.'

'Hmm.' Darac shifted his weight back against the wall. 'You know, even with Guy Vaselle's connection to Montand and the fact that he persuaded his girlfriend to lie for him, it's difficult to believe he just walked up to Paillaud in broad daylight and chucked him in front of a train. Especially with witnesses and cameras around. Your idea that he may have shoved Paillaud inadvertently to his death does have *more* going for it – they were engaged in a row, after all. But there's every reason to have doubts. And we must never forget that Paillaud was Monsieur La Chute, wasn't he? The master of...' He indicated the photo and smiled. '*That.*'

'So you think Vaselle got his girlfriend to lie simply because he thought it looked bad for him?'

'And if Flak weren't the officer she is, it would probably have stood.'

'That's true. A thought: how did Vaselle know Paillaud was at the station?'

'That was on my mind when I quizzed Caroline Rosay about Vaselle. She broke off her conversation with Paillaud to use her mobile, remember.'

Granot shook his head. 'To call Martina Sicotte. She showed us the entry on her phone.'

'Yes, that call was made but what's to say Caroline didn't make a second one? We haven't examined *her* phone, have we?'

'She did make a second call. To Martina who hadn't shown up on court.'

'I mean a second call at the time she made the first. Rafal Maso reported only that he'd seen her walking up and down outside the café, talking into her mobile. She could easily have made two calls then.'

'Just a minute. You're saying Caroline tipped off Vaselle that Paillaud would soon be at the station? Why? She professed no liking for the man.'

'We only have her word for it. They might be lovers for all we know. Or maybe she called Montand, and *he* called Vaselle.'

'It's *possible*.'

'Whatever the reason, Caroline got on her mobile and Vaselle turned up minutes later. Now those two things might not be connected. Probably aren't. But they could be.'

Granot shrugged and muttered something about the pitfalls of working for someone who never stopped asking the "what if?" question.

'You *are* right, of course,' Darac said.

'Now someone's replaced *you* with an impostor.'

'In the sense that we're getting ahead of ourselves. We're bound to pick up Vaselle sooner or later. When we do, we can take it from there.'

Granot rang the Caserne. 'I'll get an update on the search.'

Darac began checking the other books in Paillaud's library. Show-biz in all its forms dominated what was a fairly tattered collection of paperbacks, hardbacks and sheet music. One title, though, a hardback complete with slip cover, looked scarcely read. Darac prised it off the shelf.

Granot returned no more than a couple of minutes later. 'I've got the latest. It seems a lot of people know Vaselle but no one has seen him since lunchtime. On another matter, Charvet reports the wills database is experiencing some sort of problem. He's chasing some IT person in Nantes. See, it could have been us wasting time doing that.'

'Good shout again, Granot.' Darac turned a page. 'Vaselle's wife?'

'On holiday. With a group of friends which just happens to include her sister-in-law, a.k.a Mathilde Montand, wife of Hervé. Cosy little ménage. What have you got there?'

' "A Fall To Grace", it's called.'

'Shouldn't that be "A Fall *From* Grace"?'

Darac showed him the cover illustration, a familiar figure blundering blindly around the upper reaches of the Eiffel Tower.

'Ah,' Granot said, the penny dropping. 'Monsieur La Chute's rags-to-riches autobiography.'

'I think I'll borrow it.'

As Granot checked some of the other titles, Darac wrote out a receipt in his notebook and slipped it into the empty space on the shelf. 'Unorthodox but it'll probably cover us.'

Granot glanced at his watch. 'Docs and papers time?'

'You take the study, obviously.'

'Obviously. And the kitchen.'

'Watch yourself in there or I'll tell Jodie.'

'If you find a suicide note, feel free to add your own name.'

'You'd never get away with it.'


The pair didn't reconvene for almost an hour.

'Disappointing,' Granot said, hoisting himself to his feet. 'One credit card account. One current bank account. According to the statements, if Paillaud's fortune is squirreled away in *them*, he was good for just over eight-hundred euros at the time of his death.'

'So where are his reputed millions hiding?'

Granot gave a phlegm-rattling laugh. 'Hiding is exactly where they'll be. In an array of investment accounts spread around the planet, probably. I couldn't find a reference to any sort of financial advisor or solicitor but Mademoiselle Rosay would know.'

'If it proves material, we'll press her.'

'You come across anything interesting?'

'It's what I *didn't* come across that's most interesting. Was there anything you would class as memorabilia in the bureau?'

'The odd letter but not as such, no.' Granot looked tired, suddenly. 'I need to swill some water on my face. Back in a second.'

When Granot returned, Darac was taking another look at Paillaud's autobiography. 'You know, the places of some old stars are practically shrines to their former selves, aren't they?'

'I think it's been known, yes.'

'I've searched every conceivable spot: bookshelves, wardrobes, chests – you name it. I've shaken out each of those books and looked in every album sleeve.' He sat back, fixing Granot with a look. 'You found a few letters. But there isn't a scrapbook, a play-bill, programme, photo album. Apart from the book you found with the Brassaï in it, and the autobiography I'm borrowing, there isn't a single reference to Paillaud's career.' He ran a hand through his hair. 'It's strange, isn't it?'

Granot began pulling at his moustache. 'He has no living relatives either, has he?'

'That we know of.'

'Maybe there's an archive somewhere. There are such things for these old stars.'

'The Paillaud Archive?' Darac drew down the corners of his mouth. 'Maybe that's it.'

Granot indicated the vacated wall space. 'Probably where whatever was hanging there has gone, too.'

'I wonder.' Darac scrolled a couple of screens on his mobile and tapped in a number.

'Who are you calling?'

'MAMAC.'

It took him a moment, but Granot saw the possibility, also.

'Yes, good afternoon.'

Darac identified himself and, using the tried and tested tactic of stressing the difficulty of fulfilling his request, asked to be put through to the most senior person connected with the Brassaï exhibition.

'None of them is here at the moment, I'm afraid.'

Granot harrumphed.

Darac went to Plan B. 'You have a catalogue, there?'

'Hundreds of them.'

'I know you're very busy but could you check if a 1961 photograph entitled *Coming, Monsieur!* is part of the show?' He gave its rough dimensions 'The provenance will be Collection of Monsieur Ambroise Paillaud, probably.'

'Just a moment...'

They heard the sound of pages riffling.

'Hello? Yes, we are exhibiting it but it's tagged just "private loan." '

'That's fine, thanks.' Darac ended the call. 'One mystery solved, seemingly.'

'Only a couple of hundred remaining. Have we gone as far as we can here?'

'Yes, let's go.'

As they got their stuff together, Darac knew there was no need to ask if Granot had meticulously checked every scrap of paper in the place and then put it back exactly where he'd found it. 'Remember that complete murder plan you found scrawled on the back of a binned Monop' bill?'

'Ah yes.' Granot smiled as if were the fondest memory of his life. 'The Girade-Dalterre poisoning.'

Darac's mobile rang.

'Chief? We've got him.'

'Him?'

'Vaselle.'

# 14

The squad room was the usual crowd scene. Tucked away in a corner unspoiled by the Caserne's recent refurbishment was a twinkle-eyed fox of a man filling out a job sheet. Above Lieutenant Bonbon Busquet's desk, a row of unreplaced ceiling panels had left a void through which hanks of wiring drooped like a multi-coloured hammock. As if by a process of electro-magnetic attraction, Bonbon's shock of copper-red hair was rising towards it. His expression was going the other way.

Flaco handed him a cup the size of a small bucket. 'If your heart gives out, Lieutenant, I'm not taking the rap.'

'I'll sign a waiver.'

'Uh-huh.' She sat down at her desk and worked through screens as she talked. 'So you're giving up half a day's leave because of your house guest? Your cousin, you say?'

A red rag to a fox. 'Allegedly.'

'What's wrong with him?'

The job sheet went on hold for a minute. 'What would you say about a man who turns up unannounced after eight years, gets his arse under your table and wallops down your *suquet de peix* before you even knew it was on the menu?'

'I don't know. First tell me what... *sous que de pays* is?'

Bonbon picked up an imaginary microphone. ' "I'm here with Officer Yvonne Flaco of the Brigade Criminelle in Nice. Officer, explain to our audience why you chose to disrespect your immediate superior's native culture just then." '

'Native culture? I thought you were from Perpignan.'

'Exactly. I'm not French, I'm Catalan.' He displayed the FC

Barcelona socks he was wearing as proof. 'And *suquet de peix*, young lady, just happens to be the finest fish stew in the world.'

'I thought that was *bouillabaisse*.'

'Really?' Bonbon nodded. 'You think so? Come and taste Julieta's *suquet* and see what you think then. If there'll be any left. Ever again.'

'The guy is only staying a couple of days, isn't he?'

Bonbon took a mouthful of his octuple espresso. '*So* good. The last time he came for a couple of days, he stayed three months.'

Exuding a disturbing degree of menace, Flaco turned to him. 'If someone outstays their welcome back in Guadeloupe, you know what we do?'

'If it involves subjecting them to a slow and painful death, I'm all for it.'

'Worse than that.' She turned back to her screen. 'We tell them to leave. Never fails.'

'I'd like to see you tell Guim to leave. He's not normal. He doesn't even support Barça. He supports...' Adopting a hideously sour expression, he dropped his voice. '*Them.*'

'Them?'

Bonbon glanced into the four corners of the squad room. 'Real Madrid,' he mouthed, silently.

Darac walked in and performed a double-take. 'Bonbon?'

'Don't ask, chief.'

'It couldn't have come at a more opportune moment, but what are you doing here?'

'You asked.'

Granot plodded in behind Darac. 'Bonbon?'

'No – François Hollande. Gone lean and hungry for want of food.'

'Not your cousin again?' Granot said. 'Guillem?'

'No, Guillem's alright. This is Guim. A sponge in human form. Or in sponge form, more like.' The darkness already falling around Bonbon became all-enveloping, suddenly. 'I tell you, if he so much as looks at my *flaming balls*, there will be words. Possibly... a scene.'

'Easy, boy.' Darac turned to Flaco. 'Vaselle in my office?

She shook her head. 'He's in the interview room, Captain.'

'What's he doing in there? He's not in custody.'

'He complained to the uniform about your air-con. Noisy and ineffective, he thought.'

Darac's habitual half-smile widened a little. 'He's a good judge. But the sensitive type? Hadn't pegged him as that.'

Bonbon reached into his jacket pocket. 'Gooseberry grenade, anyone?'

Through force of habit, Granot examined the proffered packet. And then, remembering his own tragedy, he saw Bonbon's darkness and raised him The Day Of Judgement. 'You haven't heard, have you?'

'Heard what? And who's this Vaselle?'

'Fill Bonbon in, Granot.' Darac glanced at his watch. He had just over an hour before his band, the Didier Musso Quintet, was due on stage for their Jazz Festival rehearsal in Jardin Albert. And the excitement would not end there. Frankie had picked up his message and agreed to meet him. 'Flak? Let's you and I go and interview the man. Alright guys?'

'Yes, yes.' Granot had other fish to fry. Or grill. Without oil. 'It started only this morning, although it seems like a lifetime...'


Its air-con may have been the most effective on site but, for Commissaire Agnès Dantier and her team, the Caserne's brand new interview suite had been something of a white elephant from Day One. At great expense, an outsourced consultancy had come up with the notion that suspects were more likely to tell the truth when questioned in a four-square space painted in subtle earth colours. 'Who would have thought it?' Agnès had joked at the unveiling ceremony. 'All these years, we just needed beige.'

En route, Darac and Flaco stopped off in the surveillance room. After one glance at Guy Vaselle, Darac decided to give Flaco her head with the questioning. The suspect was seething and being ridden by a female officer, especially one young, black, and with an inclination towards directness that some interpreted as "attitude", might make things even more interesting. A riled suspect was apt to make mistakes and the still, silent presence Darac intended to maintain would only add to the aggravation. The uniform in with Vaselle seemed to be playing the silent routine himself, Darac noticed. It all helped.

The corners of Flaco's mouth set into their familiar scowl. 'Two-way mirrors? Pointless. As Lieutenant Granot says, suspects know full well we can see them.'

'They know full well that if they're in custody, we have to record interviews now, not just write them up afterwards. But they appear to be still saying the things they always have. Or not saying them.'

She turned to him. 'What do you think overall though, Captain? About these new protocols, I mean.'

'They're progressive in intention and that's good, obviously. But a crucial thing for me is that nothing in them should hinder us pursuing our first goal as police officers. Which is?'

'To uphold justice.'

'Protect the innocent; deliver miscreants for trial – absolutely.' He rummaged in his pocket and pulled out a soft leather key fob. 'And if I can continue to further either of those ends by illegally using these picks, believe me, I will.'

'So however much Luxembourg draws the line for us, we have our own line to consider as well? Does that work, Captain? Don't we need fixed standards? Rules that everyone must obey?'

'Never argue this in an exam but it depends on the standards, doesn't it? Whenever a so-called superior gives you an order, you always have to consider where *you* stand, as well. If officers in this very building hadn't toed the line laid down for them back in 1942 and '43, the deportations of Jews from the city to

Auschwitz might never have happened.'

Her scowl deepened. 'I need to think more about this.'

He gave her shoulder a pat. 'Ready?'

'Ready.'

'We'll try it this way to start,' he said, and outlined his plan.

Vaselle greeted their arrival in the interview room with a vehement protest about being kept waiting.

'You haven't been arrested or charged, monsieur,' Flaco began. 'Yet. So I won't be recording the interview. I'm just going to ask you some questions.'

Leading with his chin, Vaselle thrust his head forward and retracted it as if it were suddenly necessary to free his neck muscles. 'I said you've kept me waiting nearly half an hour.'

Ignoring the comment, Flaco outlined the scene at Saint-Laurent station, stressing the violent intent with which Vaselle had approached Ambroise Paillaud.

Vaselle thrust his head forward once more. 'Not violent. Angry, yes. But not violent. I tore the old fart off a strip and then left. Didn't even touch him.'

'Then why did you get your girlfriend to lie for you?'

Vaselle gave Darac a blokey grin. 'Which girlfriend?'

Darac remaining utterly deadpan, Vaselle shrugged and turned back to Flaco. 'I never touched him. That's the truth. But no one was looking when I left the sod so figure it out.'

'Getting her to lie for you was stupid. For that alone, you could be charged.'

Vaselle jetted Darac a look. 'I want you. Not her.'

'Tough,' Flaco said.

Vaselle sat back and folded his arms, not as a barrier to hide behind, Darac felt, but as a way of holding himself in. So far, so good.

'Stop being stupid, Monsieur Vaselle,' Flaco said, 'and you might just convince me you are not guilty of murder.'

'Fuck you.'

Flaco did something she had never done in an interview

before. She laughed.

Vaselle stiffened, his mouth hardening into a sneer. 'Listen, you're the monkey. Have you got me? The monkey. I want the organ grinder, there.'

'Monsieur Vaselle, Monsieur Vaselle... aah.' She dabbed her eyes, overdoing it slightly, perhaps. 'Let's move on. What took you to the station at Saint-Laurent-du-Var this lunchtime?'

Vaselle said nothing.

Before the Luxembourg directive, an interrogating officer might well have banged the desk at this point, screaming: "Answer the question!" Using the impolite "*tu*" form, some officers would have then told the suspect that uniforms in marked cars would be dispatched, all sirens blazing, to trash their property while looking for clues; clues which they would definitely find. For some officers, this would have just have been the start of things.

'What took you to the station?'

Vaselle remained mute.

'Do you understand the question, monsieur?'

'Of course, I fucking understand it.' Once more, he jerked his head forward. 'Paillaud asked me to meet him.'

'Why? And how? Take your time. I realise I asked two whole questions there.'

His body flexing like a racehorse in the starting gate, Vaselle's eyes bored into Flaco. It was clear that he wanted to demolish her and Darac almost wished he would try. She would have had the man on his back before he knew what had hit him.

'Let's do the "how" first.'

Vaselle shifted his weight several times before he answered. 'He called me on the phone.'

'On your mobile?'

He shrugged.

'Got that particular one on you?'

'Think you're clever, don't you?'

'Show me.'

Vaselle had been subject to a basic search but as he wasn't under arrest, he'd been allowed to retain the contents of his pockets. Cursing under his breath, he stood and tossed it on to the desk.

'*Show* me,' she said, not moving.

He grabbed the phone.

'How did he come to have your number?'

'I used to be an architect and builder. The number's freely available.'

'How did you know Monsieur Paillaud?'

'I didn't. But he knew me. Correction – knew my work.' His eyes lowered. 'It's won awards, some of it.'

And now you work for your brother-in-law, Darac thought. Making toilets.

Vaselle held out the phone half-way between them, obliging Flaco to reach for it. She stayed her ground. Vaselle began to shake. 'You...'

'Yes?' Flaco said. 'What am I?'

He bit his lip and handed her the phone. Flaco noted the incoming number – a mobile – and the time of the call. Giving no outward reaction, she handed it to Darac.

'Now *what* did he want to talk to you about?' she continued.

'A load of bullshit about wanting to sue me for putting up some properties last year that blocked his view.'

'View of what?'

'The new stadium over in Saint-Isidore. And they've only just started building it.'

'The Allianz Riviera?'

'What other new stadiums do you know there?'

'The properties you built are virtually all bungalows, aren't they?' Flaco said, doubting that Paillaud could possibly have had a case for a sightline violation. 'Second homes, mainly.'

'What of it? All of my properties are built to code and have obtained the necessary permissions. None of them block a view of anything. I don't want to speak ill of the dead...'

'Yes you do,' Darac said.

'Well now, I was beginning to think you were a deaf mute.'

'You like to speak ill of the dead because the dead can't talk back. Unlike Girlfriend Number Three, Seven or Ten or whatever she is. You're going down, mate. It's just a question of what for.'

'Bullshit!'

'We've seen how riled you get, Vaselle. Just a couple of little digs is enough to set you off. Threatening you with a law suit? That really got your goat. You pushed poor old Paillaud.'

Sweat began to show through Vaselle's shirt. 'I didn't.'

'You intended to kill him – that's murder. You didn't but he died anyway – that's manslaughter. Which is it?'

Vaselle's belligerence seemed all used up, suddenly. 'I didn't do anything! Hear me, will you?'

Darac glanced at the guard. 'All yours,' he said, getting to his feet. 'You're held, Vaselle, pending further enquiries.'

Flaco brought the interview formally to a close and the pair left to a chorus of protestations of innocence. Once they were out of earshot, Darac turned to her.

'Ask Erica to check whose number he actually gave you, will you, Flak? Paillaud didn't have a mobile.'

# 15

Crammed with hot desks and hot bodies, the Caserne's squad room was one kind of crowd scene. The palm-shaded paths, flower beds and fountains of Jardin Albert, quite another. But it was just as hectic. Picking his way between riggers, film crews, sound technicians and volunteers, Darac was heading for the more intimate of the Jazz Festival's two performance spaces, a spot he'd known since childhood. A tiered, open-air auditorium fanning out from a covered stage, the "Theatre among the Greenery", Le Théâtre de Verdure had been built in the style of an ancient Greek amphitheatre. A trio of monumental sculptures ringed the perimeter: Tragedy and Dance flanked the stage and, rising from the Promenade des Anglais above the rearmost row of seats, a Winged Victory.

Arriving backstage just as the venerable James Clarence Jazz Orchestra had concluded its rehearsal, Darac exchanged a few words with his long-time friend, jazz club owner Ridge Clay, and headed out on to the stand. If the guys trooping past him had been inspired by the verdant beauty of the setting, there was no sign of it. Perhaps they were jet-lagged. Or perhaps they were just sick of the sight of each other after decades of touring.

Ahead, a familiar bear-like figure toting a double bass was making the best of it as he foundered in the flood of bodies washing against him. Darac chuckled as he caught some of his band mate's patter, delivered in a thicker than usual Lillois accent.

'You know what they say: laugh and the world laughs with you,' Luc Gabron said, grinning as if bestowing compliments.

'Great to see you.' Everyone blanked him. 'Hi. Luc Gabron from The Didier Musso Quintet. But that's my story.'

Catching up with him, Darac nudged the nose of his guitar case against Luc's backside.

'Later, sweetie – I keep telling you.' He turned. 'Ah, it's you, Darac. I thought it was Juliette Binoche up to her old tricks again.'

'I thought Louise Bourgoin was your fantasy squeeze.'

'Left me. She's with Didier now.'

'That's rough.'

A living legend tramped past them, his gnarly upper lip the legacy of a lifetime of playing.

'Welcome, monsieur,' Luc said.

'Uh-huh.'

'And to you.' He gave Darac a look. 'Tell me, why are people like Beep-Beep Johnston rehearsing? I thought this session was just for the likes of us.'

'Whatever the reason, it's clearly not a very popular one with the guys.'

But then an explosion of laughter erupted behind them. It seemed Ridge Clay had run into some old friends.

'See that?' Luc said. 'The man has the power to bring the dead back to life. I always suspected he was God in disguise.'

'Jimmy?' Ridge called out. 'Get your shit together and haul it over here!'

'I ain't in no hurry,' James Clarence called back from the piano. 'I'll see enough of your sorry ass at the club later!'

More laughter.

'Hear that, Darac? Royalty at The Blue Devil tonight. Can you make it?'

He would if he could but he suspected that the case, as so often before, would claim him. 'I'd like to—'

'—But the usual terms and conditions apply?'

'Exactly.'

The flood having dwindled to a trickle, Darac followed Luc

out on to the stand. At the piano, Quintet leader Didier Musso was all reverent smiles and quiffy nods as he took over the stool from James Clarence himself. Seven other members of Didier's quintet – the title was nominal – listened in as the great man said a few words and took his leave.

Didier was still excited about it as he exchanged kisses of greeting with Darac. 'See these?' He held up his hands. 'These fingers are about to play keys graced only moments before by one of the all-time heroes of our music.'

'Better not fuck up, then,' Luc said, fitting the floor spike into his bass.

Trudi Pachelberg, a heavily mascara-ed blonde in a short red skirt, gave a low, throaty chuckle as she flipped open her alto case. 'Luc's available for children's parties, people.'

Thumps from the drum set behind. Some adjustment to a pedal. More thumps.

'What did you talk about?' Darac said, attending to his guitar amp.

'I know what *I* said to him; what he said to me? No idea.' Didier turned to a stocky, bald individual wearing a sax neck strap. 'Dave?'

Englishman Dave Blackstock had been sucking on a reed for the past thirty seconds. 'That'll do. He was asking about the local talent.' He fitted his mouthpiece together. 'And I don't think he was referring to us musos.'

Splintery rolls, snaps and thunky dunks from the drums.

'How old is he now?' Jacques Quille played a creamy arpeggio on his tarnished old trumpet. 'Late seventies?'

'That's what playing keyboards does for you.' Didier took a sheaf of scores and charts from his bag and began laying them out on the piano. 'Keeps you young.'

'Didier's really 62,' Trudi said, bringing laughter all round, and then blew a series of silky and snaky runs on her alto.

Splashes, crashes and clams from the cymbals.

Darac parked his backside on a chair and began his warm-up.

For reasons that had as much to do with habit and superstition as with sound musical principles, he launched into the runs and chords he always played before a rehearsal or a gig.

From the drums: thumps, rolls, snaps, splashes and crashes all at once.

'How's it going back there?' Didier called out, as the drummer exchanged her sticks for brushes and a sound like breaking surf fizzed and frothed around the amphitheatre.

'Super, Didier.' The young woman was wearing a white T-shirt emblazoned with the logo of the Young Musicians of the Côte d'Azur – JAMCA. In black marker pen, an extravagant hand had added: "Maxine – you're going to be great! Love, Marco xx." 'Thanks for asking.'

The response brought a chorus of protest.

"*Way* too polite..." "Tell him to mind his own damn business..." "Say three hail Didiers and spit..."

Maxine grinned, loving the vibe. 'Next time,' she said.

Darac gave her the thumbs-up and then scanned the arena. There was no sign of Frankie as Didier hit a middle A on the keyboard and kept hitting it until the band was in tune.

'Close enough for you-know-what.'

'Didi?' Dave said. 'We're still doing a sound check at the gig itself, I hope.'

'Of course. This is the pre-sound-check sound check – to speed things up for Yannick and his fader fiddlers on the day.' In the centre of the back row was a trio sitting with their feet up on a mixing desk. Hovering above them, Victory gazed out over the bay as if preferring not to look. 'Say hi to them.' Predictably desultory waves followed from both sides. 'Excellent.'

Didier ran a shepherd's eye around his flock. Everyone was ready. 'So let's wake Yannick and co up with...' He paused, looking all around him. 'Listen.'

All eyes settled on Maxine. A cicada had landed on one of her drum mics and was chiriking its mating call. Amplified around the Jardin, the sound, so much an emblem of a warm summer night in the south, made everyone stop what they were doing and listen. On stage, the band saw an added significance.

Dave Blackstock was the first to speak. 'Putting it out early, isn't he? It's as if Marco was...' He shrugged the thought away. 'Yeah, well.'

The cicada disappeared and for a sickening moment, Darac experienced something he usually encountered only in his nightmares: an uncannily realistic sensation of falling as if into a bottomless pit. Unlike his nightmares, the episode passed as quickly as it had come. 'Let's start with it, shall we?' he said, quietly.

'Blues For Marco?' Didier nodded and, finding solace in the activity, busily rearranged his charts.

A voice broke in through the stage monitors. 'Yannick here. Disney time's over, guys. We've got some cats from Japan coming in shortly.'

The whole band stiffened. 'They're not here yet, then?' Didier said into his mic.

'They're on site somewhere.'

'Well you can fucking wait, then.' He turned to the drums. 'You ready, Maxine?'

She gathered herself. 'Yeah. Let's do it.'

'So... Just the head and bridges, guys, OK? We'll save the good stuff for the night.' Didier counted the band in and the rehearsal began.

Darac had left a pass on the gate for Frankie but in the end, there had been no need: the gatekeeper proved to be a former beat officer from the Caserne and had admitted her without question. He had also let through the man accompanying her. The pair settled in a discreet spot and watched the Quintet work through the spines of three numbers which used up their allotted time.

Frankie's husband, Christophe, was of average height, build and looks. A designer of objects as diverse as table lamps and IUDs, he was a bright, creative individual and in other circumstances, Darac might have had more time for the man. But his tolerance, stretched to breaking point by the situation, had finally snapped a month ago. It was the day of Frankie and Christophe's 5th wedding anniversary and to mark the occasion, Christophe had laid on an evening cruise around Cannes's Îles de Lérins – a "treat for all our friends." The bay had been serene; the sunset, sensational; Frankie, superb. It had been excruciating.

'Christophe.' Darac managed a smile. 'How's it going?'

'Fine.' He clamped a hand around Frankie's waist. 'You sounded good, by the way. As far as I could tell, which isn't saying much, to be honest.'

Feeling the back of Christophe's hand as he reached forward, Darac gave Frankie two kisses in greeting. She wasn't wearing her signature *Marucca* perfume, he noticed.

'Yes you did, Paul,' she said, standing stiffly upright, not, as was her habit, with one hip thrust slightly out. 'Sound good, I mean.'

'Thank you.' Darac's habitual half-smile turned into something more wistful as he looked into Frankie's eyes. 'Were you here for the cicada?'

'The cicada? Is that a Latin number?'

He gave a little shake of the head. 'Skip it. Or hop it, or whatever cicadas do.'

'There, I can help,' Christophe said, with faux *hauteur*. 'According to no lesser authority than myself, cicadas neither skip nor hop. They fly.'

Darac found Christophe's send-ups irritating. By overplaying things, he succeeded only in reproducing the phenomena he found so laughable. If you act the part of a bore, you're a bore aren't you?

'I suppose they do fly,' Darac said. 'Cicadas.'

Christophe glanced at his watch. 'I've still got loads of time.' He gave Darac a look. 'I'm flying off, myself, later. Stuttgart.'

'Oh?' Darac's spirits lifted. 'I thought you were around for a while?'

'Don't worry, I'll be back on Sunday.' He grinned. 'In plenty of time for your act. Oh, I don't mean *act*, do I?' He was still grinning. 'Performance.'

Frankie stirred, looking around as if seeking a way out. 'Ah, there's Didier.' She removed Christophe's hand from her waist. 'Haven't spoken to him in ages. Won't be long.'

Darac turned to go with her.

'Paul – a word?' Christophe said, halting him.

Just as she had at the Caserne earlier, Frankie gave a little backhanded wave as she moved away. The two men were left facing each other. It crossed Darac's mind to open with "I'm in love with your wife." The thought returned.

'Christophe, there's—'

'Sorry but while we have a moment, Francine has told me she doesn't want a party.'

'What?'

'No party. But I don't think we should take any notice of that rubbish, do you?'

Playing jazz had developed in Darac a number of skills he'd drafted in to his armoury as a detective. The most important was not the ability to improvise *per se*; it was the capacity to react quickly and decisively to each new development in a case as it came up. Even his nemesis, Public Prosecutor Jules Frènes, had admitted that when the chips were down, no one's brain worked faster than Darac's.

'What?' he repeated, lamely.

'The leaving do, dummy.'

*Leaving do? What the hell?* 'Just... remind me where we've got to with that?'

'Well, the Marseille... Damn – what's the Commissaire's name?'

A picture was forming in Darac's head like an image developing on a piece of photographic paper. Frankie leaving? She hadn't said a word. 'Commissaire? There are several there.' Vice seemed the most likely. 'Murat?'

'That's him!'

'Her.'

Christophe shrugged. '*Her* then. The point is, the post has now been firmly offered.' He produced an almost childlike grin. 'How good is that?'

'Does Agnès know about this?'

'Your boss? No, no. It's still hush-hush.' There was something different in Christophe's expression now. Something sharper. 'She's told you. Obviously. Francine, I mean.'

'When might it start – this new role?'

'Mid October. So we've got just over three months to plan the party. Are you in? What I thought would be great...'

The image on the paper turned to black.

# 16

'At last,' Perand said aloud, as Madame Recolte emerged from the lobby, crossed the street and joined the queue at the bus stop. As if she had been looking out for it, a number 55 arrived almost immediately and Perand waited until she had safely boarded before he returned to her building. As he mounted the stairs, his friend the ginger tom sidled in from the pavement and, as if he too judged it safe to return, followed Perand up to the apartment.

The young man pressed the bell, picturing the old man's struggle to get out of bed and then the slow, dragging plod to the door.

'What did you get?' Recolte said, admitting Perand almost immediately.

'Whisky.' He produced his offering, a half-bottle supermarket cheapie. 'How did you get to the door so fast?'

'Pushed the boat out with this, haven't you?' Rolling his eyes, the old man took the bottle and turned, digging his stick into the lino tiles for leverage. 'I saw you coming. Binoculars.' He indicated a compact pair sitting on a table beside his day bed. Next to them, a glass ashtray was a graveyard for stubbed-out Gitanes. 'Fetch a glass. But you'll have to wash it up afterwards or *she'll* know.'

The cat padded into the kitchen after Perand, meowing insistently.

'His meat's in the fridge. Give it to him, will you? It's in a sandwich bag. Divide it into two and put half back. There's a bowl under the sink. If it's not there, it'll be in the cupboard. It says "cat" on it.'

'Jesus Christ,' Perand muttered, suspecting that following this unwelcome dose of low-life domesticity, he would have absolutely nothing to show for his visit. But he'd been wrong before and he was certainly in need of a result. He knew he was well behind Flaco in Darac's assessment of their talents.

Monsieur was sitting up in bed as Perand rejoined him. 'Wrong glass but never mind. Fill it, will you?'

'On one condition. Tell me what you saw this lunchtime. In detail. No embellishments. And no requests to re-tile the roof while you think about it.'

Recolte fired up a Gitane, took a deep drag, and then, wearing a look of infinite possibility, gazed into Perand's eyes.

'Reach into the bed,' he said, indicating his mid-section. 'You won't be sorry.'

Perand sighed. He'd suspected something but not this. Dog-tired suddenly, he rose. 'Keep the booze.'

'Where are you going?'

'If you want a hand job, get the cat to do it.'

' "*Get the cat...*" Come back here!'

Against his better judgement, Perand paused as, with some difficulty, the old man leaned forward and pulled back the bed cover.

'There, see!'

Lying next to Recolte's hip was the holy grail. Gold dust. El Dorado. Potentially, at least.

'I'll pour,' Perand said, returning to the bedside.

'Best quality video, this. Picture steadier – the lot. Press play.'

The first movie showed a couple of teenagers in bikinis jogging along the Marseille-bound platform toward the rear of an arriving train. Saying nothing, Perand gave the old man his exhausted patience look.

'What? Got to do something to pass the time, haven't I?'

'Is this what you wanted to share with me?'

'Go to the index page.'

Perand brought up a screen of thumbnail images, a minia-ture stained-glass window on the theme of scantily-clad girls and trains.

Monsieur took a long gulp of firewater. 'Play number 63.'

Entertaining little hope of its relevance, Perand located the clip and ran it. Two minutes and thirty-seven seconds later, he took out his phone and called Darac.

'It's definitive, Perand?'

'Watch and see.'

# 17

'Your glutes certainly needed work,' Jodie said, her oiled hands moulding and releasing the muscle in time with 'Girl From Ipanema'.

Caroline Rosay's words surfaced in a soporific whisper. 'So I'm a tight arse, am I?'

Jodie laughed. 'Pass.'

'Blame Tina. She had me sprinting all round the court, earlier. Punishing me for complaining she was late.'

'Just your shoulders now. A little more gloop...' Jodie favoured a blend of sandalwood and jasmine over an almond oil base. 'Here we go... Wow, your deltoids!'

'Yes, I'm proud of them.'

'I meant they're like bricks.'

'Can't blame Tina for that. The only shots I hit were my own serves.'

'Relax now... Relax... Listen to the music while I get to grips with this.'

' "Get to grips...." That's good.'

'Shhhh.'

The tune swayed like breeze-blown palms as Jodie slowly loosened Caroline's shoulders. It took four further songs to complete the task to her satisfaction. 'Alright, we're done.' Jodie gave Caroline's right buttock a slap and drew the towel back over it. 'I went five minutes over but I'll overlook it.'

Fully awake now, Caroline turned on to her side and flicked the towel at Jodie's retreating bottom.

'Missed! *Ah*-hah.'

'Can't hit *anything* today!' She lay back on the table, making a pillow of her interlocked hands as Jodie went to the wash basin. 'So what's with this fat *flic*?'

'Lieutenant Granot? He's a sweetie. Got to lose a lot of weight or he's going to lose his job. I said I'd help him.'

'You are so... *soft*.'

'Good job one of us is.'

'I'm not hard, just business-like. With most people. Most of the time.'

Jodie gave her a look as she picked up a hand towel. 'And how are you feeling now?'

'As loose as... what did your old tutor used to say? "Loose as a five-franc hooker." '

Jodie grinned, tilting the crescent moon scar on her cheek. 'It's really stayed with you, that one, hasn't it? Seriously, how do you feel?'

'The best I have all day, that *is* for sure.'

Fastening her ponytail, Jodie went across to her and, resting her weight against the edge of the table, gently took Caroline's hand. 'It has been strange today. With one thing and another.'

'For you too?' Caroline kissed Jodie's fingers one by one. 'Tell me about it.'

'First, my insulin stung like crazy this morning.'

'No, no, no.' Extra kisses. 'Why?'

'Thermostat on the fridge having a funny five. It's been replaced today. Or should have.'

'Supposing it wasn't?'

'You've got supplies. And so has the surgery.'

'Alright. *Then* what? Whatever it is, I'll make it better.'

'I had Mayor Almighty Montand on the table this morning. Then afterwards I saw him having some sort of contretemps with Arnaud.'

No more kissing. 'Zep?' Caroline's grey eyes sharpened a little. 'What were they arguing about?'

'I couldn't hear but Montand was bitching about me to him,

I suspect.'

'Why?'

'Two possibilities. One, he took exception to me belittling La Crague. Though how can you belittle what's little already?'

'Because to him, La Crague isn't little. It's Paris, London and New York all rolled into one. The second?'

Jodie hesitated a moment. 'I wondered if he somehow knows about us.'

'Of course he doesn't.' Caroline lifted her shoulders then sinking back, let out a long, slow breath. 'But suppose he does? It's not illegal.'

'Not very professional to touch up one's clients on the job, though, is it?' She mimicked Montand's patrician voice. ' "Are you running a surgery or a massage parlour, Zep?" '

Caroline closed her eyes. '*I* made the first move and it was in this very spot, not at the surgery or at the Centre.' She sighed languorously. 'How could he know, anyway?'

'Don't you live next door to the worst *voyeur* in France? And the biggest gossip.'

'Yes, Kerthus is a shitty little microbe. But he's never seen anything.'

'No? How many times has he turned up at your door unannounced?'

Giving in to Jodie's persistence, Caroline opened her eyes and sat up. 'It's the shared access. Makes it too easy.'

'No excuse. Remember that time he called out Doctor Zep?'

Caroline laughed. 'Jodie – he calls him out every couple of months.'

'I'm thinking about the time the poor man rushed here to find our deathbed hero wasn't even *in* bed. He'd...' She adopted the man's precious mien. '... "slipped outside for a breath of restorative air." ' Colour flushed her taut cheeks. 'He was standing there with his nose pressed to your kitchen window. Remember?'

Caroline ran her finger over Jodie's scar, a silvery-white moon in an angry sky. 'Tell me how you did this,' she said, feeling a charge as she pictured the fearless little 14 year-old working the balance beam, a blur of flick-flacks, pirouettes and somersaults. And then her final move, the one she failed to land.

'You know how I did it.' She took her finger away. 'Don't change the subject.'

'Alright, alright... Yes, Kerthus was watching me. Watching me in the highly controversial act of dressing a salad.'

'That's not the point.'

'The *point* is that I threatened him with a trespass suit if he ever did it again. He hasn't.'

'As far as you know.'

'Even if he were to do it again, I have these great new pieces of kit to counter him. *Blinds*, they're called.' She took Jodie's hand. 'And they're closed, now, aren't they?' Her words merged with the lilt of the music. 'Not so much as the tightest little opening.'

As Astrud Gilberto faded away into the sunset, a look of deep longing passed between the two women. They could have got into things there and then but allowing the conversation to build a little more, they knew, would only heighten the moment of release when it came. 'I know what to put on next,' Jodie said, padding across to the CD player.

'You know, Montand and Zep were probably discussing something completely different.'

'I hope so. And what about your day, Caro? Ambroise Paillaud!'

'Extraordinary.' Accompanied by a hybrid mix of instruments, a Latin voice stole sensuously into the room. 'Ah, Céu. I adore her.'

'I never saw Paillaud, you know. Not once. He never came to the Centre or the surgery when I was there. I was saddened to hear what happened, though.'

'You'll be the only one. Never has anyone's death been cheered so roundly.'

'Because of his bequest to the commune?'

'Precisely because of it.'

Jodie brushed her fingers along Caroline's flank as she rejoined her at the table. 'What do you make of that?'

'What I make of it is that it's a miracle the good citizens of La Crague have let Paillaud live *this* long.'

Jodie's healing hands managed something of which they were scarcely capable. They stopped moving. 'You mean... someone killed him?'

'No, he probably did it himself.' Caroline decided she had waited long enough, after all. 'Let's stop talking.'

# 18

Police driver Wanda Korneliuk glanced at her rear-view mirror and smiled quietly to herself. The man being ushered into the back seat had the mien of a caged attack dog. She enjoyed a challenge. 'Evening, monsieur.'

'Drive on.'

As the courtesy light faded, a bell chimed dully.

'Seat belt?'

'You're not going to crash, are you?'

'Who knows?'

The chiming continued. The car didn't move. Exhaling loudly, Guy Vaselle grabbed the belt.

'I'm taking you to your car, I understand.'

'You understand right. La Crague. The Place.'

'Which Place?'

'The only one there fucking well is.'

Wanda pulled smoothly away and filtered into traffic meandering torpidly along Route de Turin. Five minutes later, they had advanced no more than a hundred metres.

'Jesus. Can't you go any faster?'

Wanda drifted gently to a halt and pulled on the handbrake. 'I can, yes.'

Thrusting out his chin, Vaselle muttered a comment on the dubious ancestry of all police officers.

'Sorry, I didn't catch that?'

Vaselle grunted.

A scooter slaloming its way through the jam buzzed up behind them and squirted into the gap on their near side.

'Wrong call,' Wanda said, as the rider skidded hard to a stop. She rolled the passenger window and leaned across. 'When I move, you stay there.'

'Listen—'

'Stay there.'

In the back seat, Vaselle used the exchange to take a closer look at his chauffeuse. 'Ever shag on duty?' he said, as the window whirred up.

'My boyfriend. But only when he hasn't got a bareknuckle fight coming up.'

Vaselle leaned slowly forward, the seatbelt giving with the movement. 'Ever shag a suspect?'

Wanda considered whether to keep the thing going. Why not? It was a slow night. 'That would depend on what the suspect was suspected of. Lifting an old lady's purse wouldn't cut it.'

'Murder. That hot enough for you?'

Wanda released the handbrake. Checking the scooter was staying put, she rolled into the narrowing space. 'That *might* work for me but as I'm taking you home, I'm guessing you didn't do it.'

'Too fucking right, I didn't. But for an old cripple with a movie camera, I'd still be back in that hole.' He thrust out his chin. 'I'll find that old boy. Take him a case of Bollinger or something. I tell you, I should never have been picked up in the first place. Never!'

'Well, as you're innocent, I can't oblige. Sorry.'

'I'll make it worth your while.' He took out his wallet and leafed through it as casually as if he were ordering a round of drinks. 'How does a hundred sound?'

Wanda gave the accelerator a jab, jerking him back into his seat. 'Sit still and shut up or we're going back to the Caserne.'

The man was seething but he was savvy enough to do as he was told. Nothing more was said for the duration of the journey. Checking her rear-view mirror as she pulled into the tiny main square of La Crague, Wanda's eyes stayed on Vaselle for a moment. She saw something she had never seen to the same extent in a supposedly innocent man. She saw hate.

'Now you can fuck off,' he said, slamming the rear door as hard as he could.

'Yes, you'd like that,' she said, under her breath, as she watched him march away. 'And that is why it's not going to happen.'

# 19

A couple of hundred metres from their nearest neighbours down the hill, the two properties hunkered down in an uneasy alliance. As emphatic as exclamation marks, cypresses airily flanked Caroline Rosay's front and side gardens; on the left, her next-door neighbour, the *voyeur* Brice Kerthus, preferred the greater privacy afforded by a two-metre high wall. Neither boundary offered a serious deterrent to intruders: the properties shared a drive giving on to Avenue Montand, the road that wound sinuously above La Crague.

It was a practised routine. Jodie tipped the treatment table on to one side, retracted the legs, locked its on-board castors in position and folded it in half. As Caroline held open the front door, Jodie marched the table to her car like a porter pushing a sack barrow.

The performance wasn't over yet. The sound of crunching gravel was the signal for Kerthus's living room curtain to twitch. As rain began to fall, Jodie could feel his eyes studying her as she lifted the tailgate of her VW estate. She stowed the table, and then, exchanging a friendly but not overly familiar wave with Caroline, got in behind the wheel, turned into the avenue and pulled out of sight.


Some fifteen minutes later, a bike appeared out of the murk, its brake blocks making a sound like a honking goose as it swept on to the drive. Shifting his rucksack on to one shoulder, the rider dismounted and headed for the protection of the left-hand porch.

As if triggered by a motion sensor, the front door opened.

'Hasn't it turned horrible?' Kerthus said, waddling awkwardly to one side. 'Thank you *so* much for coming. I've been having such a terrible...'

With all the dispatch of a Venus fly trap, the door closed behind Doctor Arnaud Zep.

# 20

Decamped from Jardin Albert, musos outnumbered fans at The Blue Devil by two to one. On stage, veteran pianist James Clarence was tinkling his way through 'Stardust', a number he had assured Darac brought "sure-fire ass".

'Still has a gorgeous touch, no?' Didier said, at length. 'But the girls aren't exactly draping themselves over the piano, are they? Poor old bugger.'

'Maybe if his false teeth hadn't fallen out?' Dave Blackstock said, peering into the crowd. 'Where are our beers?'

'They didn't actually fall. Just slipped a bit.' Didier sympathetically essayed the effect. 'You should avoid those big glissandi at his age.'

Club owner Ridge Clay finally arrived with the drinks. It had taken him twenty minutes to get to the bar and back.

'Sorry for taking a while but I haven't seen some of these guys for the longest time.' He glanced at the piano and the lack of action around it. 'Ain't gonna happen, Jimmy.'

'Salut!'

Darac took a long draught of his Leffe Triple and stared at its head as he set it down. Ridge waited until the rest of the band had picked up the conversation before he turned to him. 'So, Garfield,' he said, still using the pet name he'd given Darac on their first meeting, some fifteen years ago. 'Good old Christophe doesn't give a shit for "Francine's" feelings?'

'Not about organising a leaving party for her, anyway.'

'You wouldn't ride over her like that? If you were together?'

Darac's beer was still taking his full gaze. 'I'm a sentimental slob so...Actually, no, I wouldn't or it's all about *you*, isn't it?' He heard himself. 'I majored in Self-Righteous Studies at university, by the way.' He took another long draught. 'Did quite well.'

Warm applause greeted James's final sprinkling of 'Stardust'. He played through it into 'Georgia On My Mind'.

'Did Frankie tell you why she hadn't said anything about leaving?'

'No but I could only get a couple of words with her alone.'

'Uh-huh.' Ridge took a sip of his bourbon. 'If I was Jimmy Clarence, you know what I might suggest?'

'I can imagine.'

'I'll clean it up. I'd say: "You want that woman? Then go get her, man." '

Feeling a throb in his chest, Darac looked Ridge in the eye. 'What would *you* say?'

Ridge downed the rest of his drink. 'A few years ago, she left your team, right? But that didn't kill her feelings for you because you still see each other most days. If she leaves the city... That just might do it.'

Before Darac could marshal his thoughts, he realised that the throb in his chest was his mobile. He checked the number. 'I've been waiting for this, Ridge.'

He took the call in the lobby.

'Captain? Charvet. Sorry to disturb you – I know you're off.'

'It's fine. The wills database finally playing ball?'

'No, but their IT person says it'll be up and running by tomorrow at the latest.'

'OK. Well, thanks for—'

'That's not why I'm calling.'

'If it's about my cameo appearance at Frènes's press conference later, I've told him I'll be on time.'

'They'll have to send in an understudy, Captain. You're needed elsewhere.'

# 21

As Darac took the turn to La Crague, heavier rain began to fall and Chet Baker began to sing 'Every Time We Say Goodbye'. He hit the off button.

'That's a first,' Bonbon said.

Darac knew he was on safe ground. 'I'll turn it back on if you like.'

'No, I'm fine.' Bonbon's smile morphed into a grimace as he ran an eye over the locale. 'I know few places look great in gloom but La Crague's a dull spot at the best of times, isn't it? One café bar – average. One pâtisserie – average. Boulangerie – average. Boucherie – average. War memorial – average. Pissoir – don't know. Probably average.' He reached into a pocket. 'I need a boost. Fancy a piece of this, chief? Chief?'

'What? Sorry, I was thinking about...' He was thinking about Frankie's decision to leave and he was tempted to canvass Bonbon's thoughts but until she brought it up herself, he felt he couldn't. 'Just thinking.'

'If you're worrying about Granot, he'll make it, don't worry. So long as he leaves things like this butter brittle alone.'

At first glance, the proffered bag appeared to contain a miniature green doormat. A second glance confirmed it. 'Is that the stuff with brandy in it?'

'That's butter *waffle*. From Cours Saleya. This is Brittle with a Hint of Mint. Casiprix.'

'Pass. So you think Granot will? Hit those targets?'

'Yes, especially with this...' Bonbon paused as he attempted to snap off a corner of the brittle. No go. 'Especially with this

Jodie girl...' He tried harder. Still no go. Teeth bared, the veins in his forehead pulsing visibly, he redoubled his effort. The brittle was unbowed. 'Especially... with this... Jodie girl helping him.'

'You alright, there?'

Bonbon took a deep breath and, making a noise like the start of the Monaco Grand Prix, tried once more.

'I think Jodie is the key, you're right. Anyone who can get Granot enthusing about things like "cross trainers" has to be some kind of genius.'

'What's...?' Bonbon wheezed. 'A cross trainer?'

'Dunno. But there's one with Granot's name on it at Centre Sicotte, down the road.'

Bonbon took a moment to recover, then unholstered his automatic.

Darac glanced across. 'I hope you have a licence to shoot sweets?'

'None needed. Martina Sicotte...' Bonbon pistol-whipped the brittle. To no effect. 'She's... someone I haven't thought about in a while.' A further thrashing. Same result. 'You should've seen her mother play.'

'That's what Granot says.'

'She was fantastic.' Bonbon opened the glove compartment, inserted the brittle half-way in at an angle and, holding tightly on to the end, rammed the door shut. The brittle held; the door broke off. 'Ah. It's just the hinge, I think. Popped out. How does it...?' He offered up the part and gave it a shove. To his evident surprise, it clicked into place, opening and closing freely. 'There you are.'

'Masterful.'

'Well, you know.'

'Thank God you went for the brittle and not the hard stuff.'

And then Bonbon spotted his efforts had not been in vain after all: a pea-sized nugget had landed on his knee. Snaffling it before it got any ideas of its own, he gave it the taste test. '*Uh*-huh.' He rolled the window, spat out the nugget and consigned the mother lode itself to a specimen bag. 'A waste of one euro fifty, *that* was. Unless we need to jemmy something at the scene. Like a safe.'

They passed through a deserted Place Charles Montand.

'Not exactly buzzing,' Darac said.

'Not good for you living in a place like this. The orientation doesn't help.'

'Political?'

'Topographical. La Crague sits on a ledge, doesn't it? Like a shelf in a cupboard. Because it faces east, most people who live here see the sun only in the morning. The back of the cupboard cuts it off for the rest of the day.'

'Some prefer shade.'

'As welcome relief, yes, but not all the time. Think of it: you wake up to the famed Côte d'Azur sun only for it to abandon you shortly afterwards. Every day promises more than it delivers.'

'Perhaps they should adopt that as the village motto.'

' "La Crague, Land Of Disappointment." ' Bonbon gave Darac a look. 'Considering it's a few minutes' drive from the likes of Carros and Gattières, it makes you wonder why Ambroise Paillaud chose to come back here to live.'

'Especially as he was unhappy in La Crague as a kid, according to the autobiography I'm speed reading.'

'Really?'

'Unknown father. Slightly dotty if lovable mother. Numerous kids and assorted men knocking around all the time. It was pretty chaotic.'

'I thought Paillaud was an only child?'

'The other kids weren't Madame's, it seems. She was a sort of mother hen to half the waifs and strays in the Alpes Maritimes. Animals too, and not just cats and dogs.'

'A proper circus.' Bonbon grinned. 'I bet the locals loved that.'

'Exactly. They threw Madame and her whole entourage out, basically. So off they went on their travels, losing a few here, gaining the odd one there until eventually, they pitched up near Paris. The rest, as they say...'

Bonbon's eyebrows lowered in a kind of awed bewilderment. 'Monsieur La Chute... Maybe it's fitting he died as he'd lived. Crashing into things on purpose.'

'At least we know that's how he *did* die.' Darac nosed the Peugeot into the narrow street that led out of the Place's far end. 'Thanks to Perand's video coup.'

'The way the man's body just... burst apart.' Bonbon's face crumpled. 'Ai, ai, ai.'

'You know what I keep thinking, though? Before he jumped, Paillaud stood in the one spot on the whole station that CCTV doesn't cover. Why?'

'You think it was a deliberate choice?'

'Bit of a coincidence if it wasn't.'

'He was something of a recluse, remember. Didn't like being seen. Didn't like being watched even more, probably.'

Darac turned the windscreen wipers up a notch. 'I didn't even notice the CC until Lartou mentioned it.'

'Paillaud might though, mightn't he? Especially with his life in front of the camera behind him. So to speak.'

Darac outlined the selfie scenario.

'That doesn't fit, then.'

'And there's something else, Bonbon. Something about the jump. I've watched it over and over and I can't put my finger on it. And now we've got this new death to consider. There's a lot to this thing, I think.'

'At least it's got you off TV duty with Frènes. Where did you leave it with him?'

'He's expecting me to keep him *au courant* all the way. I explained that if I did that, it would slow down the investigation hopelessly and as speed was of the essence, he should leave us to it.'

'Did you add "as usual"?'

'He knows the score. As long as I behave myself when I

eventually do get in front of the cameras or whatever, we should be OK.'

'Right. Action Boy Granot meeting us at the murder scene?'

'He'll be along later. He's got a case out at L'Escarène to sign off first.'

'L'Escarène? That's way out of our jurisdiction.'

'So is La Crague but it didn't stop Frènes allocating us.'

'Has the man never heard of the Gendarmerie? Not bad, some of them. Victims of our own success, we are.'

'Maybe we should bodge the occasional case.'

'After this one, let's try it.' Bonbon scanned the locale once more. 'Look at this rain. It's not even 8 o'clock and it's black as midnight out there.'

They followed the street to a junction with a narrower road that ascended the rising ground above the Place in a series of long traverses. Three or four hairpins later, they passed a huddle of familiar vehicles and turned at a swinging torch on to a short, gravel-laid driveway. Ahead, two dissimilar-looking villas stood side-by-side like strangers brought together at a graveside. The cordon tape glistened in his headlights as Darac drew up next to a plain black panel van. He rolled his window. The van driver followed suit, releasing a whiff of formaldehyde into the murk.

'How's it going, Ricky?'

'Sorry to tell you this, gents.' He gave his partner a wink. 'You're stuck with Doctor Mpensa – your mate Barrau's sick note's been extended.'

'Let's hope it's nothing trivial.'

'And another bit of good news. Thanks to tonight's goings-on, there's a rumour Professor Bianchi's been called back from leave. She'll be in on Sunday, they're saying.'

'*Will* she?' Darac shared a look with Bonbon. 'Thanks, Ricky. See you later.'

'Cheers, Captain.' His window rolled back up.

'Deanna back early?' Bonbon said, getting out of the car. 'You said there was a lot to this thing.'

# 22

Kicking off his sandals, Guy Vaselle slammed his front door. 'Fuck!'

He couldn't remember the last time he'd drawn a blank at a bar. Had his wife been at home, he would have even considered screwing her but he was having no luck with anything today.

'Fucking holidays! Fucking everything!'

He went to the sink and set about washing his hands, scrubbing them thoroughly. 'Look at this sink,' he announced, as if to a visitor. 'Retro farmhouse. First in the area. First!' He bent and let water from an antique brass tap cascade over his head. 'Now they're all doing it. Fuckers, I beat the lot of them. The lot!'

And then he stripped off his shirt and shorts and stuffed them into the washing machine.

# 23

'Isolated site, isn't it?' Darac said.

Suited up and signed in, he and Bonbon still hadn't entered the building proper.

'Nearest neighbours are at least a couple of football pitches away.' Bonbon clicked his tongue. 'That's two-hundred metres, by the way.'

Darac played along. 'Thank you.'

The forensic focus was on the smarter of the two villas. Darac detected a family resemblance between it and Ambroise Paillaud's larger place down in the village. Under the eaves, a lime-green box bore the lettering AMSeF.

'Alarmed. No CCTV, by the look of it. Shared driveway. Who lives next door?'

Bonbon checked his notes. 'One Brice Kerthus. Sixty-four year-old male.'

Darac indicated a newly registered Renault saloon parked alongside the cypresses. 'Where's the Porsche? If that's Kerthus's car, it's on the wrong side.'

A uniform was standing guard outside the victim's front door.

'The Boxster's in the garage, sir. Around the side.'

'OK, thanks.' Darac nodded towards the front door. 'Shall we?'

As they ducked under the tape, Bonbon spotted a top-of-the-range bike in Kerthus's porch. 'Up and down *these* hills? Must be some rider. Pity I didn't draw *him* in the Tour sweep. My guy couldn't climb stairs.'

Caroline Rosay's villa may have been a smaller clone of Paillaud's but one glance at the interior was sufficient to establish that the décor was on a different level.

'See this delicate little hall table?' Bonbon said, fighting an urge to take off his glove and run a finger across its fine intarsia inlay. 'In the trade it's called a console. This one's worth about four grand. We're in the wrong game. Should have trained as notaries.'

'Seems so.'

Bonbon's eyes narrowed. 'It's taken a bash.'

With the concern of a vet examining the leg of an injured foal, Bonbon knelt to inspect the damage as a lanky figure wearing crime scene overalls came loping along the hall towards them. The combination of a stubble-blackened face and white elasticated hood gave Max Perand the sort of look a surrealist photographer might have concocted.

'If it's not the man of the moment,' Darac said. 'The Paillaud suicide video, Perand? That call-back looked like a certain loser but you went anyway.' He gave the boy a pat on the arm. 'Good work.'

A lopsided grin rearranged the stubble.

'Anything significant there, Bonbon?'

'I don't think so. It's just surprising to see a gouge left in a piece of this quality. Looks as if someone bashed the leg dragging something past. A wheeled suitcase, maybe. Recently, by the look of it. *Possibly* today.'

'We'll bear that in mind. The body, Perand?'

'In the office at the back. The assailant broke in through the patio doors that give on to the garden.'

Along the corridor, a bald, heavily built black man hove busily into view. He looked up from the clipboard he was carrying. 'Just getting more coffins, chief,' Jean-Jacques Lartigue said, in his curiously delicate, precisely enunciated tones. He fanned the wad of paper. 'There's a lot of stuff to take away. Bonbon? What are *you* doing here?'

'I'm wondering the same thing.'

'Any CCTV around, Lartou? Couldn't see a camera outside.'

'There's none in the place, chief. Nor next door.'

'The alarm?'

'Off. The log shows it was on until 3.51 this afternoon, when Mademoiselle Rosay must have returned home. For the past three nights, she reactivated it at 11.17, 11.56 and...' He checked his notes as he moved past them and headed for the door. '10.02. Her bedtimes, presumably. Back in a minute.'

'Thanks, Lartou.' Darac turned to Perand. 'You were saying.'

'Yeah, she must have disturbed the assailant as he was turning over the office. The door into it from the house is open and there are files thrown around.'

'Who discovered the body?'

'None other than the mayor of this little burg, an arrogant shit by the name of Hervé Montand. Seems he had an appointment – that's his Renault outside. But a Monsieur Brice Kerthus and a Doctor Arnaud Zep play a part also.'

'Kerthus is the next-door neighbour, right? Who's this Doctor Zep?'

'He was visiting Kerthus when Montand arrived. Got here a couple of minutes before. By bike, would you believe.'

'Arnaud Zep?' Bonbon repeated, savouring the name. 'Sounds like a top cyclist. It was a social call, presumably?'

'Professional.'

'A house call in the evening? Kerthus is really sick, then?'

'The fat little bugger's as camp as Christmas, I'll tell you that. And he could talk for France. But he does have a serious heart condition. Acute angina.'

'Bedridden or mobile?' Darac said.

'I see where you're going, chief. He's mobile but Zep says Kerthus's condition rules him out as a possible murderer. Two reasons. First, he's just not fit enough to have carried it out. Second, if he somehow *had* managed it and survived, Zep says the effects would have been obvious in the exam he performed on him in what must have been only minutes afterwards. Flak's next door with the pair of them, taking down their statements.'

'OK, good. Montand?'

'We're holding him in the dining room off the hall here. Not a popular move. But weirdly, he showed the uniform the contents of his pockets. Voluntarily, I mean. Nothing incriminating in them.'

'Which is why he volunteered them, presumably. Walk me through his story, quickly.'

'He arrives at 7 o'clock to keep an appointment with the victim. Finding the office ransacked and her croaked, he rushes next door. Zep is there, tending to Kerthus. All three of them come here, Zep sprinting, Montand behind, Kerthus behind him. Montand and Kerthus look on as Zep examines the body. He pronounces her dead. They call us immediately.'

'Right. Let's get to it.'

The trio swept along the hall, scaring up a dust storm of voices as they passed an open door.

'*Was that the man in charge? I want to see him. Now! I'm late for a very important—*'

'*You'll see him soon enough. Sit down, please.*'

'*Our monthly commune development meeting began at 8 and I'm the chair!*'

'*Sit down!*'

'That was Montand?' Darac said.

'The same.'

Four doors led off the rear lobby, one being the side entry to the villa. A flashgun fired as they entered an office lined with prints, bookshelves and, in homage to France's long love affair with paperwork, banks of filing cabinets. The deep-pile carpet was dyed the colour of the Baie des Anges but associations with serenity ended there. The surface was littered with numbered card markers and strewn papers. And a bloodied corpse had been washed in on the tide.

Pathologist Djibril Mpensa glanced up as he handed a small

poly-bagged specimen to an assistant. 'What a bookend to the day.'

Caroline Rosay's fully-clothed body was lying on its back, her fair hair matted with what looked like brown nail varnish. Its source was a ragged-edged crater in her forehead. One arm was by her side, the other stretched out, as if she were reaching for the black leather daysack that lay against her chair. A sheet of typed A4 was resting at a diagonal across her bare left shin; and the corner of another, typed side down, had found its way on to her shoulder – a white epaulette for the pink blouse she had been wearing. Her eyes were open and Darac found himself wondering if the last thing she saw were the framed qualification certificates on the wall behind her. Perversely, it disturbed him that she would've had to have read her name upside down. He exhaled a long slow breath. 'She was playing tennis earlier,' he said. 'Running around trying to score points.' He remembered her correction. '*Win* points, I mean.' He caught Bonbon's look. 'What?'

'Nothing.'

Darac knew he had been allowing the senselessness of it all to get to him lately. 'I'm fine.'

'Sure,' Bonbon said, keeping his tone light as he took out his notebook.

Darac was keen to get the investigation up and running but first, he needed to take a step back. 'Perand? Here.'

The young man negotiated his way around the debris and joined Darac.

'I know it wasn't a definitive report but you said the victim "must" have disturbed the assailant in the act of ransacking the place. Right?'

'Ri-ight.'

'There's no "must" about it. Why?'

Perand peered at the corpse. He peered at the mess.

'Think simple archaeology,' Darac said. 'Strata.'

More peering. 'Got it. There are no papers trapped under

the body, only lying on top.'

'Exactly. It's more likely that the office was turned over *after* she had been attacked. Or at least, continued afterwards. She may well have been working at her desk when the attacker appeared.'

'Yes.'

'That's it.'

Mpensa was slowly drawing a paper glove on to the victim's left hand.

'Exchange evidence from the perp?' Darac said, bending.

'There are particles under the ring and fourth fingernail but it's not skin.'

'Ring and fourth and no others?'

'Correct.'

Bonbon made the note.

'Unlikely to be coke or some other drug, then,' Darac went on. 'Unusual for *anything* to lodge exclusively there in a right-handed person.'

Bonbon peered at the carpet where the hand had been laying. 'Is there a trace of powder there?'

'I'll get R.O. to lift it and let you know later.'

Another flash went off.

Darac straightened. 'The forehead injury. Is it the sole c.o.d?'

'I'm almost certain it is.'

An assistant opened an evidence case stencilled PATH and took out a paper bag. 'We're sure this is the murder weapon, Captain.' Flecked with blood, the object was a half-brick-sized lump of stone. 'Picked up from the rockery just outside the door.' He nodded towards it. 'You see that cavity there? It fits it perfectly.' He turned to face the room. 'That's where it finished up. Number three.'

The marker was sitting on the carpet tight into the corner of the room and a couple of centimetres above it, the adjoining walls bore deep gouge marks.

'Not just tossed aside,' Darac observed. 'Hurled furiously. One blow did it, Map?'

'Ultimately, but there were two blows, in fact. The victim was a free-standing target for the first one which made her fall back into the position she's in now. It was while she was lying there stunned that the assailant delivered the coup de grâce, a pile-driving blow more or less into the same site. The fact that the back of her head was now supported by the floor, deeply carpeted though it is, greatly added to the devastation wrought by that blow.' He played his pen torch beam over the trauma site. 'Devastation in the form of a massive depressed fracture to the skull.'

'Death would have been instantaneous?'

'Seconds, no more.'

Darac gazed at the wound. 'I know in this sort of case I always ask this but—'

'Could a woman have effected these blows?' Mpensa shrugged. 'Depends on the woman. If she happened to be a shot-put champion or something, she could. Definitely so.'

'We'll specify it on the flyer,' Darac said, essaying levity and failing. 'Let's follow a parallel line. This is an isolated spot, right? As you're aware, a Monsieur Brice Kerthus lives next door. So, he was in situ before Doctor Arnaud Zep and Mayor Hervé Montand arrived on the scene this evening. That's a big tick in the Opportunity column for Kerthus. *But* he's a 64 year-old man with a heart condition. Acute angina. Apparently, Zep believes it's serious enough to rule him out as a suspect. What do you think?'

'Difficult to say. I would have to examine him myself.' Belatedly catching on, Mpensa gave Darac a chastening look. 'I walked right into that one. A house call? Really?'

'I know it's cheeky, Map, but could you? As a favour? When you're finished in here, obviously. Just a quick assessment. A definitive answer from you and we could eliminate Kerthus as a suspect, officially. Or not, according to your findings.'

'You know what Deanna would tell you to do with your cheeky favour, don't you?'

Darac laughed. 'She would, you're right.' He remembered morgue boy Ricky's news. 'Well, she won't be back until Sunday, so I'm spared that.'

'Monday it is, actually.'

'No, no – she's been called back in for Sunday. So they say, anyway.'

'Who says?'

'Ricky.'

'In that case, it's gospel. Thank the good Lord!' Mpensa exhaled, contentedly. 'Alright, Darac, I'll look in on Kerthus.'

'Excellent.' The smile faded as he focused on Caroline's wound once more. 'So when did this happen?'

'I can be pretty precise. I began the exam at 7.40 sharp. The victim's blood had clotted but crucially, the serum hadn't separated out, and there was no rigor in the face and neck. Combined with the conditions in here and other factors, we're looking at no more than an hour at the outside. So the attack occurred no earlier than 6.40.'

'And no later than?'

'Discounting the anecdotal evidence of the witnesses – and going by the book, I include Doctor Zep in that – it couldn't have happened any later than five minutes before we arrived.'

'Right.' Darac looked more carefully at the surrounding area. 'Almost no blood spatter. The killer wouldn't have left the scene covered in it. Possibly avoided it altogether.'

'That's a question for R.O. but I agree. Anyway, I'll have more on the body back in the lab. I'll just be a little longer here.'

A serial shoulder squeezer, Darac didn't abandon the habit now. 'Thanks, man.'

'*Man*? You've been playing with your other friends this evening, haven't you?'

'You'd make a good detective,' Darac said, running his eye over a four-drawer filing cabinet away to his left.

'Detective? I doubt it. Describing the *what* is a lot easier than determining the why and then nailing the who. You guys have got the hard part.'

'A point so generously made,' Bonbon said, finishing a note, 'it entitles you to a complimentary bar of Casiprix Butter Brittle. I've got some in the car.'

'Great.' Mpensa's smile seemed genuine. 'I love the stuff.'

Bonbon's eyebrows flew up like pinball flippers. 'Really?'

'I don't *eat* it, obviously. I use it for growing cultures. It's half-way there already, let's face it.'

Bonbon looked queasy, suddenly. 'I'll pass it on later.'

At that moment, Lartigue returned and began setting down evidence cases on a cleared section of floor.

'Anyone checked those out?' Darac said to him, indicating the filing cabinets.

'I thought it best to wait for Granot.'

'It's the percentage play usually but look at the quantity of this stuff. And it's not only wills. There'll be property sales documents and so on, too. I think we should cut into it, ourselves.' He noticed that the drawer labelled Wills N-R was unlocked and had been pulled out slightly. 'I'll start with that.'

'OK, Captain.'

Darac slid the drawer fully open, revealing a tight concertina of manila folders. One was not pushed home, the corner of its white ID label protruding like a handkerchief from a breast pocket. The label read AMBROISE PAILLAUD. Darac fished it out. Inside was a thick sheaf of hand-written wills each stamped SUPERSEDED. Except one.

'Evening, gents.' Careful where he was putting his feet, Raul Ormans stepped in from the garden. 'Bonbon? I thought you were appearing elsewhere today.'

'See my agent.'

Darac looked up. 'Anything of interest out there, R.O.?'

'There's a faint but significant right footprint next to the rockery. By the angle, I believe it was made when the killer bent to prise up the rock with which he subsequently murdered the victim.'

'He?'

'Or a she with big feet. Size 42, I estimate.'

'OK. It's a faint print, you say?'

'Until it started raining just over an hour ago, it's been bone dry for weeks. However, Mademoiselle Rosay was a mulcher, bless her, or her gardener was, so that's made life a little easier. Unfortunately, the material consists of biggish pieces of bark. It's not sticky and therefore not mouldable or likely to be spread around like soil compost would have been; nor to remain lodged between the sole treads of any shoe treading in it.'

'Understood.'

'I've got spare bootees, come and look.'

Darac set down the will and followed Ormans outside. One glance was enough. 'I'm sure you're right, R.O. Whoever made that print picked up the rock. It *is* faint, though. Too faint for a cast?'

'Touch and go. We're going to give it a try, of course – it would be key evidence.'

Darac swapped his bootees at the door and they went back inside. 'As you suggest, there's no soiling of the carpet.'

'None. I've removed the doormat, by the way. There's one flake snagged in it.'

'Sounds useful,' Perand said, joining them.

Ormans harrumphed. 'It would've been *more* useful if it had remained sticking to the sole that made the print.'

Perand nodded. 'Oh, yes. Of course.'

'That said,' Darac went on. 'Providing your boys can produce a cast, and we come up with the shoe in question...'

'Cinderella *shall* go to the ball. I'll let you know if and when it's ready.'

'Excellent. Blood, now?'

'You can see the killer hasn't stepped in what is very scanty spattering. It's possible that he or she could have left the scene wearing a white suit quite untainted by the attack.'

'I was wondering if that might be the case.'

Ormans scanned the room. 'Swing that coffin over, would you, Perand? Don't want to come in any further.' He turned back to Darac. 'So it *was* suicide, then? The great man?'

As if commemorating Paillaud's life as a star, the flashgun fired three times.

'Thanks to Perand's amateur cinematographer, we know he jumped, yes.'

'Told you the boy would get something right eventually.' He jetted Perand a grin as he relieved him of the case. 'Well *done*, Max.'

As the process of investigation continued around him, Darac returned to Paillaud's active will, read it to the end and then leafed through the earlier versions it had superseded.

'So how much was the old man worth, Darac?' Ormans said.

'I feel the word "cool" coming on.'

'As in "a cool" *x* number of millions?'

'Twelve point seven of them, to be exact.'

Ormans whistled. 'All from just falling over. *Chapeau*, Monsieur La Chute!'

'I'll tell you who will also be raising his hat to him.' He set down the file. 'Paillaud has penned a number of wills since returning to the area. Signed and dated by Caroline Rosay some eight months ago, this last one names just one beneficiary. The entire estate is bequeathed to the commune of La Crague-du-Var, the sum to be carved up as Mayor Hervé Montand sees fit.'

'How magnanimous,' Ormans said.

Darac's hands went to his hips as he stared at the floor. 'How magnanimous and how connected: Paillaud kills himself immediately after meeting his notary who, only hours later, is herself killed, her body discovered by the nominal beneficiary of Paillaud's will, Montand. Earlier, Montand had left an anxious message on Paillaud's home phone, who had already left for his meeting with Mademoiselle Rosay. Montand also happens to be the brother-in-law and boss of one Guy Vaselle who told us he'd been summoned by Paillaud to a meeting, one which turned nasty seconds before the old man's death.'

'The *how, why and who* again,' Mpensa said, as he drew a technician's attention to some detail. 'I tell you – give me the *what* any day.'

'I'm certainly looking forward to talking to Montand.' Closing the cabinet, Darac saw shards of glass glinting on the carpet. 'Any thoughts on the entry, R.O?'

'Straightforward. The key had been left in the lock on the inside of the patio doors. The pane above it was smashed from the outside using the eventual murder weapon. The key turned and in came the killer.'

'Right. The safe, now? I take it your cracksman's skills haven't deserted you.'

Ormans' offended look was something of which Ambroise Paillaud himself would have been proud. 'Certainly not!'

'Anything of note?'

'Nothing that leaped out at me. Granot might find otherwise, of course.'

'Cash?'

'Petty. Petty-ish, anyway. Euros to the value of fifteen hundred and...' He closed one eye. '... sixty-two. And a small number of coins.'

'Not all that petty.' He looked more closely at the patio door. 'Fingerprinting?'

'We've dusted around where I'm standing and the other door, the safe, light switches, desk, et cetera.' He gave a nod to the file Darac was holding and the heaps of papers strewn around the floor. 'Those, we'll work on in the lab but most haven't even been listed or photographed as yet.'

'Granot will be here shortly. Could you make that a priority?'

'We're forensic technicians, Darac. Not miracle workers.'

'That's a moot point. Marcel? Nearly finished?'

The crime scene photographer fired off another shot.

'Except for all the papers.'

'Keep that thought. Lartou?'

'I can log it in, liaising with Marcel as I go.'

Darac looked back at Ormans, underlining the simplicity of the solution by raising his hands, palms upwards. 'First part sorted.'

Ormans eyeballed Darac as he took his leave. 'Make sure anyone who touches a document keeps their gloves on.'

Lartigue turned to Darac. 'Are you *expecting* any significant prints on the docs, chief?'

'Not ruling it out. The list will be key, though. There'll be an inventory of the safe and filing cabinet contents somewhere – probably on the computer. We'll cross-check it against the list to establish if anything's been taken.' His eyes slid to the filing cabinets as Marcel joined him. 'There's a lot of it to get through.'

Lartigue sighed. 'With you, chief.'

'Let's get started, Lartou,' Marcel said. 'I'm expected home some time next year.'

Darac's mind racing with theories and counter-theories, he handed over the Paillaud will file and then turned his attention to Caroline's leather daysack. A member of Ormans's team had already made a list of its contents but Darac preferred to examine the items themselves. Nothing seemed significant until he picked up Caroline's mobile. Unable to get past the password, he took out his own and called the Tech lab at the Caserne. As he waited, Mpensa appeared on his blindside. 'Finished. I'll send the boys in to move the body before too long. OK?'

'Sure. Thanks again, Map. Don't forget to look in on Kerthus.'

'How could I? It should only take a minute, actually.'

Before he could say anything else, Darac heard a voice in his ear: his call had been taken. 'So – Erica?'

'Do you believe in E.S.P. Darac?'

'Only the Wayne Shorter tune of the same name. And the Davis album, of course.'

'What, you've never been about to pick up the phone to call someone and then it rings because they beat you to it?'

'No.'

'Bet you have.'

'Alright,' he said. 'It happens all the time.'

'See there. So, what can I do for you?'

'You tell me.'

'Hey, you're clever.'

'Yeah... Listen, if we can get a mobile and a...' He peered at the desk. '... GenTec 5000 desktop over to you later, would you have time to look at them?' He outlined what he needed. 'Tomorrow would do, obviously, but you know how impatient I am.'

'I like a man who recognises his childlike limitations. How soon can you get them here?'

'I'll send them now. Forty-five minutes?'

'No problem. I won't be leaving until ten at the earliest.'

'Great – hold the line a second.' Darac called over a uniform and arranged it. 'Thanks, Erica, you're a doll.' For the $n^{th}$ time that day, he could feel Angeline buzzing around in his head. 'But a totally autonomous, non male-defined...'

'Forget it. I'll take doll, anytime.'

'So why were you going to call me?'

'I've traced the mobile used to ring one Monsieur Guy Vaselle at lunchtime today.'

As if they were videoconferencing, Darac raised a hand in apology. 'Sorry, Erica, we no longer need that, strictly speaking. I should've let you know.'

'Yes you should! For the record, it was neither Caroline Rosay's nor Hervé Montand's number. In fact, it wasn't on the list of options Flak gave me at all. It belongs to a 16 year-old named Jonah Pardère. He reported it lost or stolen last week.'

Darac didn't have time to react. There were angry voices in the doorway, and sounds of scuffling. 'Sorry again but I've got to go, Erica.'

'Monsieur! No!'

'Haven't I already seen the bloody body? It was me who found it!'

'What's going on here?' Bonbon said, as he and Flaco followed two burly uniforms and their charge into the room. 'Contain yourself, monsieur.'

'I am Hervé Montand, mayor of the ancient commune of—'

Darac was having none of it. 'Back to the other room. We'll be with you shortly.'

'I don't think you heard me. As mayor of this commune, I am titular chief of police—'

'Well, *we* are not titulars, we are *actual* police officers. Back to the other room. Now!'

'You haven't heard the last of this! I am personally acquainted with Public Prosecutor Jules Frènes.'

'So am I. We can cry about it later. Officers?'

Montand was shepherded away.

' "Bloody body?" ' Bonbon said. 'What an arsehole.'

Darac nodded. 'A very well-off arsehole after today. In a titular sense.' He updated Flaco on the will development.

'So it's control of Paillaud's entire estate that Montand has?' she said.

'Seems so.'

'Have you got this Doctor Zep and the next-door neighbour's statements there?'

She handed them over. 'They tally.'

'Alright. Anything jump out at you in them?'

'The timing. Zep says he doesn't believe it, but he conceded Montand *could* have killed Mademoiselle Rosay. Kerthus, who more or less lives at his window, clocked Montand pulling up in the drive, getting out of his car and heading for the mademoiselle's front door. Zep, who was trying to sound Kerthus's chest at the time, corroborates that. Less than two minutes later, Montand arrives hotfoot at Kerthus's own door shouting for Zep.'

Bonbon lowered his tawny brow. 'Alright, Montand was in Position A, but he gets out of his car, gains entrance to the house, brutally slays the mademoiselle, ransacks the place and then heads off next door all in two minutes? Even for a professional killer, that would be pushing it.'

'Agreed,' Darac said. 'It's not impossible, though.' And he saw another possibility.

Flaco shook her head. 'That's not Zep's point. He just meant it was possible from a pathology standpoint that Montand could have killed the victim. When he examined her, the pooling blood was yet to clot. That means she *had* to have been killed in the previous few minutes. In the conditions, no more than five, he says.'

Darac shrugged. 'Five? That puts paid to one theory I was beginning to entertain.'

Bonbon saw it, too. 'A variation on the Jacqueline Denfert ploy?'

'Exactly.' He gave Flaco a look. 'Before your time.'

'What was the ploy, Captain?'

'Denfert arrived at the scene of a murder twice: once to have plenty of time to commit it; the second, some time later, to feign discovering the body.'

'How did she work it?'

'It was your case, Bonbon.'

'It happened six or seven years ago up near the Madeleine Train des Pignes station. Making sure she wasn't spotted, Denfert called to see her lover with the express purpose of stabbing him in the heart. Which she duly did. She left the house unseen, or so she thought, and returned an hour later. This time, she made sure she was seen and even stopped to talk to the victim's neighbour directly outside. She opened the door, and while it was still open, screamed and retreated immediately. The neighbour testified that Denfert hadn't had time even to shout hello, let alone kill the man. A second neighbour had seen her leave the house earlier, though. Making matters worse, the Path team was led by one Professor Deanna Bianchi and once she had established the time of the murder within a couple of minutes of that sighting, the second neighbour's testimony put Denfert squarely in the frame.'

'Ah.'

Darac nodded. 'If Montand did kill Caroline, can you see why he couldn't have pulled a similar stunt?'

Flaco's brow lowered an extra couple of fathoms. But then she had it. 'Yes, if we accept Zep's account, we know that blood from the victim's wound had begun to flow no more than five minutes before he examined her. Any time Montand would have bought by arriving unseen first on foot would have been lost having to go back to his car and then driving it to the house. If he killed her, he *must* have arrived only once.'

'Brava,' he said.

Darac's mobile rang. Mpensa's number. 'You're on speaker, Map. So do you concur with Zep's assessment?'

'Of Kerthus's physical frailty? It's spot-on. He could *not* have committed the murder. Just hobbling around to the scene might have put paid to him. Right, I'm away.'

Noises off signalled that Ricky and his mate had arrived to bag and remove Caroline's body. Boisterous on approach, respectful on crossing the threshold, it was a signature entrance.

'Thanks, Map, that's really helpful. See you soon.' Darac shared a look with the others. 'Well, that's one suspect crossed off. Flak, before we headed off down Memory Lane, I don't think you had finished your point.'

'Not quite but what we just heard has strengthened what I was going to say. Because of what he witnessed, Zep estimated that the victim died at 6.55, which I thought was a useful steer. Now we know that Doctor Mpensa thinks Zep is sound, it's made it more than that. It's practically a working time of death.'

'Perhaps,' Darac said. 'And 6.55 is well within the initial time frame Map gave us but we have to be careful with Zep's evidence – it's technically inadmissible. The key here is corroboration. Did you ask Kerthus if he noticed that the blood from Caroline's wound was still wet?'

'I did.' She pursed her lips. 'He "bravely" looked and saw that it was, yes.'

Darac smiled. 'Well done. I'll ask Montand the same question shortly and if he concurs, too, then we'll be on much safer—'

A shriek shredded the air. All heads turned to see a figure framed in the open doorway. Too late to screen off the horror, Flaco and a couple of uniforms moved in quickly.

'Whoa! Whoa!'

'Hold it there!'

'No further!'

Sinking to her knees, the figure let out a keening cry of pain.

'Who is this?' Bonbon said.

Darac knew who it was. How she had got there, he had no idea.

# 24

The scream from next door acted like a siren call to Brice Kerthus. The combination of a heart condition, short, stumpy legs and a monumental body didn't prevent him from getting noisily to his feet.

'Sit down, monsieur!' the uniform said, his patience worn thin by the fat man. 'Now!'

Kerthus was all put-out rectitude. 'If you'd just let me sit next to the window here where I normally do, I wouldn't have to keep getting up and down.'

Arnaud Zep sighed and shared a look with the uniform. 'For pity's sake, Brice. Come back here and sit still!'

'We've given our statements. I don't see any reason—'

'Because, as Officer Flaco told us just a moment ago, the senior investigating officer will need to talk to us, also.'

Kerthus sank back on to his plump, leather-clad armchair. 'This is not doing my angina any good,' he said, his words sprawling on the hissing cushion of air displaced as he sat down. 'Especially after the shock I've had tonight. Nearly killed *me*, running round there, I'm telling you.'

The uniform took a call on his mobile.

'Find out who screamed!' Kerthus instructed him. 'Was it Daniela, Caroline's cleaner?' He turned to Zep. 'She's a screamer, that one. I bet you anything.'

'Brice,' he said, his face a mask of incredulity. 'This evening, just a few metres away, your neighbour has been brutally slayed, yes? One more word and I swear I will never trek up here to see you again.'

The fat man leaned forward, pain vying with petulance. 'You do it as much for the fitness as anything.'

Just as Kerthus the hypochondriac had latterly succumbed to a life-threatening illness, so Kerthus the prattler, it seemed, had just hit one nail squarely on the head. Folding his arms, Zep sat back, colour channelling into the whorled striations of his face.

'OK,' the uniform said, concluding the call.

'Who was it who screamed?' Kerthus said to him. No take. He turned to Zep. 'Bet it was Daniela. She's a Pole or whatever and you know how they—'

'Monsieur?' the uniform said.

'Yes?'

'Shut up!'

Kerthus's jaw dropping, he turned to Doctor Zep for succour. 'Seconded,' he said.

## 25

Jodie Foucault was holding the glass as if she had no idea what to do with it.

'Take a sip,' Flaco said. 'Hydration is important.'

'Hm? Oh.' She raised the glass to her lips.

'Better?'

Ill at ease in the role of comforter, Flaco hadn't welcomed the task of taking Jodie home. It wasn't that she felt no empathy for the bereaved; she just found it difficult adapting her direct, plain-speaking persona to such situations. Opting uncharacteristically for displacement, she'd got off to an uninspiring start, expressing surprise at the amount of rain that had fallen earlier and commenting on the state of the road surface on the ten-minute drive to Jodie's tiny bungalow a couple of kilometres shy of Bouyon. In the hall, Flaco had paused before a photo montage of a sensationally somersaulting gymnast who proved to be a young Jodie. No need for displacement there – Flaco was awed – but it had taken her some moments to realise that this wasn't the time to express her admiration quite so enthusiastically.

And then she had had to negotiate the gear change from chaperone to questioner because despite every appearance to the contrary, Mademoiselle Jodie Foucault could not be ruled out as a suspect. When the moment came, Flaco handled it smoothly.

'Better now?'

Jodie set down the glass. 'No.'

'We didn't realise there's a way down into Mademoiselle

Rosay's back garden off the Mont Crague road. The hillside is too sheer, for one thing. More a cliff.'

'It was the shrub cover. That was the real value of it.'

'Why was that important?'

'Because I could come and go without that scumbag seeing.'

'Kerthus?'

She nodded.

'And you used it just now because you were intending to spend the night with Mademoiselle Rosay?'

Jodie drew up her legs and, hugging them, lay her cheek on her knees. 'Yes.' Her voice was no more than a whisper. 'It was meant to be a surprise. We did that sometimes.'

'As you say, the route itself is more or less invisible from the garden, let alone from Avenue Montand. But what about at the top end of it? Would anyone else heading above it along the Mont Crague road know where it began?'

'No one would think to look and hardly anyone uses that road, anyway.'

'Why is that?'

'It's not really a road. It's just a lane that climbs off Avenue Montand, then loops around higher up Mont Crague and comes down to join the avenue again. There are no houses on it. Just a lot of thick scrub.'

'But you found a gap in it.'

Jodie took a deep breath and closed her eyes. 'It was the other way round. We were in the garden one day and like some stupid kid, I started climbing the cliff. Just to see how far I could get.'

'You've obviously got a head for heights.'

'I hate high bridges and things like that but as long as I'm connected to what's immediately below, I'm OK usually. Because I'm agile, I made it to the top and because I'm a skinny little arse, I got through all the vegetation on to the lane. Starting back down the cliff was more difficult.' She gave an exhausted little laugh. 'I couldn't find my way through, at first. Caro had to keep shouting out.'

164

'She guided you down?'

Josie's brows knotted. 'Yes.'

With that, Flaco rejected the theory that Caroline Rosay's killer might have entered and exited her property via this secret route. It wasn't *impossible* that someone else knew about it. And that person *might* have been endowed with the daredevil agility of a Jodie Foucault. But it was highly improbable. Unless, of course, Jodie herself was the killer. Flaco didn't believe it but she would need more than that. 'Mademoiselle, now we need to form a picture—'

'You need to form a picture of where everyone was at the time Caro... was murdered.'

When interrogating suspects in a homicide investigation, Flaco followed Darac's example of initially withholding the precise time of death. Murderers had been known to incriminate themselves by volunteering it. 'Indeed. So?'

'When did it happen?'

It was unprofessional, she knew, but Flaco was relieved Jodie hadn't fallen at the very first hurdle. But what *should* she say about the time frame? Although she gave credence to Zep's precise estimate, she thought it politic to keep things vague. 'We don't know exactly but we think it was between about 6 o'clock and about forty-five minutes before you arrived just now.'

'I can narrow your timing down. After my visit, Kerthus watched Caro wave me...' Her whole body shook and it was with a considerable effort that she composed herself. 'Kerthus watched her wave me goodbye at 6.34.'

Flaco looked up from her notebook. 'That's very exact.'

'I work to a timetable or try to. It's second nature to check my watch as I come and go.'

'I interviewed Monsieur Kerthus earlier. He didn't mention seeing you leave.'

Jodie loosely raised a shoulder. 'He maintains he never watches anyone but he sits by his window all day. I don't think

165

he would lie if you asked him outright if he'd seen me. And I think he's as precise about time as I am. Probably keeps a log. The creep.'

Flaco maintained her gravitas as she made the note. 'If he confirms that, it'll be a real help to us.' Another hurdle loomed. She didn't buy the idea but it was possible that Jodie could have driven off, turned up on to the Mont Crague loop, parked and returned unseen to Caroline's villa via the secret route, the way she did later. Flaco estimated the round trip couldn't be made any quicker than ten minutes. Probably nearer fifteen. She looked directly into Jodie's eyes. 'After leaving the victim's – pardon – Mademoiselle Rosay's villa, where did you go, then?'

'I drove down the hill into the village. I had a 6.30 with Madame Valentin. Chemin de Printemps, off Place Charles Montand.' Flaco gave her a questioning look. 'Yes, I was late – something Madame wasted no time in pointing out.'

'You drove directly to her address?'

'Yes.'

'Which takes about?'

'Three minutes but I did it in nearer two. Madame was waiting for me on the doorstep. I wheeled the table in and got started straight away. And I gave her an extra fifteen minutes to make up for my "tardiness". '

'Right.' A further hurdle cleared. Cleared in style. If the alibis checked out, Jodie could not have killed her lover. 'When you left Mademoiselle Rosay's and drove down to the village, did you pass anyone en route? Possibly someone on foot?'

'No, I didn't.'

'What about the junction of Avenue Montand with the loop road? Was anyone coming down the hill when you passed?'

'I didn't look.'

'Were you aware that Mademoiselle Rosay had an appointment to see Mayor Hervé Montand at 7 o'clock? In her private office?'

Jodie sat upright. 'She did?'

'You seem surprised.'

'It's just that we – Caroline and I – had been speaking about him earlier.' She recounted the conversation. 'I suppose I *am* surprised she didn't mention she was meeting him.'

'You say you're not sure what the earlier disagreement between Doctor Zep and Monsieur Montand was about. How did it end?'

'Arnaud had the parting shot. Whatever it was, it stunned Montand. You'd better ask *them* about it.'

Neither protagonist having referred to their meeting, Flaco intended to do just that.

'Just a moment.' Jodie stiffened. 'Did Montand keep that 7 o'clock appointment?'

'Mademoiselle...'

'Did he?'

'I can't answer that.'

'No.' Jodie looked away. 'Of course not.'

On to the final hurdle. 'Jodie, do you have keys to Mademoiselle Rosay's villa?'

'To the side door only. It's on the table there. Take it. I don't need it anymore.'

'Did anyone else hold a key?'

'Don't think so.'

'Did anyone come regularly to the house? A gardener?'

'Caro did it, herself.' A deep exhalation. 'Daniela, the cleaner, comes in one afternoon a week. Yesterday, it was, actually. But she doesn't have a key. Caro just let her in.'

'We'll need to talk to her. Do you know where..?'

Jodie gave the cleaner's name and her Vence address.

'Thank you. Finally, can you think of any reason why anyone would want to kill Caroline?' She heard herself. 'Sorry, I could have put that better.'

'No, no. Besides, I prefer straight-talking. There are people who didn't *like* her. She could be difficult. Wilful. Mischievous. I remember I didn't like her much myself until I got to know her.' As if astonished by the recollection, she shook her head. 'But she had another side. Take this evening. I stupidly scraped her console with my table when I was wheeling it in from my car. She was really sweet about it.'

'So, *can* you think of anyone—'

Jodie clicked her tongue. 'Sorry, I forgot the question. No, I can't imagine anyone could think *so* ill of her. It's to do with Paillaud's will, isn't it? I don't know what but it has to be.' A steelier look hardened Jodie's red-rimmed eyes; the look of a gymnast about to embark on a dangerous routine. 'I tell you what I do know, though. If I find out who stove my gorgeous Caro's head in, I shall take a hammer—'

'Stop there,' Flaco said, the nakedness of Jodie's feelings giving her an unexpected frisson. 'Revenge?' She shook her head. 'Bad idea. Anyone killing a killer in cold blood goes down for a very long time. And by *goes down*—'

'I know what it means.'

Over the next few minutes, Flaco built a persuasive case for allowing the law to take its course and at the end of it, Jodie acknowledged that her reaction had been forged in the heat of the moment. Flaco was content to leave it there.

'I should go now,' she said, but realising she had a final hurdle to present Jodie with, she glanced at her watch. 'Have you the time? I'm way slow, I think.'

'I have... 8.42.'

Further relief. 'Thank you.' She gathered her things, reflecting that if she were Darac, she would give Jodie's arm or her shoulder a little squeeze in parting. Expressing what he felt physically – tenderness, anger, elation – seemed to come so easily to him. Maybe another time. 'Do you have any family nearby, Jodie? Or friends? You should be with someone.'

'I'd rather be alone.'

'What about tomorrow?'

'I intend to work. It's the best thing.'

'Are you sure?'

'Quite sure.'

Their eyes met. Once again, Flaco felt a little unsettled.

'No need to worry, Officer. I'm not going to kill myself. Deliberately or accidentally on purpose.'

'What do you mean?'

'I'm a diabetic. Type One. You have to stay on top of it but I always do. And I will now.'

'Do you inject yourself?'

'Three times a day.'

Flaco's admiration for Jodie was growing all the time. 'Tough regime.'

'Not at all. I have patients who suffer from conditions such as motor neurone disease. *That* is tough.'

'Nevertheless, you're sure you wouldn't at least like to see a doctor? Under the circumstances, not Monsieur Zep, of course. But I can have a police doctor here in less than half an hour.'

Jodie steadied herself, putting her collapse on hold for just a little longer. 'No.' She reached out and gave Flaco's plump forearm a pat. 'But thank you.'

'We may need to speak again,' she said, rising, 'I'll see myself out.' After no more than a couple of paces, she heard Jodie break into a juddering torrent of tears. She turned and for a long moment went no further. Then she moved slowly to the door and let herself out.

# 26

Granot sounded exhausted on the phone. 'Any word from Flak?'

'Not as yet,' Darac said. 'Jodie had calmed down – well, *numbed* down, by the time they left for her place but of all the things you wouldn't want to see.'

'Yes, poor kid. How are you getting on otherwise?'

'We'd be doing better if Frènes didn't ring every ten minutes demanding speed, more speed and more speed still.' Darac ran an eye over the stacks of evidence cases littering Caroline's office. 'There's a lot of stuff. We're doing our best but we need you, basically.'

'Tell Divisional Command that.'

'Agnès has been telling them for years.'

'I'll be there as quickly as I can,' Granot said, and rang off.

Darac turned to Perand. 'So Montand finally gets his wish. Up for it?'

'Sure.'

'He may be mayor of one of the smallest communes in France but as you saw, he's got a Versailles-sized ego. I was brisk with him earlier and he didn't like it. I'm going to continue in that vein – make it appear I've got something better to do. He won't like it again.'

'Want me to play Good Cop?'

'Better Cop will do.'

'OK.'

In the dining-room Montand was sitting with his head resting on the heels of his hands as Darac led Perand in and sat down at the table.

'At last,' Montand said, standing. 'Are you aware that I've now had to *postpone* our monthly development meeting at the Mairie? Postpone! For the first time in living memory!'

'Sit down, monsieur. You're wasting time.'

Montand's jaw dropped. 'I... I will not be spoken to in that manner.'

'Then we'll have very little to say to one another. Sit down!'

In lieu of his mayoral sash, Montand straightened his tie and sat.

Darac took a longer look at Mayor Hervé Montand. Physiognomy, he believed, revealed little about a person's true nature, and nothing at all of their likely innocence or guilt. He'd interviewed both angel-faced murderers and evil-looking saints in his time. Yet he still found the impulse to read a face irresistible. Montand's was top-heavy, a short chin and prodigiously-domed pate combining to suggest a bias toward the life of the mind. His mouth, moist and thick-lipped, hinted at altogether more basic appetites.

Safer conclusions could be drawn from Montand's conscious choices. His carefully-shaped goatee was surely an attempt to hide the weakness of his chin, a strategy that chimed with the over-compensating arrogance of his demeanour.

'Now, monsieur – tell me everything that happened.'

'I should have a lawyer—'

'If you want me to take you into custody, I will, and you can go for any lawyer you like but as we're merely trying to put a picture together here, get on with it.'

'I understand that but I find your attitude deplorable, Captain. Not that I'm surprised. My brother-in-law, Monsieur Vaselle, told me how rough you were earlier.'

'He was stupid enough to be unco-operative.'

'Had to release him, though, didn't you? Innocent. Completely.'

*Apart from receiving a caution for coercing a witness to lie on his behalf.* 'Get on with it, Monsieur – what is it? – Montand.'

'I will *not* be spoken to in that manner.'

'No?' Darac rapped his notebook on the table and got to his feet. 'Alright, Perand – caution this person.'

'No!' He wiped a slick of sweat off his bald pate. 'I cannot suffer any further delays. Continue.'

With his strong, broad-boned face and light-heavyweight build, Darac could appear menacing when he felt like it. He felt like it. 'Let's talk money, Monsieur Montand. *Your* money.'

'What does that have to do—'

'How do you earn your living?'

'As with every mayor in France, I am paid according to the number of inhabitants residing in the commune.'

'So you're down a couple for the day.' Darac shrugged. 'Tough break.'

'I will speak to Public Prosecutor Frènes about you, Captain. Your attitude to your elders and betters is truly appalling.'

'I spoke to him just now. He says he doesn't know you from Adam.'

'That is not true! We met at the...' The handkerchief was pressed into service once more. 'We met at the—'

'I don't care if you met at the Menton Lemon Fanciers AGM. I'm not asking about your mayoral stipend. I'm asking about your principal income.'

The man seemed genuinely astonished. 'You have never heard of Montand Sanitary Ware?'

'There are pissoirs,' Perand said, nodding reverently. 'And there are *Montand* pissoirs.'

'Absolutely so, young man.'

Darac glanced at his watch. 'The company doing well?'

Montand's muddy eyes somehow managed to flash. 'It's been doing well for almost two centuries.'

'Uh-huh.' Darac gave it a couple of beats. 'Alright, tell me, as exactly as you can, what you did when you got here this evening.'

Montand began to pick at the logo on his pale-blue polo shirt.

'Very well. I... parked on the drive. I walked to the front door noticing that my dear friend, Doctor Arnaud Zep, was next door.'

'You saw him?'

'I saw his cycle leaning against the porch wall. He was visiting Brice Kerthus, the victim's next-door neighbour. Quite unnecessarily as it turned out. Poor Arnaud.'

'You're getting ahead of yourself.'

'Yes, that's right. I rang Mademoiselle Rosay's front doorbell. No one came. I rang it again and still no one came. I'd visited her before and thought she might have been playing that music of hers so I decided to try the side entrance.'

'Did you see anyone en route?'

'In retrospect, I realise there was someone. As I got out of my car, I was vaguely aware of a shape, a shadow – something – among the shrubbery in the front garden. I didn't pay it any attention at the time. I suppose I imagined it was a cat or something.' He wiped his pate and his mouth in succession. 'When I think about what happened,' he gave a dismissive nod in the direction of next door. '*I* may have been very lucky this evening.'

Darac eyeballed Montand once more. The man had no soul. And he was still picking at the logo on his shirt. Nervously. And he'd seen a mysterious presence lurking in the undergrowth? Convenient.

'You didn't see an actual person?'

'Not as such.'

'Then?'

'I rang the side door bell. No one came and then I saw light spilling on to the rear garden so I took the side path. The first disturbing thing I saw was a smashed pane in the patio door. Then I saw all the mess inside. And then Mademoiselle Rosay, lying on the floor, motionless.'

'Did you enter the room at that time?'

'No. Certainly not. I knew Arnaud was next door so I hurried there. I explained the situation and we returned to the office straight away. We both instructed Kerthus to remain where he was but he tagged along anyway. We couldn't prevent it.'

'You say you "hurried" to Kerthus's villa?'

'As fast as I could. I'm afraid a lifetime of service to the commune has left its...'

'Did you run? And did you keep to the path?'

'I went as fast as I could. And yes, I kept to the path.' Montand's top-heavy face seemed to magnify the anxious, questioning look he gave Darac. 'What... is going on here?'

'Take over, Perand.' Darac swiped his mobile and mimed looking something up.

Perand smiled. 'Someone clearly murdered Mademoiselle Rosay, monsieur. I'm sure you know that we need to establish who did what, when and how. To help us eliminate them from our enquiries, if you like.'

'Yes, of course.' Montand's thick lips widened into a weak smile. 'For a second there, I was concerned you actually suspected me.'

'Considering what you witnessed, I appreciate you probably weren't looking at your watch but how much time would you say elapsed between parking your car and knocking on Monsieur Kerthus's door?'

'I didn't knock; I rang the bell. I would say... two minutes. At the very most.'

'And on your return to the office, did all three of you enter?'

'Yes.'

'Together?'

'No, Arnaud is a very fit man and he got there perhaps half-a-minute before me; Kerthus, was probably another forty-five seconds behind that. With my official experience, I knew very well that nothing must be disturbed. Only Arnaud did in fact touch anything – when he felt for a pulse in the victim's neck. There was none as was obvious.'

Impressed with Perand's performance, Darac put away his phone. It was time to get rough again. 'You stood next to him while he did that, Montand?'

'As I said, I knew not to set foot in the room so I stood at the open patio door. As did Kerthus later, although I had to physically stop him from entering.'

That put them no more than a metre and a half from Caroline's body. 'You could see Mademoiselle Rosay's wound clearly?'

'Yes. It was horrible.'

'Describe the state of the blood.'

'Wet. Red. What do you expect it to be like?'

It seemed Zep's estimate of Caroline's T.O.D. was looking more and more secure. 'Then what did you do?'

'We called the police from my mobile and waited the five or so minutes until they came. Waited outside, I might add, in the rain. Luckily, there's a porch over the side door.'

'What time did you arrive for your meeting here this evening?'

'At 7 o'clock.' He essayed a hard stare in Darac's direction. 'Ample time, I *assumed* for a brief discussion before heading off to the Mairie.'

'Who arranged the meeting?'

'Mademoiselle Rosay herself. She rang me.'

'Why did she want to see you?'

'She didn't say in detail at the time and she was dead when I arrived here as I think I may have mentioned.'

The pulse in Darac's temple began to throb, a feeling he was used to. The tightening sensation he felt in his chest was a newer development. His pulse seemed to be racing slightly, also. 'You think *my* attitude is deplorable? Mademoiselle Rosay wasn't merely dead, was she? She had been murdered. Beaten horribly to death.'

Montand had overstepped the mark and, seeming to realise it, managed a regretful nod. 'Do not misunderstand me. I'm...

only making light of the tragedy to come to terms with it. It's difficult.'

Darac eyeballed him. 'Is it?'

Montand returned the look. 'Yes. It is.'

'You say you didn't know in detail what the meeting was about. Considering the events of earlier in the day, why do you think the mademoiselle, your local notary public, might want to see you?'

'It was to do with Ambroise's will. That much is obvious.'

'*What* about "Ambroise's" will?'

'Just to reiterate the position. Dot the i's and cross the t's – that sort of thing, I imagine.'

At 7 o'clock in the evening? On the same day as the benefactor's suicide? Darac didn't believe it. Paillaud's file had contained several wills. In the two short years since he'd moved back to the village, it seemed he'd promised money to half the local population, each will nullifying its predecessor. The last, however, had remained unchanged for the past eight months.

'Were you aware that Mademoiselle Rosay and Monsieur Paillaud had had a meeting of their own, this morning?'

'No,' Montand said, more a sound in his throat than a word. 'I wasn't.'

'Why did you ring him at home this morning?'

'How do you..? Uh, he wasn't in. I didn't speak to him.'

*But you left a message.* 'What did you want to speak to him about?'

'I often called. Just to see how he was, and so on. We were all very proud of him in our community.'

'I think he must have been pretty proud of you. You *are* the sole beneficiary of his estate, are you not?'

'Not at all.' Stronger now. More confident. 'The commune of La Crague-du-Var is the beneficiary.'

'But you are empowered to spend the money as you "see fit."'

'Only for the wellbeing of the commune and its citizens; not for my own personal gain. Obviously.'

'Obviously. You say Mademoiselle Rosay rang you to arrange this evening's meeting.'

'Indeed.'

'When did she do that? About 11.15, this morning?'

'No. It was in the afternoon.'

Playing up his exasperation, Darac exhaled deeply.

'It would be helpful to know when exactly, monsieur?' Perand said, pleasantly.

'It would be about 4 o'clock.'

Perand raised an eyebrow. 'On your mobile?' He held out his hand. 'By any chance?'

Montand gave a quick shake of the head. 'She rang my desk phone at the Mairie. I was able to intercept the call from my office phone at the factory.'

'Get on to Télécom about that, Perand.' Darac didn't give him time to react. 'Now!'

'Yes, Captain.' Perand essayed a conspiratorial look with Montand as he got to his feet. 'Just need to put in that request, monsieur. It would speed things up if you let me have both those numbers?'

'Ri–ight.' He haltingly gave them. 'I said 4 o'clock. It was about then. Give or take half an hour, perhaps.'

'I'll be back in a minute.'

'Take your time,' Darac said.

As Perand left the room, Montand's anxiety level visibly increased. Maintaining a deafening silence, Darac kept his bad cop mask firmly in place. If Montand had something to hide, and awful possibilities began to take root in his imagination, so much the better. *Go on, blurt it out, man. Get it off your chest.*

It was clear that Ambroise Paillaud's money was at the heart of this case; money that had been earmarked for the dismal mayor of the dismal village of La Crague-du-Var. And then? At Centre Sicotte, Caroline had said that her meeting with Paillaud at La Poche was a simple farewell. No transaction had taken place. Darac began to bounce questions around in his head as if trading four-bar phrases with the Quintet. What if Paillaud *had* produced a new will that, in effect, disinherited Montand? What if informing him of this was the purpose of Caroline's later meeting with him?

Darac launched further rafts of questions until he sensed he was straying too far downstream. It wasn't a question of whether an arrogant but fundamentally timorous type like Montand could commit a reckless, brutal murder for gain; nor of whether such a man could keep his head while under all sorts of pressure. One of the first lessons Darac had learned from his mentor Agnès Dantier was that given appropriate circumstances, anyone was capable of these things. Darac's concern was the timing. As it stood, it was ridiculously tight and if Montand had carried out the murder, what had he done with the new will? Secretion or destruction were the only options but...' His mobile rang. Ormans's number.

'We've got the footprint cast up and running, as it were. A word of caution. It will help us determine who didn't leave the print and to a degree, that's useful. Whether it could identify who definitely *did l*eave it, is by no means certain.'

The news was disappointing but as if the caller were relaying info that incriminated Montand, Darac stared at him and smiled slightly. 'It does? That's very interesting. Thank you.' Darac held the look as he rang off. Saying nothing, he returned privately to the question of what Montand might have done with the putative new will. If he had taken it, he wouldn't have secreted it in the house – how could he retrieve it later? Immediately outside the house presented problems, too. Nevertheless, Darac would ask Ormans to get a team on it. But Montand *might* have hidden the will under his clothing. Or perhaps folded it into one of his shoes; shoes which appeared to be about size 42 and which were slightly soiled. In order to test this, Darac would have to search the man. In order to do that, he would have to arrest him. In order to do that, he would need more than he had so far. But then he realised that Montand himself had given him the way forward and with any luck, he might be able to follow it for some distance.

'You volunteered to show the contents of your pockets earlier. Why?'

'Why?' Montand was still clearly unnerved. 'Because only hours earlier, although Guy had himself committed no crime, you had given him a very hard time.' He quickly raised a hand. 'Yes, I understand that he can be maddeningly obstinate and unco-operative. He has been that way with me on many occasions. *I* wished to demonstrate to your officers that I was being *especially* co-operative, and in so doing, of course, prove that I had absolutely nothing to hide.'

'Commendable.'

'I'm glad you realise that. Might I ask how much longer—'

'As long as it takes.' He stared at Montand, cold-eyed. 'If you really have nothing to hide, you can help yourself by handing me your shoes.'

'What?' He blanched. 'Why?'

'Your shoes.' Darac got quickly to his feet. 'I'll assist you.'

'No, no. I'll... do it.'

Darac called in a uniform and stood over Montand as he unlaced his shoes and took them off. No concealed document emerged. 'Give them to Ormans, Officer.'

'Yes, Captain.'

Montand watched his shoes being taken away as if they were themselves under arrest.

'Stand up, monsieur.'

Montand looked uneasy but seemed to feel it best to comply. 'What—'

'I'm going to pat you down. You have no objection, presumably.'

'We-ell...'

At the end of it, Darac hadn't detected a hint of anything concealed but then another, far more likely hiding place occurred to him. With a little ingenuity, it was accessible and, for once he wouldn't have to call on his lock picks.

'You may sit.' He made a moue. 'Oh, what now?' As if his mobile had buzzed in his pocket, Darac feigned taking a call. Naturally, he was irritated at the interruption. 'No, stay put, you idiot.' He ended the call. 'Some of our people can't get off the premises, Montand. We need to move your car.' He stood. 'The keys?'

The request further perturbed Montand.

'Did you hear me?'

'Yes, yes. I'd rather move it myself, if you don't mind. It's brand new and—'

'Monsieur, with all your *official experience*, I'm sure you understand that that is not permissible.'

'Indeed, I do realise that but...'

'The keys, then.'

He reluctantly handed them over as the door opened and Perand loped into the room.

'About time,' Darac said.

'Excuse the wait. I'm afraid Télécom won't be able to corroborate your story, monsieur, until...' He gave Montand a rueful smile. 'Let's just say a while.'

It would be tomorrow, Darac knew. But he enjoyed both Perand's use of the smile and "corroborate". The young man was continuing to turn in a winning performance. 'I'll only be a moment, Perand. Don't go on without me. Alright?'

'Understood, Captain.'

Outside, Darac wasted no time in getting to work. The Renault's boot yielded nothing. Nor did the door pockets or the seat curtain bags. He looked under the bonnet. Another blank. Only the glove compartment remained. He opened it. There were papers. He went through them. Nothing. After taking a further call from Frènes, Darac joined Ormans by the patio doors. The footprint test had been completed.

'Well, R.O.?'

'It's more or less the scenario I outlined just now, I'm afraid.' He handed over the shoes. 'I wouldn't rule out Montand as the killer on the basis of this but it in no way supports it.'

'I'm drawing blanks, myself. I'll just give Perand a moment or two more. I ordered him not to say a word in my absence. I'm hoping he took no notice.'

Darac pretended not to have caught the sudden silence as he strode into the dining room. 'Your car's back where it was,' he said, handing over the keys and shoes. 'No scratches.'

'I should hope not.' Montand examined the shoes. 'And what did you want with these?'

While he bent to put them on, a little eyebrow semaphore between Darac and Perand established there had been no break-throughs. 'Just routine, monsieur. Let us continue. Would you say Mademoiselle Rosay was a popular member of the community?'

Doubly re-empowered, Montand sought Perand's eye. 'No apology. No explanation. No...'

'Better answer the question, monsieur.'

'Very well. I would say... she was respected. But one doesn't live in a vacuum. Her attacker could have come from anywhere.' He gave a dismissive shrug. 'Senegal or Mali, perhaps.'

'Why there?'

Once again, Montand seemed to realise he'd made a poor judgement call. 'I didn't mean anything by that. They were just the first faraway places that came to mind.'

'Of course. Can you think of anyone who might have had a motive for murdering the mademoiselle?'

'No one.' Suddenly aware that he was picking at his shirt, Montand managed a smile and let go. The cotton crocodile looked none the worse for its ordeal. 'It's clear what happened, though, isn't it? She disturbed a burglar in the act. Hence the devastation in the office.'

It was time to test the true efficacy of Perand's play-acting. 'Keep the monsieur company for another moment, will you? You may talk.'

'Yes, Captain.'

Montand's relief at Darac's departure was obvious but so was his concern that he was once more being abandoned. 'Where are you going? And for how long?'

'Call of nature. We'll see how long.'

'Oh. Please go ahead.'

'Thank you so much. Let's just hope it's a Montand. Carry on, Perand.'

A Montand or not, the toilet was a pretext. In Caroline's office, the bad news was that Granot still hadn't shown up; the good, that Bonbon had spirited up a flask of coffee from somewhere. He handed Darac a cup. 'One of the uniforms brought this up from the village. It's not bad. I take it all back about La Crague. Montand?'

'Nervous. Defensive.'

'Guilty?'

'Some things point to it *but* his account of what he did once he'd arrived at 7 o'clock gels with what they're saying next door, according to Flak. I'm going to talk to them myself in a moment. In the meantime, I'm leaving him with Better Cop Perand. He may just let something slip.' Darac drained the coffee. 'Not bad at all. Anything new in here?'

'Granot's five minutes away, he says, and Flak just called. She'll be back from Jodie Foucault's place any second.'

'I'll wait for her outside.'

As he crossed in front of the villa, Flaco's car turned into the drive, its headlights sweeping through the murk in a wide arc. The pair wasted no time in updating one another.

'And there's something else, Captain.' She relayed Jodie's account of the confrontation between Zep and Montand in the surgery car park. 'I only talked to Montand briefly so it's not surprising it didn't come up. But I questioned Zep fully and he didn't say anything about it, either.'

'Nor has Montand to me but perhaps it seemed irrelevant. I'll get Zep alone and ask him about it directly.'

'Jodie and Caroline. They weren't just friends. They were lovers.'

Darac nodded – he'd guessed as much.

'During the massage, Jodie made a point of telling Caroline about the incident with Zep and Montand and it would have been natural for Caroline to mention she was seeing Montand in the office later. She didn't and Jodie was surprised, even a bit upset about it. Why *didn't* Caroline share that with her?'

'Preserving professional confidentiality?'

'No. I can't see that.'

'OK. So there are...' Darac's gaze settled on the glistening gravel. 'Three, no *four* possibilities: despite the caring and sharing, Caroline deliberately concealed the fact that she was meeting Montand for reasons of her own; the appointment was made after Jodie had left which, considering the timing, seems improbable and contradicts Montand's claim it was made at about 4 o'clock; it was never made at all and Montand was lying about it.' He looked up. 'Or Jodie herself is lying.'

'I doubt *that* very much.'

'Erica is going to examine Caroline's mobile. And we've asked Télécom for a breakdown of both Caroline's and Montand's landline calls. The sooner we get all that back, the better.'

Flaco made a note. 'I'll chase Télé, if necessary.'

'What about Jodie's alibi? Did this Madame Valentin corroborate her story?'

'To the letter, Captain. If Kerthus follows suit about the time Caroline waved her goodbye, and I believe he will, it means Jodie didn't have time to kill Caroline. I'm certain she didn't, anyway.'

'Certain?'

'As certain as... virtually certain. For one thing, I checked her watch against mine. It's *possible* she'd altered it subsequently but they tallied almost exactly and mine is right to the second.'

As mentor to Flaco and Perand, Darac often played devil's advocate – one of many techniques he'd learned from his own mentor, Agnès. A hint of a smile broadened into something fuller.

'So you verified Jodie's watch is more or less spot-on. And that *suggests* she was right about the times. But Jodie being in synch with *you* isn't the alibi. It's her being in synch with Kerthus and Madame Valentin that counts. Did you check their watches, also?'

Flaco's pout morphed into a scowl. 'No.'

'Look, let's just say that the odds greatly favour Jodie's innocence.'

'Right.'

'OK, let's go see Zep and Kerthus. There are a few things to check, including Kerthus's watch.'

'She's a diabetic, by the way. Injects three times a day. No word of complaint about it.'

'A tough girl, isn't she? Tough but sweet.'

'Yes,' Flaco said. 'She is.'


'Apologies for having... kept you both waiting,' Darac said, taken aback by his first sight of Zep. The man's restless eyes, spiky red hair and deeply scored skin had disconcerting echoes of something he couldn't place. 'I just need to make sure I've got everything straight.' And then he had it. Zep bore a strong resemblance to the artist Van Gogh; more exactly, a Van Gogh self-portrait. One of the more troubled examples.

'Who was it who screamed?'

Darac ignored Kerthus. 'You've already given your separate statements but I just need to make sure I've got it. What time did you arrive, Doctor?'

'I didn't notice exactly. But it took me forty-two eighteen from leaving home. The rain slowed me.'

'Nearly three-quarters of an hour?' Perhaps in sympathy with Zep's restless eyes, Darac felt his eyelids flutter slightly. He blinked to clear them. 'But you live just down the road in the village, don't you?'

'Was it Daniela?'

Zep kept his eyes on Darac. 'Just off Place Charles Montand but I went via Saint-Laurent, La Gaude and the La Crague road. I'm in training.'

Darac shared an almost imperceptible look with Flaco. 'So you arrived riding down the hill and into Avenue Montand?'

'Indeed.'

'Did you see anyone in the vicinity?'

'When I turned up the drive on my bike, I thought I passed someone moving in the bushes on the right.'

'Did the someone have a face? Our sketch artist is used to turning even the scantiest of impressions into detailed likenesses. I could have her pay a call on you tomorrow.'

'No need, Captain. I saw nothing so definite as a face.'

'Tall? Short?'

'Not a child, certainly. Beyond that, I really couldn't say anything. In fact, when I dismounted, I turned and couldn't see anyone. I wondered if it might have been a trick of the light.'

*Two* possible sightings of a figure among the shrubbery? Darac resolved to investigate further and he made a note to have R.O.'s team widen the check for footprints.

'Thank you, Doctor.' Darac turned to the fleshy and florid Kerthus. He sensed softly-softly was the way forward. 'I gather you noticed what time Doctor Zep arrived, monsieur?'

The man essayed a put-out look. 'I can speak now, can I?'

'I wish you would.'

'I've already told the young lady when it was.'

'Well, now you can tell me.'

Noises off. Granot was pulling up in the drive. Kerthus's head swivelled to the window. 'Just one of my officers arriving,' Darac said, curbing him. 'Please continue.'

'Oh. It was 6.50. And don't upset me, I've got acute angina.' He looked at Zep. 'Haven't I?'

'Yes,' the doctor said, staring into space.

'I should never have dragged myself next door. They could

have almost put me in my box afterwards, I'm telling you. But I had to see what had happened.'

'Indeed?'

'As a concerned citizen.' Conspiratorial now. 'I *have* heard, Captain, that at the station earlier, a certain person was standing quite near Ambroise Paillaud when he went *phhhtt* under the train. *Very* near, in fact.'

Zep stirred uncomfortably in his seat.

'Guy Vaselle!' Emphatically pursing his lips, Kerthus was a picture of righteous certitude. 'He's the man you want for that. There. I've said it.'

Zep's restless eyes stilled. 'Brice, honestly!'

'Vaselle?' Darac saw little point in updating Kerthus. 'Thank you, we'll look into it. Returning to Mademoiselle Rosay, just to see we're on the same page, we need to synchronise our watches. Officer?'

'It's like a movie, this,' Kerthus said, presenting his wrist to Flaco. '*Was* it Daniela?'

'That's fine.' Resisting the temptation to smirk, she gave Darac a subtle nod.

'Monsieur, Mademoiselle Rosay had an appointment with her masseuse, Jodie Foucault, this evening. Would you happen to have noticed when she left? It would be a great help to us if you did.'

'I did happen to, as a matter of fact. It was 6.35 give or take a few seconds.' A different look came over him. 'By the way, may I say, Captain, that I love that man.' He indicated Zep. 'He's an angel. But for him, I'd be dead by now. Wouldn't I?'

'Very possibly.' A tired sigh.

'When she took her leave, Monsieur Kerthus, did you see Mademoiselle Rosay, herself?'

Kerthus was still loving Zep. 'What?'

'I think you heard me.'

'Go on then – did I see Caroline? Yes. She waved little Skinny Ribs off.'

'Did you see the mademoiselle herself or just her hand or her arm protruding through the doorway?'

Kerthus gave Flaco a look. 'He's good, your lord and master. Caroline might already have been dead, mightn't she? Might have been an accomplice standing hidden in the doorway.' He turned back to Darac, smiling as if in triumph. 'Except it *was* Caroline. *Very* much alive.'

'Thank you.' Darac felt his eyelids flicker again. Just tired, probably. 'Monsieur Hervé Montand has given us his account of what happened later – as you both have. I just need to double check one point. You heard Monsieur Montand park, yes?'

'I didn't,' Zep said, gazing with a curious intensity at Darac. 'I was listening to Monsieur Kerthus's chest. Or trying to.'

'*I* heard. My watch pings on the hour so I noticed. It must have been 6.59 when he came up the drive. He had to close his door twice – got the seatbelt caught the first time. My phone pinged in between. I would've seen more after that but...' he gave Zep an offhand nod, '... *he* stopped me.'

'Did you—?'

'—hear a scream later? I'll tell you something – if I have to ask again who it was, *I'm* going to scream.'

Zep got to his feet. 'So am I!'

'Doctor?' A raised eyebrow was enough to ask the question. 'Please?'

Zep sighed, sat down and re-folded his arms.

'*Was* it Daniela?'

'Returning to Monsieur Montand's arrival. You saw him get out of his car. How much time elapsed before he reappeared at your door?'

Kerthus shrugged. 'I already told the young lady here.'

'I know. We just need to be absolutely sure on this point.'

'Why?' Kerthus's mouth dropped open. 'You think *he* did it? The mayor? Well, why not? He could, couldn't he? I never liked him.'

Zep's inflamed features seemed almost to catch fire. 'Brice, you drivelling imbecile! This isn't a spat over some stupid little trifle – the man is a suspect in a murder enquiry!'

'Well!'

'Doctor?' Darac said, conveying that he expected better from a man of Zep's calling.

'I'm sorry but one can stand only so much of this... babble.' The words burst from his mouth like water from a breached dam. 'Lord knows I'm no lover of our beloved mayor but to hear...' He took a deep breath. 'Look, may I go now?'

'A couple of quick questions and then we're finished.'

'Very well.'

'Monsieur Kerthus, once again – how much time elapsed before you saw Montand get out of his car and re-appear on your doorstep?'

'You want me now? Oh, right. Over a minute, it was. But not more than two.'

'How did he summon you?'

'What?'

'Did he hammer on the door, for instance?'

'He rang the bell, Captain,' Zep said, anxious to get the thing over with. 'Repeatedly. And he shouted my name.'

'*And* mine.'

'And I can confirm that it was no more than a couple of minutes from Montand's arrival to his ringing the bell.'

'There – told you.'

'Yes, Monsieur Kerthus, did you see anyone else lurking in or around the drive, perhaps hiding among the trees, before Doctor Zep arrived for your consultation? Or later?'

'No, why? Have I missed something?'

'Thank you. Last question to you both. As her doctor and as her next-door neighbour, you both knew Mademoiselle Rosay well, I imagine. Can either of you think of any reason why anyone might have wanted to kill her?'

'None,' Zep said, shaking his head. 'She wasn't that easy a person to get to know, as a matter of fact. She was a fit and healthy person so I hardly ever saw her in surgery. I ran into her at Centre Sicotte fairly often but not to talk to. She wasn't unfriendly as such, just... cool, I suppose is the word.'

'Monsieur Kerthus?'

The man's florid features made a perfect backdrop for tears. Gathering himself pluckily, he snatched a tissue. 'I met her the day she moved in. To think that she's...' A foghorn blow of the nose. 'I can't think about that. I can't. You see, she and me were real pals. Kindred spirits, really.' His face darkened, essaying menace. 'Whoever did it – I hope you find him. And bash *his* head in!'

'Thank you, messieurs.'

'Was it Daniela?'

The interview concluded with the usual litany of cautions and guidance. As the front door closed behind them, Zep accompanied Darac and Flaco out on to the drive. A moment later, a finger of yellow light reached out from Kerthus's living room window.

Zep filled his lungs. 'Fresh air, thank God.'

'Indeed. Sorry I had to keep you. You've had a long day, I know.'

'I'm planning on a swim later. That will restore me.'

'You have a pool at home?'

'No, no but I mean a proper swim. Madame Sicotte allows me to use the Centre's pool at night. To train or just to float around if I want to.'

'Just you?'

Zep grinned, a thing of thin red lips and yellowish teeth. 'I'm very spoiled.'

'Doctor, I didn't want to refer to this in front of Kerthus, but to return to the question of the time of Mademoiselle Rosay's death?'

'Yes. I'm sorry, I shouldn't have sounded off like that.'

'I'm aware of what you said in your initial statement but there's been time to reflect on it since, hasn't there?'

'Nothing that has been said subsequently has changed my opinion, Captain. The blood from her forehead injury was yet to clot when I arrived on the scene and that takes no more than a few minutes in normal conditions. In that context, Montand *could* have walked in and effected the blow immediately but surely, the state of the room and other indications point to it being someone else; someone who had had more time – possibly the shadowy figure I only half-saw in the front border.'

'Possibly.'

'Captain, please excuse my behaviour this evening. And you, too, Officer Flaco. My irritation is nothing, nothing at all, compared to the tragedy of murder. It's just that some people get right under one's skin, do they not?' Zep strapped on a rucksack the size of a two-man bobsleigh. 'And being confined with him like that – I'm afraid I overreacted.'

'You carrying oxygen cylinders in there, Doctor?' Darac said, the lightness of the observation intended to suggest that the formalities were at an end.

'I do carry a small one, in fact. In my profession, if you favour bikes over cars, you'd better be well equipped.' He put on his helmet. 'Apologies once more.'

'Not necessary.' Darac grinned. 'I may have cried out, myself, at another mention of Daniela and the scream.'

Zep adopted a slightly sheepish look as he began wheeling his bike. 'Actually, might *I* be permitted to know who screamed?' The yellow finger from Kerthus's window followed them like a stage spotlight. 'Most of the locals are patients of mine.'

'I don't see why not. It was a colleague of yours as a matter of fact. Jodie Foucault.'

Zep stopped in his tracks. 'Jodie? But her appointment was *much* earlier in the evening, surely? What was..?'

'We'll have to leave it there,' Darac said. 'She's not a suspect, by the way. Timings preclude it. For one thing.'

Flaco nodded, the slightest of smiles playing on her lips.

'Suspect?' Zep blew out his whorled cheeks. 'Of course *not.*'

He stared off for a moment. 'Uh... perhaps I shouldn't say this but I wouldn't pay any attention to all that nonsense about Guy Vaselle. Brice is a gossip pure and simple.' He drew down the corners of his red-barbed mouth. 'With the accent on the simple.'

Darac saw no harm in favouring Zep with the info, pre-empting the statement he knew Frènes was about to deliver to the world's media. As a solo, mercifully. 'Actually, we know for a fact that Paillaud committed suicide.'

'*Did* he?'

'You seem surprised.'

'No. Relieved, actually. In the sense that the action was his alone.'

'He was your patient?'

'Nominally. I saw him only once, I think, since he moved back here.'

'But he had cancer, didn't he?'

'Indeed he did but he was treated at Clinique Albert Magnesca in Nice. My surgery was not involved in his care at all.'

'I see. Just now you let slip that you are not the greatest fan of Mayor Hervé Montand. Why is that?'

'Where does one begin? Let's just say that his world view and mine are very different.'

'Go on.'

Zep indicated his bike. 'I mentioned I'm in training. Triathlon. I aim to do several a season.'

'Which starts in?'

'For me, January.'

Darac saw through the nonchalance. 'And goes on until?'

Zep grinned. 'Alright, yes, it's a year-round thing.'

'Montand hardly seems the sporty type but I imagine that isn't the—'

'No. Each year, I choose a different charity. This time, it's a girls' school in Angola.' He named it and outlined its *raison d'être*.

'If you visit the website, I think both of you will be opening your wallets pretty quickly.' They both made a note. 'All you need is a heart.'

'And Montand doesn't?'

'Captain, that man cares only about himself, his business and being mayor of "the ancient commune of La Crague-du-Var." '

Darac closed his notebook, wondering how to approach the crunch question, quite a leap from where he was. Disguise was the key, he felt. Build a bridge but hide it, something he'd done a million times in segueing from one theme to another in the DMQ. 'With your job, the training and charity work, I guess you don't have much time left to socialise.' *Promising.* 'When was the last time you spoke to Montand, for instance?' *Clunkily obvious.* 'Before tonight, I mean.'

Zep didn't seem to notice the jump, or if he did, he was better at hiding it than Darac. 'Lunchtime today at the surgery, as a matter of fact. He'd put his back out and needed Jodie's expertise.'

Darac turned to Flaco. 'Yes, she mentioned that, didn't she?'

'She did, yes.'

'And later, the two of you had a difference of opinion about something?'

As if running with shed blood, the furrows swirling around Zep's face reddened, suddenly. 'I had made up my mind not to mention it but I see now I must.'

Darac exhaled deeply. 'Doctor, doctor, doctor...'

'I know. I'm sorry. Put bluntly, Montand asked me about Ambroise Paillaud's state of health. In fact...' He hesitated. 'In fact, he asked me how long he thought the monsieur had left to live. I told him I couldn't possibly divulge information of that sort and he should know better than to ask.'

'Quite right.'

'He pressed me. I told him to get lost, effectively.'

'And that left him stunned as you walked away?'

Zep's eyes narrowed. 'This must be Jodie's account. I'd just been talking with her in the car park.'

'*Was* that what left him stunned?'

'No.' A longer hesitation. 'This is the part I didn't want to mention.'

Zep may have been a man with a heart but Darac was on the edge of losing it with him. 'But you will now. And fully.'

'I mentioned to him that I'd passed La Poche on my training run and seen Paillaud there in conversation with... in conversation with Caroline Rosay.'

'Did you overhear anything? Were there any documents on the table?'

'I don't know. I just noticed that the two of them were there talking as I passed. I was running at quite a pace.'

'You should have volunteered this to Officer Flaco here, and then to me, Doctor. And don't pretend it was only that you didn't want to say anything in front of Kerthus – you were going to ride away, just now.'

'Well... I realised that it made things look terrible for Montand. Everyone in La Crague knows what he is set to gain from Paillaud's death. And then he learns that Paillaud met his notary this morning? "Monsieur La Chute" had obviously changed his will, hadn't he? Montand's hopes dashed. We didn't know it then but later when he heard that the man had killed himself... Need I say more?'

'He was stunned by your news but did he say anything?'

'Involuntarily. Thinking aloud, I suppose.'

'Doctor, *what* did he say?'

'It was on the lines of "I must see Rosay. Tonight. Before the meeting." ' He shook his head. 'But I say again, Captain, despite how things may look, I'm sure Montand is innocent. He is not the type to kill anyone. For one thing, he is *far* too weak a character.'

'Doctor Zep, from now on, *share* what you know with me and my officers. Let *us* evaluate the evidence. Alright?'

'I will. I'm sorry.'

Darac held up the cordon tape for Zep.

'Now I have a question for you, Captain.'

'Yes?'

'How many espressos per day do you drink?'

The remark came so far out of left field, Darac didn't reply immediately. 'Uh... Four, perhaps. Doubles.'

The answer made Flaco almost choke. 'Sorry, sir, but I can't pass that.'

Darac grinned, quizzically. 'What?'

'You regularly drink eight double espressos a day. Sometimes more.'

'Weren't you going to interview Mademoiselle Daniela... Wienkova?'

'Wienawska.' She glanced at her watch. 'She won't be back home yet. I'm leaving in fifteen minutes.'

Darac turned to Zep. 'That's all, Doctor, thank you.'

'Not quite all. You're suffering from myokymia. Through excessive caffeine intake.'

'Nonsense.'

'It is not and I've got enough equipment on board to prove it.'

'What is myokymia, anyway?'

'Look it up.'

Flaco slipped her mobile surreptitiously out of her pocket.

Zep swung his leg over the bike. 'It's a harmless condition, in itself.'

'You see?' Darac said to Flaco. 'Harmless.'

'Harmless *in itself*, I said. Heed this, Captain. Cut the caffeine down or it might cut you down. And the chances are you won't be standing next to someone carrying a defibrillator when it happens.'

Zep pedalled away.

'A quack,' Darac said, as the man reached the bottom of the drive. 'Clearly. And thanks for grassing me up, by the way.'

'Grassing?'

Zep turned up the hill.

'A quack *and* a fanatic, look.'

There was a sound of movement among the cypresses away to their right. They held their ground as, stooping awkwardly, a figure emerged on to the drive and straightened.

'Searching for size 42 footprints,' Raul Ormans announced.

'You must have read my mind. I was going to ask you to check in there.'

'Drawn a blank, sadly. The soil around the trees is covered in a thick layer of gravel. Not the ideal habitat for them.'

'So if someone had been lurking in there earlier, they wouldn't have left a print?'

'Almost certainly not. And my legendary fine-toothed comb has not raked up a dropped handkerchief, torn fragment of clothing or any of the other clichés of the genre. As for a possibly missing will – we've looked in the drains and everywhere. No sign.' Ormans strode away to his van. 'Sorry.'

'I've got a sign of something for you, Captain,' Flaco said, scrolling her screen. 'Myokymia: fluttering of the eyelids. Sometimes caused by an excess of caffeine in the system.'

'Got a bit of grit in my eye, that's all.'

They headed back to Caroline's office.

'Would you call Professor Bianchi a quack? Doctor Mpensa? Both of them have told you to cut down your espresso drinking.'

Darac could feel his heart beating slightly out of time in his chest. 'I'll do it tomorrow. Or definitely when the Jazz Festival gig is over. And Flak – no mention of this to the others. Right?'

Pressing her lips together, she made a non-committal sound in her throat.

They found Granot sitting behind a stack of papers at Caroline's desk and Bonbon perched at a spine-contorting angle over a low table. Darac felt his spirits lift. The pair inspired the same sort of confidence in him as playing guitar with a great rhythm section.

'We should never have got rid of the guillotine,' Granot said.

'Thanks for that. Bonbon – anything?'

'Nothing in here yet and the kinder, gentler Perand hasn't elicited a confession from Montand. Any joy with the cross-checking?'

'On what happened here this evening, everyone's stories tally.'

'The guillotine, I'm telling you. Sort everything out.'

'Let's just give it a good ten minutes. We're all thinking Paillaud's estate is at the heart of this, aren't we? Zep has just told me that this morning, Montand asked him how long he estimated Paillaud had left to live. Zep didn't dignify the question with an answer.'

Granot nodded. 'As you said at the time, the message Montand left on Paillaud's phone seemed pretty cap in hand.'

'And Zep told me something else – that he'd mentioned to Montand he'd just seen Caroline and Paillaud together at La Poche. Ran right past them. Earlier, I asked Montand if he knew whether that meeting had taken place. He denied knowing.'

'On the face of it, blacker and blacker for Montand.' Bonbon made a so-so gesture with his hand. 'But how material are these lies? A lot of innocent people deny things they know look bad for them.'

'Yes and there are some flat-out incongruities here as well but let's put those on hold for a moment.' Darac ran a hand through his hair. 'The crime itself: Map puts Montand at the scene within the broad time frame of the murder. If the condition of Caroline's blood was as Zep and Kerthus said it was, and there seems no reason to doubt them, that time frame narrows to a credibility-stretching two minutes.'

'He passed the footprint test as well, didn't he?' Granot said. 'Or at least didn't fail it.'

'True. All in all, we can just about squeeze Montand into that tight time frame. But we need more than that.'

'Such as finding the new will that disinherits Montand,' Granot said. 'Especially if it's mysteriously found its way up the man's backside.'

196

Bonbon gave a rueful nod. 'Gruesome as it sounds, it's a pity we can't strip search him.'

'I couldn't go that far, obviously, but I did give him a good patting down – nothing – and managed to examine the contents of his car – ditto.' He gave Flaco a look. 'Don't worry, Flak. I didn't use my picks.'

'I wasn't going to say anything.' She returned his look. 'About *that*.'

Darac pressed on. 'But let's say Montand did see a new will. On the question of his secreting it somewhere himself, I think we've gone as far as we can for now. As for the possibility that he could have passed it on to an accomplice, he's hardly likely to have told us about the shadowy figure he claims to have seen lurking among the cypresses if he *had*.'

Bonbon began drumming his fingertips lightly against his chin. 'That's an interesting point in itself. I assumed Montand had come up with the figure as a get-out. "*He's* the man you want!" But maybe there was such a person.'

Granot gave it the full Gallic shrug. 'Maybe Montand didn't think it through.'

'Possibly.' Darac drew down the corners of his mouth 'But Zep wondered if he'd seen someone lurking there as well, remember, and just looking at the time frame angle, that person – if he exists – is a far more credible killer than Montand.'

Granot grunted. 'I haven't given up on him yet. What if he destroyed it, somehow? Burned it.' His eye went to the smoke alarm on the ceiling. 'He could have set light to it outside. Any burnt bits of paper or ashes around?'

'None detectable but there wouldn't be, would there?' Bonbon said. 'Especially on such a wet night. R.O. checked out all the rubbish, personally. Apart from a few cotton wool pads in a bathroom wastebasket, he found none of any sort.'

'Wheelie bins? How long would it have taken Montand to open and close a lid en route to next door?'

'Empty – the recycling was picked up this morning before

all this happened.'

'He didn't have a lighter or matches on him, anyway,' Darac said, glancing around. 'Shredder?'

Bonbon slapped his forehead. 'Imbecile.' He lowered his brow. 'Although now that I think, I haven't seen one.'

'It is a small office,' Flaco said. 'You'd still think she would have one.'

A search failed to find it.

'OK.' Darac steepled his hands as if he were conducting a prayer meeting. 'Anyone have any further thoughts?'

Granot harrumphed. 'Only that we've got dangerously close to concluding that Montand did exactly as he said he did.'

'And I haven't mentioned the biggest incongruity,' Darac said. 'In our interview, Caroline expressly stated that Paillaud called the meeting to say goodbye, nothing more.' Darac gave an almost apologetic shrug. 'Just maybe, that's all it was.'

'Know what I think?' Bonbon grinned. 'They're all in it together – the locals. It's *Murder On The Orient Express* all over again.'

Granot's chops took on a bilious hue. 'Don't let's go *there*, for God's sake.'

'Quite.' Darac glanced at his watch. 'So, in the absence of a guillotine, I think the feeling is that we have to release Montand at least for the time being. Several checks are going on and we can always call him back in if we need to. Agreed?'

It was agreed.

'Back in a second.'

In the dining room, Montand was apoplectic with indignation; Darac's call of nature had taken over twenty minutes.

'Thank you, monsieur,' he said. 'You may go.'

'I may go, may I? Well, thank you very much. None of this was necessary. None!'

'May I remind you not to—'

'I know all that,' he said, slipping on his jacket.

'We're going to lock down the house shortly, monsieur. So unless...'

Montand got to his feet and, wiping his toilet bowl of a head, bustled his way out of the room.

'Officer Perand will escort you off the premises.'

Darac returned to the office where Granot and Bonbon welcomed him with looks of modest self-congratulation.

'I leave the room for thirty seconds,' Darac said, recognising the signs.

'How's this for neat?' Bonbon slid open a panel on Caroline's desk top. Beneath it was a built-in shredder head. He slowly swung it to one side, exposing the caddy.

'Ah,' Darac said, staring at the contents. 'I think we're going to need more coffee.'

# 27

The manner in which Daniela Wienawska lay sprawled over her mother put Flaco in mind of an orphaned puppy seeking suckle from a field mouse.

'Daniela?' Flaco was speaking to her left ear only. 'You cleaned for Mademoiselle Rosay how many times a week?'

She uttered something that sounded like "wubs".

'I know you're upset but would you sit up, please? I can't hear what you're saying.'

Daniela stayed put.

As if the experience of having the life crushed out of her was bringing her closer to God, Sonia Bera was smiling beatifically. 'Yes, come on darling.' Her words emerging in an effortful wheeze, she tried to ease her daughter's sodden head off her chest. 'Dani?'

In an agony of grief, the young woman righted herself and blew her nose. For the first time, Flaco was able to study her properly. Face: broad and flat as a shield. Eyes: blue, perhaps green – too tear-streaked to tell. Hair: blonde, straight, short. Frame: broad, heavy-boned. Limbs: muscular. Hands: large, capable-looking. Fingernails: short, clear varnish. Feet: large, square. Toenails: short, clear varnish. Clothes: navy, calf-length slacks, white blouse. A gold chain bearing a modest crucifix completed her ensemble. If Daniela were not drowning in tears, Flaco reflected, she would appear to be made of stern stuff, a strong, even tough-looking young woman.

'Once,' Daniela said, finally. 'Once a week. Thursdays, 2 until 4.'

'And you kept to your schedule yesterday?'

'Yes.'

'How did you get in?'

'Caroline let me in.'

'You don't have a key?'

'No.'

'And that was the last time you visited the house?'

'Yes.' Another blow and then, as if a switch had been thrown, she looked vehemently into Flaco's eyes. 'She was always lovely to me! Really lovely. *And* she paid better than my other clients.'

Sonia was still smiling but her eyebrows rose slightly as she tilted her head towards her daughter.

'Except *maminka*.'

'Pardon?'

'She means me,' Sonia said. 'It's the Czech word for "mama".

Daniela drew her legs up under her and, wiping her eyes, sank back into the corner of the sofa. Finding no solace there, she sat forward, back, and forward once more, then clambered to her feet. 'I need the toilet.'

'Are you alright, darling? Do you need me?'

Already half-way to the door, Daniela shook her head.

'She'll be back presently,' Sonia said, on full beam once more. 'You're from The Czech Republic, Madame Bera?'

'I'm flattered you think I'm so young. I was born in Brno, Czechoslovakia.' Sonia's saintly eye was capable of a wicked glint. ' "Brno-born, bred and buttered," as my own *maminka* used to say. What about you, Officer? Were you born here? In France, I mean.'

'No. You work on reception at Centre Sicotte but you employ Daniela? As what?'

'I work only part-time at the Centre. Just for something to do, really.'

By ignoring the second part of the question, Sonia had succeeded only in drawing Flaco's attention to it. That it probably meant nothing did not deter her. 'You employ Daniela?'

'As a housekeeper, yes. I have three properties, one a villa over in Saint-Jeannet.' She sat forward. 'It makes a wonderful base for a week or two's holiday. Sleeps four. View of the coast all the way from Cap Ferrat to Cannes and the Esterel.' She gazed into mid-air as if she could see it before her. 'So beautiful. If you or perhaps your family back home might be interested, don't hesitate to ask me for details. Summer is usually fully booked but there are often vacancies in spring and autumn. And the rates are cheaper.'

'And the other two places?'

'Oh. Yes. Bed and breakfasts, one in this house as a matter of fact. At the back, there. Just two rooms.' Sonia hesitated, as if giving further information was something to which she needed to give serious consideration. 'The other is a B&B cum café, actually. La Poche, next to Saint-Laurent station where that awful incident happened. My son runs it. I think you may have interviewed him, earlier?'

'No, my colleagues did.'

'Ah.'

Was that irritation Flaco saw in Sonia's eyes? A sign she had given away something she needn't?

'To be clear, Monsieur Rafal Maso is your son?'

'Yes.'

Weighing a couple of considerations of her own, Flaco said nothing, It was Sonia's daughter who worked as a cleaner for Caroline Rosay. And now it turns out her son runs the café in which Rosay met Ambroise Paillaud before he jumped to his death. Connection or coincidence? The family's surnames exercised her a little, also. Maso, Wienawska, Bera? No two matched and therefore no investigating officer would have thought of connecting them. A five-minute records search, however, would get to the bottom of that one.

Daniela returned and subsided on to the sofa next to her mother.

'Alright to continue?' Flaco said.

'Suppose so.'

'Was emptying Mademoiselle Rosay's shredder part of your cleaning duties?'

She slipped her hand into her mother's and nodded.

'And you did that yesterday? Answer in words, please.'

Daniela stiffened. 'I put out all the rubbish. It goes on Thursdays.'

'And you definitely didn't visit the house today?'

'No, I said, I didn't. Why would I?'

'To be paid, perhaps? I did casual work as a student. Sometimes people don't have cash at the time, do they? You have to go back.'

'Mademoiselle always *did* have it. Always put in an envelope. And it was always right. Sometimes, a few euros more.'

The big question loomed.

'You both understand that we need to ask people where they were at the time of Mademoiselle Rosay's murder?'

Sonia was still beaming at the angels. 'No, I don't understand that.'

'Neither do I.' Daniela's words spluttered through tears. 'Maminka?' She lay her head on her mother's skinny knees. 'Tell her to go. I'm tired.'

'Tell me where you both were and I'll leave.'

'We don't know when it happened until you tell us, Officer.'

'Sometime between 6 and 8 o'clock.'

Sonia laid a finger across her daughter's lips. 'We were at Sainte Bernadette's church hall here in Vence. From about 5 until we came home just now. Père Etienne and several parishioners will vouch for us.'

Flaco made a note and stood. 'Thank you. Why were you there, as a matter of interest?'

'To take part in our summer concert series. *Puits du Sud* it's called. In opposition to, well, you know.'

'No, what?'

Sonia's smile didn't falter. '*Nuits du Sud*, of course – that awful racket that goes on in Place du Grand Jardin every July evening. Give them all headphones, I say – the audience.'

'I don't think that would work, madame. So do you sing or play something?'

'Just help out in general.'

'Uh-huh. And you, mademoiselle? What do you do?'

Daniela turned over, shutting out the world behind her broad back.

'She recites. Things like that. Now if you wouldn't mind, officer?'

Flaco issued the usual reminders and cautions and took her leave.

Sonia waited until she heard the outer door close. 'Get up, now, Dani. We need to check on Monsieur Férion.'

# 28

'Caroline Rosay's document inventory from her computer.' Erica handed it to Darac with an almost ceremonial flourish. 'And here's a list of all incoming and outgoing calls made on her mobile.' A curtain of fine blonde hair escaped the holdback of her ear as she took off her lab coat. Under it was a rugby shirt bearing the numeral 14. 'Job done.'

'Excellent.'

'Shrunk in the wash?' Bonbon deadpanned, indicating the shirt as Darac ran an eye over the back page of the inventory.

'Shrunk about ten sizes? No, Bonbon – it's mine, not Serge's.'

'Another great try haul for him this season, wasn't it? *Will* he stay with the club, do you think?'

'As staying with them means staying with me, he'd better.'

Bonbon grinned but then it was down to business. 'Any new entry for Paillaud, chief?'

'No wills or documents of any sort added today. Of course, Caroline might have been about to do just that – and perhaps set other balls rolling – when she was killed. But anyway, Granot can now start the cross-check in earnest.'

'That's a plus, chief.'

Darac turned to Caroline's mobile records. None of the numbers Hervé Montand had given them proved to be on either list. '*If* she phoned him, she must have used her landline – those records are still to come in – or someone else's phone or a payphone.'

'Don't forget our good friend, the burner,' Erica said.

'Unlikely, but it's not impossible.'

'Montand's own phone records will give us the answer to that one,' Bonbon said. 'One way or the other.'

Darac looked for the staggered calls Caroline had made to Martina Sicotte and the Centre's landline. He found them. No calls were listed in between. 'So Caroline *didn't* ring Vaselle or anyone else from outside La Poche. Another what-if answered in the negative.' He gave the sheets a rap with the back of his hand. 'Really useful, Erica. Thanks for hanging on.'

'You know me and the Caserne.' Re-anchoring her hair, Erica swept a slender arm around the lab. 'What was love at first sight has only deepened over time.'

'Let's see how you feel about it in a minute,' Bonbon said.

Erica's gaze turned to the three evidence cases the men had set down innocently between them.

'You... wouldn't be so heartless as to have brought something else for me. Surely?'

'No,' Darac said. 'But in a sense, yes.'

Erica's pale cheeks flushed the subtlest shade of coral. 'You arseholes.'

'Not for now,' Bonbon said. 'For later. Obviously.'

'Oh. Bit sensitive, there. Sorry.'

Darac smiled. 'Erica, did you enjoy doing jigsaws as a child?'

'Jigsaws? Are you kidding? I was acing Tetris when I was two.' A wary look clouded her sky-blue eyes. 'Why?'

Darac opened one of the cases and carefully lifted out the shredder caddy. 'This is why.'

Erica stared at the contents. 'You have got to be joking.'

Darac essayed what he hoped was a reassuring smile. 'It's just one document, we believe, and we haven't disturbed it. It's lying exactly as it fell. I realise how difficult—'

'No you don't. Not remotely.'

'Erica—'

'This isn't just nice long strips of paper any kid on a spectrum could reassemble.'

'I know. It's cross-cut and that would make any reconstruction—'

'It's confetti, practically. And it's not even printed. It's handwritten. On both sides of the paper. Think about that.'

He put his hands on her shoulders and kept them there. 'Will *you*? Will you think about it?'

She stared off.

'Hey,' he said, gently. 'Come on.'

She looked back at him. 'Don't give me that. I'm not scared of hard work. I'm not difficult. And I'm damned resourceful...'

The men chorused their agreement.

'But I cannot perform miracles.'

'R.O. said he couldn't, earlier. But he nearly always does. And so do you.'

She smiled, sweetly. 'That's so nice. And so bullshit.'

'No it isn't.' Darac released her shoulders. 'Look, I have no way of knowing what this document is. It could be a shopping list. But if it is, why would anyone have shredded it?'

'I realise it must be important, or you wouldn't be...' Erica's delicate features took on a sharper quality. 'Hmm.'

Bonbon shared a look with Darac. 'She's cracked it already.'

'I'm promising *nothing*.' She drew down the corners of her fine-lined mouth. 'But there may be a way. Let me sleep on it.'

'You see?' Darac said. 'Miracles.'

'I really do mean it when I say I'm promising nothing.'

'Well I'm going to promise *you* something.'

'Sorry, we forensic analysts aren't allowed to accept presents.'

'This isn't really a present, just a thank-you. A way of saying sorry for wasting your time with Vaselle's phone call.' He glanced at the caddy. 'And for landing that on you.'

Erica leaned back against her bench. 'It hasn't anything to do with what's in the other evidence cases, has it?'

Bonbon gave an involuntary laugh. 'As if we would.'

'No, no, it's just papers and so on. Homework for us.'

She brightened. 'Alright, then. Go on.'

A tension-building beat.

'How would you like a front-row seat for the Quintet's Jazz Festival gig in a couple of days?' He smiled as if he'd just offered her a free ticket for a round the world trip. 'There are two other outfits playing, also.'

'*Uh*-huh. And the thank-you part of this is?'

# 29

Tucked between a gallery and a gift shop at the intersection of two busy ruelles, Chez Pepe had been one of Darac and Angeline's favourite eateries in the old town of Nice, a quarter known as the Babazouk. She had wandered in and out of his thoughts all day and as he passed the place on his way home, Darac glanced at "their" table by the window. A woman was sitting there alone. A pretty elfin brunette wearing a strappy black dress. A woman who could have been Angeline herself. She smiled and, as if turned to stone, Darac stopped dead. Angeline just happened to be there? Or had she been waiting for him? An unopened bottle of red sat on the table. She looked at it, and then at him.

*You're over her.*

She turned the label towards him. Their favourite, he guessed. He didn't look.

*After four years, she dumped you by text.*

She raised her brows. An invitation.

*"Make love, hit someone, or play the guitar." That's how she thought you dealt with every problem you couldn't immediately solve.*

Her eyes were dancing.

*And think of Frankie. A true soul mate. A woman of true heart and wit. A true beauty.*

Angeline pursed her lips.

*And yet...*

He managed a smile but, indicating the case he was carrying, he tapped his watch, mouthed "work – got to go" and walked away. Walked away without a backward glance. But when he was out of sight, he stood for some moments looking back, looking around, wondering what the hell he was doing.

*Are you hoping she'll come after you? After everything that happened then and is happening now?*

He moved on, any thoughts of continuing the debate scotched when his mobile rang. Unless the caller were Angeline herself, of course. Steeling himself, he checked the ID.

'Granot?'

'I know it's late but this is important. I'm working through Caroline's diary. She's supposed to have made or agreed to a meeting in her office at 7 o'clock with the odious Mayor Hervé Montand, right?'

'Go on.'

'Accordingly, she has entered a name in that slot. Only thing is – it's not Montand's.'

Darac ran a hand into his hair. 'Who, then?'

'Guess.'

# 30

It was the sort of morning that had attracted artists and tourists to the Côte d'Azur before there even was a Côte d'Azur; a morning of such vibrantly intense light that the atmosphere seemed to thrum. To a couple of sleep-deprived officers heading along the busy A8 autoroute, the effect was less appealing. On the opposite carriageway, vehicles strafed by the low sun flashed past like glitter balls in an endless strobe-lit parade.

'We played a jazz festival in the U.K. a couple of years ago,' Darac said, squinting behind his shades. 'Marsden. It was great. Great and grey. Ever been to the north of England, Bonbon?'

'North London's as far as I've got. Wembley, to be exact.'

'Was it grey? Flat? Dull?'

'As ditch water.'

'How much would you give to be there right now?'

Bonbon closed his aching eyes. 'Think of a number and double it.'

With the diary entry bombshell vying with Frankie and Angeline for headspace, Darac had had difficulty concentrating as he'd worked on into the night. It was almost 2 o'clock before he finally went to bed and to unwind, he decided to read just a few more pages of Ambroise Paillaud's autobiography. It was a mistake, the narrative sweeping him along until he'd finished it.

If his compelling account were to be believed, Paillaud's life story was a true rags-to-riches affair, his talent to amuse evolving as an antidote to the deprivations of a chaotic childhood. His "family", loose around the edges but tight-knit inside, had always loved his antics but taken them for granted. He was just "the funny one", a rubber ball of a kid who "always bounced back". Harbouring no showbiz aspirations, it was almost comically apt that the future Prince of the Pratfall's first great stunt was to "stumble into the profession itself". But for an off-duty studio executive spotting him larking about on a Paris street, cinema fans the world over may never have got to see anything of Ambroise Paillaud. The trajectory of his career – obscurity, rise, peak, decline, obscurity – was, Darac recognised, a familiar one. But if Paillaud had slipped out of the public eye in his latter decades, the star maintained that it was only because he had wanted it that way. As he finished the final chapter, Darac couldn't shake the conclusion that the rubber ball of a boy who had always bounced back was still bouncing back even in death.

After finally turning out the light, Darac had been able to snatch only a couple of hours' sleep. He had spent most of it having dreams and nightmares. In one episode, he and Frankie, dressed in clothes made of shredded paper, had been charged with unspecified offences and put on trial. Perhaps it was inevitable that Angeline had appeared, acting as both judge and jury. Darac had been convinced that the misunderstanding could be straightened out if he and Frankie were allowed to speak in their defence. But every attempt to do so resulted in a part of their clothing disappearing, and with it, the flesh underneath. It wasn't until the pair of them were almost invisible that the familiar chasm of oblivion opened up beneath him and he fell down, down, down.

He had awoken with a great wrenching shudder. As he came round, he felt better about the situation with Frankie until he realised he was comparing it only with his nightmare. He was desperate to talk to her. Just the two of them. And what had Angeline been up to at Chez Pepe? If she had wanted to speak to him, why hadn't she just called? She still might. Angeline never gave up easily on anything she wanted.

After showering and dressing, he'd needed an espresso to kick-start his day. Once again, it had given him a slight flickering sensation in his eyelids. Worse, his heart had spent a couple of bars beating out of time with itself. But he'd be alright, wouldn't he? The Daracs were a long-lived family. On his father's side, anyway. When things had calmed down at work, he resolved to discuss the condition with Deanna Bianchi. As a renowned medic, she would give him as much detail as he wanted; as an enthusiastic smoker, she would advise him what to do about it without delivering the sort of improving lecture his own doctor was wont to do.

The sun was still blinding.

'This may just be a first,' Bonbon said, his Perpignan accent lacking its usual percussive energy.

'Because you haven't sucked a single sweet since we set off?' A delay on the feed from Darac's brain to his lips gave him an involuntary beat. 'How's that for alliteration?'

'Super.' Bonbon gave the CD player a tap. 'I was thinking you hadn't given Sonny Rollins yet one more shot at turning me on to jazz. Or Louis Armstrong. Or that Ornate fellow.'

'*Ornette*, Bonbon. Ornette Coleman.'

'Him too.'

'So how come *you* didn't get a decent night's sleep?'

'A case full of papers doesn't make the best bedtime story. But I was finally just going off when cousin Guim came back with his girlfriend. And two new mates. Who rang three others. Six of them turned up in the end. I threatened to arrest them.'

'And?'

'They're probably...' Bonbon yawned. '...still partying.'

Darac came off the autoroute near the construction site for the Allianz Riviera stadium and headed for what he still referred to as the "new" bridge over the Var at Les Baraques. As if it were a requirement, he waited until they had crossed it before collecting his thoughts on the case. Several details puzzled him and he went over them one after the other, returning to the most pressing only as he began to skirt the racquet-shaped grounds of Centre Sicotte. By the time he made the turn on to the narrow shelf of La Crague itself, he'd formed a few tentative theories.

'It looks almost strange like this, doesn't it?' Darac couldn't recall seeing the village bathed in sunlight before. Not up close, anyway. It was like encountering a taciturn neighbour wearing fancy-dress. 'You awake?'

Bonbon gave his head a clearing shake and sat up. 'Am I a what?'

'Wake.'

'Definitely. Ready for anything.'

They pulled up outside a neatly kept villa washed in Roman red.

'Good. Anything is just what we may need.'

# 31

'Jodie?' Martina Sicotte's expression managed to temper concern with reproof. 'I didn't expect you to work *today*.' Tossing her pen on to her desk, she rose and enveloped Jodie's slight frame in her arms. 'Sonia has cancelled your morning appointments.'

'I've just uncancelled them,' she said across Martina's broad chest. 'I need to work.'

'Caroline has not vanished,' a voice intoned behind her. 'She has merely moved on to a different plane.'

'Thank you, Deepak,' Martina said, holding on tighter still to Jodie. 'Not now'. She gave him the hard eye. 'OK?'

'As you wish.' He put his hand on Jodie's shoulder. 'I'll be in the Pilates room if you need to talk. Stretching.'

'You can stretch yourself right up your arse for all I care, *Denis*.'

Jodie's use of Deepak's true given name hastened the man's exit.

'He means well,' Martina said, finally releasing Jodie as the door closed.

'Does he?'

'He believes all the wishy-washy crap, trust me.' She looked into Jodie's weary eyes. 'But forget him. Let's us talk. Girl to girl.'

'No – thank you. But I do need to say something.'

'Yes?'

Jodie raised her eyebrows, chasing a line as straight as a balance beam in her forehead. 'Caroline wasn't just a client.'

'I know. She'd become a good friend.'

'She wasn't just a good friend.'

Sympathy giving way to surprise, Martina sat back against the edge of her desk. 'Ah, I had no idea.'

'No idea that I'm a lesbian? Why should you? My sexual preference is no one's business but my own. My own and my lover's.'

Martina's face hardened. 'So why are you telling me now?'

'Because it may come out anyway, and I wanted to stress that I haven't abused my position here. I've never once...' The beam bit more deeply into her forehead as she searched for the term. '... *preyed* on a client. Clothed or unclothed. And it certainly didn't happen that way with Caro.'

'I'm sure it didn't.' Martina's lips widened into a smile; her eyes remained cool. 'But thanks for the reassurance. My business motto may be "Do whatever makes the punters happy", but we also have a duty of care, haven't we? Even Deepak knows that.' The smile disappeared. 'And if he ever did cross the line, make no mistake, I would fire him immediately.'

Jodie returned Martina's look. 'Yes? I'm glad to hear that.'

Martina stood, taking Jodie's hands. 'Now I know what Caroline meant to you, I'm even more certain you should go home.'

A knock at the door.

Martina frowned in irritation. 'Come in.'

An outsized figure wearing an antique tracksuit appeared in the doorway.

'Ah, Lieutenant,' Jodie said. 'I'll be right with you.'

# 32

'Go through to the kitchen.'

In the daylight, the livid whorls and swirls of Arnaud Zep's face seemed even more Van Gogh-like to Darac.

'Coffee, gentlemen? I'm test driving a chocolaty little Costa Rican number at the moment. Cartago farmers collective.' He nodded. 'Promising.'

Darac would have given anything for a decent espresso at that moment. Or any espresso. A single, even. A thimbleful. A dry bean to crunch between his teeth. At his shoulder, Bonbon gave him a curiously questioning look.

'Not interested,' Darac said, aware Zep was testing him. 'But my lieutenant—'

'Me neither. We're here on business.'

'*Not interested* was the right answer, Captain.' Zep followed them along the hall. 'A power juice, perhaps?'

'Pass.'

'Lieutenant?'

'Ditto.' He lowered his voice. 'Whatever *power* juice is.'

The kitchen was all white planar surfaces. Except for the bike sitting wheels-up on the tiled floor and a basket of very *bio*-looking vegetables, it had the appearance of a lab, a place for scientific experiment rather than preparing meals.

'Nice machine,' Bonbon said, indicating the bike. 'Admired it last night. Expensive?'

'It's worth more than any car I've owned, put it that way.' Righting the bike, Zep wheeled it out of the way and gestured them to sit at the table. They remained standing. 'Could we be reasonably quick? I'm due at the surgery in twenty minutes. Appointments.'

'Are you cycling to work?' Zep was wearing chinos and a blue, short-sleeved shirt. 'Or isn't this a training day?'

'Every day is a training day, Captain. No, as you see, I'm not dressed for it. I have kit stationed at the surgery.'

'And the bike?' Bonbon said. 'How does that get there?'

'I have a roof rack on my car.'

Bonbon, looking fully awake at last, smiled his foxy smile. 'I see. Handy. '

'Indeed.' Zep's eyes narrowed. 'Didn't you spot it? It's the grey Ford Focus parked outside.'

'There are several cars parked outside. Didn't notice it, particularly.'

'Are you sure about that juice? I could up the carotene. Good for vision.'

'I'll muddle through, thanks.' Bonbon grinned. 'As always.'

Darac judged that now was the moment. 'So you have appointments this morning, Doctor. Last evening, Caroline Rosay made an appointment of a different kind, didn't she? With Hervé Montand, 7 o'clock.'

'So I believe, yes.'

Darac brandished a sheet of A4. 'A photocopy of the appropriate page from her diary. How do you explain this?'

Zep glanced casually at the page but then froze. 'I... don't understand.'

'You were very selective in what you told us, yesterday. I warned you about it and you swore you had revealed everything.' Darac eyeballed the man. 'Didn't you.'

'Yes and I assure you I did.' He re-examined the entry. 'I *can't* explain this. I made no appointment with her nor vice versa. My 7 o'clock, as I think you know, was with Kerthus. A home visit.'

'Then why did the mademoiselle write *your* name into that slot in her diary and not Montand's?'

'I don't know. If I remember correctly, he said she had phoned him to make the appointment. Why would he say that if she hadn't?'

Darac was nursing a theory about it but he kept it to himself. 'I have to tell you that we're checking Mademoiselle Rosay's landline phone, computer and mobile records.'

Zep produced a peculiarly tight-lipped smile. 'Good because it will establish that we haven't communicated in... it must be months. Last year some time, I think.'

Once again, Darac had another theory. 'Uh-huh.'

'Feel free to examine *my* records if you wish. Including for phones at the surgery. I hereby give permission.' He slipped his mobile out of his trouser pocket. 'And by all means check this in the meantime, if you can be quick about it. I need it for work.' He selected a page. 'Go into emails and texts as well, if you like. Naturally, I would appreciate it if you refrained from reading the messages themselves. Inevitably, some of them are medically sensitive.' He handed the mobile to Bonbon. 'It is the only one I have, by the way. You can check that out, too.'

As Darac continued, Bonbon began cross-checking Caroline's numbers against Zep's call log. Dead end. He then delved into the wider picture; the electronic back story of the man's last several days. It was some moments before he handed the device back. 'As far as this goes, it checks out, Doctor.'

'Naturally.'

'You have computers, laptops?' Darac said, pointlessly making a conscious effort to keep his eyelids still. 'Here and at the surgery?'

'Of course. And as long as our work and our patients' confidentiality is in no way compromised, everything can be made available to you.'

'I'll send someone over.'

'Fine.'

'Thank you, Doctor. For the time being. We'll see ourselves out.'

In the car, Darac turned to Bonbon. 'Open access? How helpful was he?'

'A little too helpful, you think?'

'I wonder.'

'I liked the fact that he had no explanation for the diary entry, though. Had the ring of truth, I felt.'

'What about not mentioning he was at Centre Sicotte yesterday afternoon? *That* didn't.'

'He was there at the same time as Caroline Rosay?'

'According to their booking records, he was indeed. They could have made the arrangement to meet then.'

'So they could. But why? And why did Montand insist she had arranged to meet *him*?'

'I don't know. When we get word from the provider, we'll know whether she called Montand. Of course, what was actually said...' He shrugged. 'Who knows?'

'You know, but for Caroline putting Zep's name in that 7 o'clock slot in her diary, we probably wouldn't have even questioned him again.'

'That's true.' Darac still felt uneasy about the man. 'Liked your insinuation about the bike, by the way.'

'It's funny what you don't see, isn't it? With or without carrots. Or rather what you don't think of looking for, even after all our years on the job. Zep's a human dynamo, right?' Bonbon mimicked a movie trailer voice. ' "Is it a man, is it a bird, is it a plane? No, it's Zeperman!" ' He dropped it. 'If he's not running, he's swimming, and if he's not swimming, he's riding his bike everywhere. So we've been assuming he takes at least bike-sized chunks of time to get to the places he's going.' His eyebrows going in search of his shock of red hair, Bonbon gave Darac a look. '*Except*, he might not.'

'Absolutely. He could drive anywhere at speed, unhitch the bike and pedal say, just the last couple of hundred metres.'

'Not that I think it will prove material to the case.'

'And it does leave the car unattended and potentially spottable.'

'And now we come to the really serious business of the morning. You refusing coffee.'

'Ah.' Darac would trust Bonbon with his life. Indeed, he had done so many times. But now didn't seem the time to come clean. 'As you said, we were there on business.'

'So it's not that you're suffering from myokymia, then?'

Darac exhaled deeply. 'Flak?'

'No, I guessed... Yes, Flak! And she was right to tell us.'

'*Us*? How many of you know?'

'Agnès wasn't surprised, I must say.'

Darac slid to a stop. 'You got hold of Agnès? In New Zealand?'

'Me? No. Charvet. Drive on.'

Bang to rights, Darac did as he was told. 'Look – *suffering* is a very strong word. I'm going to talk to Deanna about it but as far as I can gather, it's just a reaction, this myokymia thing. All I'll need to do is cut the caffeine down a bit.'

'No other symptoms?'

'Uh... No. Not really.'

'No palpitations, then? Irregular pulse?'

'Bonbon, for God's sake! I'm as strong and fit as I ever was. You know I am.'

'Really? How much do you weigh?'

'How much do *you* weigh?'

'Same as I did fifteen years ago. Can you say that?'

Darac could have lamely repeated the phrase but he resisted the temptation. 'Virtually.'

'Virtually? How about *truly*? I think you'll find that would yield a slightly different result.'

'Fifteen years ago, I was twenty. Still a kid. You were what – twenty-eight, twenty-nine? Makes a lot of difference. I bet I weigh the same as I did at *that* age.'

They had reached Place Charles Montand. Ahead, someone was rolling down the awning on the imaginatively named Bar de la Place.

'All I'm saying is, you need to start thinking more about your health. Take care of yourself.'

'Take care? You'll be telling me I need to join Granot on the... cross trainer next.'

'You could do worse.'

'I *need* coffee now. Shall we stop?'

There appeared to be only one paying customer. 'It might be a squeeze.'

They took a table out on the terrace and ordered espressos from a waiter who would have been a certainty for La Crague's Bored Person Of The Year Award. If he could have been bothered to enter.

'Despite appearances,' Bonbon said, 'the coffee we had last night – the stuff they brought up from the village? This is where it came from.'

'As Zep would say, "promising."'

The coffees did not disappoint. On flavour, at least.

'Just because I'm on the wagon, you didn't have to order a single.'

'Do me good to cut down, as well.'

Punctuating the conversation with irritatingly bee-like sips of the nectar, they were running over the case's main points when Darac's mobile rang.

'Erica?'

'The confetti I was going to sleep on? I decided to work on it a bit first.'

Darac's eyes met Bonbon's. This could be the breakthrough. As if staying a clamouring crowd, he absently raised a hand. 'And?

'I can reconstruct it.'

'You can?'

'Yes.'

'Brilliant!'

Darac and Bonbon bumped fists and, without thinking, downed the rest of their espressos in one.

'Those weren't coffee cups I heard clinking in the back-ground?'

'Might have been. Why?'

'You know what the doctor said.'

Darac cast his mobile an exasperated look. 'As does everyone in the Alpes Maritimes, it seems. But enough of that. *How* do you stick the confetti back together?'

'I was hoping you'd ask. First, you photograph every shred of paper separately, upload them and make an image file of each. It wasn't that many pieces actually when I added it up. I've got Marcel on it already. That's the easy bit.'

'I'm with you so far.'

'Then it's a matter of applying a sorting algorithm to those files. Do you know what I mean by that?'

'Broadly. Very broadly. Not really, no.'

'It doesn't matter. The clue's in the word "sorting".'

'Will it help that we didn't disturb the order the paper fell into the caddy?'

'To an extent. And we have other useful things going for us. Although it's written on both sides, the document is a single sheet and it was the only one in the caddy. The handwriting appears to be very small so each shred contains more graphic information than would otherwise be the case. As a control, I got Lartou to bring some samples of Paillaud's handwriting over and I can already see some congruence, especially in the squashed-up size of the letters. I then realised that if the original is a will, as you believe, it would contain certain phrases and patterns of words common to all such documents – "this is my will", "I bequeath" and so on. In this case, it would contain the notary Caroline Rosay's name and address and if it *is* Ambroise Paillaud's will, it would contain his, too. So we have a contextual steer as well. That leaves us with this simple equation: sorting algorithm plus standard code-breaking techniques equals reconstruction. *Quod erat demonstrandum.* I'm curtseying, by the way.'

'Erica, you are fantastic.'

'I know.'

Grins at the table. 'How long do you think it will take?'

'Perhaps only a day or two but it could be weeks, I suppose. Especially if the document turns out to be not what you think it is.'

'That in itself would be significant.'

'I see that. I've requested the shredder head itself, by the way. The state of the cutters needs to be taken into account. Right, it's coffee and croissant time for me. No more for you until lunchtime.'

Erica rang off before Darac could respond.

'What a talent.' Bonbon was still grinning. 'Amazing woman.'

'You know, from front line *flics* to back-room boffins, almost all our female colleagues are exceptional, aren't they? If only we had some espresso in these cups, we could toast them.'

They shared a look. It was a tempting thought. And who would know about it but them?

'No, we must be strong, chief. You, especially.'

Darac let out a long breath. 'You're right.'

Bonbon brightened. 'All is not lost. As luck would have it, I've got something even more celebratory in my pocket.'

'A nice chilled Krug?'

'It *is* fizz.' He produced a crinkle of pink and white-striped paper. 'Flying saucer?'

Darac took one. 'To our women in uniform!'

'And to those out of them!' Bonbon performed a double-take. 'So to speak.'

Rice paper and sherbet may have been a poor substitute for champagne but the pair were soon chewing over more substantial fare. To open out the discussion, Darac decided to set a team meeting for later in the day and so for the moment, he turned to the less obvious elements of the investigation, the in-between stuff; things that were neither leads nor evidence but might yet have a bearing on the outcome. Eventually, they arrived at a topic that had exercised Darac from the beginning.

'You know, Ambroise Paillaud's suicide is still on my mind.'

'That's old news, surely. Perand's footage is crystal clear. The man jumped unaided.'

'There's no doubting that.' Darac ran a hand into his hair and kept it there. 'There's *something*, though. I'm thinking of discussing it with Paillaud's ghost.'

Bonbon gave him a look. 'Ghost? I think your flying saucer may have been spiked. What are you talking about?'

'Paillaud's ghost – the ghost-writer of his autobiography. If he's still alive, that is.'

'Might be difficult to spirit him up even if he is. They don't always name them to make it look as if the star wrote the thing all by themselves.'

'In this case, it's in the preface. A Monsieur Férion. Maurice... Robert? No – Rémy.'

Bonbon grabbed the laptop from his bag. 'No time like the present. Spell?'

'It's Férion as in the mountain.'

'Maurice... Rémy... Férion...' Bonbon finished tapping in the name. 'Hang on.'

As Bonbon began the search, Darac's thoughts turned back to Frankie. Ever since Christophe's cheerful announcement of her decision to leave, questions concerning the finality of that decision had been falling over one another in Darac's head and he had formulated hopeful answers to most of them. Curiously, it was one of the more seemingly trivial that exercised him most, a question that wouldn't occur to most people. Darac was the son of a perfume house Nose and he had inherited both a heightened sensitivity to smells in general, and an understanding of the connection a person can feel to their preferred fragrance. Frankie's scent was *Marucca*. He had never known a day that she hadn't worn it and she never wore anything else. Might the fact that she hadn't been wearing it at the Théâtre de Verdure be a sign that she had indeed decided to move on? The pragmatist in him hoped she had simply run out of supplies, temporarily. Whatever the truth, he couldn't wait to talk to her.

'Ah.' Bonbon angled the screen to Darac. 'This our Férion?'

'Uh...' Darac came to and read the entry. 'That's him.'

# 33

It seemed to Granot that his skin and bone had dissolved in his own sweat. Through the blur, a large blue ball appeared at his feet. 'Hope you don't want me to kick this thing. It looks as if it might kick back.'

'No, you're just going to sit on it.' Jodie raised an eyebrow. 'And stop being so negative. You did very well on the treadmill and the cross trainer.'

'I did three minutes on each.'

'That's quite enough for a first session.' She glanced at her watch. 'We'll do five on the ball, then go into our cool-down and that will be it for today.'

'All I do is sit on it?'

'To begin with. But take your time. It's trickier than you might think.'

'And what is this going to help with?'

'Your core strength.' She looked him in the eyes and nodded. 'Your powerhouse.'

'Core strength,' he repeated, lowering himself. 'Powerhouse.'

'Make sure your starting position is...'

'Whoaaah!'

Granot's powerhouse flobbed up to meet his face as he performed an involuntary backward roll.

'... square on.' Despite all she was feeling, Jodie couldn't resist a smile. There was nothing like a little slapstick to lift the spirits. 'Let's try that again. Without the fancy move, this time.'

Granot checked to see he was still in one piece. Concluding

that he was, he hauled himself off the floor in a series of instalments.

'Think I'm ready for the pommel horse yet?'

'Might give that one a miss just for the time being.' She retrieved the ball. 'Stand facing me.' She held out her child-sized hands, inviting him to grasp them. 'I won't break.'

'I bet you won't,' he said, searching for a dry patch on his tracksuit. 'Uh...'

'You think I've never encountered sweaty hands before?' She rolled her eyes. 'Give!'

A tugboat to Granot's container ship, Jodie took only a moment to manoeuvre him into position. 'OK, that's good and square.' She let go of his hands. 'So slowly... Down. That's it. You're there.'

He felt the ball compress under his weight. All he was doing was sitting on an inert blob of rubber but riding a bucking bronco would not have caused him greater difficulty. Muscles he didn't know he possessed began working in ways he didn't think possible.

'That's really not bad, Roland. Not bad at all. Let's bring your arms into it now.'

On the mezzanine, two figures were looking on with more than passing interest.

'This is bad,' Deepak Abhamurthi said. 'It's blocking my chakras. All seven of them.'

Tina kept her eye on Granot. 'What is?'

'Having that barrel of lard around the place. For one thing, it looks as if he could drop dead at any second. Has he been cleared for physical training?'

'By a police doctor, yes.'

Deepak nodded but then another doubt stressed his chakras. 'He is paying, I hope?'

'Of course he is and if anything, I'm going to encourage his and Jodie's relationship. A tame *flic* could be useful. No?'

'I didn't think of that.'

'You don't have to think.' She glanced along the mezzanine. 'Especially when we're alone.'

'What if it all goes wrong?'

'It won't. The Lord will protect us. The Lord and Hervé Montand.'

'Think so? I don't trust either. Have you rung him yet?'

'Which one?'

'Per-lease.'

'Alright. I'll do it in a minute.'

'Good.' He ran his hand around the curve of her buttocks. 'You'd better make that half an hour. I can feel my energy beginning to flow again.'

Behind them was a door marked CLEANERS.

'In there.' Tina brandished a key card. 'Now.'

They stepped back from the rail and Deepak followed her as if they were on a routine inspection of the building.

'I see you're wearing black-soled trainers,' he said. 'That's against the rules.'

'I had to bin my indoor ones. Got them dirty.'

'Naughty. I could have you banned.'

'Doubt it.' She opened the door. 'I'm in with the bitch who runs this place.'

'So am I.'

The room smelled of damp cloth and lemon cleanser. He reached for the light switch.

'No. Leave it.' She locked the door. 'Do it to me in the dark.'

With light from the mezzanine outlining the doorframe behind her, she pulled Deepak toward her. He slid his hands under the waistband of her sweatpants and, slowly pulling them over her hips, he put the tip of his tongue in her navel and began tracing an ever wider arc.

'Tell me about her.' She dug her fingers into his scalp. 'The little Bambi in the locker room, yesterday.'

'Who?'

'You know the one. Sixteen going on thirty-six – if she's made sixteen yet. I want to hear what you did. Tell me.'

Deepak stood and pulled Tina's pants back up. 'Listen. I haven't been in there in weeks. OK?'

'I saw you go in. What else would you be doing? Come on, baby, don't be mean. Tell me —'

A strip light sputtered on overhead.

'I didn't.' His eyes had lost all their fawn-like lustre. 'And if you tell anyone I did, you could get me into a lot of trouble. Do you understand?'

She nodded.

'Good. Now pull down your pants and get on your knees.'

Tina did as she was told but the look she gave him made it clear that in ceding control, she was getting what *she* wanted, too. He threw the switch and once again, light from the mezzanine rimmed the door. It was the closest Deepak Abhamurthi had ever come to seeing an aura.

## 34

While Bonbon snored in the passenger seat, Darac received two calls on the way back from La Crague. The first was a barrage of questions, demands and cautions from public prosecutor Jules Frènes. The Paillaud-Rosay case was already a staple of news programmes worldwide and Frènes was clearly relishing his role as its official voice. Press conferences, statements to camera, interviews with everyone from TF1 to CNN – the little man was working on building a big reputation.

Darac couldn't look such a gift horse in the mouth. 'You'll probably be a regular on TV now, monsieur. Commentating on world affairs and culture. Even sports.'

'I doubt the latter.'

'A second Bernard-Henri Lévy.'

'What will be, will be.' The ceasefire was soon over. 'Are you aware that odious layabout Recolte sold the video he took of Paillaud's suicide? And that it went viral on the internet before it was taken down? What do you say about that?'

Darac could see where Frènes was heading. 'I say that Recolte, the video uploader, and any branch of the media showing a clip or still of the footage will be in trouble. So no blame can be attached to Perand.'

'Are you certain of that, Captain?'

'Absolutely certain.'

'You recall your former intern Christian Malraux, now in Marseille? You lost a good man when you lost him. He has informed me several times of Perand's slackness.'

How could Darac ever forget Malraux? And he and Frènes were still in touch, were they? It had slipped Darac's mind that the young man had been transferred from Cannes, his posting after the Caserne. And of course, it would be to Mar-fuck-ing-seille, wouldn't it? Just the mention of Frankie's future base had made Darac's blood run cold.

'Perand may have been a little slow to reveal his strengths but he has become a valued member of the team. Valued and trusted.' Once more, Darac saw an opportunity to ridicule the ridiculous. 'On another matter, when would you like me to take the platform with you, monsieur?'

'Pardon?'

'Yesterday, you were adamant, quite rightly, that I share the media burden with you. Working in harness. Shoulder to shoulder.' He resisted the temptation to say *close-up for close-up*. 'I have some things to go over but I will be available later.'

'Yes. Right. On mature reflection, I feel that at the moment, you might be better employed in the field. The investigation is still in a comparatively early stage and—'

'That's most considerate of you, monsieur. Oh, I'm going into a...'

Darac rang off and noticed he had missed a call from Angeline. He hadn't heard her voice in two years. Did he want to hear it now? He gave it a moment and pressed play. Nothing. She had rung off without leaving a message. First Chez Pepe and now this? She wanted to see him, clearly, and he didn't really know why he was so resistant to the idea. Was his hurt that deep? Was he trying to punish her? Show that he didn't care? But he did care and resolved that if she tried a third time, he would agree to meet her. What could possibly be the harm?

Approaching the Caserne, Darac was wondering how best to awaken Bonbon when he remembered he had Kenny Barron's *Minor Blues* cued-up in the CD player. Before he could select a suitable track, his mobile rang again and did the job for him.

'*Wassat?*'

'For a minute there, I thought you'd nodded off, Bonbon.'

'No, no.'

'Go ahead, Perand.'

'Télécom have come through. Caroline Rosay *did* ring Montand yesterday afternoon in that re-routed call he mentioned – 4.22 pm from her home office phone.'

'She did, eh?' Darac recalled Montand reporting that very little had been said. 'Duration?'

'It was... thirty-nine seconds.'

'OK. Any other significant calls? To and/or from either of them?'

'I just got this. Hang on.'

'Thirty-nine seconds is not long,' Bonbon said, as they waited for Perand to check. 'But probably long enough to get more than just the meeting arrangements sorted.'

'Touch and go, I'd say.'

'Chief? Caroline made no other calls at all nor received any. Montand took a couple, both from business numbers, and made one to... I think that's Vaselle's mobile... Yes, it is. That call was made at 5.37 pm and lasted one minute forty-one.'

'Twice as long but not hugely involved,' Bonbon said.

'OK, thanks, Perand. Team meeting at 1 o'clock, right?'

'Wouldn't miss it.'

# 35

Hervé Montand knew he shouldn't have glanced up and down the landing before ringing the bell. It looked suspicious. As if it were any ordinary Saturday, he'd opted for a *chic-décontracté* outfit: pale-blue, short-sleeved shirt, stone slacks, tan loafers. The black eye he was sporting wasn't part of the look but he was sure Mathilde's camouflage make-up was doing an effective job.

Guy Vaselle opened the door wearing nothing but underpants. His eyes adjusting to the light, he took a moment to react. 'Well, come the fuck in if you're coming.'

'I can smell your breath from here.' Montand stepped quickly inside. 'And you need a shower.'

'Phone before you come round next time.' Vaselle led his visitor along the hall. 'I could've had a woman here. *Should*'ve had a woman here.'

'And how is your wife?' Montand said. 'Enjoying her holiday?'

'Don't give me that bullshit. How's my sister? And how did you get that shiner? Rosay or the flics?'

'Neither.' He tentatively patted the site of desecration. 'It was a creditor. One of them. He came to the house last night.' His eyebrows rose in bewilderment. 'The bastard wouldn't listen to reason, Guy.'

'And then?'

'He punched me and drove me to an ATM.'

Vaselle laughed as they walked through an open-plan lounge towards the kitchen. 'Anything else come up?'

'Martina Sicotte rang. Wanted to know when she was going to get her new all-weather courts. And the spa.'

'What did you say?'

'I said "in due course," naturally.'

On the breakfast bar, a half-eaten croissant lay submerged in a bowl of coffee. Next to it, the broad, dimpled base of a shot glass was balancing on the open neck of an empty whisky bottle.

'If you want anything, get it yourself.' Vaselle rearranged his balls and climbed back on to his high stool.

'I ate my breakfast two hours ago.' Montand said, looking anxiously at the precariously balancing glass. 'Like any normal human being.'

'Stoving the bitch's head in didn't put you off your food, then?'

Montand's top-heavy face coloured like litmus dipped in acid. But he said nothing.

'Good for you, Hervé. I didn't think you had it in you.'

'Yes. Well...' Montand smiled slightly as he dabbed at his mouth. 'My family is used to making sacrifices for the commune. We've been doing it since the Middle Ages.'

'You're all heart.' Vaselle laughed. 'And it's full of shit.'

'That's enough! Now listen, Guy, I thought we agreed you were to steer well clear of Rosay's place.'

'What...' Raising one buttock, Vaselle squeezed out a fart, '... are you blabbing about?'

'If Zep had come the other way, he would have passed your car on the road. As I did. Alright, you'd parked it practically under the hedge but it was still visible. And he *did* see a shape skulking in the garden. As I did.'

'You didn't tell the *flics* about the car or they would have come for me already.'

'I didn't tell them anything.' The endangered glass took Montand's eye once more. His hand moved towards it but he brought it back. 'How could I?'

Vaselle gave him a sideways look. 'Upsets you, doesn't it? The tumbler. The way it's sitting there like that. Above a granite bar top. What's to stop it falling off? And smashing?'

'You were to stay away, we said. We agreed that explicitly. That's why I'm here. To ram home that from now on, you *must* stick to what we agree.'

His eyes fixed on Montand's, Vaselle gave his little balancing act a backward nod.

'I didn't do that just now, sober. I did it last night after I got back from La Crague. The bottle wasn't far off half-full when I started. I drank it all and then set the glass down right on the button. First go.'

Guy got casually to his feet but then suddenly grabbed his visitor by the collar. Montand tried to wriggle free, mewling like a rabbit caught in a trap.

'I keep calm under pressure, Hervé. I keep a very cool head. I don't make mistakes. Ever.' He pulled Montand's head down his stomach to his groin and held it there. 'Like it, do you? That's how a real man feels.' He pushed him away. 'It wasn't me you saw in the garden, fuckwit. Got that? Not me!'

For the moment, Montand could only cower, riven with anxiety and disgust. But as Vaselle calmly lit a cigarette, he began to recover slightly. The immediate threat appeared to be passing. At length, he straightened, adjusted his clothing and after a further moment to think about it, sat down at the bar.

'So what did you do with the new will?' Vaselle said.

As if he was unable to resist any further, Montand's hand moved toward the shot glass. 'Nothing. I never saw it.'

'I don't think I believe you.'

'You've got no alternative.'

As Montand's fingers went to close around the glass, they twitched suddenly, knocking it from its perch. Vaselle extended his left hand, catching it just before it hit the bar top.

'Maybe you're not as cut out for a life of crime as I thought, Hervé. Or maybe you just want me to think that. Either way, I'm glad you came, it's saved me a trip. If you've still got a business when all this is over, it'll mean one thing, won't it? It'll mean that Paillaud's previous will held. If it does, Hervé, I'm giving up my poxy little post. I had a chat with Mathilde about it last night on the phone.'

Montand could scarcely contain his delight. 'We've had our ups and downs Guy. And yes, there's been fault on both sides, I admit. But I should be very sorry to see you go.'

'Don't worry, I won't be going far. In fact, I'll be sitting right next to you.' Making a hollow chinking sound, Vaselle repositioned the glass in one crisp movement. He turned to Montand and smiled. 'As third co-owner of the company.'

# 36

Darac had been back in his office no more than a few seconds when Djibril Mpensa's preliminary autopsy reports on Paillaud and Caroline Rosay buzzed in to the fax machine. As if Mpensa were present, Darac thanked him aloud and, for once sans coffee, settled down to read them. Turning to Paillaud's first, Darac was put in mind of a Steely Dan song lyric in which its subject had "died in fifteen ways". Any one of the hundred or so traumatic injuries suffered by Paillaud would have killed him. With the cause and exact time of death indisputably established, the only further factor to have been examined was the state of the deceased's health prior to his suicide. Mpensa had indeed found evidence of the terminal cancer – a rare form of leukaemia – for which Paillaud was being treated at Clinique Albert Magnesca in Nice.

Mpensa's preliminary report on Caroline made altogether sadder reading. Detail after detail offered no, or only minor, revisions from his analysis at the scene. He had adjusted his estimate of the time of death to between 6.50 and 7.10. In a separate memo, Mpensa recorded that having interviewed Zep, he was satisfied that the doctor's account of events was consistent with his own but that the man's time-of-death estimate – between 6.55 and 6.58 – while probably correct, particularly in light of the corroboration of two other witnesses, could not itself be entered into the record.

Now that Mpensa's reports were in, Darac circulated them with a note bringing the team meeting forward to midday. He spent the interim tying up as many loose ends as he could and initiated an email exchange with the Police Nationale's crime lab in Lyon. He also rang ghost-writer Maurice Férion's number in Paris and left a message. Most importantly of all, he arranged to meet Frankie in her office at 2 o'clock.

As if synchronised with Château Park's midday maroon, Granot appeared in Darac's doorway slap on the appointed hour. Considering he must have been to hell and back with Jodie earlier, he looked surprisingly chipper. 'Still alive, then, Granot? How's that for stating the obvious?'

'Haven't felt so alive in years, my friend.' He glanced back down the corridor. 'Bonbon? Playtime.'

'Can Yvonne and Max come, too?'

'Only if I don't have to run them home later.' He waddled into the office, tapping the lid of the document box he was carrying. 'Got some interesting things here.'

'Want to open with it? My stuff can wait until the end.'

'OK.'

Feeling a rare headache coming on, Darac eyed the chromed temptress that was his Gaggia espresso machine. Gorgeous. Loyal. Caring. And cruelly forsaken. A noble thought struck him. 'Feel free to make yourself a coffee.' He got the words out without faltering. 'I don't really need one at the moment.'

'No, no. I'm fine.'

Bonbon, Flaco and Perand walked in as Granot began setting out the contents of his box on Darac's desk.

'No surprises in Map's prelim reports,' Bonbon said, offering Flaco his usual seat and being put politely but firmly in his place. 'Sure? OK. And you can see Deanna's mentoring all over them, can't you? Clear, concise, thorough.'

'Yes, they're perfect.' Darac gave Granot the nod. 'Go for it.'

'First, a few updates. I've been able to verify what we suspected from the beginning. Thanks partly to the incompetence and profligacy of Mayor Hervé Montand, it seems the commune of La Crague is practically bankrupt. Montand owes money all over the shop and his bog business, as Perand here puts it, is struggling also.'

'That fits.'

Bonbon grinned. 'I've just been on to an antique dealer I know up in Carros so he hears things from La Crague. The talk is that Montand's shiny new fire engine might have to be repo'ed. Great boost for the local morale in wild fire season.'

'Great vote loser for Montand,' Flaco said. 'Come election time.'

'Absolutely right. Update number two: or rather, non-update. Although I enjoy nothing more than a spot of fiscal ferreting, I haven't bothered trying to locate Paillaud's probably numerous investment accounts. With his death now registered, it will emerge all by itself in due course, anyway. Update number three: in our visit to Paillaud's villa, we were struck by the lack of memorabilia on show or stashed away out of sight. I wondered if the existence of an archive somewhere might explain it. I've discovered there isn't one.'

Darac raised his eyebrows, etching a stave of fine parallel lines on his forehead. 'Hmm.'

'In one of the smaller display cases at the Cinémathèque Française in Paris, there's a waxwork Monsieur La Chute dressed in one of his waiter outfits, a few props, posters et cetera, but that's it. Not much for a man being posthumously garlanded as a national treasure. Annie Provin went as far as calling him "an irreplaceable star in our firmament" on Télé Sud last night.'

Darac gave a derisive little laugh. 'Of course she did.'

Without stirring from his seat, Perand mimed Paillaud's death leap. 'Suicide's one of the best career moves there is, it looks like. What's left of the guy is in kit form but he's never been so big. They're already planning retrospectives, a biopic, a major tribute at next year's Cannes Film Festival.'

Darac was still exercised by Granot's finding. 'So what *did* Paillaud do with his memorabilia?'

'It seems glamorous to us,' Bonbon said. 'But maybe it was just a job to him so it never occurred to him to keep any of it.'

'Except one thing.' Darac sat back in his chair. 'His original Brassaï photo – *Coming, Monsieur!*'

'That's my final bit of news. The version of it in the MAMAC exhibition – the one we established was a private loan? I got hold of one of the exhibition curators. It's not Paillaud's. It was lent by a collector in the U.S. One Mrs Edna Clayton.'

Darac knew Granot's methods as well as he knew his own. 'And she's a collector of—?'

'All the Paillaud memorabilia there has ever been?' Granot said, seemingly aware he was playing to type and enjoying it. 'No, she collects photographs. Loaned three others by Brassaï to the exhibition. Cityscapes.'

'And when did she acquire—?'

'Her version of *Coming, Monsieur!* ?' Forty years ago. And not from Paillaud, then.'

For the second time in as many days, Darac felt a very particular pleasure: the synergy of working in a great team. But it was a feeling tempered by concern. If they had to go on without Granot, Darac wondered how on earth they would cope without the big man's savvy, doggedness and above all, his meticulous attention to detail. Flaco was cast in the same mould and she had strengths Granot had never dreamed of possessing but she was nowhere near the finished article. He banished the thought. 'God, the rhythm section's on fire today.'

'Fire?' Bonbon's foxy eyes twinkled. 'In that case, we'd better give La Crague a miss.'

Granot had finished laying out his bric-à-brac. 'OK – show and tell time. Everything has been dusted. No alien prints.' He opened Caroline Rosay's diary. 'This little gem has already given us the anomaly of the 7 o'clock appointment entry for Doctor Zep. Investigation on-going.' He gave Darac a look. 'More later?'

'Absolutely.'

Granot held up the diary. 'Now look at this.' He pointed out a series of entries going back to the start of the year. 'Notice anything?'

'Dots,' Bonbon said.

'Succinctly put. Dots — the simplest note there is. Caroline didn't need to specify what it meant, because it must have been something obvious to her and happened the same way each time.' A fat finger bumped the page. 'Three dots in pencil, look — like a colon with an extra one on top. Three dots every final Friday in the month. Including February.'

'Marking the start of her periods?' Darac said, failing to see the mystery. Angeline, he recalled, had annotated her diary in a not dissimilar way.

Suppressing a smile, Flaco shook her head. 'Periods that start on the final Friday of each calendar month? Unlikely, Captain.'

'Yes — that was ridiculous.' He eyeballed Flaco. 'Brain isn't working through lack of coffee.' And his headache was worsening.

With the exception of her mother and her two aunts, Flaco could stare down anyone on the planet. 'You have to reduce your caffeine intake and that's all there is to it.'

'Welcome to the world of deprivation,' Granot said, transparently enjoying the moment. 'Now look at this. Yesterday for the first time, the day she is murdered, Caroline, or someone wearing gloves, rubbed out the dots.' He handed it to Darac. 'Check it out and pass it round. You can see the indentations of the pencil, a slight smudging and a fleck of rubber from the eraser.'

'So you can,' Darac said, almost always mistrusting coincidences.

Bonbon had a different take. 'Remember what Agnès always says, though. The banal interpretation usually turns out to be the true one. The dots are probably just a reminder to pay a monthly bill or something. This month, she couldn't get to the bank or had run out of cheques or whatever.'

'Maybe it's club subs for Centre Sicotte,' Flaco said. 'And with all the Paillaud business, she forgot to pay.'

'She had copies of her bank statements up to last month in

the safe. I've cross-checked them and couldn't find anything obvious. Early days though.'

'*This* month's?'

'Requested through global superstar Monsieur Speed, a.k.a. Frènes. Might come today.' Granot's grizzled chops shook with the relish of it. 'Don't tell Salaries, but I'd pay *them* to let me do this stuff.'

Granot, it seemed, had momentarily forgotten the precariousness of his situation. In the deafening silence that followed, Darac was the only one to maintain eye contact with him.

'Bless you,' Granot said. 'All of you. But that wasn't a slip. *I* am going nowhere.'

Observers had frequently commented on the camaraderie of Agnès Dantier's teams, never more evident than in the banter and ribbing that fuelled so many of their conversations. Sometimes though, speaking straight from the shoulder was the way to go.

'This sodding directive,' Darac said. 'We've cursed Divisional for it. We've made jokes. We've bigged up the alternatives. But it's really just whistling in the wind. Are you sure you'll be able to lose the weight, lower your cholesterol and meet the other demands?'

'Done deal. Thanks to Jodie.'

Hoping the big man wasn't riding for a fall, Darac joined in a chorus of positive voices.

Granot bowed gracefully. 'And as we're on Jodie, I have another thought about the diary. We're agreed that she couldn't have killed Caroline: logistically, for one thing.'

'You're wondering if she might be able to shed any light on the dots?'

'I know it's not best practice but what do you think? Shall I show her?'

Darac pursed his lips while he thought about it. Granot was a pro through and through but it was clear that he had warm feelings for Jodie. Warm enough to skew his judgement?

'Jodie and Caroline *were* a couple, after all,' Granot said, tacitly dispelling concerns about his own possible sexual interest in her. 'I could just *mention* the dots to begin with.'

Darac returned Granot's gaze. 'I think it's what Agnès would do.'

'That's good enough for me.'

Flaco unzipped a pocket in her cargo shorts. 'When I interviewed Jodie last night, she said that if she ever discovered who killed Caroline, she would...' She found the line in her notebook. ' "... take a hammer" to him. Or her.'

'It's a natural reaction.' Massaging his temples, Darac went across to the water cooler. 'So soon after the event, particularly.'

'Of course it is,' Granot said, joining him. 'I'll have one with you. Hydration's essential for... health.'

Showing just a hint of irritation, Flaco shifted her weight from one foot to the other. 'I know it's natural.'

'So how did you respond, Flak?'

'I explained things to her and she seemed to drop the idea. I'm not sure she completely meant it.'

'Time's a great healer.' Granot gulped down his water. 'I'll be seeing Jodie most days for the next three months. I'll keep an eye on her, don't worry.'

'*Most* days?' Bonbon gave the others a look. 'How?'

'Before work. After work – whatever fits. Or there may be no work for me ever again. Not the work I want to do, anyway.'

'When you put it that way.'

'Can't promise anything,' Darac said. 'But when this is all over, I might be able to get you some time off, as well.'

Perand put his hand up. 'Can I have some of that? I could do with losing a few kilos.'

Granot gave him a look. 'A few kilos? You'd disappear altogether.'

Perand turned to Bonbon. 'Ever notice that it's OK to diss us thin types?'

'Wouldn't know, mate.'

Darac took his cup back to the desk and mounted a search for the painkillers he had bought ten years ago. 'What's next, Granot?'

'Something even more interesting than dots. If it looks as if it's been hit by a train, that's because it has.' He produced what had once been a cheque book. 'R.O.'s street combers found it snagged under that clump of aloes between the platform and the fence. Opposite La Poche, more or less.'

The level of anticipation in the room rose as Granot slowly pulled back the front cover. 'Three blank cheques left. You can just make out the account holder's name.'

'Ambroise P. Paillaud,' Bonbon recited, squinting. 'P – yes, I'd forgotten that. It's in the back of my mind that it stands for something peculiar.'

'The P?' Darac found the garish yellow packet he was looking for. 'It's Pernod.' He popped a couple of capsules and chased them down with a health-giving mouthful of hydration. 'Named after his mother's favourite tipple, according to the autobiography.' There was little point quizzing Granot about the potential value of his discovery. One glance was enough: the raised left eyebrow; the nonchalant cant of the head. Darac was happy to play along. 'Does it give us anything, Granot, this cheque book? Anything interesting on the counterfoils, for instance?'

'The last filled-in one is dated yesterday. Is that good enough for you?'

If it could have been measured, the anticipation level rose several degrees.

With the coyness of a conjurer, Granot slowly pulled back the cover to its full extent. The quartet leaned in as one. The counterfoil had been completed in a small, childish-looking hand. Dated yesterday, it had been made out to Mlle Caroline Rosay in the amount of €8.96. Sacred and profane oaths were uttered. The quartet straightened.

'Anyone get the significance of that piffling little sum?'

Granot said.

'Let me guess.' Darac ran a hand through his hair. 'It's the fee charged by a notary for registering a new will. Complete with taxes.'

'Exactly.'

Flaco's scowl was more deeply etched than ever. 'But Caroline categorically denied that Paillaud had written a new will. He was just meeting her to say goodbye, she said.'

'She lied. The question is why.' As if the answer might be found in his pockets, Bonbon patted them one after the other. 'And I'm all out of flying saucers.'

Staring at the floor, Darac began reprising the what-ifs he'd entertained already and began adding a few more for good measure. 'You haven't got the cheque itself there, have you Granot?'

'Interestingly, there's no sign of it – not in Caroline's office, daysack, handbag, anywhere. So that's another item to look for on this month's bank statement.'

Flaco looked doubtful. 'A busy woman like that wouldn't have called in at the bank or even stopped at an ATM to pay in a cheque so small. Unless she was paying in several or needed to make a withdrawal.'

'We'll know that part soon enough.'

Darac's black desk phone rang. An internal call. 'It's Erica.' The room hushed. 'Go for it. We're all listening.'

'Breaking – I don't know what the document is yet but Paillaud's signature is on it. Well, it was just the capital P, to be exact, but it's definitely his. The two cartoon-like eyes he draws in the counter – that's the closed round part – is a giveaway and quite easy for my sort programme to split out. The rest won't be so easy but it's a start.'

'Brilliant, Erica.'

The call ended on an upbeat note and for the first time, Darac began to feel a little more positive about the case.

'This feels like a good moment both to recap and to take

things on a bit. We've got a couple of possible new scenarios here, haven't we? There are some troubling details missing and the truth may lie in between but you have to start somewhere.'

Bonbon turned to Flaco. 'I like a good recap and scenario.' Preparing for the long haul, he twisted himself into an unlikely knot and draped his legs over the side of the chair. 'Action.'

'Are you sitting uncomfortably?' Darac had another swig of water. 'So what do we think we know? To spare himself a slow death from cancer, Ambroise Paillaud decides to bow out in a style that even those who had never heard of Monsieur La Chute would remember him for. Immediately beforehand, he arranges to meet his notary, Caroline Rosay. It's looking increasingly likely that his intention was to present her with a new will superseding the previous one that syphoned his assets into the empty coffers of the commune of La Crague-du-Var, coffers to which Mayor Hervé Montand is the sole key holder.

'As we stand, we have no idea what the new will stipulates but thanks to Erica, we may not have long to wait. Back to Paillaud. Unseen by any witness, he hands over the new will, writes out a cheque for Caroline's services and shortly afterwards, takes a running jump into oblivion. Caroline hears of the suicide later that afternoon. For a working hypothesis, it will do for the time being, right?

'Now it's speculation time. We'll go into more detail in a minute but let's fast forward to Caroline's office last night and look at the basics. Two possibilities emerge. Either her killer proposed that she destroy the new will in return for a kickback and she wouldn't play along, so he then killed her and shredded the will. That's the Good Caroline version, right? Now the Bad. The proposal to lose the will for money came from Caroline herself. The killer agreed to it and *she* shredded the will. To ensure her silence, the killer then smashed her head in and made off into the cypresses.'

'Erica nearly always come through,' Perand said. 'Once she's reassembled the will, she can hand it over to R.O. for fingerprinting. That could help us big time.'

Darac's ancient painkillers were starting to work and to test them, he shook his head. 'No prints. She's not reconstructing the paper document itself. It's a computing exercise.'

'That's right, yeah.' Perand nodded as if owning the correction. 'Makes sense.'

Granot shook his chops. 'I favour scenario one. Caroline wouldn't have destroyed the will on just the *promise* of a kick-back.'

'Perhaps the killer put a wad of cash on the table. Not for the whole amount, probably, but a reasonable down-payment. Then he took it back after the deed.' Darac's absent half-smile made a comeback. 'Do you know any good money followers, Granot?'

'The best. This all blew up in one day, didn't it? So it would be easy to find out if any of our principals or secondaries withdrew a large cash sum, or had an authorised cheque made out or did anything else that leaves a record. And I'll get on to that. But if the killer had cash lying around in a personal safe or if they turn out to be someone we haven't come across yet...' Granot let a forlorn shrug finish the thought.

Perand had the look of someone needing to claw back lost ground. 'What does it matter whose suggestion it was to lose the will? We have to find Caroline's killer whether it was her idea or his.'

Flaco, Darac noticed, seemed to take no pleasure in the boy losing more ground still.

'That's true, Maxie,' Bonbon said, as if to a 10 year-old. 'But the better we understand exactly what happened at the scene, the more likely we are to find that killer, aren't we?'

Once again, Darac felt a sudden overwhelming desire for coffee. Not risking so much as a glance at his beloved Gaggia, he ploughed on. 'Let's look in more detail and see what we can tease out by rewinding a little. When we interviewed Caroline at Centre Sicotte, she categorically denied that Paillaud had made a new will. Why did she lie to us? Here's what might have led to the Good Caroline scenario. Since Paillaud's previous will would have benefited virtually everyone living or working in La Crague, she understood what a crushing disappointment his new will, which she had presumably read, would prove to cash-strapped Mayor Hervé Montand. As a courtesy, she decides to break the bad news to him in person and so picks up her phone and summons him to a meeting at 7 o'clock in her office.'

Flaco raised a hand. 'The Zep entry in her diary?'

'Stay tuned.'

She nodded.

'When we interviewed him, however, Montand told us that the summons, improbably, was a formality. It gave no hint of anything unpleasant.'

Perand's grin was at its most lopsided. 'Just a bit of the old "Congratulations, Paillaud's topped himself so you get to keep your fire engine, your title and your factory. And maybe line your own and your mates' pockets while you're at it."'

'Perhaps. But if that was the status quo, why call Montand to remind him of it? He knew what was coming to him. Surely, she would have called only if something had changed. Perhaps she hinted that all was not well with this new will. Or even that it was an unmitigated disaster. What does Montand do then? Say "Never mind, I'm looking forward to losing everything, destroying the community, facing charges of mismanagement and possibly prison?" No, he resolves to stop the will being registered even if it means killing the registrar. And a few minutes before that meeting was due to start, Caroline was killed.'

'Was she ever,' Bonbon said. 'A vicious blow.'

'Indeed. We've been over everyone's movements at the scene in some detail and concluded, mainly because of the time frame, that it's improbable Montand could himself have killed her. But he could have had an accomplice. We've speculated about the shadowy figure he *and* Zep, remember, mentioned seeing in the front garden. From the timing alone, that figure could have been Montand's bottom-feeder of a brother-in-law Guy

Vaselle, whom we had released and returned to La Crague at 5.35, about an hour and twenty minutes before the murder. At 5.37, he took a call from Montand on his mobile which lasted almost two minutes. It looks as if Vaselle, though not the only possible suspect, may well have been in Position A to have killed Caroline. We need to trace where he went after Wanda dropped him off. I've put in a call to her and I've already got a couple of uniforms on it.'

Granot had been tugging away at his moustache for the past five minutes. 'We've said before though, that if the figure *was* Montand's accomplice, it's unlikely he would have drawn our attention to him.'

'Which could be exactly why he *did* bring it to our attention. For that and a reason I'll come to in a moment, I'm having Guy Vaselle picked up a second time. Bonbon – I'd like you to lead this time.'

'Sure.'

'Flak – you free to second?'

'Definitely.'

'Sorted.'

A dubious-looking Perand gave his stubble a scratch. 'Vaselle and Montand make weird accomplices, chief. They can't stand each other, I hear.'

'I hear that as well but a common goal can unite anyone. Especially when the stakes are high. Let's look a bit closer at the Bad Caroline scenario. Put this together: when she leaves Paillaud in La Poche, she knows she is carrying a highly significant document, one that takes on a different connotation when she hears that Paillaud is dead and so no longer around to interfere. What if, she says to herself, I don't register this utterly disastrous new will? What if I suggest to Montand that I shred it? Everyone in the community would benefit. Although no one but Montand, obviously, would know that. It must be their secret. So she tells us that Paillaud had arranged to meet her only to say goodbye – an implausibility. She tells us he had made no new will – a lie, it looks like. In a conversation she has about Montand with her lover, Jodie, she doesn't tell her that she was meeting him shortly afterwards – not a lie but a suspicious omission. She doesn't write Montand's name in the appropriate slot in her diary – another suspicious omission.'

Flaco raised a hand. 'Now, the Zep entry, Captain?'

Perand rolled his eyes. 'It's Kerthus, the human tape loop all over again.' Mugging imbecility, he bleated, 'Was it Daniela?'

Flaco turned slowly towards him.

'What?' Perand said, avoiding the flaying gaze. 'Just a joke. Jesus.'

Her point made, Flaco turned back to Darac and raised a questioning eyebrow. 'Zep?'

Unflinching tenacity, a hint of menace; Flaco's characteristic performance made Darac smile. Perand's reminded him that despite recent signs to the contrary, the sardonic kid he didn't particularly care for was alive and kicking. 'It's coming, Flak, but what do you think of this Bad Caroline scenario?'

'Jodie told me that to begin with, she didn't like Caroline. She could be wilful and mischievous, she said. But it's a long way from there to venal, Captain.'

'The promise of, say, a hundred-thousand euro kickback might get you there quickly.'

Flaco folded her arms, considering the point. 'It could and the scenario does fit better with the facts as we know them.'

The black desk phone rang.

'Go ahead, Charvet.'

'The FCDDV have finally got back to me. No new will for Ambroise Paillaud was registered by Mademoiselle Rosay yesterday.'

'Or by anyone else?' Darac said, voicing a what if question he had been keeping to himself.

'No one else.'

Darac ended the call. 'I don't think we're surprised by that, are we?'

'It went in the shredder, alright,' Perand said. 'Go, Erica.'

'Indeed.' Darac opened Caroline's diary. 'So – the famous Zep entry. I've been studying those three hastily penned characters. More importantly, Louise Ouârd has been studying them. Or rather a scan I sent her along with a load of other stuff.'

'Who's Louise Ouârd?' Bonbon heard himself. 'To sound as if I'm talking gibberish.'

'R.O. put me on to her,' Darac said, resisting the urge to add further euphony. 'She's a graphology specialist. Works out of Lyon.'

Bonbon seemed a little put-out. 'Outsourcing? I know it's not her speciality as such but Erica's not too shabby in that department.'

'She's got enough on with the recon job, hasn't she? Besides R.O. reckons Ouârd is the best in Europe now Filliard's retired.'

'I didn't even know he had.' Granot shook his head. 'A good man. They come and they go... What does Madame say?'

'Even without seeing the originals, she is convinced that whoever wrote the name Zep into the 7 o'clock space, it was not Caroline herself. The forger was obviously trying to implicate him in her murder. The good doctor was right next door at the time, don't forget.'

Bonbon's face fell. 'So Zep's open access routine with us earlier was genuine? Pity. I'd taken an irrational dislike to the man. Did she have any thoughts on who might have written it?'

'Oh yes. Of the samples I sent, she reckoned it *could* have been Monsieur Guy Vaselle; Vaselle trying to disguise his hand as Caroline's. Only *could*, though, partly because I was only able to send the signature from his statement and from various official docs. We'll harvest some of his freehand shortly.'

'What about Montand?' Flaco pressed her lips together. 'Although he didn't make a signed statement.'

Perand grinned his lopsided grin. 'We could always photograph a urinal.'

'No need. There are plenty of examples of his handwriting

around.' Darac's gaze fell on the Gaggia and lingered. He got to his feet, thought better of it again and headed for the water cooler. 'Interestingly, Ouârd thinks his is the least likely hand to have mimicked Caroline's. Again, she can't be certain without seeing the materials themselves. But she was pretty sure.'

'Vaselle,' Bonbon said. 'It's feeling like him, isn't it? The violence of the blow, alone. Vicious. Powerful.'

Perand shook his head. 'There are cases of kids doing worse. Young girls, even.'

'Yes but it's rare.'

The black desk phone rang once again.

'Hit it, Erica. We're hanging on your every word, here. Almost literally.'

'In that case, you'll be glad to know I've just put together a couple of complete words from the document.'

'And?'

'We're on track.'

# 37

The receptionist held on to Jodie's hand as if fearing her imminent collapse. 'Listen to me. Yes, you're a little marvel. Yes, you have a big heart.' Her face, round as a melon and garishly made-up, creased in matronly concern. 'But I know what I would be like if my best mate had been butchered like that. You have to take some time off. I'll ask Doctor if you don't want to.'

Jodie tried to free her hand. 'I know you mean well but I need to work.'

'I am not taking no for—'

'Listen. She wasn't my best mate. She was my lover.'

The receptionist was thrown momentarily but she gripped Jodie's hand all the tighter. 'Think I'm shocked? I'm not. I had crushes on girls at school.' She indicated the photo of a horse-faced, joyless-looking man on her desk. 'Until dreamboat there came along.'

It took Jodie a good couple of minutes to extricate herself. After the final client on her list, she found herself in a similar lockdown with Arnaud Zep.

'Have you checked your blood-sugar levels today? A shock such as you've suffered can wreak havoc, you know.'

'Of course I have.'

He nodded. 'Of course. Sorry. But I do want you seriously to consider taking some time off.'

He offered no resistance as she withdrew her hand. 'Arnaud, thanks. It's very nice of you. Everyone, well, almost everyone, is being very nice but I need to keep busy. Surely you of all people can see that?'

Zep's whirlpool of a face took on a more turbulent roil. '*Who* isn't being nice? Tell me and I'll punch their lights out.' He smiled thinly. 'Unless it's Captain Darac, of course. Or that female officer. Falco? I suspect both of them could wipe the floor with me.'

'It's Flaco. No, all the police are being very sweet.'

'Being or been?' Zep said, bending to lace up his running shoes.

'What? Oh, I see. I think they've probably finished interviewing me but one of the lieutenants is using the gym at the Centre. He needs to lose a lot of weight. I'm helping him.'

Zep got to his feet. 'Just make sure *you* don't lose any. So who is giving you grief?'

'Oh, Tina. She has a hard side that comes out now and again. But I can look after myself.' She looked into his eyes. 'Arnaud, I need to tell you something about Caroline and me.'

He essayed the smile once more. 'Oh?'

'We were lovers.'

Zep's face fell. 'Oh.'

'Don't tell me *you* disapprove?'

'No, no, of course not. It's just...'

'Yes?'

'She was...You're so different.'

'You can't judge. You hardly knew her.'

'Well, that's true.'

Zep's intercom buzzed. He kept his eyes on Jodie as he pressed the receive button.

'Sorry, Doctor, but is Jodie still with you?'

He raised his eyebrows. She nodded. 'Yes, she is.'

'A gentleman staggered in just now complaining of a severe rick in his back. I sent him packing.'

'Oh, Lord,' Jodie said, the words carried on an exhausted breath.

'I know what we said but Jodie's adamant she wants to work.

We should respect that.'

'That's not why I got rid of him. He asked for her by name and when he got outside, he skipped off towards his car like a spring lamb. He's a reporter. Press.'

'Press?'

Jodie was away and through the door before Zep could stop her.

She caught sight of the interloper as he was climbing into his car. 'You! What the fuck do you want?'

'Mademoiselle Foucault,' he shouted. 'The old bat in reception said no one of that name has ever worked here. Funny it's on your Meet Our Staff board, then, complete with photo. Crap though it is.' He took out his mobile and pointed it at her. 'Let's do better. Smile.'

The look on the man's face only strengthened Jodie's determination to kick him in the balls, headbutt him – whatever would cause the most pain. But flying out in her wake, Zep caught her by the waist and, turning his back on the reporter, held her close into him. 'This will be in the papers tomorrow, Jodie. Don't make it any worse. For you, for Caroline, for everyone.'

The reporter was advancing towards them. Jodie knew she could wriggle free but she saw the sense in Zep's words. 'How does he know about me?'

'Tina?'

'She wouldn't say anything.' But she knew who might. 'I'll kill the gossiping old bastard.'

'No you won't, Jodie. Let's go back in. Don't rise to his bait. Come on.'

The reporter followed, circling them, shooting, firing off questions, goading. In her head, Jodie was back on the balance beam, the camera tight-in as she gathered herself for the pirouette into three forward somersaults that no one else in France was attempting; the move she had only just landed the time before; the move that this time, she didn't. *That* cameraman got his money shot, alright.

The reporter was faring less well. Wherever he pointed his camera, Zep and Jodie turned away as if by magnetic repulsion. As one gyrating entity, they reached the entrance doors where the receptionist was waiting, a bumper edition of *Immo D'Azur* rolled up in her fist. As Zep pushed through the door, Jodie thrust out a hand, grabbed the reporter's mobile and hurled it as high and wide as she could.

'Bitch!' He spun around. Gazing upwards, he was a sitting duck for the receptionist who gave him a good clump on his ear with the magazine. The mobile was dropping towards a seating area surrounding a small pond. 'No!' The reporter gathered himself and, thrusting out a hand, ran off in pursuit. With perfect comic timing, he arrived just as the projectile plopped pleasantly into the water. All that was missing was a headlong plunge into the pond and the sequence would have been pure Monsieur La Chute. If Jodie hadn't been so fired up, she might have laughed.

'Well done, both of you,' Zep said locking the doors. 'Hell of a throw. Hell of a smack.' He turned to them. 'Now I'm calling the police.'

## 38

Darac gave the desk a rap as he closed the report and then rang Mobile Control. 'Patch me through to Wanda Korneliuk, will you? Unless she's in active pursuit, of course.'

'She isn't, Captain, but it wouldn't worry her anyway. Just a moment.'

Pursuit or not, when she came on, her car sounded to be going 200 kms per hour.

'Yes, Captain?'

'Wanda – if you ever tire of scaring half the drivers in the Alpes Maritimes to death, would you consider a move to the P.J.? Officers who think on their feet as well as you do are always needed.'

'Thanks but no thanks, Captain. *Out of the way, sweetie...* Glad what I did helped, though. *That's the boy.*'

Darac could picture the driver scurrying out of Wanda's path. 'We were getting Vaselle in again anyway but you've given us enough to arrest him this time.'

'It's a pity I couldn't have got back to you sooner. *You stay there, darling...* But I didn't realise I had anything. On the night, I was ordered away on a call before I saw anything material, then after that, I went off shift. I assumed Vaselle had pulled up where he did at random – I didn't know anything about Caroline Rosay, where she lived or anything. *A quad bike, seriously? Nearside lane, buddy.* I didn't hear about the murder until I came back on an hour ago and you contacted me. If I had, I'd have rung you at the time.'

'You would, I know. Just need to be clear on the timings you recorded. You're certain about them?'

'Completely.'

Darac thanked her again, emailed the report to his team and called Bonbon.

'Job for you.'

'Yes?'

'Look in your inbox.'


When he finally left the office, Darac had been glancing at his watch every ten minutes for the past hour. Carrying an espresso cup and a steaming earthenware mug, his destination would have been obvious to anyone he passed – Frankie's love of mint tea was almost as legendary as his own for coffee. What was different was the shallowness of the nut-brown nectar in his cup. The deeply anxious feeling in his heart, he hoped was far less obvious.

First, he had to sign out of the building. Charvet was working the duty officer's desk, chatting with a man who looked less like an off-duty *flic* than an Italian film idol of the '60s. It was partly his outfit: crisp, button-down black cotton shirt; pure white cotton slacks; tan loafers. It was partly his looks: crisp, button-down black hair; pure white teeth, tan skin. Somewhere down in the compound, a young Claudia Cardinale just had to be waiting for him at the wheel of a blood-red convertible.

'Darac!' the man said as if he hadn't seen him in years. 'How goes it?'

'Want the truth, Armani?'

'No.'

'Then it's going brilliantly.' He indicated the tray. 'I'm on a mission here.'

'She can wait. Listen...' Slipping an arm around Darac's shoulders, he took him almost furtively to one side. 'A little bird told me you drew Evans.'

The words were meaningless syllables in Darac's head.

Armani drew the tips of his fingers together and shook them. 'The Tour sweep? Cadel Evans? The red–hot... no hoper from Australia?'

'Ah, yes. Evans. I thought he was the favourite?'

Armani's eyebrows rose. 'Says who? Granot? Bonbon? Pah! *Imbecilli*! Both of them.'

'Yes, well while you find your way back to central casting, I'll just take this—'

'Wait. I'll give you twenty euros for your Evans ticket. Here and now. Last offer. No bidding war this time.'

'Hold this.' He handed Armani the tray and began fishing around in his pockets.

The smile was dazzling. 'You accept?'

'If I can find it.'

Armani's smile disappeared. The brow lowered, darkly. 'No strings, now. No trips to the jazz club or anything.'

'No strings.' He found the ticket. 'Here and keep your money. If he wins, buy me a drink.' He took the tray. 'Charvet?'

'I hope that's a decaffeinated espresso you've got there, Captain?'

'There's no such thing.'

*Bzzzzzzzut!*


Darac hesitated outside Frankie's office.

'Oh, Paul. Is it that time already? Come in.'

No smile. No softening. No chair pulled up next to hers. He set out the drinks on the desk and sat down opposite her. He was used to arriving at a crime scene not knowing what he would find and taking it from there. He was used to turning tunes inside out on the bandstand having no preconception of where he was going with them. He needed something of the same spirit now. As full as his heart was, his mind was blank.

'I've just had some tea. I should have asked you not to bring one over.'

'Shall we just leave the cup there between us?' His words emerged as if someone else were saying them. 'Like in a Douglas Sirk movie?' *What the hell am I doing?* 'Remember the Sirk season at Cinéma Mercury? We managed to see a good few of them together.'

'I remember it.'

Her orange-flecked green eyes hadn't lost their lustre. Her hair was the luxuriant black mane it always was. But she looked drawn, nevertheless, and the expressive touches – the eyebrow choreography, the purses and pouts of her lips, the one-shoulder shrugs – were all conspicuous by their absence.

She went to the door and locked it. As she returned to the desk, his hand lifted towards hers but she had already passed. Passed without the familiar slipstream of her perfume.

She picked up a phone. 'No calls.'

'Have you run out of *Marucca* at the moment, Frankie?'

'No.'

'Right.'

Nothing was said for a moment and then both of them spoke at once. Darac hoped Frankie hadn't caught what he'd said. It sounded ridiculous. Perhaps she had had something better. 'You first.'

'The world's media are all over Paillaud/Rosay, aren't they? How's it going?'

Was this how it was going to be? A reporter asking a prepared question could scarcely have sounded more dispassionate.

'It's... puzzling. Erica's being brilliant, though. We gave her a seriously shredded handwritten document and she found almost straight away that it had been signed by Paillaud. An hour or so ago she was able to put "my will" together, too, as in "This is my will." And we've just had what could prove a break-through on the murder itself.'

'Good. And Granot tells me he's knuckling down to his new health regime.'

'To the point of obsession which is perfect, of course.' Darac sipped his coffee. 'And while we're on the subject, forty-eight cups of this stuff a day isn't good for you, apparently. It's given me myokymia.' *Playing the sympathy card, now? You snivelling shit, Darac.* 'Which is a serious-sounding name for a trivial condition. But it seems that cutting down the caffeine is a good idea. You've always said that, I know.'

'And did you listen?'

'I'm listening now.' Another small sip finished the espresso. 'But anyway, Granot's on track. That's the main thing.'

'Absolutely.' Her expression didn't change. 'You don't want to lose *him*, do you?'

A chill splintered Darac's sinking heart. 'I don't want to lose you, Frankie. Ever.'

'No?'

'Stop it. Of course I don't. You know I love you. Deeply.'

'And just how am I supposed to know that?'

'Frankie—'

'No, Paul.' Her eyes were wide. '*How* do I know? Because of all the hand-holding and kissing in corners and then a phone rings, and so we still haven't been to bed? Because, as the very model of a modern man, you never seek to take the lead, prompt or even offer advice when I can't decide what to do for the best? Whether to tell Christophe? Whether to grin and bear it? Whether to just leave him?'

Wasn't she forgetting something here? Hadn't they *agreed* to try and keep their feelings in check?

'Frankie, think back to February when we finally accepted what was happening between us. The flood gates were about to open and we knew it. It was then that your concerns for Christophe's wellbeing deepened and you asked me to help you keep those gates firmly closed.' He shook his head. 'My God, Frankie, I have put my back into that effort. Like nothing ever before.'

'I know I asked for your forbearance at the beginning and we both found that difficult. But haven't we moved on since then?'

Her eyes misted. 'I know you understand that for me "no" could never mean "yes". I'm a feminist, after all, a woman who knows her own mind, a leader, strong. Yes I am those things but let me tell you something you should have understood weeks ago.' Her hand went to her forehead. 'Sometimes, *everyone* needs a sign.'

Darac couldn't bear to see Frankie like this. He made to get to his feet, 'Let me—'

'No, stay there. Please.' She dabbed her eyes. 'I haven't finished. You have known for a whole month that Marseille have been trying to lure me. Your reaction? Nothing. Let her go, if she wants to. Of course, if you'd said "No, I forbid it," that would have destroyed—'

'Wait a minute, wait a minute. Known for a *month*? And only an *offer* of a job? I didn't hear a word about this until yesterday when Christophe told me you were definitely going. And I've been trying to talk to you about it ever since.'

'But Christophe broached it on that awful evening on the boat.'

'What?'

'The cruise – the anniversary celebration. He took you to the back of the thing, the stern or whatever they call it, specifically to tell you.'

In his bewilderment, Darac found a seed of hope. 'No, he didn't, Frankie. When we got there, all he talked about was something to do with... plastics recycling. It was riveting, let me tell you.'

'And so you switched off for a minute. I would have, too.'

'I swear to you he didn't say a word about Marseille, a possible move, or you at all, come to that.'

Frankie's expression changed so rapidly, it was like watching a time lapse movie. 'He *didn't*?' She smiled, bewildered, her words spluttering through tears. 'He didn't tell you?'

'If he had, I might have pushed him off the boat there and then. The bastard.'

'He isn't a bastard.' She looked exhausted, suddenly. 'But he is still in love with me. I see that more than ever.'

Darac saw something, too. 'He told you he *had* mentioned it?'

She nodded.

'Did he say how I'm supposed to have reacted?'

'That it was a great opportunity for me but that you'd all be sorry to see me go.' As if hugging herself, she drew her arms across her torso. 'Which is what you probably would have said. To him.'

Darac looked away, trying to put the thing together in his head; trying to temper hope, anger, blame, self-recrimination. 'If you had just asked me then what I really thought about the news, this... horrible distance would never have opened up between us.'

'I was waiting for you to say something.'

'Waiting... I guess you were used to that.' He let out a long breath. 'Christophe and me. I think one of us is going to be in a very lonely place, soon.'

'I think so, too.'

'And Marseille?'

'I'm flattered they courted me so assiduously. And there have been times over the last few days when I was on the verge of saying yes.' She shook her head. 'I can't tell you how relieved I am that I didn't.'

It was only then that Darac felt the full force of what had happened. The yawning chasm of loss, the stuff of his nightmares since his mother's death when he was just twelve, opened up at his feet as if making a final attempt to claim him. Even as he managed to step back from it, he felt as if he was going to weep as all the tension drained from his body. 'I thought you were gone for ever.'

'Paul...'

'Tonight.' He took her hands. 'No more waiting.'

She looked into his eyes. 'No,' she said, softly. 'No more waiting.'

# 39

'Don't be ridiculous!' Bonbon said. 'That's shit and you know it, Vaselle.'

The lawyer gave him an outraged look.

Bonbon was a study in contrition. 'I'm sorry. Old habits die hard.' He turned once more to the suspect. 'That's shit and you know it, *Monsieur* Vaselle. You have a problem with that? You see, until this interrogation concludes, our friend here can do nothing for you but look daggers at me over his specs occasionally. And *then* all he can do is ask questions and talk through a few technicalities with you. This isn't the good old U.S of A. "Don't answer that!" etcetera doesn't work here. You may as well dismiss him. Wouldn't you, Flak?'

She treated the lawyer to a full-on scowl. 'I'd take it under advisement.'

Vaselle eyed the man as if he were seriously considering the move.

'Although his presence does ensure one thing,' Bonbon went on. 'It means I won't set about you.'

'You, you scrawny bastard?' Vaselle laughed. 'Fuck off!'

Bonbon bared his teeth. 'I'm a biter.' He mimed the action. 'Lethal. But back to my question. Where did you go and what did you do when the police driver dropped you off at your car on the evening of Mademoiselle Rosay's murder? Just to remind you, dropped you off a mere three-minute drive from her villa?'

'I told you. I drove home.'

'You drove home straight away?'

Vaselle's eyes slid sideways.

'He can't help you. Answer!'

Vaselle readjusted the lie of his gonads while he thought about it. 'Now that I think—'

'Steady, boy.'

Vaselle got to his feet. 'Fuck off!' A forefinger stabbed the air. 'I mean it!'

'Sit down, for goodness sake.' Mugging concern for the man's sanity, Bonbon leaned in to Flaco and muttered 'Talk about a violent temper' just loud enough to carry across the table. 'And have you seen the size of his hands? Wielding a rock is no problem to him.'

Flaco nodded and made the note on her pad.

'Sit, sit, monsieur,' Bonbon said, lightly.

Vaselle sat down, folded his thick forearms, and then, as if realising it was a counterproductive look, unfolded them and laid his hands in his lap.

Bonbon smiled at him. 'I don't know why you weren't thinking before but now that you are, let's hear what you've come up with.'

'I didn't drive off straight away and I never said I did.'

Thanks to Wanda's report, Bonbon knew where Vaselle had gone and for how long.

'I went to Bar de la Place and had a couple of drinks. I needed them after what I'd been through with her.' He tossed Flaco a nod. 'And that other f—fellow.'

'Acting Commissaire Darac, you mean?'

'Dunno. Didn't catch the name.'

Wanda had noted that Vaselle had sunk three large tumblers of whisky with beer chasers at the bar. He had stayed for an hour and four minutes. 'What did you drink? How long did you stay?'

'Two small cognacs. A quarter of an hour. They'll vouch for me.'

'Uh-huh. Then what did you do?'

'Drove home, like I said.'

'Does your route normally take you past Mademoiselle

Rosay's villa?'

Vaselle jerked as if he'd been jabbed in the ribs. The lawyer twitched as if he knew he was on a loser.

'No.'

'But on this occasion?'

'Yeah, well... To be honest—'

'Honest?' Bonbon broke into a laugh. 'Well, why not? Give it a go.'

Vaselle's hot temper seemed to be cooling. 'I had a few more drinks than I said. The car was pointing in the wrong direction and I didn't want to reverse it. So I set off up the hill and went round. It was easier.'

'Did you stop en route?'

'No.'

Bonbon brought his hand down too hard on the table but he hid his pain. 'Liar!'

'Hang on. Now that I—'

'You've done that one.'

'Yes, uh... I did stop. But just to pee. That's the honest truth.'

'The "few more drinks" you had were actually industrial quantities of whisky and beer, right?' Bonbon glanced at his notes. 'Canadian Club and Peroni, to be exact.' He looked up, grinning. 'We have eyes everywhere.'

Vaselle froze. He was in trouble and he knew it. The lawyer looked away and sighed.

'*Where* did you stop to relieve yourself?'

'Just on the road. On the roadside.'

'You know, Guy... I may call you that? I really think you'd better start telling the truth.' Usually, Bonbon's eyes were things of twinkling merriment. But he knew how to level a suspect in a cold stare. 'We're waiting.'

Vaselle's shoulders slumped. 'I... I don't know why I did it.'

'Did what, monsieur? Kill Mademoiselle Caroline Rosay?'

'No! *That* I didn't do.'

'You're a brute of a man, Vaselle. Violent. Hot-tempered.'

He also had terrible taste in leisure shorts but Bonbon decided to keep that to himself. 'You have also lied. Repeatedly. As the brother-in-law and employee of Mayor Hervé Montand, you stood to lose a great deal if Rosay registered a new will that effectively disinherited the commune.'

'*Everybody* connected with La Crague stood to lose. And why aren't you talking to Hervé? He would be the biggest loser of the lot.'

'Because he wasn't seen in Mademoiselle Rosay's front garden at the time of her murder. You were.'

'By the fat fairy who lives next door, no doubt.' He sneered. 'Brice fucking Kerthus.'

*No*, Bonbon thought to himself. *By your tail, Wanda 'The Wheel' Korneliuk.* But Kerthus was the natural assumption and Bonbon saw no reason to correct it.

'He's a pervert. Probably jerked himself off watching me.' Vaselle's expression said he was about to offer irrefutable proof of innocence. 'I had my dick out, right? How could I kill anybody? I was pissing on the bitch's precious gravel. And up her trees.'

Eyes wide, the lawyer emitted a series of restraining sounds in his throat.

Bonbon was equally incredulous. 'Out of all the places you could have stopped, you chose the home of a woman you clearly detest; a woman who was battered to death a few minutes later? To summarise: you've placed yourself at the scene of a murder *and* you had motive, means and opportunity. Think of the odds against you *not* being guilty! You killed her. Admit it!'

'No! I didn't go near the house. I went no further than the drive. Just a couple of metres off the road.' He shook his head. 'Look, it was stupid, what I did. Childish. But that's what my life is now. Working for my fucking brother-in-law...'

There was no stopping Vaselle and as the LED on the recording device blinked off the seconds, Bonbon remained silent and still. Under the table, a knee-to-knee signal told Flaco to follow suit.

'... I used to have my own building business. I've won awards.

You know the ranch-style bungalows on the La Gaude – Peyron road? I built them. The Santina Apartments in Saint-Laurent? They're mine as well. What's Hervé ever built? What's he ever done? Nothing. Everything he's got has been given to him. Inherited. And he's still at it. You think he's a milksop, don't you? A puffed-up sissy. And he is. But let me tell you something you don't know. He's a madman. Yeah! A fucking little Hitler.'

Bonbon waited to see if anything had been left in the pipe-line. There appeared to be nothing. 'Let's rewind. There you are, sprainting Mademoiselle Rosay's greenery—'

'I told you I was. And the word is spraying.'

Bonbon knew from Wanda's report that, having ignored several calls already, she had been ordered back to work at this point. Since Kerthus hadn't seen Vaselle on the night, Bonbon had no more eyewitness testimony to call on. He also knew that Vaselle didn't realise that.

'Tell us what you did *after* you finished relieving yourself,' Bonbon said. 'And if I were you, I'd think carefully before you answer.'

'I went straight back to my car and drove home.'

Bonbon gave Flaco a look, then the lawyer, then Vaselle.

'Think *carefully*, I said. One more chance.'

'I swear on my mother's life, I went back to my car and drove home. Kerthus must have seen that, right? Because it's what I did. Ask him again!'

Vaselle's entreaty gave Bonbon pause. In mistakenly believing that Kerthus had followed his entire performance, Vaselle, ironi-cally, had succeeded in making a persuasive point in his defence. 'Did you see anyone else arrive? Doctor Zep? Montand?'

'No. They must have got there after I'd left. And I didn't see them on the way, either.'

'Did you see anyone else lurking in the shrubbery? Or down the side of the villa?'

'No.'

Entertaining the possibility more and more that Vaselle was

telling the truth, Bonbon changed the angle of attack. 'You're innocent of this crime, right? Nothing to hide.'

'I keep telling you.'

Bonbon thrust a pen and a piece of paper across the desk. 'Dictation time, Vaselle. No difficult spellings, don't worry.'

'What's this? What are you trying to do? Trick me?'

'You've got nothing to hide, remember.'

Vaselle picked up the pen as if it might be booby-trapped. 'What shall I put?'

'Your name. Not a signature. Just your name. In full.'

He completed the task without mishap.

'Leave a space and write Caroline Rosay's name.'

'Why?'

'Do it.'

Vaselle obliged and Bonbon continued in the same vein until Vaselle had written the names of all the principals in the case except one. 'Who's left?' Bonbon said to Flaco.

'We haven't had Doctor Zep.'

'Oh yes. Put that as well for luck.'

Vaselle did as he was told. Bonbon took the paper and without looking at it, put it between two sheets of white card and slipped it into a document box. 'Thanks for that.'

Somehow, the writing test seemed to calm Vaselle but as he sat back in his chair, signs of strain began to show once more. 'How long are you going to keep me here this time? Before you have to let me go? Eh? How long?'

Flaco dropped her pen, bent to pick it up, and then leaned into Bonbon. 'Thought so,' she whispered. 'He's wearing the same sandals as yesterday.'

'What's your shoe size?'

'Forty-two wide. What's yours?'

'Take them off.' Bonbon opened a paper bag. 'And put them in there.'

## 40

Taking a call from Ridge Clay, Darac stood and gazed out of his office window at the compound below. The same bodies on the move as yesterday. The same cars. The same conversations. Same joshing. Same arguments. Except that yesterday, it all seemed random and meaningless. Now everything was back in its proper place. Everything made sense; real life playing a version of Coltrane's 'My Favourite Things'.

'So Frankie, huh?' Ridge said, his bass voice almost too deep to register in the mobile's earpiece. 'I'm stoked for you, Garfield. And I've got news, too. Those Phronesis boys – the trio playing the second set at the festival? Busy guys, right? But I asked them if they'd like to play the club sometime. They said they would.'

'Yeah? That's great. When?'

'A.S.A.P.'

Darac understood hundreds of Ridge's Gallicised English idioms but the abbreviation flummoxed him. 'Again?'

'*Aussitôt que possible.*'

'Ah. But much as I rate them, not a Thursday, OK? Thursdays are ours.'

'Listen, I'd never bump the DMQ for anyone.'

'Thanks, man.'

'Except Sonny, of course.'

'That's fair enough.'

'And Kenny. Dianne. Herbie...'

Darac's external desk phone rang. 'Saved by the bell, I suspect, Ridge. Got to go. See you tomorrow night.'

'You guys opening with Blues For Marco?'

Reminded that not everything was in its proper place, a chill ran down Darac's spine. 'Oh yes. Has to be.'

'That's right.'

Darac ended the call and picked up the outside line.

'Captain Darac? This is Maurice Férion.'

# 41

Fresh from the locker room, Granot was the colour of a boiled lobster – one with immaculately combed hair. Jodie was waiting for him in the corridor.

'Done twenty-five steps already,' he said, indicating the new toy clipped to his belt. 'Cumulative.'

'It will record tranches of other data too, but you're wise to stick just to the step counter at the moment.'

He beamed at it fondly as they set off toward the foyer. 'Like my very own offender's tag. How many steps should I do in a day?'

'Ten thousand or so.'

'Seriously.'

'I am serious but don't get paranoid about it.'

He was never so sure of anything in his life. 'I'll try not to.'

'And what about me, Roland? Am I getting paranoid? Chucking a mobile in the pond, I ask you. What happened to the reporter, in the end?'

Granot saw no harm in answering. 'I reckon he'll be having an uncomfortable time of it at Commissariat Foch.' In fact, he knew the man would be – Granot had had a word with one of his many mates there. 'He'll get off with a warning but it might make him think twice next time. You know *why* he stooped to harassing you like that?'

'To get a reaction.'

'Indeed and that's because he's a scandal sheet hack who has no other weapons at his disposal. But be careful, Jodie. This case is big news and there'll be worse than him out there. In fact, there'll be reporters of every stripe. If anyone approaches you again, the best thing to do is say nothing.'

'I'll try.'

It was only a few metres from the locker room but reaching the foyer prompted Granot to check his step count. 'Fifty-six. Soon be cracking the hundred. Right, it's time to have a word with your boss and one Denis Golou.'

Jodie grinned, tilting the scar on her cheek. 'So you've discovered our Deepak's secret.'

'Wouldn't be much of a flic if I hadn't.'

'Why...' Jodie looked over her shoulder. Sonia was at her desk but out of earshot. 'Why do you want to talk to them? If you're allowed to say.'

'I couldn't divulge their replies but I can tell you what I'm going to ask them.'

'Yes?'

'I'm going to ask where they were at the time your...' As a police detective of over twenty-five years standing, Granot had witnessed just about everything of which human beings were capable. And yet the lobster had turned a shade redder at the prospect of coming up with an appropriate term. '... at the time Caroline was killed.'

Jodie's face fell. 'Caro and I loved each other, Roland. You don't approve?'

'Of love? Of course I do. There isn't enough of it in the world.' He shook his chops. 'I suppose I'm just set in my ways about some things.' He smiled, ruefully. 'It's a weakness. Forgive me.'

'No forgiveness necessary. If I didn't think it would embarrass you all over again, I'd give you a kiss.'

'I said I was set in my ways, not a shrinking violet.'

He offered up his cheek and she obliged.

'Jodie, I want you to have absolutely no doubts that we are doing everything we can to find Caroline's killer.' He thought of Erica. 'We have people doing the most extraordinary work to get to the truth.'

'Thank you. I know you are.' She seemed to brighten. 'You were going to ask Tina and Deepak where they were at 7 o'clock last night? Don't be surprised if it turns out they were together.'

Granot raised a shaggy eyebrow. 'They're an item?'

'Not exclusively. Especially on his side. Teenage girls are his thing. And he's theirs, believe me. They can't get enough of him.'

'Impressionable young girls is one thing. But what does Tina see in him?'

'He has a hidden talent. The sort she likes.'

'Oh?'

'Actually, in those pyjamas he insists on wearing, it's not all that hidden, half the time.'

'Ah. I see.'

As if spirited up by the mention of Deepak, a couple of scantily clad girls sashayed past, necks craning all around. At the reception desk, Sonia trained her beatific smile on them and then, eyes rolling, shared a look with Jodie.

'I love Sonia,' she said. 'She's so funny.' Her expression losing all its animation suddenly, Jodie stared into space and when she spoke, her words emerged in an absent diminuendo. '*Caro* could be really funny. At times. She used to... have me in stitches.'

Granot thought it best to move on. 'Jodie, there is one thing I've been meaning to ask you. Jodie?'

She was still staring off into the distance. 'Fell off a balance beam. I was 14. Am I scared of high places? No. Am I scared of things like rope bridges? Yes.'

'Pardon?'

Exhaling deeply, she lightly grasped his forearm. 'I'm sorry, Roland. I wasn't listening. I've got so used to people asking me how I got this scar on my cheek.'

'I would never ask that.' Flaco had already told him, anyway. 'No, no.'

'Sure.' She withdrew her hand. 'What did you want to ask?'

'It's about something that's been puzzling us. You might just have the answer.'

'I have another client in a couple of minutes.'

'This will only take a second. It's about Caroline's diary. Against the final Friday of each month, a three-dot pattern appears in the margin. Irrespective of the number of days, February included. Next to yesterday's entry, the dots were rubbed out with an eraser we found in the same spot. Why the dots? Why the erasure? Can you enlighten us?'

It seemed that Darac wasn't the only one to look for answers in the floor. Finally, Jodie shook her head. 'Sorry. I can't.'

'I don't have them with me but perhaps if I showed you the pages?' He remembered there had been a droplet of blood on the diary cover. 'Just photocopies. Might that help?'

'It *might*.'

Hearing the sound of approaching footsteps, they turned and saw Tina stomping towards them carrying a large cardboard box. She looked less than happy with life.

'I'm thinking of installing headsets in this place. Your buttock strain has been standing outside the treatment room for the past two minutes, Jodie.'

*Buttock strain? And you're another one*, Granot thought, but he said, 'It's my fault, madame.'

'I'm going now, Tina.' Jodie shook hands with Granot. 'Good work today, Roland. I'll think about that question in the meantime.'

As the two women crossed, Tina looked past Jodie at Granot. 'Lieutenant? Ever heard that if you want something doing properly, do it yourself?'

'Heard it? I invented it.'

She set down her load. 'Would you swap my and Deepak's interviews around? He's waiting over in my office.'

'Of course.'

She indicated the box. 'I've got this to sort out.'

Granot looked at it and noticed something else. 'Could I ask you something just informally for a second, Madame Sicotte?'

'Tina, please.'

Inclining his head, Granot smiled as if he'd been granted a long-held wish. 'Tina. I've always been fascinated by professional sportswomen. Their capabilities in relation to men. Their natural advantages and disadvantages, and so on.'

'We get paid squat compared to the guys. That's all you need to know.' She hoisted the box easily on to her hip. 'I'll be free in about fifteen minutes.'

'This will take five seconds. I was wondering what size shoes you wear?'

# 42

Darac suggested he meet Maurice Férion at Thurién, one of Promenade des Anglais's more upmarket cafés. Glimpsed through an exuberance of palms, the azure sparkle of the Baie des Anges promised a picture-perfect backdrop – if you ignored the multi-lane drag strip in the foreground. On the terrace, Darac seated the visitor facing the view and, fanning himself with a menu, ordered a single espresso.

'You don't mind if I have a glass of wine?'

'Be my guest,' Darac said.

'This on expenses?'

'If you like, sure.'

As the waiter stood tapping his foot, Férion examined the list. Darac examined Férion. Wearing a navy and white Breton-style shirt, he was a fit-looking bald man in his late-sixties. There was something of the older Pablo Picasso about him, a Bohemian who looked as if he could have turned his hand to anything. The battered old leather shoulder bag at his sandaled feet might have contained anything from tubes of paint to plumbing tools.

'Yes. The Fleurie looks good. It is summer, after all. A bottle alright?'

'You're not driving anywhere after this?'

'No, no.' He turned to the waiter. 'The Lacombe.' Having dismissed him, Férion reached easily into his bag and took out a pack of Gitanes. 'Use these?'

'I don't but...' Férion was already lighting up. 'Feel free.'

'So you enjoyed my book, Captain? The Paillaud autobiography.'

'I did.' Darac had a raft of forensic questions for Férion but he decided they could wait. 'Very much, actually.'

'You think I caught his voice?'

Darac's habitual half-smile widened a little. 'It's hard to say. The Ambroise Paillaud of Monsieur La Chute days let his films do the talking for him and the older Paillaud seems to have had almost nothing to say on anything. Publicly, at least. And even privately, except to you and a few locals.'

'Fair point. Did anything surprise you?'

'His decision to retire to La Crague was one thing. Considering his childhood.'

'I hoped I'd hinted clearly enough at the end of the book that it was his way of giving the finger to the locals. Especially to the mayor whose father was responsible for kicking out young Ambroise and what passed for his family. Kicked them out and ordered them never to return. "Or else!" So here was Paillaud the film star returning in glory. "Look what *I* became, you losers. Now you can all lick my arse." Plays, doesn't it?'

'It makes a kind of sense. It's just that it's something I wouldn't want to do myself, I suppose.'

Férion blew out a long column of smoke. 'But I wasn't writing about you. I was writing about him. Trying to get into his head. Heaven help me.'

'Why do you say that?'

The drinks arrived, muting Férion for the moment. Quite unbidden, Darac's conversation with Frankie came back to him and a feeling of deep happiness rose in his chest and broke over him like a wave.

'Only one tray?' Férion said, as the waiter walked away. 'A disgrace to the uniform.'

'Ah, *Coming, Monsieur*! I follow you. But you were saying?'

'Yes. Paillaud was far from being cute little Monsieur La Chute in real life. Most of the time, he was an out-and-out bastard. One of the most horrible individuals I've ever had dealings with, professionally or otherwise.'

'In the book, you make it clear he was difficult.'

'Difficult?' The idea seemed to amuse him as he poured a glass of wine, flicked ash off his fag and took a slug in one almost continuous movement. 'Do you know any comedians, Captain? Personally?'

In a sense, didn't everyone? 'We-ell...'

Férion shook his head. 'I don't mean your Aunt Alice who has you in pieces when she's had a few. Or your desk sergeant who does hilarious impressions of your workmates. I mean a real, hardened, professional comedian. Do you?'

If Darac hadn't been in such a joyous mood, Férion's bullishness might have got to him a little. 'No, I don't know any.'

'How can I explain this?' He had it. 'OK, you play in a jazz group, don't you? In fact, I know you do. The Didier... Musso Quintet. That's the old journo in me, coming out: "Whatever else you do, don't screw up the names." But think of—'

'A second? Would you mind telling me how you know that? It may not be the world's best-kept secret but we never advertise the fact that I'm a *flic.*'

Férion grinned, pleased with himself. 'I know. On the group's website, for instance, it says just that you "work for the city." But your name appeared with other so-called "poètes policiers" in an article I read recently – *France's Cultured Cops.* Patrolling the mean streets one minute, writing novels and so on the next – she thought you were all the bee's knees, didn't she, the writer?'

Darac shook his head. ' "Poète policier" is one stuffed-up case away from being a pejorative term, believe me.'

'Be that as it may, when you called me, your name rang a bell. So to speak.'

'Uh-huh.'

'Anyway, I was trying to explain comedians to you. The Quintet is a pretty good outfit, I read. So you're playing somewhere – say the Jazz Festival like you're doing tomorrow night. It goes brilliantly. Crowd loves it. How do you comment about that when you leave the stage? Or the *stand*, you call it, don't you? What do you say to each other about how it went?'

Darac wasn't sure he was enjoying this level of scrutiny. 'As in "Top stuff, guys. That was great." Is that what you mean?'

'Exactly.' A second slug drained his glass. 'Now consider the language a comedian uses in that situation. They'll say "I killed them out there!" "I slayed them!" "I knocked 'em dead!".' He raised his almost hairless eyebrows. 'See what I'm saying? Comedians are by nature aggressive. Violent, even. They have a need to dominate others. And that makes them *very* difficult people to deal with.'

'Interesting.' It was time to open out. 'My team has been struck that Paillaud seems not to have kept any career memorabilia. There's nothing at the Chemin des Mimosas villa and it appears he owned no other property. You don't refer to it in the book but can you shed any light on it?'

'You've been to the villa, then?'

'Of course.'

'Yes. Makes sense. Memorabilia? Cinémathèque Française has some pieces on display and several more in store. All Paillaud bothered keeping was my book – and I do call it *my* book, Captain – and that's it, more or less.'

'The space on the wall between the two bookcases? Something appears to have been hanging there until recently. Any thoughts on that?'

He flicked ash off his fag. 'It's where the aforementioned *Coming, Monsieur!* lives. Or used to. The original print. Given to him by the photographer.'

'Brassaï.'

'Top marks!' Férion slurped down more wine. 'Jazz and photography? You're a groovy cat, Captain.'

'What happened to it? Do you know?'

'I don't.'

'Never mind. There are a few other things you can help me with if you would.'

An attractive young woman walked past the table en route

to the promenade. Férion's gaze followed her gently swaying hips.

'If only I were six months younger, eh?' he said, neither slaying Darac nor knocking him dead. 'Help you? *That*, my young friend, is why I'm here. In fact, if you hadn't contacted me, albeit *in absentia*, I was going to call you today.'

*Really?* 'What a coincidence.' Darac sipped his espresso. 'So let's start with that. Why are you here? In the area, I mean.'

Férion smiled and, keeping his eyes on Darac, took a long drag on his cigarette. 'You're going to love this. Paillaud *asked* me to come. A week ago, it was. Oh, I was wary. When I finished the book, I never wanted to have anything to do with him again. And I didn't, for years. But he offered to pay my travelling expenses, B&B accommodation – the lot. He even sent the cash! So more out of curiosity than anything, I decided to come. Got here on Thursday. Going home tomorrow.'

'Why did he want to see you?'

'The kernel of it was that he told me he was dying, that he was going to kill himself, and that it was going to be the most dramatic stunt of his life.'

Darac had been down this same avenue with Caroline. 'Kill himself when?'

'He didn't specify. I was as shocked as anyone else when I heard why he hadn't turned up at MAMAC.'

'You had arranged to meet him for the Brassaï show?'

'Yes. I'd spent several hours with him at his place on Thursday. It was agreed then.'

'Did he want you to write an exclusive on the story? Is that it? A sensational coda to the book? Because if he did, I'll have to caution—'

'No, no, I'm not writing anything at the moment. What I *am* going to do, after due process, is move into number 11, Chemin des Mimosas, La Crague-du-Var.'

'You're moving into Paillaud's villa?'

'As its new owner.'

Darac ran a hand through his hair. 'He's bequeathed it to you?'

Férion grinned, contentedly. 'Uh-huh.'

'So he *has* written a new will?'

'Within the last couple of weeks, yes.'

'Have you seen it?'

'No.'

'Then how confident are you of your position? Between us, Paillaud has written several wills since returning to La Crague.'

'All that matters is that I'm named in the most recent.' He took a long drag on his cigarette and blew out the smoke. 'I'm an heir, can you believe it?'

He would be an heir, Darac reflected, only if Erica were able to resurrect the will; and if they could prove it had been destroyed mischievously and not at the wishes of the testator. 'Congratulations.'

'Thanks.' Férion poured another glass of wine with the air of a man who had pulled off the coup of the century. 'There are a couple of caveats: one, that I don't say a word to the media about what we discussed in our meeting on Thursday. Two, that I have to live in the villa for at least the next ten years. After that, I can move out and sell it if I want.'

'Didn't you think that this bequest was something of a bolt out of the blue, monsieur?'

'I did, but between you and me, it couldn't have come at a better time. Except for the occasional article, I haven't had anything published in years and all in all, things were looking pretty bleak. So as much as I never thought I'd say this...' He raised his wine glass. 'God bless good old Monsieur La Chute.'

Darac's mind was still rife with questions. 'This is more than just a windfall, though, isn't it? It's quite bizarre that Paillaud should bequeath something of such value to you, someone he hadn't had any dealings with in years and with whom he didn't particularly get on, anyway.'

'I thought you said you'd read my book? It's Paillaud *to a T* to do things like this. I said most of the time he was a bastard, right? And he was. But he was also unpredictable. Unpredictable some times more than others, as I've joked elsewhere. Listen to this. It's Paris about thirty years ago. Paillaud's on his way to the Saint Ouen flea market and he's carrying quite a bit of cash. Out of nowhere, this raggedy-ass kid jumps him with a knife. About 14, he was. He's shaking so much, he almost stabs *himself* but he's shouting, pushing – the whole shtick. Somehow, Paillaud manages to sweet talk him into giving up the knife and the kid starts crying. Paillaud gives him a slap and makes him promise never to rob anyone again. But this is the kicker – he then gives the kid nearly all the cash he's carrying anyway. Gold dust, right? I *begged* him to let me put that in the book but he wouldn't listen.'

'It does make a great story but I can see his point.'

'I can picture him now: "I don't want every damn freeloader out there thinking they're good for a hand-out." ' He poured another glass. 'Which, in the light of all the speculation following the murder of Paillaud's notary yesterday evening, is pretty ironic, isn't it?'

'Ironic is one word for it. Monsieur Férion, this is an entirely routine question...'

'Where was I at roughly 7 pm last night? Yes, I know when it happened. Thanks to the blurtings of that next-door neighbour.'

'Monsieur Kerthus has been cautioned for speaking out of turn and may yet be charged. As may the so-called newspaper concerned.'

'Good – some years ago, those ingrates turned down a piece of mine. Anyway, where was I? I'm staying up in Vence and went to a restaurant around the corner for dinner. Le Nid de... Merle. It was good. Good value, too. Do you know it?'

There wasn't an atom of Darac's hometown that he didn't know. 'Not sure.' He made a mental note to pass on Férion's comment to the staff, most of whom were friends from school days; friends who had blossomed under the teaching of Darac's mother Sandrine; friends who still gathered in Vence's old cemetery every February 27th to mark the anniversary of her death at just 33. 'Is that the place near the Jardin?'

'*Too* near, yes.'

Darac grinned. 'It's certainly in Position A for *Nuits du Sud*. If you like that sort of music.'

'And if you don't, you're stuck with it anyway.'

'What time did you arrive?'

'Six on the dot. I had a glass of wine with a couple of locals, then dinner. Several people will vouch for me. Left at about 9.30.'

If the folks at Le Nid would indeed vouch for Férion, it was as good as alibis got for Darac. 'A three-night stay in Vence – lovely. Quite a change from Paris.'

'It's a lovely little town. And the views all around are fabulous, of course.' There was still some smoking left in his cigarette as he stubbed it out and lit another. 'Actually, I checked into a different place down the road on the first day. Bit of a shithole – sort of place the lights go out if you take more than ten seconds to get to your room. So when Paillaud told me what he was going to leave me in his will, I thought I'd treat myself to an upgrade. Could've found somewhere there and then, I suppose, but I left it to the next morning. I'm up in Saint-Jeannet tonight. Best 'til last.'

Darac was starting to get a strange feeling about Maurice Férion. 'Over three nights, you'll have stayed in three different places?'

'It was all last-minute so I was lucky to find anywhere nearby to start with – at the sort of money Paillaud had given me, anyway. He must have thought it was still 1980.'

'Why didn't he put you up, himself? That would have been cheaper still.'

Férion gave Darac a disappointed look. 'Because he hated sharing his living space, didn't he? Back in '71, he even baulked at putting up Jeanne Moreau for the weekend.' He shook a loose fist. '*Jeanne Moreau*, my friend. He's hardly likely to have made an exception for me, is he?'

'I remember that from your book now you mention it. And he knew he wouldn't be returning to the villa, of course.'

'Seems so.' Férion poured another glassful, stagily extracting the last few drops from the bottle. 'This soldier's dead,' he said, pointedly holding on to the body.

The old journo was certainly true to the drinking traditions of his trade but Darac needed him sober and a second bottle might be pushing it. 'May he rest in peace.'

'Fair enough.'

'Monsieur Férion, you must have conjectured about the meaning of Mademoiselle Rosay's murder? Are you still confident about your windfall?'

'I am.'

'Why?'

Férion hoisted the shoulder bag on to his knee and took out an envelope marked: "Not to be read until Friday evening." Dated Wednesday, in it was a note apparently written in Paillaud's hand and bearing his familiar cartoonish signature. 'Read this, Captain.'

*My dear Maurice,*
*By now you will have learned that I am dead. At least, I hope you will or my final stunt will have been something of a damp squib, won't it! Whatever the days and months ahead may bring, I want to reassure you that so long as you abide by the terms we agreed upon, your future is secure.*
*The showbiz media may well want to talk to you. I know you demur on this but if they refer to me as a second tier star, don't argue with them. If they trot out that Cahiers jibe about my films being "hopelessly formulaic", don't argue with them. If they assess my latter years as those not of a recluse but simply of a forgotten man, again, don't argue with them. But if anyone says that as a child, I was dragged up by an uncaring, drunken whore of a mother, you have my posthumous permission to shoot them.*

*When everything has died down, Maurice, and you've taken over my old villa, keep an eye on the locals. I wouldn't trust most of them as far as I could throw Gérard Depardieu.*
*Cordially, Ambroise P Paillaud.*

Férion held out his hand. 'Well? What do you think?'

'Interesting.' Darac held on to the page. 'Articulate. Touching. No trace of the bastard.'

'Don't be fooled. He could turn on the charm when needed. And turn it off as easily.'

It prompted a thought. 'I don't think it's strictly necessary but...' Darac brandished his mobile. '... just to authenticate that this *is* Paillaud's handwriting.' Maintaining eye contact with Férion as he spoke, he fired off a few covert, and probably poorly aimed, headshots. 'Would that be alright with you?'

'Be my guest.'

Darac held the letter flat, took several shots and handed it back. 'One thing – you do realise it's not a legally binding document?'

'Not in itself, true. But I know him. The offer is genuine, alright.'

'His comments on the showbiz media, as he calls it, are interesting. Have they contacted you?'

'The Cinémathèque have already approached me for an interview and there will no doubt be others. Have no worries, Captain. I'll speak up in time but I won't pull a Monsieur Kerthus job on you. I can't afford trouble.'

'I'm relieved. Paillaud was wrong about the critics, wasn't he? They're all queuing up to say how brilliant he was.'

'That's because he's dead, he killed himself, and he had cancer – in that order. The ones who used to trash him feel guilty about it, that's all.'

'But you never did. Trash his talent, I mean. Even though you're writing in his voice, your admiration for that side of him is... I was going to say obvious but you know what I mean.'

Mugging displeasure, Férion looked uncannily like his muse for a moment. 'I'll let that pass, my young friend. But you're right. Paillaud's talent for physical comedy was entirely natural. He didn't have to work at it and as a result, he didn't value it. That was what the studios mainly wanted him to do, though. But if you look at some of the work he does in between the stunts?' Férion shook his head. 'Amazing. In my opinion he was a better actor than Tati, Funès – all the comedians. Except Michel Simon. But he was of a different generation, of course. And he could do anything.'

'He's unsurpassed, I agree.' Darac's brain teeming with possibilities, he said nothing for a moment. For the jazz player in him as well as the detective, it was a familiar state of mind. Some ideas would collide and crash; others would connect, forming sequences that would gain in significance as they led to others. Just such a sequence suggested itself to him now. 'Tomorrow, monsieur. When are you returning to Paris?'

'I have a reservation on the 18.02 TGV. Not long before you'll be strutting your stuff with your group. Or band, do you call it?'

'In that case, I wonder if you might be able to help with something else. You're the one man in the country who could and as we have you here, it would be a pity not to draw on your expertise.'

'Depends. Will it take long?'

'No.'

'So what's the problem?'

'There's something about Paillaud's suicide that has been nagging me ever since I saw the footage. Just to indulge me, my team has agreed to view it just one more time, at the Caserne Auvare here in the city. Tomorrow at 1 o'clock. We would send a car, naturally, return you afterwards, and as a bonus, run you to the station later. How's that?'

Férion blanched. 'You want me to view the suicide?'

'Not the moment of impact, of course. In a sort of compare

and contrast exercise, we're going to run a couple of Paillaud's shorts first.'

'Which?' He was all business, suddenly, then smiled, nervously. 'Out of interest.'

'I believe it's...' Darac quickly pictured his DVD collection. '*Président La Chute* and *Three Coins In The Jukebox.*'

'What are you looking for? And if you found it, what good would it do?'

'I have no idea. But you might.'

Férion lit another cigarette. 'I don't know about this, Captain.' He turned the packet around in his hand. 'I don't know at all.'

'I quite understand. I shouldn't have asked.' One last play. 'We'll just draw our own conclusions from the clip.' Darac slipped the bill from under the ashtray. 'Well, I think that just about—'

'Wait. It will be very difficult but I suppose I ought to come along.'

'Thank you, monsieur. Most appreciated.' He brandished his mobile. 'Let me just check something.' Darac kept his eyes on Férion as he waited for Bonbon to pick up. 'Officer Busquet – good, you're there. You know the screening of Paillaud's suicide jump you booked for tomorrow at 1 o'clock?'

'Since I've done no such thing, somebody's obviously with you.'

'That's right. We've pulled off something of a coup. The ghost-writer of Paillaud's autobiography is going to join us.'

'That fellow I looked up before? Just to check he was still alive?'

'That's him, yes – Maurice R Férion.'

'So now you need something else.'

'Indeed. Just the autobiography? No, he's done a lot since. And previous work, too.'

'Got you. I'll get the database up.'

'Good. He has to return to Paris tomorrow evening so we're lucky to have caught him.' Darac listened to silence, nodding. 'A car, yes, absolutely. To Vence – correction: Saint-Jeannet, it will be. I'll get the address.' Buying time by not supplying a pen, he tore a page out of his notebook and pushed it across the table. 'If you would, monsieur?'

As Férion fished a pen out of his bag, Bonbon came back on.

'OK – a couple for drink-driving, the most recent 2009. Paris. Just fines. Then we have to go way back... to summer 1968. Affray. Bound over. Again Paris. Ah, but it's '68. Student unrest time. He's clean, basically. Very.'

Férion handed over the note and Darac recited the address into the phone. 'Got that?'

'So we are actually doing this, then?' Bonbon said. 'The films?'

'Yes we are. I'll bring them.' Darac turned to his guest. 'We need a pick-up time. Shall we say noon to be on the safe side? And don't worry, it will be an unmarked car, plain-clothes driver. Alright?'

'Yes, I suppose so.'

'So that's 12 noon in Saint-Jeannet, Officer. See if Wanda Korneliuk is free. Thanks.' Darac rang off. 'Summon the waiter, will you, monsieur?'

While Férion turned his back, Darac carefully laid the torn-off page back into his notebook.

## 43

'You have palpitations?'

'Terrible ones,' Hervé Montand said, following Doctor Zep into the kitchen.

'And you have chest pain.' Zep wheeled his bike to one side and motioned Montand to sit at the table. He himself remained standing. 'Anything else?'

'Yes. My left arm is numb and I have pins—'

'When did this start?'

'About three hours ago.'

'And you didn't see fit to make an appointment at the surgery. Instead, you leave it until the evening, arriving here just as I'm about to go on a long, restorative training ride. After which I am going to run to the Centre where I'm going to swim until I've washed away every single irritant that has attached itself to me during the day. Such as this moment.'

'Commendable. Heroic, even. And I'm sorry, Arnaud, but you see the sweats started only ten minutes ago as I was leaving the Mairie and then—'

'*Sweats*... Monsieur Montand, you have been looking at an internet description of someone about to suffer a heart attack, haven't you?'

Montand's mouth moved but only hesitant sounds emerged.

'A black eye isn't part of the symptom profile, by the way.'

Montand's toilet bowl head dropped on to his chest. He started to weep.

'Oh, Jesus Christ... Stop blubbing!'

After a couple of false starts, Montand managed to stop.

'That's better.' Zep took a closer look at the man and took his pulse. 'Your trip hasn't been entirely wasted. You are clearly stressed and I'm going to give you something for it.'

'Thank you, Arnaud.' He blew his nose. 'Thank you.'

Zep glanced at his watch. 'And I'm going to give you ten minutes to tell me why you have really come here.'

Montand composed himself and in no more than a matter of seconds took on an air so imperious, Zep began to doubt the man's sanity.

'As mayor of this ancient—'

'You have nine minutes fifty left. Cut to the chase.'

'Alright! The first thing is my brother-in-law, Guy Vaselle. He's in police custody again.'

'They've charged him?'

'Held, pending further enquiries. For up to forty-eight hours, initially. Then another forty-eight upon application – the *garde à vue* situation, as we term it in law.'

Zep sat down. 'So they have grounds but they also have doubts.' He took off his bike helmet. 'What about you, monsieur? Do you have grounds for believing Vaselle killed Rosay?'

'May I have a drink? Cognac?'

'I have water, tap and filtered, various juices and electrolytic fluids. I also have coffee but there isn't time.'

'Never mind.' Montand stared at the table. When he looked up, a layer of pretence seemed to have been stripped from his pink skin. 'Yes. I do believe Guy did it. You recall the figure we both saw in her garden? Hiding in the shadows?'

Zep seemed unconvinced. 'It was him, you think?'

Lowering his voice, Montand leaned forward. 'And so would the police, Arnaud. If we said it was definitely Guy we saw and we hadn't said so originally because we are scared of him. *Then*, the police would have all they need to charge him. Especially when I tell them that Guy hated Caroline Rosay. Hated her with a passion.'

The assertion seemed to pique Zep's interest. 'Did he? Why?'

'Probably because he propositioned her and she turned him down. Women don't usually do that.' Montand was beginning to get into his stride. 'He's a brute. And he'd been drinking that night. Heavily. And when he's like that he can do anything. Believe me.'

'A man meets his notary public minutes before he kills himself. Only hours later *she* is killed. And you contend that those two events are not connected? Most of the local population and half of the world's media believes the opposite. And with good reason.'

'The two may have been *connected*, of course. We all know what a disaster it would be for *every* citizen in our commune if that moron Paillaud had at the last minute disinherited us. But they haven't found a new will, have they? And Rosay is most definitely dead. Everything that was promised to me...' He raised both hands palms outwards. '... Promised on behalf of the commune, I mean, *everything* may just be days, even just hours away.'

Zep's hand went to his chin. 'There are problems with your suggestion, monsieur. Let's leave the ethical part of it aside for the moment, a policy with which you are more than familiar, as is obvious.'

Montand climbed on to the overworked animal that was his high horse. 'I take grave exception—'

'When everything is taken into account, I agree with you on one point. The shadowy figure we both glimpsed last night is the likely killer of Caroline Rosay. However, unless he has lost a good 15 cms in height since I last saw him, that figure was not Guy Vaselle. And if he is charged with her murder, I will impart that information to the police.'

'Arnaud, please—'

'I may also remind them that you are around 15 cms shorter than Vaselle, yourself.' His eyes bored into his would-be patient. 'Aren't you, Monsieur le Maire?'

The observation threw Montand but he recovered with surprising speed. 'You have already said that I couldn't possibly have committed the murder. It was your professional opinion that there wasn't time.'

'If I think of an explanation, be assured that I will tell *that* to the police also.'

'That would be a bad mistake.'

'Get out.'

Montand stood. 'First, go and get my pills. *Doctor.*'

# 44

Darac could conceive of no better place to experience the magic of a Babazouk night than the roof terrace of his Place Saint-Sépulcre apartment. The sights alone were gorgeous: the way light faded on walls washed in tones of cayenne, cumin and turmeric; the darkling embrace of the vast Alpes Maritimes; the slow churn of the star-scattered sky. And Darac recognised a synergy, almost an alchemy, in the way sounds and scents rising from the streets combined with the jazz soundtrack invariably drifting across from his living room.

At the moment, those scents included the slipstream of Frankie's *Marucca* perfume as she and Darac left their champagne glasses and walked arm in arm to the bedroom.

There was no frenzied ripping off of clothes. Instead, they stood facing each other as they slowly undressed. When they were naked, they stood for a moment, revelling in being fully revealed at last but feeling vulnerable, too, as if to say: "Is this alright? Is this what you were hoping for?" Darac was certain of one thing. As he took Frankie in his arms, he knew that she had opened a space in his heart and his head that only she could fill.

'Paul.'

His lips met hers. His manhood rising, he felt her hands exploring the muscles of his back. They fell back on to the bed. And then quite suddenly, she pulled away.

'Frankie?'

'I'm sorry, Paul. And after everything I said yesterday.'

'What is it?'

'Would you...' She took a deep breath. 'Would you just hold me?'

## 45

For a second, Darac wasn't aware of where he was or how he had got there. But he felt a woman's head resting on his shoulder, the soft impress of her breasts against his chest, and he felt something else: he felt gloriously, unprecedentedly, indecently happy.

Frankie's eyelashes brushed his chest and he realised she was already awake. He gently touched her cheek and she rolled on to her front, contemplating him. Nothing was said for some moments.

'So that was your idea of "just holding" me, was it?'

'Ah.' Feeling he couldn't explain himself properly lying down, he sat up, a manoeuvre that obliged Frankie to do the same. 'I was more than content to, Frankie. But when you started...'

'You didn't *have* to respond.'

They smiled, kissed and began just holding each other all over again.

Darac was first to shower and dress. The morning had dawned in the most spectacular way and for a moment, he considered abandoning his 'morning detox' – picking up his lounge guitar and playing along with a CD of choice until he felt ready for the day – but more in a spirit of celebration, he decided to go for it. Besides, it wouldn't disturb Frankie. She had risen but was still in the shower.

As he scanned the shelves, he found himself wondering about the adjustments the two of them would inevitably have to make;

how they would reconcile the routines and habits that made up the small print of their lives. The bigger stuff, he felt sure, would take care of itself. They knew each other's predilections and passions inside out. Trips to the movies, plays, exhibitions – the prospect of openly sharing these things was delicious. And work permitting, they would be able to do whatever they wanted on impulse. No elaborate planning. No last-minute dramas. No lying to Christophe.

But then there was jazz. Suffering through lessons on a variety of instruments as a child had virtually strangled Frankie's feeling for music. When melody plus harmony plus rhythm equals distress, it was hardly surprising. She had developed some interest over the years but it hadn't taken her as far as jazz and, he realised, possibly never would. Would this difference between them matter? Would it get in the way?

His musings subsided as he slipped *Djangology* into the player and picked up his guitar. Adopting his usual perch, he parked his backside on the rolled arm of his chesterfield and began chunking away four to the bar.

Darac was duetting along with 'Ménilmontant' when Frankie, wearing only a towel around her waist, appeared in front of him as if in a vision. He looked up and smiled, for effect crashing the sequence he was playing in a random flurry of notes. The corniness of it made her laugh but then life played a random card of its own. Taking a sharp intake of breath, Frankie looked past him into the room. Her eyes widened in disbelief. Her hands went to her breasts. The guitar slid off Darac's thigh as he turned. 'Ménilmontant' swung happily on without a pause.

'Modesty, Frankie?' Angeline said. 'No need for that. Your hands are too small for the job, anyway.'

Darac was dumbfounded but then words came in a torrent. 'Angeline? For God's sake! What are you doing here? After all this time, you think you can just let yourself in? As if nothing had happened? Jesus! How dare you?'

Angeline's smile was sour as she watched Frankie walk

quickly away. 'So,' she said, turning to him. 'You finally got your mother back, didn't you?'

Frankie slammed the bedroom door behind her.

Angeline turned on her heel. Darac stood poleaxed, a maelstrom of thoughts and emotions hitting him all at once. It was some moments before they coalesced. 'Back soon, Frankie!'

He hurried out, his anger propelling him down the stairs two and three steps at a time but he still hadn't caught sight of Angeline as he emerged into the courtyard at the bottom. The gate in the far corner was open. He ran towards it, knowing that unless he overhauled her in the doglegged alleyway beyond, she would disappear in the tangle of the Babazouk.

There was no sign of anyone as he began jinking through the alley's many turns. Half-way along, he glanced at his watch. *Yes!* There was hope. Suzanne, his friend and neighbour, often returned from her shifts at the nearby Saint-Roch hospital at about this time. She had known Angeline well. If the pair were to bump into one another, she was bound to detain her at least for a moment. More turns... One turn left... *Come on, Suzanne!*

No. There was still no one as he reached the junction with Rue Neuve. Now the options multiplied. The chances of catching up with Angeline in the tangle were slim so he jogged into a Place Garibaldi waking up to a slow-mo Sunday. There was no sign of her in the broad expanse of the Place itself so he made a tour of its flanking colonnades. It proved the wrong call. Where now? République? Cassini? Segurane? His chest heaving, he decided to head back into the Babazouk after all. Rue Pairolière offered a couple of possible sightings but neither worked out. It was hopeless. Over ten minutes had elapsed by the time he made it back to his apartment.

'I'm so sorry about that, Frankie.' he said, hitting stop on the CD player. 'Can you believe it?' He glanced into the bedroom. And then tried the bathroom door. 'Frankie?' He went out on to the terrace.

She was gone. He went back inside and saw a note threaded

through the strings of his lounge guitar: *I cannot compete. Nor will I try.*

'What? Compete? No, this can't be happening!' For the first time in his life, he picked up an instrument with the intention of smashing it. Smashing it to pieces. A variation on Angeline's *Make love! Hit someone! Play the guitar!* mantra from two years ago came back to him and it stopped him. He picked up his mobile and called Frankie's. No answer. He tried again, willing her to answer. Nothing. He tried again. And again, walking from room to room. It was only then he noticed Angeline had dropped a CD-sized FNAC bag in the living room. Or rather, tossed it into a corner. He left it where it was. He thought about leaving Frankie a message but he wanted to speak to her directly. He thought about driving to her place in La Turbie but Christophe was due back and Darac had to see her alone. What to do? And there was the small matter of going to work – a team meeting had been scheduled, something Frankie herself often attended. He looked at his watch. It was due to start in an hour. Leave now? Stay put? He decided on the latter. Frankie may have had similar thoughts and return.

She didn't. He left the apartment half-an-hour later, picking up Angeline's discarded offering en route. She had annotated the cover: "I've been enjoying this lately, A x"

Bobby Watson's *Love Remains* was a favourite album of Darac's. As he tossed it into the recycling, he never wanted to hear a single bar of it again.

# 46

'No music today, Captain?'

'What?'

'Had a row with the girlfriend, I know.'

The barrier rose and Darac drove into the compound faster than usual. At the turn, he sat forward, his eyes trained on Frankie's space. *Be there.* If she was, there would be time to talk to her before the meeting.

Empty.

He pulled into his own space and tried her number again. His pulse quickened. The call connected.

'You fucking bastard. Don't think I'm ever going to forgive either of you for this.'

'Christophe – where's Frankie?' Darac's chest tightened. 'What are you doing on her phone? Put her on. Now.'

'Screwing behind my back? You arseholes. Arseholes!'

'Where is she, Christophe?'

'Shall I tell you where she is? She's in the house calling Marseille on the landline. Marseille, Darac! Yes! I don't know what you've done but congratulations—'

'Listen, I don't know what Frankie saw in you in the first place but it's over between you now. Have you got that? Over! Put her on the phone.'

'Don't tell me what to do, you shit! Do you think I'm going to take this lying down? She does, though, by God. She takes it lying down, standing up—'

Darac tossed the phone on to the passenger seat and, slamming the Peugeot into reverse, floored the pedal. Scattering officers like chickens in a farmyard, he jagged back through the compound and attempted a handbrake turn as he neared the barrier. He stalled. It was then he heard Frankie's disembodied voice. He picked up the phone.

'Frankie? I'm coming to you now.'

'No.' Her tone was calm but firm. 'Stay there.'

'Alright, let's talk. *Marseille*, for Christ's sake? And earlier, I was just as perplexed as you by what Angeline—'

'I have to go, Paul. I'll call you later.'

'Let's aim to—' She rang off but she would be as good as her word, he knew. What was far less certain was what she was going to say to him when she did call. The stupidity of his actions infuriated him. Chasing Angeline all over the place so he could have it out with her face to face when all he needed to have done was yell "never come back!" down the stairs? 'Idiot!' he shouted, punching the steering wheel hard. He took several moments to recover sufficiently to put the car in gear. Eliciting a range of reactions from the scattered ones, he threaded his way slowly back between them to his space.

Darac's task now was to appear sufficiently upbeat not to alert Granot and the others; Granot who had been against Darac's love affair with Frankie from the start. In the sure and certain hope that all was not lost, he got out of the car and set off to Building D.

'What was *that* about?'

The man was wearing torn jeans and a soiled basketball jersey. Despite his build and his looks, a few adjustments to his body language was all it would have taken to convey the impression that he was a crackhead on the edge.

'Sorry, Armani.' *If only I had your acting talent.* 'False alarm. Going in?'

'Narco meeting. That was the saddest attempt at a handbrake turn I've ever seen, by the way. Wanda will give you a lesson if you ask her.'

'She has. Twice.'

Armani threw his head back and laughed, threw his arm around Darac's shoulders, and threw a spanner into the works. 'You crack me up. I don't know what the divine Frankie sees in you.'

'Nor do I.'

'Yeah?' Squeezing Darac's shoulder, he leaned in. 'I was working the Babazouk last night. Found myself in a doorway in Ruelle Saint-Augustin. Just a few metres from your private little Place Saint-Sépulcre. You walked by, the two of you. Almost home so you relaxed.'

'We didn't see you.'

'No?' He grinned. 'Maybe that's because you stopped to kiss each other. And not like the time you did...' He extended a finger. 'Just over there. You *really* kissed.' He put his finger tips together and shook them. '*Eating* each other.'

There was no avoiding it. 'Armani, I'd be grateful—'

'Hey! Back then it was fun. This time, it's serious. It goes no further. Does he know? Piss Face?'

'Christophe?'

'A rose by any other name.'

Darac was too worked up to laugh. 'He does know, yes. Just a few minutes ago.'

'And so?'

'So things are in the balance, I guess. Not with him – that's over, I'm pretty sure. But there are complications.' He glanced at his watch. 'Listen, I've got to go.'

A slap on the back was Armani's signature sign-off. 'You know where I am.'

'Except when you're standing in a doorway in Ruelle Saint-Augustin.' Darac gave him a pat on the cheek. 'Thanks, man.'

A couple of steps later, Frènes called, berating Darac for keeping him in the dark and issuing the usual litany of threats and sanctions. Darac gave him as full an update as he wanted to give and, knowing his enemy, suggested he join Frènes to relay the information to the world's media. Frènes thanked him for the suggestion, offered a lame counter and rang off in quick order.

Darac was the last member of the team to arrive in his office. 'Sorry I'm a little late, everyone. I got...'

'Held up?' Bonbon said. 'At a rough guess?'

'That bodes well for the session.' Darac grinned, playing the carefree card perhaps a little too obviously. 'Remember we have Maurice Férion coming in later, the man who believes he's about to inherit Paillaud's villa.' Darac took a DVD out of his bag. 'This is our control – a pair of Monsieur La Chute's finest shorts, as it were. I've sent a copy of Férion's handwriting off to Louise Ouârd, as well, by the way.'

'Think he may have been in Caroline's office around the time of the murder?' Flaco seemed almost put out at the thought. 'That opens up a whole new line of enquiry.'

Darac shook his head. 'No, he has as solid an alibi as is possible. I was just riffing on a few ideas and as we have Madame's services at our disposal at the moment, it seemed churlish to ignore them.'

'I see.'

Darac's head was beginning to throb. 'You know, I feel like a coffee.' He gave his caffeine monitor a look. 'And I haven't had one yet today, Flak. Who wants to join me?'

'Just one wouldn't hurt,' Granot said.

Bonbon pulled his elastic band of a mouth into an upside down U. 'A small one.'

'Flak?'

She brandished a litre bottle of Evian. 'I've got my water.'

'Perand?'

'I've got her water, too.'

'OK, then.' As the others talked among themselves, Darac set about making the three espressos. When they were ready, he handed them out and parked his backside on his desk. 'Go for it, Granot.'

'Let's start at Centre Sicotte. What size shoes do you think former French Open chump Tina might wear?'

Darac had seldom welcomed the distraction of work more than he did at this moment. 'I don't know how you finessed it out of her but would it happen to be 42?'

'The size of the cast R.O. took from Caroline's rockery? Bullseye.'

'Tina?' Bonbon's brow lowered. 'Map did say a sportswoman could have delivered the blow that killed her.'

'Hold your horses. What size shoes do you reckon Monsieur Denis Golou, a.k.a. Deepak Abhamurthi, wears? On the rare occasions he does wear shoes, that is. I'll tell you – also 42. *But.*' Granot glanced at his notes. 'He and Tina have given each other alibis for the time of the murder and they look solid.'

'Any news on Vaselle's footprint?' Bonbon said. 'I have grave doubts about his guilt but we're still holding him.'

'I've just made a one hundred and sixty-step round trip to the lab.' Granot indicated his new toy. 'They're a bit behind over there but R.O. says he'll have a result within the hour.'

'Excellent,' Darac said. 'Before you tell us how far it is to every corner of the Caserne, how's Erica getting on?'

'I was saving this for a big finish.' Granot owned the moment for as long as he could. 'She's still some way off completing the reconstruction but there'll be a rapid acceleration towards the end of the process. She's predicting a result within the hour, too.'

'This is going to be quite an hour.' Darac's words washed around in a general wave of enthusiasm. He waited for it to fall back. 'Anything else, Granot?'

'A few things. I've got progress on Caroline's bank accounts – and no cries of "boring", please.' He opened a second file. 'The news here is that she *didn't* pay in Paillaud's will fee and a thorough search for the cheque itself has come up with nothing.'

'Hmm.' Darac ran a hand into his hair. 'How's this? Paillaud knows he's going to hand over his new will to Caroline in what would perhaps be a rushed meeting at the station, right? So he fills out the cheque *before* meeting her. Here's Good Caroline in action: after telling his sad story, Paillaud goes to pay her and she, thinking it unnecessary or even in the circumstances unseemly to take his money, says forget it. She doesn't know he's already filled in the cheque. Even though she fully intends to register the new will, she has no cheque to pay in. We know what happened next.

'Now Bad Caroline: Paillaud goes to pay and she demurs because she wants no paper record of a new will having been written. Why? Because she's going to use the will as a bargaining chip she intends to destroy when the hush money is coughed up. She doesn't realise Paillaud had already filled in at least the counterfoil of the cheque. And but for the thoroughness of the crew at Saint-Laurent station, neither would we. Again, we know what happens next.'

'I like that,' Bonbon said. 'I'll especially like it when we see Erica later.'

Perand made the effort to sit up. 'You might just have something there, chief.'

Granot shook his grizzled chops. ' "Might *just* have something." Listen to him.'

'Next, Granot?'

He produced a third file labelled INVENTORY CROSS-CHECK.

Bonbon set down a paper bag on the desk. 'Jelly bears from Cours Saleya.' He took one. 'Help yourselves.'

Granot stuck out a fat hand but Flaco's death stare stopped him. 'Quite right.' He returned to the file. 'This is the interesting one. The property sales documents all tally with the lists. However, I've discovered a discrepancy elsewhere.' He handed round a page bearing the names of three former citizens of La Crague. 'Messieurs Blé, Martot and Colle. As you can see, each had a will registered with Caroline and each died at a reasonably ripe old age. The wills themselves though, are missing.'

Darac pursed his lips. 'Are they connected in any other way? Have you had time to dig?'

'Only to establish that they are not related by blood or marriage. I've asked Erica to search for any further details on Caroline's computer – a job for when she's finished the reconstruction, obviously.' He produced a wad of photocopied pages. 'Caroline's diary, now. I've got nowhere with the dots business and from my description, Jodie can't explain them either. So I'm going to show her these as we agreed. Alright?'

Darac felt a tremor in his chest and his heart jumped but there was no moment of confusion about the cause this time. His pulse quickening, he grabbed the mobile out of his breast pocket and juggled with it before getting it under control. He looked at the screen. A text. But it was from Didier. He'd read it later. When he looked up, all eyes were on him. 'Bit nervous about tonight's gig, I guess. Any more, Granot?'

The big man tugged at his moustache. 'This would take more digging still but hasn't it occurred to anyone that Caroline lived very well for a notary?'

'It did to me,' Perand said. 'The Porsche, the clothes, the house itself.'

'Don't forget the furniture.' Bonbon scrolled his mobile. 'This is in the dining room where you interviewed Montand. A kind of cabinet known as a credenza.' He showed it. 'It's eighteenth century, I'd say. Worth about five grand. And there are several other pieces of note. Found any receipts?'

'A couple from the 1970s. Payments were made by cheque in the joint account of her parents, both no longer with us.'

'I felt she came from money,' Darac said.

'And she was an only child.' Granot let go of his moustache. 'Before you ask, she doesn't appear to have handled the parents' wills.' He set down the file. 'That's all I have at the moment.'

'Good work. Flak?'

Before she could answer, the grey desk phone rang and Darac put it on speaker.

'It's Louise Ouârd, Captain. I've now thoroughly examined the new samples you sent.'

In the room, voices hushed; ears pricked up.

'Thanks for coming back so quickly.'

'First, the name Zep as written in the diary of the murder victim, Rosay.'

'Tell me Guy Vaselle made that entry and there'll be a cheque in the post.'

'I was hopeful but my conclusion is going to disappoint you, I'm afraid. Vaselle did not make the entry.'

No one swore or threw up their hands but the news took the mood back down.

'Alright. Now you have the diary itself to work with, have you revised your opinion on Caroline Rosay?'

'Only to strengthen my first thought. She *definitely* did not make the entry.'

The mood hadn't lifted by the time Darac arrived at his final question. 'The letter Paillaud purportedly wrote to Férion – *is* that his hand?'

'I'm only going on the jpeg you sent but I'd say there's little doubt it is.'

'Thank you, Louise.'

Assurances of future co-operation were made and the call ended on a cordial if downbeat note.

Bonbon pressed his lips together. 'So Vaselle dodges another bullet. If R.O.'s footprint doesn't work for us, we'll have to release him. Again.'

'Agreed.' Darac massaged his temples. 'Flak – we were coming to you before all that.'

'I've been looking into Sonia Bera, and her children Rafal Maso and Daniela Wienawska. First, none has a conviction, an arrest or even a parking fine to their name.' The scowl deepened. 'The name inconsistencies are easily explained. Sonia has been married twice. She divorced the first husband and lost the second to a heart condition. The children took their fathers' surnames. Sonia reverted to her maiden name following the death of husband number two. The interesting thing is the connection they have with Paillaud and now Férion.'

Darac ran his hand into his hair and kept it there. 'Go on.'

'We know that La Poche is managed by Rafal on behalf of his mother, Sonia – a detail she didn't have to volunteer but did. On the day of Paillaud's suicide, Rafal told you and Lieutenant Granot that he'd had a male guest staying the night before who'd left after breakfast. That put it well before the time of the fatal incident so no further enquiries were made about him.'

'I think a "but" is coming,' Darac said, giving Granot a look.

Flaco added a full pout to her scowl. 'That guest was Maurice Férion.'

Darac waited for the reaction to subside a little. 'In referring to that night, Férion said only that he'd spent it in a "shithole down the road" from Vence.'

Perand shrugged. 'Saint-Laurent *is* down the road from Vence. And if La Poche isn't a shithole, I don't know where is.'

'You're overlooking the significance to the case of that shithole,' Granot said. 'The question is: did Férion simply fail to mention he'd stayed at La Poche or did he deliberately conceal the fact?'

'That's my concern,' Flaco said.

Bonbon helped himself to another jelly bear. 'It mightn't be sinister even if he did the latter. Routinely concealing what they get up to is second nature to journalists. Take my uncle Jaume. He's been a scribbler on *Diari de Girona* for nearly thirty years. If that man played his cards any closer to his chest, he wouldn't be able to read them himself.'

Darac nodded. 'It is part of their craft, I think. Anyway, we can tease the truth out of Férion when he comes in later. Flak, how did you discover this?'

'Rafal's never seen me so after you sent your update last night, Captain, I went there incognito. Had a drink. Went to the toilet. Stuffed the paper towels into my bag and told him he'd run out. While he went into the back to get a new roll, I took a quick look at the guest book.'

Granot gave a little grunt of pleasure. 'Voilà!'

'Not all *that* close to his chest,' Perand said. 'Signing in.'

'What made you *think* of looking, Flak?'

'You mentioned in your update that Férion had stayed in a dump somewhere "down the road" on his first night; then decamped to Vence, and was finally heading to Saint-Jeannet. I interviewed Sonia and Daniela on his second night. As well as revealing her connection to Rafal and La Poche, Sonia mentioned she let out a couple of nice rooms in the Vence house but that her best place was her villa up in Saint-Jeannet.'

Perand shrugged. 'In other words, you took a punt on the coincidence and got lucky.'

'Guilty.' The observation clearly didn't trouble her. 'On both counts.'

The internal phone rang. 'Hang on to your hats,' Darac said, putting it on speaker. 'So, does the shoe fit, R.O.?'

'Guy Vaselle? I was hopeful but sadly, no.'

'Ah, well. Thanks, R.O.' He hung up. 'That's Vaselle out of here. I'll ring the cell block after the meeting.' He exhaled deeply. 'Let's go back to the Sonia/Paillaud/Férion connection.'

Granot's thumb and forefinger once more found his moustache. 'How did a Parisian like Férion know about La Poche? I didn't and I live only a few kilometres away. It's not advertised. There's no website.'

Bonbon shifted in his chair, exchanging one contorted posture for another. 'We can't call and ask Rafal without alerting the boy, and therefore his mother and sister, to our sudden interest, can we?'

Darac's headache was returning but at least he hadn't felt his eyelids flutter since yesterday. 'Maybe a lack of coffee in my system has destroyed my imagination but again, there could be a simple explanation. Férion told me that Paillaud virtually begged him to visit for a few days, yet offered no hospitality and stumped up only the minimum for board and lodging. Controlling and cheap – that absolutely fits my picture of Paillaud. We know *he* knew of La Poche – that's where he arranged to meet Caroline – so he may have simply recommended the place. Férion told me that, buoyed by the promise of an unexpected windfall from Paillaud, he decided to upgrade after that first night. Again, we can quiz the man about it when he comes in. Artfully, if need be.'

'The banal explanation usually proves to be the true one,' Perand said, consciously or unconsciously quoting their absent boss, Agnès Dantier. 'But do we need a break this morning.'

Darac moved the meeting on. Issues were discussed, leads followed, ideas thrown up, but after a good half an hour, no conclusions had been reached except that they needed Erica's reconstructed will more than ever. No more than a minute later, the door opened and in she stepped.

'Here comes the cavalry,' Bonbon said, his voice the first in an upbeat chorus of welcome.

She was wearing a crestfallen expression, a routine favoured by her mentor Raul Ormans, a piece of harmless shtick aimed at ramping up the triumph of the eventual reveal.

'Take my spot, Erica.' Darac swung his weight forward off the desk and joined the others.

Erica's expression did not change as she turned the laptop screen towards them.

# 47

The teaspoon hung suspended half-way to Sonia's lips. 'Are you sure you wouldn't like some tabbouleh?'

Jodie shoved the cabinet drawer home with a flourish and crossed behind her. 'I would like some.'

'Ah.' Sonia lowered the spoon.

'But I won't, thanks.'

'Ah.' The spoon began its ascent once more.

Jodie grabbed a form and, scrolling a couple of screens on her tablet, began transferring some of the figures. 'Lieutenant Granot *is* doing well.'

'He reminds me of Oliver Hardy,' Sonia said, beaming. 'Fat but graceful.'

'He's less fat than he was. Lost two kilos already.'

As if daunted at the prospect of further spoon-work, Sonia set her barely touched lunch aside. 'Do you talk to him?'

'Of course.' She hit the off button and picked up her schedule for the day. 'What do you mean?'

Sonia turned to her. 'Do you talk to him about what happened? Dani is still devastated, poor thing, so heaven only knows how you must feel. We do worry about you.'

Jodie managed a smile. 'I know you do. But I'd just as soon not talk about it.' She glanced at her schedule. 'I've got a pair of tight quads in Room Two in a minute and I don't want to weep all over them.'

'And who is going to massage you, Jodie?' Sonia rose and held out her arms. 'Come here. Let me give you a hug.'

Jodie hesitated but she didn't really know why. The two women, short and slight as young girls, came together.

'We would love you to come and stay with us for a while, Dani and me. You need company. You need to be able to talk. But you'd be completely self-contained, too. Whenever you wanted it, you could be by yourself.'

As Sonia's almost weightless hand rubbed her back, Jodie felt as if she were 12 years old again, being consoled by a teammate at having been awarded a low score.

'Will you think about it?'

Jodie smiled. 'I just might.'

# 48

The atmosphere was flat.

'I'm putting Erica up for the Edmond Locard Medal,' Darac said. 'Alright, it didn't work out for us, but from conception to execution, she devised a programme that put together an image of a shredded handwritten text, every cross-cut speck in place, in just two days? Amazing.'

'It will become the norm, this method.' Granot nodded. 'They'll name it after her.'

'Here's to Erica.' They essayed smiles as they chinked cups. 'And the Lamarthe Process.'

'It takes nothing away from the achievement but it's a pity she hadn't been able to reconstruct the date at the beginning of the exercise, not right at the end.'

Darac shrugged. 'It was just the way the pieces played out, I guess. But this is a bad break, there's no getting away from it.'

'Another one.'

'Yes.' *You don't know the half of it.* Darac still hadn't heard from Frankie.

'As a notary, Caroline shouldn't have even kept Paillaud's last-but-one will!' Granot's chops took on a more bilious hue. 'Not without marking it superseded like the others in the file.' He let out a long breath. '*And* it wasn't recorded in the inventory.'

'So where are we with all this now?'

'I'm seriously wondering if there actually *was* a new will. Although Férion has joined the ranks of those promised the earth by Paillaud, he didn't *see* the document, did he? And alright, Paillaud may have filled in a cheque counterfoil payable to Caroline but there's no sign of the cheque itself. And she did flatly deny he'd produced a new will.'

'We're going round in circles, Granot.'

'With no real evidence that a new will exists, the old one will be processed at some stage, you realise.'

Darac ran a hand through his hair and kept it there. 'Not while we're still investigating Caroline's murder.'

'I know but Monsieur Toilet Head will be cock-a-hoop when he finds out it's only a matter of time. That really sticks in my craw.'

A new possibility occurred to Darac. He stared at the floor, running with the idea until it attached itself to another. And then another. He felt a frisson of excitement as a whole sequence of connections put itself together in his head and kept going.

'I know that expression,' Granot said, brightening. 'You've got something. Come on, let's hear it.'

Darac gave it a couple of beats, then looked up. 'How does this play? On the day Caroline was killed, someone shredded an old will in her office, the sole document found in the caddy. Why? Because, never imagining it could be reconstructed, whoever did it wanted us to believe it *was* Paillaud's new will, the one Caroline denied being given, the one it looks as if he at least *intended* paying her for.'

'Yes, go on.'

'It all points to one thing, doesn't it?'

# 49

Clad only in boxer shorts, Hervé Montand sat up and said "ah".

'Again?'

'Aaaaah.'

'That's fine. So they have released Vaselle?'

'Yes. Now I have a question. Why the urgency for this? My annual check-up isn't due for nearly two months. And on a Sunday?'

'I deemed it necessary to bring it forward. Your medication profile has changed. Stand, please.'

Montand clambered off the exam bed.

'I'm going to check for hernia now. Look to the side and cough for me?'

Montand thought he knew what was coming but as he felt the gloved hand slip under his shorts and close firmly around his testicles, Zep added an unexpected variation. With his other hand, he produced a sheet of paper.

'As a distraction, look at this.' He kept the gloved hand where it was. 'Can you read it or do you require glasses?'

'What on earth—?'

'Monsieur, I'm sure your ancestors were no strangers to the art of torturing captives and I could make this as hellishly medieval as you probably deserve but I'd prefer to give you just a small indication of what I could do to you if you don't co-operate.'

Montand's whole body shuddered. Among the cries and whimpers that emerged from his gaping maw over the next few seconds, only one word was distinguishable: 'Why?'

'Read the document.'

'But—'

Zep began to squeeze again.

'No, stop! Stop...' Montand tried to focus on the page. 'I'll... I'll read it!'

Zep relaxed his grip but held on. 'Aloud.'

Montand's eyes were streaming and, at first, he couldn't make out that the handwritten page bore Ambroise Paillaud's address and had been signed both by him and by Caroline Rosay. As his vision cleared, he failed to notice that Zep's thumb was concealing the document's date. ' "This is my will..." ' He turned to Zep. '*Which* will and how did *you* come by—? *Aaaaarggghh!*'

'Read.'

'Alright! Alright...' He slowly gathered himself. ' "*I... hereby bequeath my villa known as no 3, Chemin des Mimosas, in the commune of La Crague-du-Var, Alpes Maritimes and all of its contents to Monsieur Maurice Rémy Férion...*" '

'Skip this paragraph. The remainder will be of more interest to you. Don't worry, once inheritance tax is paid, you may still get the millions you were promised last year.'

'I may?' Montand closed his eyes and he would have sunk to his knees in gratitude if he hadn't understood the likely consequences for his sex life. 'Oh, thank God, thank God. But only *may* get it?'

Zep smiled. 'You will not receive a cent of that sum unless La Crague meets its constitutional obligation to provide social housing for its citizens.'

'What?' Montand's eyes flashed open. 'I... I recognise no such obligation! I shall just continue to pay the fines. As they do in the likes of Neuilly, I might add. And elsewhere.'

'And there are other stipulations. Read the details. To yourself, if you like. I'll turn the page for you as and when. Just don't forget where my other hand is.'

Over the next two minutes, a complex of emotions fought

their way across the sweating face of Hervé Montand; a struggle between triumph and tragedy that any classical actor would have been pushed to equal.

'Well?' Zep said. 'What do you think?' He gave a mild squeeze. 'Speak!'

Montand gasped but he complied. ' "Permanent apartments for the deprived and destitute?" "Offender rehabilitation centre?" "The renaming of Place Charles Montand as Place *Annette Paillaud*"? And all the other garbage? It's an outrage!'

'Make no sudden moves, Montand. We are far from finished but first, I'll answer the question you asked earlier. After I had sprinted off to tend what proved to be the corpse of Mademoiselle Rosay, I saw that she had fallen back on a document of some sort. Although only a small part of it was visible, as I knelt to examine her head wound, I realised it was a Paillaud will. I thought it best to remove it. You bustled in thirty seconds or so later none the wiser. And here we are.' Zep finally moved his thumb. 'Look at the page again.'

Montand's face was a mask of astonishment. The document was dated the day before yesterday. 'So this *is* the new will,' he said.

'Yes.'

'What... What do you intend?'

'What I intend is that we destroy this will together. Here and now.'

'Destroy?' The whimpering began again but it sounded different this time; a sort of pre-orgasmic moan that bubbled up and up until it gushed out in a joyful cry of release. 'Yes!'

'But we will *only* do so if you sign two other documents I have prepared. The first is a bank transfer of €250,000—'

Montand began to laugh. 'Oh, *what* a relief! Thank God, thank God! Arnaud, I always knew you were one of us. Of course I'll sign. It would—' He juddered to a halt, his mouth agape in agony.

The channels and pools of Zep's face running red, he yanked

Montand roughly to the floor. 'How dare you liken yourself to me? You corrupt bastard! The €250,000 is a donation to a clinic in Burkina Faso. The other document is a standing order for €1000 per month to the same institution. The commune of La Crague, humbled by inheriting such a great deal of money, wants to share its benison abroad. Have you got that? Now get to your feet and sign those orders.' He brandished Paillaud's new will. 'Or I will jump into my car and take this to Captain Darac immediately.'

Montand was panting. He was awash with sweat. But he managed to stagger to his feet. 'Where do I sign?' he said.

# 50

It was 1 o'clock by Darac's watch – six hours before he was due at the Théâtre de Verdure to play one of the most important gigs of his life; about a minute before a uniform delivered Férion into his supervision; and all of four hours since Frankie had said she would call him.

In his unease, he had entertained a series of increasingly tortuous scenarios to account for the delay. It had even flashed across his mind that Frankie's instruction to wait for her call might have been a test, the sort of lose-lose situation to which he had occasionally been subjected by Angeline. But he knew Frankie would never do that and he was being stupid. Nevertheless, he felt it something of a miracle that here he was waiting around outside Building B at the Caserne and not blasting along the A8 towards La Turbie.

The escort duly arrived with Férion. He looked nervous and before they entered the building Darac reassured him again that he would not be witnessing the moment Paillaud suffered the coup de grâce.

'Whoever's finger is poised over that pause button had better have a steady hand, Captain.'

'I realise it will still be a difficult watch but you can relax on that issue. I've had one of our technical people record a separate file. The footage will blank out at the appropriate moment irrespective of who is operating the machine.' Darac hadn't seen the new clip himself but Erica had prepared it and his confidence in her was total. 'Shall we?'

Férion nodded and Darac buzzed them into the building.

'You are screening the two shorts, also?'

'Just for my team. You know them backwards, I'm sure.'

'That I do.'

'They should just have finished. *Three Coins In The Jukebox* is particularly successful, I think.'

'It still holds up?'

'To be honest, I haven't seen that particular one in some time.' They had arrived at the viewing room. 'The team is watching them purely in a forensic context – to establish a control for comparison with the suicide jump.' Darac opened the door. The tinny twang of a rock and roll guitar cut the air. 'Ah – still a moment or two to go. After you.'

They were just in time to catch the celebrated climax of *Three Coins* in which a young Monsieur La Chute has to clear tables while performing a lively jive dance at the same time. A series of increasingly surreal obstacles had been set in his path and, complicating things further, he is both blindfolded and wearing roller skates.

Looking on, Darac's team displayed a degree of forensic rigour that was remarkable. It was entirely absent. From Bonbon's desk-slapping shrieks through Granot's guffaws to Flaco's lawn sprinkler *tst tst tst*, every one of them was helpless with laughter. Even Perand.

'Play that bit again!' Granot roared. 'When he limbos under the chaise-longue!'

'How'd they get the zebra...' Perand could hardly get the words out '... to sit on it?'

'Cross-legged!' Erica squeaked, wiping her eyes. 'Reading... reading... Vogue!'

Darac turned and was about to say, 'Yes, I think it probably does hold up, monsieur,' when he noticed Férion was wiping away a tear, also. But he wasn't laughing.

Erica rewound the sequence and it was only then that the team realised Darac and their guest had joined them. Attempts to curb their hysteria seemed only to make matters worse but like a class of giggling schoolchildren, they eventually settled down.

Granot was the first to say anything coherent. 'Sorry about that, Monsieur Férion. They don't make like them like that any more, do they?'

'No. Thank God. Nice to meet you all, by the way. Let's get it over with, shall we?'

'Alright, Erica – cue up the AV file you recorded, will you?' While she ejected the DVD, Darac turned to Férion. 'So how's Saint-Jeannet looking this morning?'

'Very nice.'

It was small talk and if it relaxed an increasingly tense Férion, so much the better. But Darac had a point, too. 'And the accommodation?'

'Ah, yes. Lovely.'

Erica signalled to Darac that she was ready to roll the clip.

'Nicer than the dismal spot you stayed that first night?'

'God, yes.'

'Where was that, out of interest? Always useful to get a personal recommendation. Or the opposite.'

Granot shared a discreet look with Bonbon.

Férion didn't hesitate. 'Place called La Poche down in Saint-Laurent. A Paillaud recommendation, you won't be surprised to hear. The boy who runs it – if you can call it running – put me on to the Vence place and my feet didn't touch.'

'The boy suggested another place? Altruism is alive and well in Saint-Laurent, clearly.'

Férion appeared to be returning to something like his form of the previous day. 'Altruism? More like typical small-town incestuousness. It was his mother's place – Sonia. And you probably know this but her daughter Dani cleaned for the murdered notary, Rosay.'

'Indeed she did. Between us, have you heard them say

anything about the murder? Facts, gossip, it's all grist to our mill.'

Férion grinned. 'Between *us*? I hope you don't mind me saying this, Captain, but I hope you can play the guitar better than you can act. In fact, I know you do. I read in one of the music magazines that you're "rewardingly explorative" and... what was it? "Versatile". Pretty good combination.'

As if accepting it as a compliment, Darac smiled but he felt a little unnerved. Good journalists prepare for interviews – he knew that. But Férion's interest in him seemed out of all proportion. '*Have* they talked about the murder in front of you? Perhaps speculated about its possible meaning?'

'No, except to go on about how awful it was. The girl seems to be able to turn the waterworks on and off at will. Make a good actress.'

'You don't think it's genuine?'

'I wouldn't say that exactly. Some people just love a good wallow, don't they?'

'It's been known.' That was as far as Darac wanted to take it. 'OK, the footage we're going to run was taken from an apartment overlooking the station. You'll see various things that happened before the suicide itself. I'll warn you when that's coming. Ready?'

Férion took a deep breath and slowly let it out. 'As I'll ever be.'

Darac gave Erica the nod. The footage rolled and he kept his eye squarely on Férion. He was rapt, it was clear, in Paillaud's arrival at the station, his confrontation with Guy Vaselle, and perhaps most of all, the selfie sequence.

'Hold it there, Erica. A comment on any of that, monsieur?'

He gave a grimly knowing smile. 'The way he behaved with that fan. "Come here my friend, come here! Go away you bastard, go away!" That's his personality in a nutshell. But that's by the by.' He shook his head as if clearing it for what was to come. 'OK. Do it.'

'It's very brief. Just a few seconds, alright? Roll it, Erica.

Twice initially, please.'

During the first take, Darac was more interested in watching Férion's reaction to the sequence than the sequence itself. The man was clearly moved, any dispassion he may have felt for Paillaud dissipating with each running step. By the time the old man leaped up and out from the platform edge, Férion's eyes were firmly closed.

On the second take, Darac watched the footage carefully and afterwards, he asked Erica to run it three more times. On the third, he again studied Férion's reaction. Half turned away from the screen, the man had at least watched the sequence through.

'Thank you for cutting that so accurately, mademoiselle,' Férion said, breathing deeply. 'Squeamish, you see.'

'You're welcome.'

He looked older suddenly. 'Can't imagine how those war zone guys do their job.'

Darac turned to him. 'But...' He stopped himself in time. 'I'm sorry, monsieur. I hadn't anticipated quite how difficult that would prove for you. Some water?'

Férion waved the thought away.

Darac pressed on. 'I've mentioned that something was nagging me about Paillaud's suicide jump but now I'm not so sure. However, you're the expert. Did you see anything strange there?'

'No but I tell you what I did see. Whatever else I may have thought of him, Paillaud really was a star, wasn't he?' He threw out a hand at the screen. 'He called that the stunt of his life and it was some way to bow out, by God.'

'Hear, hear,' Granot said.

'And now I need a drink.' Férion got to his feet. 'Several, in fact. Anyone free to join me?'

Darac felt a small surge of satisfaction. 'I'm afraid not monsieur but Officer Korneliuk, your driver, will take you anywhere you want to go.' He failed to add that he'd just dreamed up a second task for her to perform. 'Or wherever *she* does – she knows all the good bars in the city.'

'I wouldn't be surprised.' He grinned. '*Quite* a girl.'

There were handshakes, thanks and goodbyes as, moments later, a uniform arrived and led Férion away.

'Narco are due in here now,' Darac announced. 'We'll reconvene in the squad room in an hour.'

As the team members filed out of the room, a lively debate sprang up about which of Paillaud's stunts had been the funniest. 'The last one,' Perand said, predictably.

Erica slipped in next to Darac. 'Don't want to anticipate the meeting but having seen the edit, you say you've lost the feeling that there's something odd about the suicide jump?'

'The feeling? Yes, I have. Now I'm absolutely certain there's something odd about it.'

Erica put a hand on his forearm, halting him. 'What? Tell me.'

'I will.' He smiled as he unhooked his arm. 'In the squad room. An hour. Now, I have a couple of quick calls to make.'

# 51

Guy Vaselle helped himself to a brandy. 'Limping, Hervé? Wincing?'

Montand said nothing as he lowered himself into his chair.

'One of your creditors kick you in the balls, did he?' He threw down the slug and poured another. In the yard outside, a train of empty carts rattled past. 'Or was it the bank manager?'

Montand lit a cigar. 'I was delighted they released you, Guy. I've been petitioning on your behalf.' He savoured a mouthful of smoke. 'Just in the background. Quietly.'

Vaselle's eyes narrowed. 'You're different. What's changed?'

'Everything, Guy.' He swivelled in his chair and gazed up to the massif of La Crague. 'Everything.'

# 52

Depleted numbers in the squad room meant that the usual pre-meeting hubbub – what Agnès Dantier was wont to refer to as "the storm before the lull" – was little more than a buzz of voices. Nevertheless, Darac was finding it difficult to hear Frènes in his earpiece.

'The shredded will *wasn't* Paillaud's newest, Darac?'

'No, monsieur. Sorry about that.'

'But this is a disaster.'

'Look, it was not what we were hoping for but thanks to it, we're a step nearer the truth. Tell *that* to the world's media.' Darac ended the call, checked that he hadn't missed one from Frankie in the meantime – he hadn't – and trying to set his increasing frustration aside, parked his backside on the front desk and prepared to address his team. But first, there was time for a much-needed pick-me-up.

'Your Gaggia sends her love, chief,' Perand said, flashing Flaco a grin as he handed it over. 'One *double* espresso. Enjoy.'

Darac followed Perand's gaze. 'Thanks for your concern, Flak, but this meeting could be our case breaker, alright? I need more than a thimbleful.'

Everyone stopped talking.

'Wait a minute.' Bonbon looked dumbfounded and delighted in equal measure. 'We're close? We could have sold tickets and there's only us here.'

'Let's see how we go but some things have fallen into place. Astrid will be joining us later, by the way.'

'*Will* she? Interesting.'

'I was going to open, Granot, but you've picked up something by the look of it.'

'I'm still ruminating on it. You kick off.'

Darac savoured a sip of nut-brown nectar and felt instantly, almost ridiculously, on track. 'OK, now you've all seen Paillaud's shorts – forget the gag, Perand – consider the following. Leaving aside that his stunts were hysterically funny, Paillaud was a terrific gymnast, wasn't he? Balance, flexibility, power, nerve – he had it all. I've watched scores of his routines over the years and I've re-run many of them this past few days. From the outset, something was nagging me about the suicide jump but it wasn't until we saw Erica's stop frame just now that I pinpointed the reason. It's this: in every stunt Paillaud performed that involves a jump, whether it's a fall into mid-air, or a leap over an object, even when wearing roller skates, he did something the same way each and every time.' Darac raised a quizzical eyebrow. 'Anyone?' He gave them a couple of moments. 'No? It's that he always took off on the same foot. The left. But for the suicide jump? He took off on his right. That's why it looked somehow wrong to me.'

Around the room, lips were pursed and brows lowered as, testing the theory, everyone ran a personal Paillaud show reel in their heads. Nods and murmurs of agreement were not long in coming and then Bonbon said, 'Bravo. You're right, chief.'

Darac ran a hand through his hair. '*Now* the question is: does it mean anything and if it does, what?'

'It's a great observation,' Granot said. 'But there's no mystery here, surely? The jump at Saint-Laurent station wasn't a comic routine, was it? It was life and death. And he was a much older man, suffering from terminal cancer, remember.'

Flaco raised a hand. 'But according to Férion, Paillaud thought of it as the stunt of his life. All the *more* reason to stick to his usual method.'

'Perhaps.' Granot waggled his head as if physically weighing the assertion. 'Perhaps he tried to and couldn't.'

Bonbon drew his knees up under his chin. 'The history of sport is littered with people who favoured one leg, foot, or hand over the other. But the illness and his age notwithstanding, maybe Paillaud had simply injured his left leg.'

Darac had thought of that possibility already. 'Perfectly valid counter theories but if they were correct, wouldn't it be apparent in the way Paillaud moves on the platform? It isn't. Yes, of course it's slower and less fluid, but for me, the run-up looks remarkably similar to the way the young Monsieur La Chute would have performed it. And apart from the switch of feet, so does the jump itself.'

'I thought that, too,' Perand said. 'Tough, these old pros.'

Darac turned to Granot. 'Just had a thought. Where will Jodie be at the moment – do you know?'

The question took him by surprise. 'Why? I mean, she's off until later this afternoon.'

'Got a mobile number for her?'

'Yes I have.'

The big man's protectiveness was obvious. But why, Darac wondered, did Granot feel Jodie might need protecting from him?

'I'll try it if you like.'

Darac swiped his mobile. 'Just let me have it. I need to ask her something.'

Granot gave the number. All eyes were on Darac as he called her.

'It's Paul Darac here...' He listened. 'Yes, *Roland's* colleague,' he said, drawing smiles from the team, except from the man himself. 'I'll put you on speaker... Do you have a minute?'

'Sure.'

'I need to pick your gymnastics brain.' Darac saw Granot visibly relax. 'A hypothetical question.'

'I didn't think policemen were interested in hypothetical questions.'

'You'd be surprised. Jodie, when you were performing a sequence that required a one-footed take-off, would you always use the same foot?'

'Always, yes. For me, the right.'

'You wouldn't suddenly switch to the left?'

'Oh no. Unless I was carrying an injury but if it were severe enough to make me consider a change as radical as that, I probably wouldn't perform the routine at all.'

'Well, thanks, Jodie. You've been a great help.'

'Is that it?'

'Except to say a big thank-you for all the work you're doing with your pupil.'

'No thanks needed. Would you tell him I'll meet him *outside* reception later? We're going to begin with a power walk around the grounds.'

'You just have,' Darac said, and ended the call amid some good-natured ribbing of the big man. 'So we've identified what seems odd about the jump. On what we take from that, let's add something else into the mix. When Férion complimented you on your editing prowess earlier, he referred to his squeamishness, didn't he? A former journalist, he said he couldn't imagine what it would be like to cover a war zone. Well, he should have been able to imagine it because for almost twelve months back in the early '80s, Maurice Férion was part of *Libé*'s ground team covering the Iran–Iraq War.'

Perand shook his head. 'No way. The man is strictly showbiz.'

'I agree. The man we met is exactly that. He shed a tear, you know, when he saw just how much his comedy can still make an audience fall about.'

'You mean *Paillaud's* comedy?' Perand said.

'What I mean Perand, or at least, what I'm wondering, is that Maurice Férion may *be* Ambroise Paillaud.'

A medley of disbelief, doubts about Darac's sanity and general protests went up.

'I know. I can hardly believe it myself so talk me out of it, someone. Granot, you first.'

'The first thing that comes to my mind is... Map's autopsy on the jumper. He found clear evidence of precisely the rare form of terminal leukaemia Paillaud was being treated for at Clinique Albert Magnesca here in the city. Explain that one.'

'What if Paillaud and Férion have been planning and indeed working this switch for years? It may have been Férion in the guise of Paillaud who was being treated for cancer, then Férion as Paillaud who jumped in front of the TGV − off the wrong foot, as it turned out. So of course, there would be traces of the cancer in his remains.'

'Given your scenario, there would.' Granot began twisting the ends of his moustache. 'It is possible, this.'

'And there's another telling detail. If the Férion who just watched the suicide jump *were* actually Férion, an expert on Paillaud's routines, he would have spotted that wrong-footed jump immediately, wouldn't he? And he would have said so when I asked him about it. He didn't because he didn't want us tumbling to the fact that the jumper wasn't Paillaud.'

Granot was still working on his whiskers. 'That's a persuasive point, too.'

'Bonbon? You shoot me down.'

'So far so interesting, chief, but what about Paillaud's *everyday* life? Yes, he hid from the public eye but he must have been known to many people in La Crague.'

'But was he? Caroline Rosay seems to be the person he knew best and she described him as a recluse − if indeed it was him she knew and not Férion. She is also dead and cannot help us with that question. And there's another factor. Paillaud, as the true Férion asserts in his book, was a superb actor. Brilliantly observant and subtle. Partly because you're so dazzled by the stunts, you don't even notice that he *is* acting. You believe him completely.'

'That's true on screen.' Bonbon scrunched his forehead. 'Real life is one hell of a movie, though, isn't it? Think of what we've just witnessed. If *that* Férion turns out to be the miserable recluse Paillaud, it was an *amazing* performance.'

'Certainly was,' Perand said. 'And what about situations where acting doesn't come into it? What about the various photo IDs you need nowadays? The *carte vitale*, for instance. If you're being treated for cancer at somewhere like Clinique Magnesca, you'd have one, wouldn't you?'

Granot shook his head. 'We didn't find one but anyway, you're talking about the *carte vitale* smartcard that was introduced only recently. The originals were quite basic things. Didn't even carry a photo. And usually, once you get on a system with a particular identity, you can keep it through any number of upgrades. And it can serve as a springboard for obtaining other cards, and so on.'

The point met general agreement.

'This puzzles me,' Erica said. '*Why* would Paillaud and his ghost-writer want to exchange identities? What was in it for Férion except to die a grisly death now when in a couple of years or whenever, he could have just slipped away in a haze of morphine?'

Darac nodded. 'Quite. That exercises me more than some of the more technical issues of this thing. There are a couple of pointers, perhaps. To save anyone bringing up the database...' He flipped open his notebook. 'What Férion refers to in the auto-biography as Paillaud's "travelling circus of a family" eventually fetched up in Paris after being kicked out of La Crague. Férion, now 67, was himself born in Paris, registered as Maurice Rémy Férion. The mother is named as one Scarlett O'Hara, spinster, which I think we can safely assume was an alias, as was Scarlett's Elysée Palace address.'

'Do you think?' Bonbon said, his foxy eyes twinkling.

'The father...' Darac continued, squinting at his entry. '... *Jonny* Férion is cited as a musician of no fixed abode. I'll come back to Jonny shortly.' He closed the notebook. 'Remember Paillaud's mother, real name Annette, gave Ambroise the middle name of Pernod, a favourite tipple of hers? Férion's middle name is Rémy as in Rémy Martin, the cognac house. I'm putting the conclusion a bit before the proposition here and I know it's tenuous but I'll bet Paillaud and Férion were half-brothers. So there might have been some filial loyalty there, a bond strengthened by the chaotic circumstances of their childhood, a time of unusual license for the young Paillaud but also of deprivation and humiliation, something he firmly attributed to the odious Montand dynasty of La Crague.'

'If all those ifs hold good,' Bonbon said, 'Férion and Paillaud *could* have bonded over something like that, and dreamed up a long-term plan to deprive and humiliate Montand. Armani always says revenge is a dish best served cold. Even though in this case, only one of the conspirators would live to see it.'

Paillaud wouldn't even have to move house for the pleasure, Darac thought to himself. 'And that brings us back to the new will I'm absolutely sure Paillaud made precisely to deliver that dish to the table.'

Bonbon wrapped himself into an affirmative sort of position in his chair. 'Agreed, on that one.'

'Flak – we haven't heard from you yet.'

'Question, Captain: if Paillaud *is* passing himself off as Férion, what do we do next? Practically, I mean.'

'Answer: act on the results of a DNA swab test I set up just now.'

'Férion agreed to take one?' she said. 'Or did we have enough to sanction it?'

Darac shook his head. 'All we have are anomalies and some pretty compelling theories which *might* explain them. So no, I felt we didn't have enough, officially. However...' His customary half-smile made its first appearance in some hours. 'As we speak, Wanda is plying Férion with drinks. A *sympa* sort of person, she's going to clear the table of glasses at the end of the session and while Férion goes to the toilet, or waits in the car, she will go to work with a swab kit. And now I come back to said Jonny Férion,

Maurice's father who died seven years ago. He had a record of drug abuse, some minor dealing and got into the occasional fight over it which led to an arrest and a swab taken. Our new test couldn't prove for certain if the Férion we know *is* Paillaud, but it would determine if he is Maurice, son of Jonny, half-brother of Ambroise through mother Annette.'

'All well and good,' Granot said. 'If your scheme with Wanda works, I have no objections. But will it work? And obtained like that, there could be legal implications. With Luxembourg calling the shots, increasingly.'

'A positive result, though, would provide grounds to authorise a proper DNA test.'

Granot gave a qualified nod. 'Let's hope so.'

'Just to show I'm still paying attention,' Erica said. 'I have another question. If Paillaud is pretending to be the down-on-his-luck Férion, he isn't fraudulently assuming the identity of someone who is rich and famous for gain, is he? He already *is* rich and famous. And you are certain he didn't kill Caroline.'

'As certain as makes no difference – his alibi is one of my oldest friends. And just to trail our brand new blockbuster, Granot and I are now seriously questioning whether Caroline's murder *was* directly connected to Paillaud's new will.'

Everyone talked at once.

'Hey, hey! We'll get to that. We're still on the B-Picture at the moment. Go on, Erica.'

'Paul, honestly. You are *such* a tease!'

The observation met general support.

Darac retired to safe ground. 'Remember Agnès's dictum? "Everything in its time, everything in its place." '

Scarcely mollified, Erica continued. 'As you've outlined it, Paillaud hasn't coerced or robbed anyone. He hasn't committed actual bodily harm. And if there is no causal connection to Caroline's murder, has Paillaud committed any crime at all?'

'As a rule, deception is too low down the scale to interest us but it is definitely a crime and if Paillaud is alive, he has definitely committed it.'

'Even if he stands to gain nothing from it?'

'Well, we don't know what he may gain from it yet, do we? But I take your point.'

Granot stirred in his seat. 'Erica, have you had time to look at Caroline's computer?'

'For anything on your missing will files, you mean? No, but I'll get to it later on.'

The door opened and in walked a young woman with feather-cut pink hair, grey shorts and a navy blue T-shirt bearing the word OOF in large pink letters.

'Hi, people. Hot one out there, today.'

'If it's not Astrid,' Bonbon said.

'Then I don't know who is.' Darac gave her a smile and motioned her into the chair drawn up next to him. 'Or you can join me here on stage.' He indicated the desk. 'If you like.'

'Flying visit. I'll stand.' A large cardboard-backed pad flopped out of her tote bag as she set it down and with a soft slap, performed a forward roll on to the floor.

'You haven't gone digital then yet?' Perand said, channelling bonhomie from somewhere.

'No. Still skin and bone.'

'Not you. Your media shit, I meant.'

The pad made an effective if unwieldy fan. 'You can lap a lot more air with this than a tablet.'

Darac took out his mobile. 'How have you fared with the photos of Férion I took at Café Thurién, Astrid?'

'You tell me.' As Darac scrolled screens, she riffled pages. 'Beat you. I call it *Man Minus Breton Shirt, Garrulous Manner And Glass, Wearing Toupée, Dyed Eyebrows Et Cetera, Doing The Splitz.'*

'Catchy,' Bonbon said.

In a sort of non-digital reprise of Erica's earlier presentation, Astrid displayed her handiwork to the team.

'This anything like your Ambroise Paillaud?'

# 53

On summer evenings, the palm-flanked arc of the Promenade des Anglais pulsed to a complex rhythm: road traffic, strollers, joggers, skaters, cyclists. Darac joined a loose knot of pedestrians at the kerbside and took the opportunity to stand still for a moment.

On the far pavement, members of the headlining James Clarence Orchestra were arriving *en masse* for their set, trudging past the Winged Victory monument that stood sentinel over the Jardin. Darac was irresistibly reminded of a New Orleans-style funeral band, the solemn march before all heaven broke loose.

Darac glanced at his watch. Paillaud or Paillaud's ghost would be well on his way back to Paris by now. Earlier, Astrid's mock-up likeness had succeeded only in preaching to the converted. Those who, like Darac and Granot, leaned towards the theory that Férion and Paillaud were one and the same person were not persuaded otherwise; the rest remained unconvinced. Uniforms were then dispatched to enlarge the test group. As Rafal Maso had entertained both the man calling himself Férion and Paillaud at La Poche, he was shown relevant photos alongside Astrid's work. He could draw no firm conclusion. Hosting Rafal's Monsieur Férion in Vence and then Saint-Jeannet, Sonia Bera and Daniela were drafted in to help, also. Neither had a definite view. With blanks drawn all round, Darac decided to wait the three days for Wanda's unauthorised DNA sample to come back from the lab before taking this aspect of the investigation further.

The traffic stopped and Darac crossed. Setting down his guitar case at the agreed meeting place, he gazed back through the helter skelter towards the Baie des Anges. He loved these on-the-cusp times of day. Orange-streaked azure over glittering sapphire, the sky and the sea would soon lose the horizon that separated them, forming a vast continuum of bluish purple. Two infinities becoming one, it was a thing of immense promise. Tonight, he felt it more than ever.

Away to his left, a woman wearing a white sundress was picking her way through the crowds towards him. A woman with luxuriant black hair and green eyes. Darac was still gazing out into the bay when an unfamiliar perfume filled his nostrils and he felt a hand close on his. He turned. They kissed for a long time.

'Frankie, your call was the happiest of my life.'

'Christophe and me. It's over. For good.'

Darac closed his eyes and held her tightly. He went to say something but no words came. It didn't matter. He felt sure they would have all the time in the world to talk and besides, they had gone over a couple of things that needed to be said during the call. Yes, Frankie had been on the line to Marseille when Darac had rung her mobile from the Caserne – but only to decline their offer formally. For his part, Darac had explained that he'd spent so long trying to find Angeline because he felt the need to tell her face to face that he never wanted to see or hear from her again. Other things were not broached and possibly never would be. How Frankie could have believed that Darac might have welcomed Angeline back into his heart at her expense was something he couldn't fathom. That Angeline's spiteful dig about re-finding his mother might have given Frankie even a moment's pause had not occurred to him at all.

It was Darac who finally spoke. 'Where will you sleep tonight?'

'At my place, I think, Paul. Join me. And it is *my* place, incidentally.'

'Christophe?'

'Gone to stay with a fellow designer. Laura. Lives in Miramas. Tall. Trim. Blonde. She's 27. And *so* creative.'

'And lives *so* near Marseille.'

'Yes, what a coincidence. It transpires they've been lovers for the past five years. Half the time he goes away...' Her tone supplied the inverted commas... "on business", they couple up. Laura has been ever so good about sharing him with me, he says. By default, she's had the lion's share, actually. I can't even remember when I last slept with Christophe.'

The self-denial. The guilt. The heartache. Darac couldn't believe what they had put themselves through. 'Frankie – all this time, we've...'

'I know. Great detectives we are, aren't we? I was even wrong about him not wanting to lose me. It wasn't love. It was owner-ship. And on that theme, he will no doubt want to move his things out in stages. To make life as difficult as possible.'

Darac cradled her face in his hands. 'Let's make it easier. I'll load everything of his into a van and drive it to Miramas.'

'Paul...'

They kissed once more.

Should an old friend have caught sight of Darac at that moment and tried to sneak past unnoticed, a double bass would not have made a helpful accessory. Neither would a companion announcing to anyone who would listen that Darac was with a woman and *jo!* how fabulous she was!

'Roll call. The one with the big fiddle and his head down – that's Luc Gabron who you've met before. The one walking backwards with her eyes on stalks...' He gave her a wave. 'That's Trudi Pachelberg. Not sure you've had the pleasure.'

'She looks fun.'

'And then some.' His eyes slid to the security guards. 'Shall we? I've got your ticket.'

'Uh-huh.'

He picked up his guitar case and they walked towards the entrance arm in arm.

# 54

Hervé Montand's hand hovered over the plan like God reaching towards Adam.

'The new buildings and courts increase Centre Sicotte's overall footprint by some 15%.' His kickback on the deal was a mere 10% but it all added up. 'So we're agreed then?' He looked into Tina's eyes and smiled. 'Work can start immediately once everything is settled.'

Deepak whispered something in her ear.

'Yes, that's right.' Tina eyeballed Montand. 'We spoke of a 20% footprint increase originally, monsieur.'

'You don't know how close you came to having flats crawling with *racaille* from Paris and Lyon overlooking your grounds, each with a free membership to your new facilities, and called *Apartements Yolande Bertrand* in honour of your hated, sorry *beloved*, mother. Better a slightly smaller spa, isn't it? But if you can stomach the other thing, *don't sign*.'

Tina grabbed the pen. 'That limp of yours,' she said, as Montand rose. 'Although everything's officially closed now, Jodie Foucault is still on site. If I asked her nicely, she might just squeeze you in.'

Just hearing the word "squeeze" made Montand feel nauseous and he took his leave without further comment. Seeing Zep's bike chained outside the swimming pool did nothing to improve his discomfort and for a reckless moment, Montand considered letting its tyres down. But the good doctor was sure to materialise and catch him in the act. Besides, the man was Montand's co-conspirator as well as his tormentor and for the time being, he knew he owed him everything. He also knew that next year or the year after, or the year after that, he would see to it that Doctor Zep would not return from one of his runs, bike rides or swims. No one got a Montand by the balls and lived to tell the tale.

# 55

For fans of the Didier Musso Quintet, the only surprise of their set was that no one had turned up on behalf of "the city" to whisk away guitarist Paul Darac half-way through. Concluding with a scorching ten-minute version of Billy Cobham's 'Taurean Matador', a number chosen partly to showcase the talents of young drummer Maxine Walda, the DMQ's performance was an unqualified triumph.

The band left the stage high as kites, and when they floated back to earth, they gathered around club owner Ridge Clay as if he had been pulling the strings throughout.

'I'm proud,' he said, the gravity of his expression matching the weighty rumble of his voice. 'You were stars tonight, each one of you. And Maxine?' He gave it a beat. 'Special.'

Didier led the cheers and whoops for the young woman.

At that moment, Frankie drifted in next to Darac and slipped her hand in his. She seemed proud, too. Proud and something less positive. 'I loved Ridge's "special". "Awesome" is an over-used word, I think.'

'Agreed,' Darac said, taking her to one side. 'Listen, I know you don't love this music. I also know you understand that I do. That's good enough for me.'

'Don't give up on me yet. But...' Brandishing her mobile, she pressed her lips together in apology. '... an operation we've had going on up in Ventabrun for three months is coming to a head. I'm needed.'

He clicked his tongue. 'A police detective's life, eh? Who would marry one?'

She took a key off her ring and slipped it into his hand. 'I wonder,' she said.

# 56

In the fitness room, Granot was feeling exhausted but happy. The session had begun with an eight-lap power walk around the grounds, a whopping 3000-step addition to his total for the day. Next, Jodie had put him through his paces on the rowing machine, the cross trainer and his new best friend, the stability ball. The results at his post-session weigh-in had him punching the air.

'They thought they were going to fire you?' Jodie said. 'No way. Well done, Roland.'

'It's all down to you.'

'It isn't me who's lost three kilos in as many days.'

'If I keep going like this, I'll have reached my target weight in three weeks, not three months!'

'I won't lie to you. The rate of loss will slow down considerably as you get further into the programme. But with your attitude. you'll do it, I have absolutely no doubt. Everything else will follow. Hit the showers and I'll see you back here in fifteen.'

By the time he emerged from the locker room, Granot was even more upbeat. 'I feel so much better for all this, too.' A look of magnificent confidence suddenly ennobled his grizzled chops. 'I may even take up pétanque again.'

It took a couple of seconds but Jodie couldn't help laughing. Granot couldn't help joining her.

'Let's go. We'll have to use the emergency exit. Sonia will have gone home by now. Have you have got everything, by the way? Once I close the door, we won't be able to get back in.'

'You don't have a key?'

'Not to any of the outside doors. And I've learned never to disturb Michel.'

'Your night security man?'

'More of a night watchman. When he's awake.'

'Right. Would you mind a couple of questions on the case?'

'Anything to help.'

'Anything?' Still in high good humour, Granot felt like asking: "According to Caroline's inventory, three processed wills are missing – those of Messieurs Blé, Martot and Colle. Any idea where they've got to?" Before he knew it, he'd done just that.

'I knew all three of them – they were my patients. You think the killer took their wills? Is that why you want to know?'

'Forget I asked you that,' he said, coming to his senses. He lost them again immediately. 'Unless you can think of a reason.'

She shook her head but it appeared that she was still thinking about it when Granot asked his next question.

'We've been wondering about Caroline's background. Her parents were well off, it seems?'

'Uh... Caro's parents? Both of them had died before I came on the scene. They were comfortable, I think. Some of the furniture was theirs. What Caro called the good stuff.'

'The house, the car – Caroline lived well, herself.'

'She worked very hard, Roland.'

Granot decided to drop the line. 'I'm sure.'

They arrived at the exit.

'Was there anything else?'

'Yes.' Granot unzipped his holdall and produced a sheaf of photocopied pages. 'The diary entries I mentioned.' He handed them over. 'Check out the last day of each month.'

Jodie ran through them in sequence, shaking her head each time. 'No. I'm sorry, I'm none the wiser.' But then she turned to the final page and froze, staring through the paper as if to a deeper truth beneath. Her face flushed pink, throwing the scar

343

on her cheek into sharp relief.

'I'm sorry, Jodie.' Granot took back the pages. 'I shouldn't have reminded you of that day so graphically.'

'No, I'm fine.' She clicked her tongue. 'Stupid me. I've just realised I've left something in my locker. Diabetes stuff.'

'Ah. Are you sure you're alright?'

'Yes, yes. You go on. Just follow the path around the building and you'll come out in the car park.'

'My sense of direction is unerring, don't worry.'

'*Very* good work today.'

She turned and was gone before Granot could reply.

# 57

With his *non-sympa* immediate superior, Doctor Carl Barrau, still off sick, and with senior pathologist Professor Deanna Bianchi called back from leave a day early, Djibril Mpensa had grounds for a double celebration. And it meant he finally had time to look into the more peripheral evidence from the Paillaud/Rosay case. He had begun by mounting a proper examination of the substance he'd found under Caroline's fingernails. When it came, the result shocked him to the core. He prepared a second slide and then re-examined her bloods. The result was the same. He thought about it, glanced at his watch, and picked up the phone. A nicotine-rasped voice answered.

'Bianchi.'

'It's Map, Deanna. I've got a problem with Caroline Rosay's subungual findings. Have you a moment?'

'A moment, yes. I'm due at the hippodrome shortly.'

'Listen, I don't want to make you late for the theatre but—'

'The hippodrome at Cagnes, you naïve young thing. Horse racing under the lights. What's the problem?'

He gave a concise summary.

'Only in the wound blood?'

'Yes.'

'I'll be in as soon as I can.'

A dark-eyed woman with the quick, alert mien of a small bird, Professor Deanna Bianchi looked at Mpensa over the gold rims of her glasses and said: 'Alright, let's run it again. I'll wait for the second race to lose all my money.'

Mpensa shook his head as he set about it. 'If only I'd discovered this before.'

'A grain of *this* here, a grain of *that* there? You've done well to isolate and then link them at all.'

Twenty minutes later, the machine made a buzzing sound and stopped. LEDs pulsed in rapid sequences as if they themselves were making the effort to analyse the sample. Finally, the screen went blank, blinked, and then displayed: $NA_3C_6H_5O_7$. Mpensa recited the formula slowly, each element a dagger in his heart. 'That and raised calcium levels in the wound blood only? A first-year student knows what that could mean.'

'The first thing it means is to give Darac a call.'

'He's playing at the jazz festival this evening.'

'If you can't raise him, leave a message and try the others. Then call R.O. and ask him to re-examine the carpet where the victim was lying.'

'And Frènes?'

'No, not yet! Have I taught you nothing? And it's because of his incessant demands for quick results on the case that this has happened.' She took her leave. '*Courage!*'

# 58

Darac was chatting with Didier and Ridge in the back stage area when his mobile buzzed.

'Paul?'

'Can't talk now, Erica. I'm suffering from Phronesis, which, if you've never encountered it, is paralysis of the larynx brought on by a surfeit of listening pleasure. And you could have been here to witness it.'

'So-o glad I wasn't. Listen, I've been looking for the three will summaries Granot wanted me to find on Caroline Rosay's GenTec 5000. An obliging machine – wish we came across them more often.'

On stage, the James Clarence Orchestra chose that moment to get their set underway.

'Hang on a couple of seconds, Erica.' Darac retired to a quieter corner. 'Now, I can just about hear. You've found them, you say? Good work.'

'I was going to send them to Granot but he's unavailable. I've put all three on one file which should ping in any second. It's only a few lines.'

'It's just coming in.'

'Right, I'm going home. Serge is learning to cook so I may never see you again.'

'It was lovely while it lasted.'

They ended the call and to the accompaniment of 'One O'Clock Jump' from the stage, Darac read the file. When he had finished, four links between the three original wills had emerged. Each of the elderly decedents had been resident in La Crague; each had been a patient of Doctor Zep; and each had left their quite modest estates to the same institution, a children's medical facility in Ouagadougou, Burkina Faso, named for one Arnaud Zep. The fourth link was the reason that Granot had wanted to find them in the first place: all three original wills were missing. Darac stared at the floor.

'I enjoyed your set, man,' a Scandinavian-inflected voice said in passing.

'Thanks,' Darac said, absently, not looking up.

He would never know just whom he had impressed because his mobile rang immediately.

'Darac? Good, I caught you.'

'Yes, Map?'

'Listen, I've got bad news. The powder I detected under Caroline Rosay's fingernails at the scene? As you implied, although it clearly wasn't the direct cause of her death, it might still have been significant if it proved to be cocaine, an opioid, methamphetamine, whatever. It transpired that it wasn't and with all the Frènes frenzy, I decided to shelve a proper examination until things quietened down. Now that Deanna's back, I have been able to look at it.'

'And?'

'It's Trice.'

'Trice?'

'Sorry – Trisodium Citrate. And the bad news doesn't end there. I also found traces of it in her wound blood along with a raised calcium level. People can have raised or reduced levels of all sorts of things in their bodies, quite naturally, or as a result of drug or meds regimes. Neither was the case here. In the levels we're talking about, both were crucially absent from her blood chemistry itself.'

'And this is crucial because?'

'If Trisodium Citrate is added to blood in a 1:9 ratio, it prevents it from clotting, keeping it liquid, and that means, I'm

348

afraid, that my estimate of the time of her death is out.'

'Out?' As if under the weight of clotting blood, Darac's heart sank. From Jodie to Férion/Paillaud, he and the team had discounted suspect after suspect for Caroline's murder because of that estimate. 'Out by how much, potentially?'

'In lab conditions, Trice will keep blood in a liquid state almost indefinitely. On the ground, kept cool in a sealed container of some sort – many hours.'

Darac exhaled deeply. 'So just in terms of the pathology, the killer could have struck *hours* before we thought?'

'Hours, no – other factors preclude it. We're talking keeping the killer's window of opportunity open by another twenty to thirty minutes. I realise that puts many suspects back in the frame but there it is.'

Darac's mind was racing. 'How did the stuff find its way into her blood?'

'That *how* is key and it brings us back to the raised calcium. As it flowed following the blow, I believe the wound blood was drawn off into a syringe to which the Trice was added. A couple of grains spilled and, in her death throes, Caroline scratched them up off the carpet. It seems the killer didn't notice, beat a hasty exit, and returned, let's say, twenty minutes later. First adding the re-coagulant calcium, the liquid syringe blood was then squirted back into the wound, making it appear that the murder had just taken place. It's worth noting that without the addition of the re-coagulant, the deception wouldn't have worked – the clotting schedule would have been greatly delayed.'

'I said you would make a good detective. Who could have pulled this off, Map?'

'Someone who's used to handling syringes. And under the circumstances, someone with nerves of steel. The materials themselves? Obtaining them is no problem.'

'No problem?' A familiar complex of emotions came over Darac. 'Especially,' he said, 'if the killer has access to a doctor's surgery.'

# 59

A stark concrete box topped with a flat roof, the swimming pool building was an example of an architectural style known as brutalism. Jodie found it an apt term. For her, it had always conveyed a palpable sense of threat, an effect heightened at night when the grounds were deserted, as was the case now. And she had felt that way before she had learned that the building had originally been the Centre's gym, a place where parents sent little girls to be put through their paces and who sometimes fell short. Brutalism, indeed.

Zep's bike was still chained to the rail. Jodie walked around the perimeter of the building, looking for a door or a window that may have been left open. None had.

She cursed her luck, realising she would have to wait outside somewhere. Wait in the shadows, jump out and catch him by surprise. But he was a strong man and fit. Surprise alone may not be sufficient. If she really wanted to catch him unawares and vulnerable, her original plan was best. And she had to succeed. Had to. There was only one thing to do. She shone a torch up the moonlit side wall of the building.

Jodie knew that one of the roof skylights was stuck open; its metal frame distorted in a heat wave the previous summer and not yet replaced. Instead, cash-strapped Tina had had a roll of fine-mesh chicken wire stuffed roughly into the gap, a simple but effective means of performing a vital task – keeping out the local wildlife. The last thing the Centre needed, she had said, was for a bird, or worse, a bat to have entered through the gap and got into the storeroom below. All it would then have taken was for their fool of a maintenance man to have left the door ajar, or one of the inspection hatches open, and the creature could have found its way into the pool area itself. No swimmer wants to swallow bird shit, she had said. No one balancing on the end of a diving platform ten metres above the water wants to be buzzed by a bat and fall off. With a straight face, she had added "Things like that cause ripples." Jodie and Caroline had laughed about it until it hurt.

Glad of the full moon, Jodie tightened the straps on her rucksack, took a deep breath and began the ascent. As a 10 year-old, she had routinely shinned up ropes in free air and not been allowed to descend until she had touched the gym's ceiling. Compared to that, the prospect of climbing up a fixed drainpipe with a solid wall either side seemed simple.

In the event, the poor state of the pipe and of the wall made for a slower, more difficult climb than she anticipated but as she reached the top, she hadn't once succumbed to the feeling that she might fall. The eaves, mercifully, were shallow and with her feet clamped firmly above a collar on the pipe, she pulled herself up and on to the roof in one supple movement.

The easy part was over. Checking that no one was below and that her VW Estate was the only vehicle left in the car park, she scampered towards the skylights on the opposite side of the roof. The chicken wire plug had been compressed and twisted into a tight tangle, its cut mesh ends a jagged challenge to unprotected hands. In lieu of gloves, Jodie took a towel out of her rucksack, wrapped it around both hands and pushed hard. Snagging on the frame, the plug hardly moved. She gave it a series of hard shoves. Finally, it tore itself free and fell harmlessly into the storeroom beneath.

She took out her torch and shone the beam through the gap. There was a clear landing space on the floor immediately below. No more than a three-metre drop. No problem. Playing the beam around the room, she found a door set into the far wall and realised it must have been the one that gave on to the landing. From there, a flight of steps descended to the poolside. Her pulse quickened.

But first, she needed to negotiate the gap. As slight as she was, she knew there no way she could squeeze through so she grabbed the window's metal frame and pulled. It groaned. She pulled harder and, testing her theory that Michel was the least attentive night watchman in France, wrenched it open to the accompaniment of a loud, metallic squeal. She stuffed the towel into her rucksack, tossed it through the widened gap and dropped easily in after it.

The torch beam found a light switch. She turned it on. A bare room. To her right: open shelving. A bench. Exposed pipe work. An inspection cradle set over a hatch in the floor. A corridor receding into the distance. Two further cradles. To her left: the door. Metal. No handle. Flush-fitting lock.

She opened a drawer in the bench. No key. The shelves contained nothing but replacement light fittings and tubes. She looked for a hook. None. She returned to the bench. No tools.

'Shit!'

She tried the door again but there was nothing to hold, nothing with which to lever it open, nothing protruding to bash off.

'Shit! Shit!! Shit!!!'

Her eyes slid to the inspection cradle, a contraption used by the maintenance man mainly to replace bulbs in the pool's ceiling lights. It was a fearsome looking device. Yellow-painted steel. Black lightning bolts. Cables. Counterweights. The words TRAINED PERSONNEL ONLY.

It was during one of the annual pool closures that Jodie had seen it in action. 'Why doesn't Tina get rid of these cradle things?' she had said to Sonia, realising that the pool's hanging lights could be replaced by ones set into the ceiling. 'That way, the maintenance guy could change bulbs and so on from directly inside the storeroom. Much safer. And quicker.' 'Why doesn't Tina do it?' Sonia had said, beaming away as usual. 'For the same reason as always. It's cheaper to keep things as they are.'

As Jodie tried to work out a plan, she was for once glad of Tina's penny-pinching. Deploying the cradle – if Jodie could work out how to do it – would give her access to the pool. But what good would hanging a couple of metres beneath the ceiling do her? For the first time in her life, Jodie regretted not owning a gun. All she had was a rock.

But then another possibility occurred to her. It made her blood run cold.

'*You can do it.*' She began to hyperventilate. '*Stop your nonsense. You can do it!*' She ran through the idea once more. A lot could go wrong. *No negative thoughts now.* She took a deep breath and moved towards the cradle. The platform was surrounded by a rail-topped safety cage, the height of a tall man's waist; chest level for Jodie. Grasping the rail, she sprang up and side vaulted over it into the cage. The words HOLD RAIL WHILE MOVING. Footprint outlines. The words PUSH BUTTON TO DESCEND/ASCEND. She took another deep breath. Her finger moved to the button.

# 60

'Where are you, Granot? Still at Centre Sicotte?'

'No, on my way home. Just crossed the Var on the 6202.'

'Got to the roundabout yet?'

'Coming up to it.'

'Go right round and head back. I'm a few kilometres ahead. I'll wait for you in the car park and we'll take it from there.'

'Take what from there?'

'Arresting Caroline's killer.'

# 61

If Jodie had not been so entirely focused on the coming ordeal, she might have wondered what she would do if her quarry were not obliviously reeling off laps in his preferred front crawl. If he switched to backstroke, he might be gazing up at the ceiling at the very moment the cradle began to descend. Or what if he was already on his way to the changing rooms? She asked herself none of these questions.

A whirring sound. A sudden jerk. Keeping her eyes on a fixed point on the ceiling, she held on tightly as the cradle dropped slowly away and the dim confines of the storeroom gave way to a bright, reverberant vastness smelling of chlorine. A second jerk. The whirring stopped. All she could hear now was her heartbeat thumping in her ears and the slap, slap of water far below.

She was still staring upwards. *Jodie, stop your nonsense!* Lowering her gaze until she was staring straight ahead, she took a deep breath and looked slowly over the rail into the abyss. Her stomach came up into her mouth. *Stop that! Think!* She calculated she was a full twenty metres above the shallow end of the pool – too high to risk a fall into such a meagre splash of water. *But you won't fall. Think about your next move.*

For the moment, she couldn't see the swimmer. He must have been immediately below, turning at the end of a length. And then a red swimming cap emerged, heading back up the lane. A pale back. Tanned forearms. Zep.

What now? She looked across to the landing outside the

storeroom, and to the steps leading off it. Both were too far away to reach with a standing jump. But there was an alternative. Three reinforced steel joists spanned the length of the pool, i-bar sections of steel about twice the width of a gymnast's balance beam. The nearest was all of four metres below the cradle and about two metres to the side. Reachable? Just. If she aced it. *You can do it.* She stood for a moment, trying to put the routine together in her head. *Break it down.* The whole thing would require two dismounts, first from the cradle on to the i-bar, then from the i-bar on to the back of the high diving platform at the far end of the pool. That last part would be easy, a drop of a few metres on to a wide landing area – if she made it that far.

The cradle floor extended beyond the cage on all four sides, forming a ledge about 10 centimetres deep – sufficient to accommodate only the balls of her feet. That would be her take-off point but first, she had to negotiate the rail fixed to the top of the cage. She decided to pull herself up and roll over it on the turn so she would finish facing into the cradle, a simple bailout option if she got it wrong or couldn't get her balance. It was a manoeuvre guaranteed to rock the cradle and that was good because she needed to assess how much resistance it would provide for the dismount.

Another visualisation, another deep breath and she went for it. Her Lycra leggings sliding freely over the rail, she found the ledge with her feet and stood still. The cradle had hardly moved.

Switching her grip on the rail, she kept her gaze level as she pivoted on the balls of her feet. Her balance held. Now with her back to the cradle, she had to banish the thought that, the i-bar apart, there was twenty metres of empty air beneath her. Her heart was thumping. Sweat began to sting her eyes. No! She *must* be able to see clearly. She blinked repeatedly. No use. She needed to wipe them. Her hands were behind her. She had to release one. The right. No, the left. She let go and flicked away the blur. She would have to make the jump before it happened again. She looked down. Zep was embarking on a new length.

Face down in the water. Blind.

Now look at the i-bar. *Look at it*! She lowered her eyes and her stomach turned over as the pool dropped further away from her. *Concentrate*! Her legs were shaking. Her feet were cramping. Her palms were sweating. Chalk! Where was the chalk? Forget it. *Visualise*! *Deep breath*! From somewhere far away she heard a crowd hush; she saw the faces of the judges; and her coach, intense, exhorting. And then quite suddenly, they disappeared. Knowing that if she took an extra couple of steps on landing, they would be her last on this earth, Jodie took one final look. Flexing at the knees, she let go of the rail and, splaying her limbs like a human grappling hook, jumped off her right foot into space.

Jarring every bone in her body, she landed hard on all fours. She overbalanced. She made a couple of gut-wrenching adjustments. And hung on.

Now she had hit the target, she could see that the i-bar was about 30 centimetres across, three times as wide as a balance beam. She could have straddled it and shuffled along quite safely on her bottom to the far end. But wouldn't that increase the risk of being spotted from below? *Walk. That's all you have to do. No somersaults. No flick-flacks or handstands.*

As the red cap continued to plough a lone furrow, Jodie slowly stood. She let the void on either side of her settle. Another visualisation. Another breath. Standing tall, she put one foot in front of the other and moved steadily away. She had already run through what she was going to do when she got to the other end. The easy drop on to the diving platform. The stealthy descent of the steps. Surprising him. The blow. With every passing moment, it came a little closer.

What she couldn't know was that Zep was completing his final length of the evening.

# 62

Darac was grooving to Omar Puente's 'Samba Para Dos' as he
pulled into the Centre Sicotte car park; grooving and smiling at
its almost ridiculous aptness for his future with Frankie. There
was just one car left in the lot: Jodie's VW Estate. Keeping it in
sight without giving his own presence away, he backed into a
deeply shaded pocket outside the pool and turned off his lights.

It was then he saw Zep's bike chained to the rail outside
the entrance. He called Granot immediately. No reply. He left
a message. Best practice now was to wait but what would be
the harm in having a preliminary recce? Darac headed for the
entrance. The lights were on but the doors were locked. Hoping
agents from the European Court weren't lurking in the shadows,
Darac took his picks out of his pocket and, resolving to leave the
door open for Granot, set to work.

Officers sometimes had a sixth sense that they were walking
into danger. Darac always had to fight that feeling around swimming pools. It wasn't just that, as a non-swimmer, he was scared
of deep water. What was more beautiful to him than the Baie
des Anges? And he had made the crossing to Corsica from the
old port several times without a qualm. He had no problem
with being *on* water but a swimming pool meant going *in*. That
was what it was for. Just the thought of it made him feel claus-
trophobic and light-headed. And as the son of a perfume house
Nose, he detested the disservice done to his nostrils by the
pervasive reek of chlorine.

At first, there appeared to be no one around but as he walked through the changing room, he heard noises in the distance. Voices. Echoing shouts. And then silence. He unholstered his automatic and ran. The smell of chlorine ever stronger, he hurried on to the poolside as something splashed into the water ahead of him. A small projectile. Already feeling nauseous, he looked up. There were figures on the highest of three diving boards. Zep standing. And Jodie, it had to be, lying on her back, a limp arm draped over the edge.

'Captain? Why weren't you here two minutes ago! Jodie tried to kill me. By smashing my head in. That was a rock hitting the water. I took it off her.' He bent over her. 'She's just unconscious. I had to knock her out.'

A hundred things went through Darac's head; Granot being no more than five minutes away, the first of them. He holstered the automatic. 'I'll come up.'

'Good. Be easier getting her down with two.'

'I must apologise, Doctor. We were far too slow cottoning on to her.'

'I can't believe this. Eight years I've worked with her. Eight!'

'Murderers don't wear placards, alas.' As he reached the tower, Darac's gaze was drawn to the diving pool. *It's just water.* 'Pull her back from the edge, though, will you?' *No, it's not just water. It's a bucket of bleach ten metres deep. Maybe fifteen.* 'I want to question her, not visit her in the morgue.'

'Yes, of course.'

Darac began to skip up the steps as if diving were something he did every day. He glanced up at the platform. En route, landings for two lower boards appeared to offer breaks in the sightline. At the first, he swiped his mobile and, without breaking stride, texted "*jod zep pool*" to Granot. 'The myokymia's abated, by the way. No fluttering at all. Thanks for that.'

'You're welcome. Coping with the headaches?'

'You know your stuff.' At the second landing, Darac texted "*danger.*"

Zep, two backpacks drawn up at his feet, was still crouched

over Jodie as Darac emerged on to the dizzying height of the platform. He felt sick. *Look calm.* He could see she was breathing and there was no blood. But she hadn't been moved any further inboard. 'Hey, bring her in a bit, will you?' *Stay away from the edge.* 'I must commend—'

'Your mobile was in your shirt. Now it's in your jacket. Called for back-up?'

'Not back-up. Just letting the Caserne know—'

'Stop there, Captain. Don't take another step.' Zep stood, revealing the umbilicus fastening his wrist to Jodie's ankle. 'Zinc oxide tape. Forget the gun! Shoot me and she's dead, too. Whether we hit the water or the poolside.'

*Give it one more try.* 'What are you doing?' Darac edged forward. 'I'm here to arrest her.'

'Stop, I said! Here for *her*? I knew immediately you were here for me. Rosay was a blackmailer, Captain. She bled me. At the end of every month for over a year, I paid her. Like a service bill. Two hundred euros. Clever, keeping it modest. But Christ, it adds up. There were two others, did you know that? Three of us paying. Paying every month on the dot. She thought that was very funny.'

Blackmail? Yes, Darac believed it. *He'll want to say more.* 'How did you pay her?'

'Cash. I put it in her daysack in her locker. She gave me a key. Nice of her, wasn't it? I was late last month. Paid in the end, though. And so, my God, did she.'

*Keep him talking.* 'Three you say? Who are the others?'

' "Even Deepak pays on time," she said. A slip. I think Vaselle may be the other but I don't know.'

'What did she have on you, Zep?'

'It doesn't matter.'

The missing wills of Blé, Martot and Colle were surely at the heart of it. 'You persuaded three people to leave everything to your charity, right?' He glanced at Jodie. No change. 'That's not a crime.'

'They were no longer *people*. They were sick, worn-out old carcasses. But their money helped sick, *young* people to have a life. I feel no guilt at all.'

'No? You felt guilty enough to remove the wills in question from the scene. That was a mistake, by the way. It only drew our attention to them.'

'*Did* it, now.'

*Accuse him further. He may argue.* 'I suspect you did more than just *persuade* the three you deemed to have gone past their live-by date. I think you eased their passage into the grave, didn't you? And somehow, Caroline found out about it.'

'We'll have time to debate morals on the way.'

*On the way? He's going to take me hostage. First, he'll have to jettison Jodie.* 'Listen, Zep – you killed Caroline solely because she was blackmailing you, right? The court will take that into account. They'll show some leniency. What you're planning to do now—'

'Will make no difference.'

'Yes, it will.' Darac glanced once more at Jodie. *Where are you, Granot? Keep Zep talking. Try flattery.* 'Incidentally, it was ingenious, how you killed Caroline and made it appear that you couldn't possibly have had time. Oh, yes, we know how you did it.'

'So do I and you're stalling. Here's what we're going to do. There will be no negotiation or hesitation on your part or I'll end this here and now.'

*Yes, you're just mad enough.*

'Throw your mobile into the water.'

Darac did as he was told.

'Take your gun out of its holster and set it down in front of you.'

*Have you ever fired a handgun, Zep? You may just have bought me some seconds.*

'Now go back down to the landing below and walk to the end of the springboard.'

*Shit, shit, shit.*

'Understand?'

'Sure,' Darac said.

'Be careful. It's not wide and stable like this. You wouldn't want to fall in.'

*Does he know?* Darac shrugged. 'OK.'

Zep grinned. 'You'll make your driving seat all wet.' The grin disappeared. 'Do it!'

'I'm going.' Darac took a step backwards. Another step. And another. 'Listen, Doctor.' His eyes were still on Zep. 'I beg you not to compound your—'

'Watch where you're going. You're going to fall down the steps.'

Darac went to glance over his shoulder but he saw Jodie jerk her foot and it stopped him. One wrong turn and it would be all over for her. 'Zep! She's stirring! You'll both go over!'

Zep turned, tearing at the tape.

*Now!* Darac rushed forward. *Go low. Pitch him back over your shoulder.* Using the platform as a break, Darac threw himself on to his side, rolled over and then sprang forward, arms flexed. He saw too late that Zep was not bound to Jodie, but merely holding one end of the tape. He dropped it and stepped away. Teetering sickeningly, Darac grabbed at nothing but air as he pivoted on one foot, the drop at his back. A syringe darted at him, grazing his throat, a kill shot but a lifeline, too, as Zep's forearm offered itself as a grab handle. Off balance, both of them fell, Darac jumping to his feet in one quick motion, Zep landing hard against Jodie, pushing her over the edge. One arm trailing behind her, she was already at the point of no return before Darac could react but he lunged anyway. Just as her hand was about to disappear, he dived headlong and reached out. *One chance!* His hand collided with flesh. He grabbed for it... and he felt her whole body weight tug on his arm. *Haul her up!* But Zep had other ideas. He came again, shouldering Darac in the back.

They fell as one tangled mass. Somehow, Darac writhed free

as he tumbled over and over. And then blue flew up towards him. A blue wall. He slammed into it head-first, feeling a chemical stab in his nostrils, in his forehead, in his brain. His lungs filled with water, choking him, bursting him from inside. He flailed and thrashed and pain seared his chest. A chasm opened up, beckoning him into infinities of dark space. He saw Frankie somewhere beyond, a world gained and lost. He fought harder but sank deeper and deeper. Before his eyes closed, he saw Jodie, a stone, Zep, a fish. He didn't see the creature diving in from the poolside; an altogether bigger fish.

# 63

Directives from Divisional Command rarely brought good news. The one sitting on Darac's desk bore the heading: "Re: Lieutenant Roland B. Granot, award of the Police Medal of Honour; & Re: Technician Principal Erica N. Lamarthe, award of the Edmond Locard Medal."

'Agnès will be back for the ceremonies,' Darac said. 'Perfect, huh?'

Erica was peering at herself in a hand mirror, attempting to gather up her fine blond hair. 'Can't wait to see her. Think I'd suit a bun?'

'No.' Flaco shook her head. 'Loose on the shoulders is your look.'

'Right.' Erica made a moue and let the remaining strands fall free. And then her gaze fell on Flaco's cornrows. '*Love* those. How long does it take?'

'A couple of hundred thousand years.'

'Ah.'

'Loose on the shoulders!'

'Having Agnès there will be the cherry on the cake,' Granot said. 'And not glacé, either. The genuine article.'

'Those from Ceret are by far the best but the season's finished,' Bonbon said, helpfully. 'The Monts de Venasques are still around. And the cake itself?'

'A croque-en-bouche, obviously. A ten-tier tower of heaven. That shall be my reward for hitting my health targets.'

Perand gave him a look. '*Our* reward, you mean. They're

supposed to serve about fifty people.'

'We'll see.'

'Could we stop the cake talk?' Darac said. 'I still feel queasy from swallowing a diving pool.'

A look of splendid self-satisfaction softened Granot's chops. 'So – the Police Medal of Honour. And for valour. In the field.' He gave a circumspect nod. 'Not bad for someone who isn't the action hero type. More a desk jockey. A paper chaser.' His brow lowered quizzically. 'Who was it who called me that?'

Darac went to his Gaggia machine. 'Just because you look like a walrus, how was I to know you could swim like one? Thanks for rescuing Jodie first, by the way.'

'You're welcome.'

'She *was* unconscious,' Perand said, looking half asleep himself. 'You know what I find incredible? After all the amazing stuff she did to get to Zep, she then blew the easy bit.'

Granot bristled. 'Yes, thank you, Perand. Thank God she *didn't* succeed. Arresting her for murder? An appalling thought.'

'It was definitely *Bad* Caroline, wasn't it?' Bonbon shook his tawny head. 'Bent as they come.'

'Jodie still can't believe it.' Granot gave a sad little smile. 'She even feels a little hurt that Caroline hadn't told her what she had been up to all that time, I think.'

Perand looked unconvinced. 'She didn't come out with that in her interview yesterday afternoon.'

'Nevertheless.'

Erica turned to Granot. 'I know what Caroline had on Zep. What about Vaselle?'

'Property swindle. When I compared the deeds to the plans of his Ensoleillé development in Cagnes, I discovered he'd shaved enough off each unit to build an extra bungalow on the site. Caroline discovered it too – she handled the sale.'

'I see. Deepak Golou or whatever he's called?'

'We can't find any documentary evidence but Jodie suspects she may have caught him having sex with an underage girl at the Centre. The bastard. Caroline probably had a photo of it somewhere.' Granot gave Darac a look. 'When do we expect the DNA result on Paillaud/Férion?'

'Later today. Who's for coffee?' A chorus of voices answered. 'So that's... one, two, three singles, a double and a noisette for you Erica. Flak – nothing? Right.'

Bonbon took a paper bag from his pocket. 'And what goes better with a decent espresso than a chocolate chair-o-plane? Help yourselves.'

Flaco took one and handed them on. 'Commissaire Dantier always says that in any contest...' Her lips stopped moving, running aground on a sandbank of mush.

Measuring out beans at the Gaggia, Darac couldn't resist a smile. Flaco talking with her mouth full? Unheard-of nonchalance. 'Yes, Flak?'

'Sorry – these chocolates are chewy. Yes, she says that in any contest, mistakes are inevitable and the winner is the one who makes the fewest.'

Perand produced one of his trademark half-sneer, half-grins. 'Zep made plenty, although making it look as if he was tethered to Jodie on the diving board – that was clever.'

'He *wasn't* tethered to her, Paul?' Erica said.

'No, he was just holding his end of the tape. He yanked it to move her foot which he knew would alarm me. Then when he stood feigning helplessness as he pretended to disentangle himself, I rushed forward. He suckered me, basically.'

Perand was still grinning. 'The mistake he made then was then missing your neck with the syringe he was holding behind his back.'

'Thanks for the thought.'

Perand turned to Erica. 'You wouldn't think that injecting caffeine into someone could kill them, would you?'

'If you had no knowledge of biochemistry, you wouldn't.'

'OK.'

'I'll make yours a quadruple, if you like, Perand.'

As he began grinding the beans, Darac retired into his own thoughts. For him, among the more remarkable aspects of the case was the extent to which the mistakes he and the team made had worked *for* them. In showing Jodie photocopied pages from Caroline's diary, Granot had unwittingly allowed her to see something she shouldn't − Zep's diary entry in the slot Caroline had reserved, though tellingly not recorded, for Hervé Montand. Encountering the good doctor's handwriting virtually every day and recognising the sort of sticky, threadbare ink line his job-lot surgery ballpoints made, Jodie realised immediately that it was Zep himself who had written his name in that slot, saw how it incriminated Montand and diverted suspicion away from himself. Pondering why and when he had done that, she could come to only one conclusion.

Granot had also *told* Jodie something he shouldn't − the names of the testators of the three missing wills whom Jodie had known as patients. In her subsequent interview, she recounted that in hours of chat on the massage table, none had ever given the slightest indication of an interest in the welfare of African children, nor of anyone else. It had always struck her as strange, therefore, that their names appeared on a list of benefactors to Zep's eponymous clinic; a list reproduced on a charity T-shirt, one of many such garments Jodie had bought over the years. And then, after her workout with Granot, there he was telling her that the trio's wills were missing from Caroline's files. Again, like a good detective, she put these things together and arrived at an inescapable conclusion. Like a bad detective, she had kept that conclusion to herself.

Assessing that Zep would be at his most vulnerable in the swimming pool, her plan had been to confront him just as he climbed out but he had caught sight of her when the cradle descended and was waiting on the diving platform. Brilliant and brave though her performance had been, she had risked her neck for nothing, a serious misjudgement which had almost cost her and Darac their lives.

As with some jazzers Darac knew, Zep's own misjudgements resulted from overdoing things when he should have been underplaying them and vice versa. Partially erasing the end-of-month dots in Caroline's diary was a case in point. In his interrogation, Zep recalled that he had no sooner started to remove them when he heard sounds from outside – sounds, the team now believed, made by Vaselle – and abandoned the idea. Erasing all the dots, or better still, leaving them all extant, would have worked better for him; as would leaving the 7 pm appointment slot empty instead of tricking up an entry to further incriminate Montand. And as Darac had told Zep when stalling for time at the pool, all he achieved by removing the wills of Blé, Martot and Colle was to draw the team's attention to them.

Not taking other matters far enough had cost him more dearly still. Having delivered his ultimatum on the diving platform, he should then have waited until Darac was clear of his automatic, picked it up and shot him. Armed and alone, he might well have made good his escape.

Darac hadn't been slow to recognise that he himself had made mistakes. In his whole career, few had had such a fortuitous outcome as his decision to enter the swimming pool building alone. He had had no idea of the life and death struggle going on inside and by the book, he should have waited for Granot to join him. If he had, they would have found Jodie dead.

Darac's mobile rang. Ormans's number.

'Where are you?

'My office. Is everything OK?"

'Go into the squad room and turn on the TV.'

'What?'

'Put it on Télé Matin. Or any news channel. Now!'

'Squad room, everyone!'

The picture faded in. A stack of trays. Monsieur La Chute about to stride into the Seine. 'It's the *Coming, Monsieur!* photo,' Darac said.

The camera reframed, lingering on a handwritten signature.

'And it's the original Brassaï.'

The camera pulled back. The photograph was hanging in an alcove over a writing desk. Panning now. A living room. Quite large. Untidy. A chaise longue. Doors. Posters. Play bills. More framed photos. A low table. Then, the familiar face of the TM interviewer, speaking. Now a two-shot. The interviewee was Ambroise Paillaud.

'They're running an old interview.' Perand yawned. 'So?'

Darac's heart jumped. 'No, it isn't. Look at the ticker.'

BREAKING: AMBROISE PAILLAUD ALIVE       PACT WITH GHOST
WRITER MAURICE FÉRION TRUST FUND GIFTS   MILLIONS
TO LA CRAGUE–DU–VAR       STRINGENT CONDITIONS APPLY
BREAKING: AMBROISE PAILLAUD ALIVE       PACT WITH GHOST–
WRITER MAURICE FÉRION...

Gasps in the squad room. Then uproar.

'Hey, hey!' Darac called out. 'Listen.'

*'Monsieur Paillaud, commentators are already referring to this affair as Monsieur La Chute's last laugh.'*

*'Last laugh? No, I hope there'll be many more to come. I'm particularly looking forward to the biopic. Quite a twist for the third act, my brother Maurice and I have given them, haven't we? And I can't wait for next May. Cannes should be a real hoot. I had thought it would be more fun to attend as Maurice but I'm now thinking it will be even more special to appear as myself.'*

'Granot? Chief? You were right!' Bonbon said, lapping it up. 'The bugger!'

*'Shouldn't you be contrite? You and Monsieur Férion have perpetrated a hoax on such a scale—'*

*'A hoax implies a lack of serious intent. Our intention was deadly serious.'*

*'In the case of murdered notary public, Mademoiselle Caroline Rosay, particularly so.'*

*'In all our years of planning, it never occurred to Maurice and me*

*that Mademoiselle Rosay was anything other than honest. If it had, we would have gone to a different notary. Ultimately, it was the fact that the mademoiselle was a blackmailer that got her killed.'*

'Hear, hear,' Granot said.

*'Nevertheless, in his confession, Doctor Arnaud Zep stated that he would not have murdered Mademoiselle Rosay if you hadn't presented her with a new will and then apparently taken your own life just minutes later.'*

*'So to spell it out, Zep used my will as a cover, a smokescreen he thought the police, like an entire troupe of Monsieur La Chutes, were bound to stumble blindly through to the wrong conclusion...'*

Erica grinned. 'I *love* that connection.'

*'... He thought, "No one will suspect me – they'll suspect the beneficiaries named in the previous will." You think that makes me responsible for the murder of a blackmailer?'*

*'I didn't say that. But what about the question of your own motives, here? Are you not laughing at the expense of your home village, at the police, the judiciary, and your millions of fans throughout the world?'*

*'One can only laugh at the laughable – is that not true? People such as the public prosecutor in charge of this investigation. A pompous buffoon if ever there was one...'*

Laughter.

'Shhh!'

*'... Nevertheless, like the majority of people in our country, I generally fear rather than revere the police.'*

'Too right.' Perand nodded, a tough guy, suddenly. 'But piss off.'

*'But I have come to have a grudging respect for Captain Paul Darac and his team in Nice...'*

Cheers. Fist pumps. Desk slaps.

'Shhhhh!'

*'Yes, they did stumble blindly through the smokescreen at first. But unlike Monsieur La Chute, they didn't fall over at the end.'* Paillaud looked into the camera and smiled. *'Sorry for stealing your thunder by coming clean, ladies and gentlemen, but I knew that despite my*

*brilliant performance, you were about to work out the whole thing. Just a couple of missteps on my part were all you needed. Chapeau! But I'm sure you...'*

Erica could scarcely contain herself. 'He's talking to us!'

'Shhh!'

*'And this...'* Paillaud swept an arm across the scene. *'... plays much better for me than being bundled into the back of a police car, don't you think?'*

'That, my friend,' Granot said. 'Is coming anyway.'

'How about this guy?' Bonbon was wide eyed. 'I love him. Can't help it.'

'Shhh!'

The interviewer was beginning to look impatient. *'Monsieur, if I may—'*

Paillaud sailed on. *'Good girl, that Wanda. Very quick with my glass at the bar. If you're wondering how Maurice and I worked it at the station, he was waiting for me in the toilet at La Poche. First he passed on a note about his stay. Then we swapped clothes. I gave him my toupée and my blessing. We hugged. We wept. And then off he went as me. I came out as him. The boy at the bar didn't suspect a thing, as we knew he wouldn't. And Monsieur Vaselle? About a week before, I'd filched the phone on which I later summoned him to the station. Slipped it right out of a teenager's pocket while asking him for directions. Were Maurice and I hoping Vaselle would lose his temper with the man he thought was me and do something he shouldn't? That was up to him, wasn't it? Just as it was up to Caroline Rosay to do her duty as a notary. By the way, Maurice used to throw himself around almost as much as the future Monsieur La Chute when we were boys. He just didn't do it for laughs as I did. And I owe it to him to say that he performed his final leap much better in rehearsal. A back garden wall is obviously a poor substitute for a railway station platform. Anyway, I've written you a letter, Captain. Should receive it tomorrow.'*

'Wonder if he signed it,' Perand said.

'Shhh!'

The interviewer had finally wrested back control. *'If we could continue? I'm sure officers from the local commissariat here in Paris will be with us very shortly.'*

Paillaud tossed his toupée aside. '*There. Now they won't recognise me. Yes, we were discussing the question of respect. How worthy of it is La Crague's Mayor Hervé Montand, would you say? How much is he entitled to?'*

Ignoring the question, the interviewer held up a wad of A4 pages. '*This is a copy of Monsieur Férion's trust fund holdings, a sum which will be made exclusively available to the commune of La Crague-du-Var, even if said mayor remains in office and agrees to your various provisos. This document was received here at Télé Matin at precisely the same moment broadcasters and print media throughout France received theirs. Quite a publicity coup.'*

'*One might almost say "stunt", if it weren't in such poor taste.'*

'*Indeed. We are sitting in the modest apartment Monsieur Férion owned for the past thirty-eight years. Although the trust fund is vast, he lived simply. Explain that, monsieur'.*

Perand jumped in. 'It's a chunk of Paillaud's own money, you fuckwit! A Plan B in case the will shtick didn't work for some reason – like people spotting Paillaud wasn't dead.'

'Shhh!' Erica clicked her tongue. 'I missed the reply.'

Bonbon leaned into her. 'I think that's what Paillaud said, more or less.'

The interviewer continued. '*Monsieur Hervé Montand, the mayor of La Crague, is unavailable for comment at the moment...'*

'I'll bet he is,' Darac said.

Granot punched the air. 'Jodie for mayor!'

'Shhhh!'

'*... but the social housing provision and several other conditions spelled out in the Férion document send a clear message to him, and to the community, do they not?'*

'*I would hope so.'*

'*And that message is?'*

'*Your family chucked mine out like so much rubbish all those years ago. But look what that rubbish contained. Me, for one. You might just find another national treasure among the outsiders you're going to be rubbing shoulders with from now on.'*

'*A fine, improving sentiment, monsieur. But are you entirely sincere about it?'*

'*Yes, of course.*' Paillaud gave it a long couple of beats and then grinned. '*But we did get you, didn't we, Montand? We really knocked you dead!*'

The interviewer looked away, listening intently. '*Monsieur Paillaud, we have a live link now to someone you have already referred to, a significant player in this saga. Monsieur Jules Frènes, one of the public prosecutors…*'

Derision. Cat calls.

'Guys,' Darac called out. 'Better listen.'

Once again, the interviewer paused. '*I'm sorry but I'm going to have to hold you, Monsieur Frènes. I'm advised, as predicted, that officers have arrived to take Monsieur Paillaud in for questioning…*'

The screen blanked out.

Bonbon shook his head. 'That might just have been the best thing I've ever seen on TV.'

# 64

To Darac, for whom leading a double life was second nature, a rooftop apartment suspended between the tangle of the old town and the Nice of the boulevards was a perfect place to live. But sometimes, the Babazouk was all he needed. The buzz on the streets was not always sonorous; the smells not always sweet. But harmonious and discordant, delicious and sour, it was a world that was alive and kicking and he loved it.

The sun lounger on his roof terrace was supposed to be a single seater but he and Frankie were managing somehow. The conversation, low and slow, had drifted to the topic of Frankie's new perfume.

'So this is the... third you've tried since *Marucca?*'

'Fourth.'

'I like it, this new one.'

'It's lovely but it's still not *quite* there.'

'You realise if I mention this to papa, he would have every Maison Darac perfume in the range sent round? Or work with you in the lab to design your very own?'

'Tell him immediately.'

It was meant light-heartedly, Darac knew, but he made a mental note to do it anyway.

'How are you going to spend the rest of your time off?'

'The usual,' he said. 'Deep sea diving.'

'In that case, I'd better teach you to swim.'

'Only if you promise to wear that white bikini.'

'Haven't got one.'

'Mine, I meant.'

'Paul, Paul – seriously, you have to learn. I don't mean to any great standard but just so you feel reasonably comfortable in water.'

'God, that night... I've been told before that if you fall into deep water, the key is to relax. But I couldn't. And of course the more I thrashed around, the more exhausted I became. Classic vicious circle.'

Frankie squeezed Darac's hand. 'You know, gruff curmudgeon though he sometimes is, I've always been fond of Granot. Now I positively adore him.'

'He drags three people out of the diving pool, two of them half-drowned, the third trying to kill him. He cuffs and arrests him, revives the other two... Astonishing.' He stroked Frankie's hair. 'What was the name of that Hollywood glamour puss who used to be a swimmer? Esther Somebody.'

'Esther... Williams?'

'That's it. One of the moguls said of her, "Wet, she's a star." Or something like that. Well, that was Granot.'

'While we're on remarkable men, what about Ambroise Paillaud?'

'Apart from all else, has there ever been a more effective unmasking of a self-serving bigot than that of Hervé Montand by Paillaud? I can't think of one. He could have just *funded* the building scheme, couldn't he? But by dangling the bequest in front of him, he brought every venal instinct he knew Montand possessed to the fore. And talk about revenge being sweet.'

As if applauding the observation, someone whooped in the street below.

'I wonder how much of the brave new La Crague that Paillaud wants will actually go ahead?'

'Most of it, I should think. Certainly enough to thoroughly piss off Montand. Especially when he gets out of prison and sees what's happened to the place with his own eyes.'

Rolling her shoulders, Frankie nestled back into Darac's

arms. 'Paillaud was complimentary about you and the team in his letter. I liked that.'

'His comments might not have been quite so positive if he'd known how many mistakes we made on the Rosay murder. A double-arrival killing just like the Jacqueline Denfert case? Bonbon and I even cited it to Flak. We realised pretty well straight away that Montand couldn't have done that so we dropped it. Partly because we paid too much respect to the watchdog capabilities of Monsieur Brice Kerthus, it didn't occur to us that *Zep* might have arrived at the scene twice.'

'Map's first estimate of the time of Caroline's death was the main problem.'

'But there again, the blame lies with me. I should have waited for his full report before I acted. I went too far and too fast on just the preliminary.'

'And why? Because of the time pressure you were all put under by Frènes. Yes, Map initially fell for Zep's trick with the blood. But in the usual scheme of things, the investigation wouldn't have advanced half as far as it did before he discovered it.'

'That *is* true.'

Bill Evans's 'But Beautiful' began to drift across the terrace. Darac gave it a good couple of bars and said: 'I'll tell you something else that's true, Frankie. Before Granot worked his miracle in the pool, I really thought I'd had it, you know. And I never, ever, wanted so much to be alive.'

Frankie stood, took Darac's hand and, saying nothing, they walked back inside.


END

## ABOUT THE AUTHOR:

Peter Morfoot's writing credits include plays and sketch shows for BBC radio and TV, and the "cult classic" (Time Out) satirical novel, *Burksey*. He has lectured in film, holds a PhD in Art History, and has spent 30 years exploring life on the French Riviera, the setting for his crime series featuring Captain Paul Darac of Nice's Brigade Criminelle. The first Darac Mystery, *Impure Blood*, was U.S. Library Journal's Pick of the Month for April 2016; the second, *Fatal Music*, was listed in *Strand Magazine's* Top 25 Books of 2017; and award-winning critic Mike Ripley selected both *Fatal Music* and the third novel, *Box of Bones* for his 5 Crime Picks of 2017 and 2018 respectively (Shots E-zine).

## ACKNOWLEDGEMENTS:

As ever, thanks must first go to my wife Liz and to Rob, Clare, Katey and Bryan, without whose love, sage counsel and all-round support, writing the Captain Darac Mysteries would be an infinitely tougher call. For sharing their insights and giving generously of their time, many thanks to Susan Woodall, Lisa Hitch, David Gower, Alex Carter, Boris Blouin, Jacky Ananou, and Gosia Wisinska. I owe particular debts of gratitude to Commandant Divisionnaire de Police, Jean-Baptiste Zuccarelli of Commissaire Foch, Nice, and to the doyen of all booksellers, Richard Reynolds. For her many kindnesses and for her translation work both from texts and during live interviews with officers of the Police Nationale, my special thanks to Katherine Roddwell. Finally, warm thanks to my publisher Robert Hyde of Galileo, and to my agent, Ian Drury at Sheil-Land.

Sonny Rollins: Darac's favourite tenor sax player. His go-to album: *Newk's Time.* Darac's track choice: 'Asiatic Raes'.

Bill Evans: 'But Beautiful'. Title track of the Evans trio album featuring Stan Getz.

Rahsaan Roland Kirk: Reeds instrumentalist, sometimes playing many simultaneously. Track: 'Three For Dizzy' from *Kirk's Work*

'Tina' Brooks: Darac rates the hard-bop sax player's stylish inventiveness. Track: 'The Way You Look Tonight' from *Minor Move.*

Astrud Gilberto: Bossa Nova singer loved by Caroline Rosay. 'Girl From Ipanema'.

Céu: Contemporary Brazilian singer utilising electronica. Track: 'Mais Um Lamento' from *Céu.*

Nara Leão: Darac's preferred Brazilian singer. Track: 'Corcovado' from *Des Anos Depois.*

Elis Regina: Another Darac favourite. Track: 'Águas de Março' from *Elis & Tom.*

Hoagy Carmichael: 'Stardust'. Track: Louis Armstrong's 1931 version.

Carmichael and Gorrell: 'Georgia on my Mind'. Track: Billie Holiday's 1941 version.

Chet Baker: Track: 'Every Time We Say Goodbye' from soundtrack album *Let's Get Lost.*

Wayne Shorter: 'E.S.P.' Title track of the Miles Davis album.

Louis Armstrong: Unlike Darac's band mate Didier Musso, Darac loves all early 'Pops.' Track: 'Potato Head Blues,' *Louis Armstrong & His Hot Seven* 1927 version.

Ornette Coleman: Showing his wide-ranging tastes, Darac loves O C's avant-garde sensibility. Track: 'Ramblin' from *Change of the Century.*

Kenny Barron: 'Minor Blues.' Title track of the album. Darac's all-time favourite pianist.

Steely Dan: Darac enjoys the band's jazz-inflected approach. Track: 'Your Gold Teeth' from *Countdown To Ecstasy.*

John Coltrane: 'My Favourite Things.' Title track of the album.

Dianne X: Blue Devil Club owner Ridge Clay's allusion is probably to singer Dianne Reeves Track: 'I'm In Love Again' from *When You Know.*

Herbie X: Ditto, keyboard giant, Herbie Hancock. Track: 'Cantaloupe Island' from *Empyrean Isles.*

Phronesis: Explorative, ever-evolving trio supported by Darac's group at Nice Jazz Festival. Track: '67000 mph' from *Parallax.*

Django Reinhardt: 'Ménilmontant' from *Djangology.* Django is Darac's hero.

Bobby Watson: *Love Remains,* the title track from what is a significant album for Darac and former lover Angeline.

Billy Cobham: 'Taurean Matador' from *Spectrum.* A favourite of Darac's.

Count Basie: 'One o'clock Jump.' Played by the 'James Clarence Jazz Orchestra' at the festival. Track: 'One o'clock Jump' by Oscar Peterson, 1953 version.

Omar Puente: 'Samba Para Dos', from *Best Foot Forward.*

## SPOTIFY PLAYLIST: